CW01509327

THE MISTRESS & THE RENOWNED

BOOK TWO
IN THE

LOVE & FATE
SERIES
BY
JEANETTE ROSE & ALEXIS RUNE

ROSE & STAR PUBLISHING

This book is significantly different than the first and explores some potentially triggering themes. A list of content warnings can be found on the Rose & Star website.

To All Long Distance Best Friends:
No Matter the Miles.

To those who raised Alexis, both here and gone:
Thank you.
J

Chapter One

Persephone

WELCOME HOME, YOUR MAJESTY."

The words echo in the room that was previously silent save the fire crackling homily behind me. My ears ring, blood pumping through my veins. Adrenaline courses through me, my chest constricting as I struggle to take in sufficient oxygen. My head swims, making the room spin.

Your Majesty?

I whip around to face the strange woman, her expression a mixture of awe and bewilderment, a careful smile tugging at her lips.

"Your Majesty?"

Hekate nods. "Yes, Queen of the Underworld, Dark Spring, the Mistress of the Obsidian Throne."

My brows furrow, and I look down at the ground, trying to find some understanding and make sense of what this woman is saying. *Dark Spring?*

I shake my head and look up at her. "No. You've got the wrong person. I'm just… Persephone."

Hekate lifts a brow. "If you're so sure that you are the wrong person, why is your outfit changing?"

I frown and look down, gasping as Hades' shirt slowly transforms into a floor-length black gown, the silk whispering against my skin as it hugs my every curve perfectly, the thigh slit tracking almost to my hip. I slide my hand over my waist, my fingers gliding over the soft material, watching it shimmer under my touch.

I lift my head, as a weight settles atop it. I slowly raise my hand, frowning as my fingers meet cool hard metal. On shaky legs, now supported by feet in sky-high black heels, I walk to a large mirror on the wall. A dark obsidian frame encases the window to my reflection. Small delicate roses and intricately carved vines climb up the frame. The sharp thorns are so pronounced it reminds me of myself.

A rose with a bite.

I step into the path of the mirror, blinking at the woman staring back at me. My reflection is somewhat familiar to what I usually see, yet so foreign at the same time. The crystal blue eyes looking back at me belong to me but look clearer, brighter. My face looks paler, drawing attention to the rosy blush high on my cheeks and the redness of my lips. My hair, the same reddish brown, still fell in loose curls down my back. I tilt my head slightly, my breath hitching as the light catches on the heavy crown perched proudly atop my head.

It is solid gold imbued with small diamonds and large rubies. The stunning coronet sits perfectly, making me look every bit the queen Hekate seems to think I am. The spikes point threateningly toward the ceiling, and the entire piece holds an air of power.

Hekate silently moves to stand behind me, her hands clasped. "All Hail the Queen."

My eyes meet hers in the mirror, and I turn to face her, shaking my head. "You're crazy..."

"What I am is the Goddess of Witchcraft and ruler of Propylaia, the land of lost souls."

My eyebrows draw, and I decide to hold off on this conversation until later when I can discuss everything with Hades. My eyes snap back to Hekate. "Where is Hades?"

She lifts a shoulder in an unconcerned shrug. "It is not my job to know where Hades is. My job was to find and escort my queen here when the curse activated."

I blink. "Curse?"

Hekate glances at one of the grand doors at the far end of the room, clearly avoiding my question. She purses her lips and blows, emitting a sharp, cutting whistle. A moment later, I hear something barreling down the hallway. Is that the sound of... paws? The walls of the building seem to shake as the sound gets closer, the chandelier above us tinkling musically. I blink as a massive canine-looking beast bursts through the heavy door. The animal is large. It must come up to my chest when standing, but the thing that makes my eyes go wide in terror is that it has three heads, all of them barking and panting as it barrels toward Hekate.

I stand frozen in fear, watching as it skids to a halt just in front of Hekate. Its faces all look menacing and intimidating. Hekate keeps her face neutral as she looks at it.

"Cerberus. Sit." Hekate's voice is firm, but you can hear her underlying affection for the animal. Cerberus falls onto its back, begging the ancient goddess to scratch its stomach. She breaks out into a smile as she crouches to scratch it, softly crooning to the beast.

My mouth drops open at the sight. Cerberus's face goes from menacing to goofy in an instant, its tongues lolling out of each of its mouths. Hekate bends to kiss his stomach, one of its heads licking her face happily.

I blink once, twice, three times before I burst out laughing.

What the fuck is going on?

Obviously, I have gone completely insane, or this is a dream, but this absolutely cannot be real. My laughter stops almost instantly when a stray thought enters my mind.

Could this be one of my mother's tricks?

Cerberus ceases licking Hekate, his body tensing as he finally notices me. The animal jumps to its feet and pads over to me. All three faces convey his mistrust. I go still and hold my breath as it leans in to sniff me, my heart thumping in my chest. A second head leans in,

8

inhaling deeply. I close my eyes, trying to calm my heart and dampen my fear, guessing it can sense it. I feel the third head move in, its cold, wet nose brushing against my bare leg. It huffs an exhale before all the heads pull back. I slowly open one eye, expecting to see the beast snarling and baring its teeth. Instead, Cerberus is bowing all of its heads, submitting to me.

I glance up at Hekate uneasily. "What are they doing?"

"He is bowing to his queen."

I look back at him and tilt my head. Tentatively taking a step forward, I reach out and gently scratch behind the ear of the middle head. Cerberus's back leg starts kicking in delight. My lips twitch, and I scratch him a little harder.

Just like a regular dog... With three heads...

I move my hand to the left head, giving it the same attention, and use my other hand to scratch the right head behind the ear. Cerberus's leg kicks more, and his eyes grow heavy as I pet him. I look up at Hekate again, her gaze meeting mine.

"Why am I here, Hekate?" I pull my hands back from Cerberus. "And no more riddles."

She clasps her hands again, resting them against her stomach. "Because of the curse."

Cerberus nudges my hand, wanting more attention. I smile at him and start scratching him again. "What curse?"

Hekate looks away from me. I think she's going to ignore the questions again when she speaks, her voice even, as if reciting a prophecy, "The Lord of the Dead will rule alone, the solitary sovereign to watch the souls pass through. But every lonely winter is thawed with the arrival of Spring. With the burial of seed, spring will grow in the desolate darkness. Tied to the realm of the dead, even more tightly than its lord."

I blink, her words replaying in a loop in my mind as I try to make sense of them.

9

"In what world is that not a riddle?"

"I did not write it. The Moirai did."

I sigh in frustration. "Fine. But what does it mean?"

"It means that Hades was cursed. When the curse activated, you became queen." She pauses, appearing to study my face. "The second he came inside you, he sealed your fate."

I flush, my cheeks burning. I look away from Hekate, unable to meet her eyes, knowing she knows what went down between Hades and me.

Hades told me there were consequences to doing what we did. I remember him lying on the bed next to me after the first time. He was trying to tell me, but...

"I don't understand."

"The second Hades gave you his seed, everything was as it should be," Hekate replies simply.

I blink at her. Her words and tone are so casual as if she has not just informed me that I am now Queen of the Underworld. Me. Persephone. The Goddess of Spring. *Spring*. Fuck.

"But he..." I swallow, "he didn't tell me."

Hekate nods solemnly, but I can see her joy beneath the surface. "Those bound by fate cannot speak to change it. It is the heavy price one pays to be told their future." Hekate's eyes glaze over as if she is gazing upon her own fate. She goes silent and stares eerily ahead but is pulled back to the present by Cerberus sniffing her hand, her haunted look replaced with a bland smile. "I must go. Until next time, my queen."

A loud snap fills the air, and it looks as though she is compressing in on herself before she vanishes.

I stumble back, my head still spinning. *What the fuck is going on? Where is Hades?* My head snaps to the dais when I hear something fall. A small black duffel bag sits on the edge. I cautiously move toward it, Cerberus on my tail, looking at the bag with mild interest.

As I get closer, I realize it's my bag from Hades' apartment. Relaxing slightly, I open it and am relieved to find my phone sitting on top of a pile of clothes. I pull it out and call him immediately. I tell myself I'm going to yell at him, tell him how angry I am with him about this whole situation, and demand that he come here right now and give me a full explanation. But there is no answer.

Hades always has his phone.

I call the office, hoping he's just in a meeting.

"What?" Minthe snaps.

Fuck, of all the people I don't want to talk to right now, she is just about at the top of that list, right below my mother. I try to center myself and remain calm. "I need to speak with Hades."

"He's not in." Her cutting voice sounds like nails on a chalkboard.

I take a deep breath, but my blood is boiling. "Cut the bullshit, Minthe, and put me through. This is important."

"He's not here. And if he's not with his newest fuck buddy, I guess he's moved on." I can hear her smirk through the phone. Gods, I wish I could slap that look right off her smug face. "Ouch, must hurt."

My body thrums, practically shaking. If she were here, I'd tear her limb from limb. The anger seems to fill me, the darkness inside me completely muting the light, fueling my rage. Pain pierces my forearm, sharp enough that I hiss and drop my phone. I look down, and my eyes go wide. A black thorn protrudes from my skin. I blink and slide a finger over the point, pulling back with a yelp when it slices through my skin.

I suck the drop of blood from my finger and look down at my phone, cursing when I see the smashed screen.

Fuck!

Another three thorns break through my flesh, and I cry out, a tear sliding down my cheek.

"What is happening to me?" I whisper.

Cerberus whines and moves to my side, his left

head nuzzling into me. I look down at him, the knots in my stomach easing slightly. I stroke his head, but my anxieties renew when my gaze snags on the thorns again, although they seem to retract slightly.

Is this my power growing? What good are thorns piercing my skin when I get angry?

Cerberus rubs his face on me again, and I start to calm, the thorns disappearing beneath my skin. I sigh, my heartbeat slowing slightly and my breath coming easier. I gaze at the dog, the corners of my lips tugging into a smile.

"I bet you know the castle really well. Can you show me to my room, boy?"

Cerberus's middle head barks, and he paces, panting with excitement. He turns and runs toward the door, looking back with his right head when he gets there, waiting for me. I smile warmly, and follow him as he leads me from the throne room.

I try to get a sense of the place as we go, but my head is too busy, too full of all the information to take in any of the stunning details of the castle. I try to focus on the deep red wallpaper, the gold sconces, and the dark marble of the floors. This is every bit the home of the ruler of the Underworld. I'll explore it all later. Right now, I just need to get to my room and lie down for a while.

After climbing stairs and taking endless turns, Cerberus stops outside another grand door, just as expensive looking as the rest of the castle. Palace? I wrap my hand around the gold doorknob and suppress a shiver, the cool metal just as cold as my crown. I push open the door, and I am immediately enveloped in *his* scent. *Hades.* My eyes land on the large four-poster bed in the middle of the room. Like in the throne room, flames crackle in an enormous fireplace, warming the space.

I kick my heels off, almost groaning as my feet sink into the plush rug. I step into the room on the right and turn on the light, Hades' scent in my every breath. His large closet is neatly organized with all of his clothes. I want to explore, to examine everything, but exhaustion tugs at me. There is so much information, so many questions, so much change. I grab one of Hades' suit jackets, pull it off the hanger and return to the bedroom. I look at Cerberus, who's taken his place on the largest dog bed I've ever seen, right in front of the cozy fire.

"This is where Daddy sleeps?" Cerberus whines. "You'll tell me when he gets here?"

Cerberus's middle head barks once in answer. I smile at him and climb into bed. Carefully, I remove the crown from my head, taking some time to examine it. The sharp points are pregnant with diamonds, and three large rubies spark at the base. I place the crown on the bedside table and grab Hades' suit jacket, holding it to me. I should be furious with Hades, but I don't have it in me right now. Right now, I just need him here. I need his comfort, his touch, his voice telling me everything is going to be okay, and I need to not feel so alone. I bury my face in his pillow and inhale deeply, praying for sleep to take me, praying that he will be here when I wake.

Chapter Two
Hades

***I* SLAMMED INTO THE GROUND AFTER YEARS OF FALLING.** *I grew up in the fall, from infant to child to teen, all in the air, during a never-ending descent, a plummet with no bottom, a prison with no escape. But, then the ground rushed up at me, and I hit so hard I thought I had arrived to wherever gods went when we died. I had learned in the fall. I don't know how, but it felt like knowledge was provided to me. The whispers in the darkness kept me from going insane. Sometimes I thought it was a woman's voice, but it was too low and fleeting to make it out. But there was nothing else to do but listen and learn. A voracious thirst for knowledge grew and grew within me but could never be satiated.*

I was a god. Consumed by my father at birth, my body grew as I descended, my immortality keeping me alive even though I didn't eat or drink. Life clung to me like a disease. I got used to sleeping even as I fell, though it was more small bouts of unconsciousness. My limbs grew in painful, quick moments. I could feel them pushing against my skin. I was little more than a skeleton, a shell of a god who shouldn't have been born. A god trapped in a never-ending abyss.

Somehow, I learned my name was Hades. I was the middle sibling, the second to be swallowed, but I was alone. Where was my brother? Was my brother a lie? A comfort told by the voice to soothe me during the fall? To make me forget I was alone?

Then I slammed into the hard, unforgiving ground. It took several moments for me to realize I was no longer falling. My body, as emaciated as it was, tried to throw up the contents of my stomach, but there was nothing, only years of the air and descent. Maybe this was the end, my body finally giving out from the strain and years without sustenance. This could be the end, and this was where gods went when they died. I hadn't expected it to be so... bright.

My eyes, so used to the never-ending darkness of the plummet, burned when I looked up into something like a blazing star, but then a dark piece of cloth was pulled over them. A soothing voice, young and male this time, spoke into my ear. "You don't want to look directly into the star. I was practically blind for days after I landed."

Maybe I'm not dead. I didn't think I could feel the coarse fabric across my face if I was. But what would I know about death? I didn't even know about life. All I knew was the fall.

I tried to speak, but my voice was broken, never having been used. A slightly fractured gasp was all I could manage. The air rushed into my lungs, creating pinpricks of pain in my chest as I tried to adjust. I only managed strangling breaths that felt torn from my throat, not filling my chest with what I needed. Maybe I was dead. I didn't think it should hurt this much to breathe.

The other boy continued, putting something to my lips. "Drink this. It will help you heal."

I pushed it away at first, the movement so pathetic that the other boy easily batted my hand away. He grabbed my face and forced me to drink.

I protested at first, then drank it greedily. It tasted sweet, but I immediately tried to shove it away. He should just let me die. My body felt odd, out of place. But the other boy kept it to my lips, refusing to stop until it was empty. I rolled onto my back, my body shaking from whatever he'd forced on me. My bones rattled so loud I had to cover my ears. Curled into a ball with my face covered, I wished for death again. It had to be better than this. My skin was too tight, and though my body was warming, I thought my bones might force their

15

way out of my skin at any second. I didn't know how long I shuddered before my body stopped shaking, and the other boy spoke again.

"Your name is Hades," he said. His voice wasn't as harsh to my ears as before. Was I healing? Not dying?

I might have nodded, but my skin felt raw. That blinding light was burning my skin. I reached over to cover my arm, surprised to find that it was covered in some material. Had he put a blanket over me while I was shaking?

"My name is Poseidon," the boy whispered. Poseidon. I was not alone.

My lips cracked when I tried to speak, my throat still dry. Would I be able to speak? "B-B-Brother..."

"Yes. We're brothers," Poseidon responded. Now that the ringing in my ears had finally dimmed, I could understand him better. It didn't hurt to hear him. His voice was soothing and how I imagined the ocean would sound. I'd never seen the ocean, and I never would. I'd only know it from the stories told to me from the whispers during the fall. Ambient sounds filtered in as my hearing recovered.

I tried to speak again. "F-Falling?"

I felt his hand against my shoulder. "No more, Brother."

Something wet filled my eyes, dampening the blindfold. My hand trembled as I touched the blindfold. Poseidon's hand covered mine, his fingers rough and calloused. It made me flinch to feel them. My skin was hypersensitive, never having been touched.

"N-No more?" I whimpered, my voice breaking over tears rather than the cracked pain in my throat. They were tears soaking the cloth. I didn't know I could cry. I never cried during the fall, but now I couldn't stop.

His arms wrapped around me, and I felt his head shaking next to me. He whispered, "No more."

My weak, spindly arms embraced my brother for the first time.

Chapter Three

Persephone

I LURCH UP, RETCHING ON... AIR? My chest heaves as I try to gulp down the oxygen I was never starved of.

Just a dream. Just a dream.

Tight space. Darkness. Pain. Weakness. Helplessness.

My brows furrow as I think of the ultimate feeling that sparked within me in the nightmare. I'd felt it deep in my chest, the smallest glimmer of something... Love? Hope? It was so small, so buried, that I almost missed it.

I wipe my damp brow, once again my stomach rolling, just as it had earlier when I woke in Hades' apartment. I try to remember my previous dream but only recall the smell of rot, earth, and roots. Cradling my head in my hands, I try to get control of my stomach. Cerberus pads over to me, nudging me with one of his noses. I put on a smile and look at him, his enormous eyes glimmering with concern.

"No Daddy yet?" I stroke his middle head.

Cerberus whines, nudging me with one of his other heads.

"I'm all right, just missing him like you are."

Cerberus lifts a paw onto the bed, releasing a huff. My lips twitch.

"You want to be in the bed with me?" The idea of letting Cerberus in the bed makes me smile when I consider Hades' reaction. Hades, whose apartment is so neat and tidy, would never let the dog in the bed with him. A wave of anger washes through me.

Well, he also trapped me here against my will, so…

I shuffle over and pat the bed, gesturing for Cerberus to join me.

"Don't tell Daddy."

He happily jumps up, settling into the bed. Under his weight, the bed groans slightly, and the legs give out. I yelp in surprise, and Cerberus releases a concerned bark.

I lift my eyebrows, sitting still in the bed. When my gaze meets Cerberus's, I burst out laughing. I scratch his ears and lay back. I mean, it can't get any more broken. He shuffles under the covers, but they don't cover his big body. He rests one of his heads on Hades' pillow, one on my stomach, and one on my thighs. I smile down at him.

Spoiled boy.

I lay my head back on the pillow, stroking his head absentmindedly. "Tomorrow, we will get bigger blankets."

Cerberus lets out a little yelp and sniffs Hades' pillow before moving it closer to me and resting his colossal head on it again. My heart aches for him. He obviously misses him deeply.

So do I.

I try to resurrect my anger with Hades. While I understand he couldn't tell me about the curse and that the chokehold must have been endlessly frustrating for him, I can't help but feel betrayed. I know I pushed him for it. I wanted it.

Would I have chosen this had I known the consequences? Would I have chosen him?

I sigh. Of course, I would. I will always choose Hades. But I need him, and he's not here. I need to know the ins and outs of the curse, and I need to know what exactly I have signed myself up for by activating it. Maybe there is an *Idiot's Guide to Ruling the Underworld.*

I look back at Cerberus. He's watching me, obviously sensing my unease.

18

"I hope your daddy's back tomorrow."

He licks my cheek before closing his eyes.

I lay awake, staring at the ceiling. The grand chandelier above me reflects the moonlight streaming through the balcony doors. The crystals sparkle, trying to lull me to sleep. Two of Cerberus's heads snore softly, but that is not the reason I'm not sleeping. Neither is the fact my head is busy with unanswered questions. It is fear. I am afraid that I will fall back into that dream, that confined space, that rotting smell, that feeling of weakness.

When I finally fall asleep, the second I fade into the blackness, I return to that airtight coffin and the increasingly familiar feeling of my power slowly being drained from me. I gasp, trying to take in any oxygen I can, but there is none. My heart thuds in my chest, my lungs tight, unable to expand with the air they desperately crave. My stomach knots. No one knows where I am. No one will find me. I am alone.

My body tenses, and a faraway voice calls to me. It is almost indiscernible at first, but the harder I focus, the louder it becomes. My eyes flutter as I feel a tug, an invisible string being yanked on, trying to pull me closer. I concentrate harder on the voice.

"Persephone?"

I thrash in the bed, kicking at the blankets. My hand goes to my throat as I wake up, finally able to breathe, sweat covering my skin. I practically fall out of bed in my haste to get free. I reach behind me, scrabbling for the zip of the silk dress. My hand shakes as I try to grasp the tiny metal pull tab, needing it off. My skin feels as if it's on fire, my lungs burning with every breath. I yank the zipper down and shimmy out of the dress, letting it pool on the floor. I pull up my falling bra strap and hurry to the balcony door. Wrenching it open, I gulp the cool, fresh air as it rushes into the room. I rub a hand over my face, wiping away the thin layer of sweat and squeezing my eyes shut as I try to come back down from my nightmare. But the memory of that voice remains, my heart racing as I hear it over and over.

"Persephone?"

It was too faint for me to discern who was speaking. The accent was morphed from the strain, or maybe from my weakness, but the way my body reacted to it... It was so familiar.

I take another deep breath and blink my eyes open, letting them slowly adjust to the light. The sun is slowly rising, forcing the shadows to recede and with it, my nightmare.

I step onto the balcony, my heart thundering in anticipation of seeing my kingdom. Even thinking of it as *mine* sounds completely ridiculous. The Goddess of Spring is not a title that inspires much of anything except maybe the awe of middle-aged women into gardening. I am hardly a feared or strong leader.

Sunlight floods the Underworld, and I blink as I behold the sight. A low-lying mist clings to the ground, leaving a mysterious air in its wake. Directly below, a garden of dark flowers sways lazily in the gentle breeze. I frown. There isn't much color anywhere. The dark petals almost blend into the even darker soil. I lift my gaze, looking further afield. Groves of tall, dark trees cover the landscape for as far as the eye can see.

My fingers wrap around the wrought iron of the balcony, entranced by the allure of the Underworld. Nothing about it holds obvious beauty, yet I have never felt more at home.

I turn, heading back into Hades' bedroom. Once again, his scent envelopes me, my hand going to my aching chest.

What to do now?

I look at the other door in the room, the one I didn't explore yesterday, and pray to every god in Olympus that it's a bathroom. I'd love a shower. Not only do I feel gross from waking up covered in sweat, but my skin is grimy, the last remnants of my dream still clinging to me. I can't see the mud covering my skin, but I can still *feel* it.

The rug is plush beneath my toes, and I can admire the grandeur of the room now that I'm not completely exhausted. I had slept for most of yesterday and all of last night. The four-poster bed sits proudly against the back wall. The dark mahogany wood looks sturdy, though obviously not sturdy enough to hold a three-headed dog. Its headboard is the same dark wood, and the detailing is as intricate as that of the thrones. The sheets are the softest of cotton, and the wine-red color fits the theme of the palace. The back wall is paneled in dark wood, even darker than the bed frame, but the rest are lined with dark gray wallpaper with the faintest pattern of flowers and vines. Every fine vine seems to have the smallest amount of gold through them, making the decor sparkle a little in the light. The chandelier is large and more modern than I would have expected, with solid gold curls and flows and small light bulbs dangling like droplets of water.

I push open the door to reveal a large bathroom, the white tile such a contrast from the dark room I've just left. I close the door behind me and lock it before stepping further into the room. It surprises me to see that the bathroom was designed for a couple. There are two sinks side by side, both with their own large mirrors in front of them. The one closest to the door is obviously the one Hades uses. A black monogrammed towel sits folded on the shelf with a golden 'H' proudly on the top. I chuckle, running my fingers over the stitching. I would not have expected my King of the Dead to enjoy monogrammed linens.

I open his medicine cabinet and stare at the contents. It's so strange seeing his things here, thinking of him living here for six months of the year. My eyes drift over his toiletries, so normal, so human. I close the cabinet again and move over to my sink. The towel left out for me simply has a crown, a perfectly stitched image of the one I found on my head yesterday. I lift it, tracing the delicate embroidery with my fingers.

How long has this been here? How long has Hades had to endure seeing this towel here, not knowing if he would ever find who it was meant for? Not knowing if he would ever find... me?

I swallow the lump forming in my throat. It's almost unbearable to think about Hades being alone. But, I am currently alone, and Hades has made no moves to reach out to me. I make a mental note to try to fix my phone after I've showered.

Sighing, I place the hand towel back on the counter and open the medicine cabinet above my sink. I look at the empty shelves, I doubt the Underworld has a CVS.

I click my tongue. "Hm. Where would the queen of the Underworld get toiletries?"

The second the words leave my lips, the cupboard fills with all of my preferred hygiene products. I blink, pulling out my favorite moisturizer.

"Huh..." I look at it, opening the cap and smelling the product to make sure. I lift my eyebrows and replace it in the cabinet, turning to face the huge shower and bathtub. While I would love a bath, I don't fancy sitting in a tub full of the imaginary grime I feel coating my skin.

Grabbing two large fluffy towels, I step into the shower and turn it on. The water emerges at the perfect temperature and pressure. I allow myself to just stand under the stream for a couple of minutes, enjoying the warmth cascading over me, washing away the last remnants of my nightmare.

After I've scrubbed every inch of my body and hair clean, I leave the shower, wrapping the towel around my body. I'm not convinced I feel much clarity after the bombshells dropped on me yesterday, but I'm at least clean and rested.

I walk over to the mirror, wiping the condensation

from the glass. Tilting my head, I study my reflection. I look the same as I always have, but there is something so unfamiliar about the goddess staring back at me. I can't put my finger on what the difference is. My fingers slide over the completely healed skin of my arm. The memory of the thorns piercing my skin is a whisper of pain in the wake of my touch. I frown and hold my hand out, my palm raised. A small flower sprouts in the center, its sharp petals black with blood-red veins stretching through them.

I am not who I once was. I am the queen who was promised. I am the rose with a bite.

Chapter Four

Persephone

I SIT ON THE STILL-BROKEN BED. Hades' and my bed.

Where the fuck is Hades? Could he be hiding from me? I know he was worried about the curse and that he was desperate to tell me, but how could he activate it and then disappear off the face of... well, everywhere? I've been trying to repress my thoughts and feelings less, but how am I supposed to work through these with so many unanswered questions? Questions that won't be answered until I find my... Hades. I sigh heavily.

That begs another question. What are Hades and I? We didn't have that discussion before he disappeared. I'd bet we're exclusive, given his reaction to Jackson, but *boyfriend* seems like too weak a term for your fated mate.

A faint knock pulls me from my thoughts. Cerberus lifts his heads and bolts to the door, the sheets strewn all over the place in his haste to jump off the bed. He barks loudly, all three of his heads making it sound like a loud echo. I stand with a frown, wrapping the towel tighter around my body.

"Cerberus, you need to..." I try to shift Cerberus out of the way, but he stands on his hind legs, his huge paws against the door as he continues to bark. I sigh and stand back, raising my voice.

"Cerberus. Sit."

He looks at me, all six of his eyes wide. He whines softly and sits heavily on the floor.

"Cerberus, bed."

He whines again and slowly pads off to his bed, his heads low. My heart squeezes with guilt, but I steel myself and open the door.

A tall, cloaked figure stands in the hallway, his face hidden in shadow. The cloak covers him almost entirely, but I can tell from his build that he's huge and muscular. The only patches of skin showing are his hands, and they are covered in what looks like tattoos, ancient script and runes painted on his otherwise pale skin.

"Y-your Majesty! M-my apologies!" I blink. "I… um…" he stammers, turning away.

I look down at my towel-covered body and blush.

"Oh, sorry. I-I don't have any clothes."

"I-I'm sure the palace will provide whatever you require, my queen."

I frown. *The palace will provide?*

"Just speak whatever it is you require, and it will appear," he continues, still looking away, his tattooed fingers held over what I can only assume are his eyes.

I turn back to the room frowning and glance at Cerberus, his head lying on the bed morosely, his large eyes staring up at me sadly. My heart squeezes again. I'll need to fix that.

I look at the bed, half worrying that this may be some elaborate prank, but then all of my toiletries appeared in the bathroom after I thought about them. I reach behind me and close the door before taking a breath.

"I sure wish I had some yoga pants."

A pair of black yoga pants appear on the bed. I walk over and pick them up, feeling the soft material.

25

My brows draw as I hold the pants up. They look like they'll be the perfect fit. I look back at my bed.

"I certainly could use some panties... and a bra."

They materialize instantly. I narrow my eyes at the two scraps of lace and place the pants back down beside them. Slipping on the panties and bra, I am again surprised at how well they fit. I pull on the pants and decide to just wear one of Hades' shirts. I walk to the closet and pull out one of his crisp white shirts. The ends hover just above my knees, so I tie it at my waist before asking the palace for socks and a pair of Converse.

When I'm fully dressed, I walk back to the door and open it to find the man still standing outside, his back to the door. "I'm decent," I say, trying to hide the smile in my voice.

He doesn't immediately look at me. His body is tense, and he's acting as though he would rather be anywhere but here. I gently tap his arm, and he jumps away, his body flying against the opposite wall. I blink, looking at him, my eyes wide.

"I'm sorry!"

"Y-you shouldn't touch me."

I blink again, frowning. "Sorry."

He slowly drops his hand and turns to face me, immediately dropping to one knee, his head bowed.

"Forgive me, my queen. I am Thanatos, God of Death, humble servant."

I lift my eyebrows. "Persephone. You can call me Persephone."

He raises his head, the light catching him so that I can only see his mouth. His skin looks like porcelain, and his pink lips are pleasingly rounded. Well, they would be if he wasn't currently gaping up at me. "My queen, I could not disrespect you in such a way."

"Please stand up."

He bows his head again and slowly stands. There's an awkward silence, and I can sense his reluctance to be here. I clear my throat, looking around, taking in more of the decor in the hall. The wallpaper looks so plush and exquisite. I resist the urge to brush my fingers over it. "So… Thanatos?"

He bows his head more. "My queen."

I tilt my head. Will I ever get used to being called that? "You came to see me?"

He gives a slight nod. "Yes, my queen. I came to ask if you would like a tour of the palace and grounds?"

My lips curve in a small smile. "Oh, that would be lovely."

Thanatos drums his fingers against his thigh. He turns on his heel and gestures for me to proceed him. I glance back into my room, guilt sitting heavily in my chest.

Cerberus is looking at me sadly, not having moved from his bed. He whines softly, his enormous eyes fixed on me. My lips twitch at the sight of him. He is such a giant, intimidating beast, but I can tell while his exterior looks tough, he's a marshmallow at heart. I pat my leg and smack my lips. "Come on, boy! Let's go!"

Cerberus lifts his heads, all three of them, with his tongues lolling out of his three enormous mouths. I swear he's smiling. Clumsily, he scrambles to his feet and bolts toward me. Thanatos regards Cerberus, and his lips curve in a fond smile, but he doesn't reach out to touch him.

The three of us start down the long hall. Thanatos keeps his hood up, only affording me the briefest glances of his jaw when the light catches him just right. He points to the various pieces of artwork lining the halls, explaining the history and the stories behind them.

We stop before a large picture. A large black chasm spirals down the center, and there are two objects in the middle of it. Something about the image makes my stomach churn. Hopelessness, fear, and anger seem to radiate from the oils on the canvas. Thanatos shuffles on his feet behind me, and I can practically feel his unease as I study the piece. I tilt my head, and right in front of my eyes, the small colorful shapes seem to slowly descend, the black chasm moving with them. I lean in, my brows drawn.

"M-my queen?"

Thanatos's voice pulls me from my trance. I blink, and my frown deepens when I notice the painting has stopped moving. I straighten and look at Thanatos. He can obviously see the questions in my eyes, and he shifts from foot to foot.

"Shall we?" He gestures down the hall. The edge in his voice doesn't escape me, as if he's working hard to keep it even.

"Tell me about the painting."

"Which?" Again, I can hear the strain in his voice as he tries to sound at ease.

I nod at the one I was just looking at.

He sighs heavily. "A story for my king to tell."

"Yes, well, he isn't here, is he?" I pause. "Speaking of Hades, where is he?"

Thanatos doesn't immediately answer, almost as though my question has truly caught him off guard. "My king is not due back for another few weeks."

"Yes, but I am here," I say, watching him closely.

"Yes. Because the…" I can feel the discomfort rolling off him. "The curse was…" He clears his throat. "The curse activated."

"But given I have never been to the Underworld before, and he has cursed me, would you not expect him to pop on down here a little sooner than expected?"

Thanatos considers. "He is not due back for another few weeks, my queen."

I sigh in frustration and turn back to the painting. "Just tell me about the painting." When he hesitates, I decide it's time to try out how far being queen will get me. "Now, Thanatos."

He inhales sharply, the internal war between loyalty to his king and his duty to serve his queen is clear.

I wait a moment, and I'm surprised when he steps forward and stands beside me. We stand side by side, looking at the painting, his voice rough. "When my king was born, he was the second son to the King and Queen of the Titans. The gods before the Olympians. But the king was a cruel father who had been told by the Fates that one of his sons would supplant him on the throne. His solution was to swallow his newborn sons whole, trapping them within his body in a realm outside of time. Poseidon went first, then my king." He pauses, staring silently at the abyss in the painting. "He grew up in a prison."

I stare at the painting in horror. Nausea rolls in my stomach. How did he survive that? How could anyone have done that to their own child?

Thanatos clears his throat, and I pull my gaze away from the painting.

"I wouldn't advise looking at it too long, my queen."

I look up into the shadowed darkness of his hood, only able to see the slightest glint of his eyes. "Why?"

"It has been known to… entrance its patrons on occasion."

"Entrance?" I ask.

He nods solemnly and backs up a step. "Let us continue our tour, my queen."

I look back at the painting, tilting my head as I observe it. So many mysteries about this place, so much darkness seeming to pull at me. Even now, I feel it growing inside me, not having realized I had been holding it at bay for years. What if I'm unable to resist the siren's call? Do I even want to?

Chapter Five

Persephone

THE HALLS BLEED INTO ONE ANOTHER. The same dark wallpaper lines the walls, and the same black wood covers the floors. Gold runners stretch the lengths of the corridors, the gilded borders starkly contrasting with the flooring below. We wander, and just like the corridors, my sense of time seems to fade away. We walk in a comfortable silence, save for Thanatos dropping interesting facts or supplementary information about the seemingly endless guest rooms we pass. As we pass the doors, I notice them disappear the second my eyes drift away. I stop in my tracks, frowning as I look at the wall. My eyes go wide as the door slowly materializes once again.

"The palace is a living thing. If it is required, it will appear. If it is not, it will vanish into the Void."

"So, if I were to require a restroom?"

Thanatos tenses. "It would appear."

I nod once and turn, continuing down the hall. Thanatos hurries behind me, and relief drips from him.

After a few moments, we arrive at a large pair of double doors, red, blue, and purple stained glass, taking up the main panels of the door and casting colorful light against the dark floorboards.

"The king is an avid collector. He once…" Thanatos trails off.

I glance at Thanatos. "Once what?"

Thanatos pauses at the stained glass doors, his hand on the handles but not opening them. He speaks so softly that his voice is closer to a whisper in a howling wind. "He said that reading was the only time he didn't feel alone."

I feel like the rug has been pulled from under me for the second time today. How can I feel so deeply about this perfect, complex man but also know so little about him? Cerberus nudges my leg with his left head, whining softly, almost as if he feels the pain that Hades felt, the pain that I feel. I give him a halfhearted smile and look at Thanatos expectantly. I should be having these conversations with Hades. It should be him giving me this tour, him telling me how to be a ruler of this realm I know nothing about. I squash the feelings before the anger burns too hot, already feeling the sharpness of the thorns beneath my skin. I close my eyes and take a breath.

Thanatos pushes open the doors, the wood groaning. "This is the king's personal library."

I open my eyes, grateful for the distraction. Thousands and thousands of books stare back at me, lining bookshelves that stretch from floor to ceiling. I look up in awe, taking in the hundred-foot ceilings and the grand chandeliers hanging proudly, lighting the room. Not that they're currently needed. Along the back wall, amongst the stacked shelves, floor-to-ceiling windows allow the muted light of the Underworld to cast the room in a warm orange glow. I step into the room, completely awestruck. I wander to the closest shelf and glide my fingers over one of the countless leather-bound spines.

"He spends a lot of time in here, then?" I ask Thanatos as I pull one book from the shelf and leaf through it.

"More than anywhere else."

I return the book and move farther into the library,

31

strolling between the stacks. "Does he have a favorite?"

Thanatos walks to a small section of the library, slipping a book from its shelf. "This one."

He holds out a copy of *Fellowship of the Ring*. I take the book from him, smiling at how worn it is, clearly well-loved and well-read. I hold the book to my chest and look back at Thanatos. "Where to now?"

He gestures to the exterior doors. "The palace gardens."

I smile, genuinely excited to visit them. Thanatos holds his hand out, gesturing for me to lead the way out of the stacks and to the glass at the back of the library. As we get closer, I see a large door leading to a balcony area encircled by the same wrought-iron railing as the balcony upstairs. Cerberus barrels into the library, his tail wagging as he runs to the door. He barks with his middle head, his whole body wriggling in excitement to go outside. I laugh and open the door for him. Cerberus rushes past me and down the stairs, jumping and leaping as he goes.

I glance at Thanatos. "Is he always that excited to go outside?"

"He is excited to go outside with his queen."

I lift an eyebrow. "His queen?"

Thanatos looks at me, revealing a sliver more of his face, the bottom of his cheek just barely visible. "Yes, my queen. He is as honored as I am to be accompanying you on this walk."

Cerberus happily smells the flowers and rolls in the grass. I smile warmly at the sight and set the precious book on a small table before stepping onto the balcony. I stand at the railing and look out over the garden. "There's not much color," I say to no one in particular.

Thanatos steps up beside me, impassively looking at the gardens. "Whatever is not to your liking can be changed, my queen."

"I'm sure I can." I hesitate and look down at my hands, thinking about my powers and how they feel like an unknown entity. Everything about me feels foreign now. This has always been who I truly am. I am no longer half of a person. Two hundred years of suppressing one side of me has taken its toll, and I'm only realizing that now. Only now am I feeling the weight of what my mother took from me. She is so ashamed of that other side of me that she worked tirelessly to hide it.

I hold out my hand, the dark daisy sprouting from my palm. The red veins on the petals pulse in even beats. "I don't know who I am anymore," I murmur, my gaze fixed on the flower.

"You are who you were always meant to be," Thanatos states softly. I close my hand, trying to swallow my anxiety.

"My powers are changing."

"The Underworld shows us as we truly are. No artifice." Thanatos looks at my fist. "Your powers are simply becoming what they always were."

I open my hand and twist it, watching as my vines curl and twine around the balcony railing. It doesn't even surprise me to see that they're no longer bright green. Now they are much darker, almost purple. They no longer emanate the cheerful air of spring but something darker, more powerful, more sinister. Tentatively, I reach out and touch the leaves. They're waxy and malleable between my thumb and forefinger, but they're strong.

I step back and start walking down the stairs into the garden, shivering when I cross into the ankle-deep mist. It clears for me as if it, too, bows before me. I watch the mist as I move farther into the garden. It curls and sways almost playfully as I walk, my feet always visible. My eyes latch onto the rose garden. Black and purple flowers are landscaped perfectly. I wonder if I can change the rose color as I did when I was young. My mother would always be furious with me when I would turn her pink roses red and the white roses orange. She took such pride in her always pristine garden, with no thorn out of place.

I bend, looking at the delicate petal of a black rose right in the middle of the patch. I reach forward, brushing the very tips of my fingers over it. Being in gardens has always made me feel more powerful; this one is no exception. Being here has increased my power tenfold.

I concentrate on the rose, stroking the petal again, the softest whisper of a touch on such delicate silk. I wait for the rose to change color, but nothing happens. Disheartened, I sigh but try once more. I cup the full flower in my hands, concentrating with all I have, pushing against the powers of the Underworld, of my kingdom, which clearly wants this rose to remain black.

But the Underworld will have to bend to my will as the petals of this rose. I am the Queen of the Underworld, but I am also the Goddess of Spring, and I have lived too long being one without the other, existing as half of myself, ashamed of an entire part of me. My hands shake with the power I'm exerting, but I continue. I am Persephone. I am spring. I am the ruler of the Underworld.

A bead of sweat slides down my temple, and my hand trembles, but finally, a bloom of red appears in the center of the rose, like a droplet of blood. I take a breath, pouring my power into this one rose, needing to succeed at this, to prove to my mother, Hades, and myself that I can be both. The red slowly stretches, covering the whole rose, only the faintest of black ringing the edge of the petals, showing what it used to be. I slide my thumb over the outer petals once, twice, and then stand, stepping back out of the flower beds. My blood-red rose sits proudly in the middle of a bed of black, no less powerful, no less beautiful, but definitely different.

I stretch my fingers, my gaze fixed on my rose. My eyes sting with tears. I glance over my shoulder at Thanatos to find him watching me. "I'll tend to the garden from now on."

Chapter Six
Hades

DAYS TURNED INTO MONTHS, *months into years. I marked the passing of time by carving notches into a rock, and created ways to satiate my thirst for knowledge. Rather than living beneath a scrap of cloth as Poseidon was doing before I arrived, I built what we needed from the world around us. I didn't know how he'd managed before me. Poseidon was content with just surviving, whereas I wanted more. I needed more. So, I used the one thing that I never seemed to exhaust: my mind. I honed it like Poseidon sharpened his ax.*

Eventually, my form filled out as I grew into adulthood, no longer the skeletal teenager I was when I landed. I irrigated a large garden from the nearby lake and grew food. Poseidon and I spent the never-ending days hunting or building our homes from whatever we could find inside this prison. As the years passed, we developed a routine, or what could pass as one. We spent most of the morning working on the crops and hunting. In the afternoon, we'd work on our houses, or I would create languages. I couldn't read or write, but I created things to keep my mind occupied. I'm not sure what Poseidon did when he was alone. Not sure I wanted to know, but at least we had each other.

It was a realm outside of time, and nothing made sense inside it. Why were we able to sustain ourselves? Why were there animals and trees and water and seeds? Why were they forced to live their life in a prison? When we wandered too close to the edge of the world, we would end up right back where we started. Poseidon didn't have any answers, and he didn't seem bothered by it.

I no longer heard the voice that whispered to me during the fall. The allure of her soothing syllables and the knowledge she'd promised faded into forgotten memory. Had I imagined the voice? Had it been something to cling to during the fall?

Poseidon shoved me out of the way as we hunted, trying to gain the upper hand in our competition. He excelled in brute strength and not much else, but I was cunning. I smirked as he landed in one of my traps, giving me enough time to close the distance and overtake him. I laughed as he glared at me and jumped out of the way when he tried to grab my ankle.

I pulled back the string of my bow, my eyes narrowing on the hide of the golden hind in my sights. My favorite.

I held my breath, even as I heard Poseidon catching up. He'd gotten out of my trap faster than I expected, but I'd prepared for that. I prepared for everything, every eventuality, and every possibility.

Just a moment more.

My fingers released the bowstring, and my arrow flew.

BOOM!

My arrow went wide, the very ground beneath us moving. I barely kept my balance as the world rocked under my feet. I looked back at Poseidon, whose eyes were wide and panicked, identical to mine. The ground shook, throwing us into trees. I clung to the bark until the tremors subsided. My eyes locked with Poseidon's, and he nodded silently. The years had given us a form of silent communication. We raced through the forest toward the source of the sound. Neither of us spoke or barely breathed.

It's the clearing where I landed, where Poseidon landed.

We burst through the trees, both of us freezing when we saw what was there. Our houses were still perfectly misshapen, but right in front of them was... a boulder? The rock was sitting in a crater, the dirt having sprayed in a halo around it.

"I'm guessing this isn't a typical occurrence?" I whispered to my brother, not taking my eyes off the boulder as if it would disappear if I looked away from it for too long.

Poseidon shot me a dry look before storming closer. I reached out to pull him back, the words of caution dying on my tongue. Not that Poseidon would have listened, anyway. Pain in my ass. I sighed heavily, following my brother, hurrying to catch up to him.

"It's a rock," Poseidon murmurs.

"Your observation skills are unparalleled," I responded drolly. I walked closer to the massive boulder, looking it over. It was bigger than I thought and wrapped in some sort of blue fabric. "Is it wearing a blanket?"

Poseidon fingered the material wrapped around the rock. Part of it was trapped beneath the stone, and I doubted that even together, Poseidon and I could free it. It was almost as if the boulder and blanket were one. "A boulder in a blue blanket."

My brother and I circled the strange stone. I lifted a hand, touching the rock. The smooth surface was cool under my fingers, the slightest scent of clean linen wafting from the fabric. But with every passing second, the smell dissipated. Something about the scent was so familiar. Familiar enough that it made my chest ache. For a moment, I felt the warmth of someone's arms holding me, a soft voice humming as I fell asleep.

"This makes little sense," Poseidon murmured, pulling me out of the memory. Dream?

"We are trapped in a pocket realm with only each other for company. Why would anything make sense?" I mused.

Poseidon came around the side of the stone, and for a moment, his shadow aligned perfectly with the stone. Realization settled over me like an icy finger down my spine.

"It's another one of us," I whispered shakily, taking a step back from the stone.

Poseidon looked at me, his light brows furrowed over his eyes. The same eyes I had. "The fuck does that mean?"

38

I took another step back from the stone. "It's another brother."

Poseidon inhaled sharply as he came to the same realization. The stone was a replacement, a trick that our father fell for.

"He's been swapped out," Poseidon said, staring at the rock.

I took another step back from the stone. "Someone wrapped him in a blanket."

"And pretended he was a child."

"A baby," I whispered hoarsely.

Poseidon stared at the stone, and his eyes flickered, the blue turning to crashing waves as anger roiled within him. I could feel it radiating from his body. With the mental connection between us, I heard his question echo my own without a word leaving our lips.

Why didn't they switch me?

Chapter Seven

Hades

FOR DAYS AFTER THE BOULDER'S APPEARANCE, *Poseidon and I waited for another thing to land. Would our father know he had been tricked? Would our actual brother come hurtling to the ground soon? When nothing happened, we returned to our routine, but the boulder still sat in the same place, almost mocking us. The rock became a point of constant contention. Poseidon wanted it destroyed. I caught him multiple times punching the boulder as if he could somehow shatter it with just his fists. I said it was better to just ignore it and pretend it didn't exist. Maybe one day, it would disappear as mysteriously as it appeared, and then we could go back to trying to survive in this tiny pocket realm.*

Forget about the worlds outside. They'd clearly forgotten about us. Why should I care about them? My hands fist as I looked at the house I'd built. I'd spent decades toiling in front of it, sourcing materials and tools, agonizing over every part, every corner and crevice. Each part of this building was a part of me; the crooked cabinets that held nothing; the lopsided table I tried for days to get flat; the mattress filled with straw, and the slightly skewed bed frame. I looked at the front of my home and saw the stone just on the edge of my vision. My hand found the crooked cabinet, the one I'd slaved over and spent hours trying to make perfect.

I ripped that fucking cabinet from the wall, hurling it at the other furniture I'd struggled to make. My hands found the next thing, a stupid plate I'd tried so hard to make flat and smooth. It went the way of the cabinet. I kept grabbing things I'd struggled to make and create, seeking a way to ease the ache inside me. What did it matter how long I'd spent on them? No one cared. They sent me here and forgot. Fuck them. I didn't care what they thought. I didn't care how long I'd worked on the chair as I broke it against the wall.

I didn't even realize I was crying until Poseidon grabbed my hands, stopping me from throwing the table against the wall. I struggled against his hold, needing to destroy. Why was he stopping me? It didn't matter.

"Hades!" Poseidon shouted.

I looked at him, barely seeing his face through the haze of tears. "Let go of me!"

I slammed my shoulder into him, but he clung to my hands. I snapped my head forward, hitting his forehead with a crack. Golden ichor spilled from the cut above his eyebrow, and his eyes turned stormy.

"You need to calm the fuck down, Hades!" he shouted.

My powers responded, the shadows of the realm clinging to me, a helm of darkness surrounding me. Of course, my powers would choose now to finally manifest. I'd spent decades watching Poseidon manipulate water and shake the world, and I'd been unable to do anything. How many times had I wished for something similar?

Now it manifested.

Poseidon responded, water flowing from the lake to him. His mouth was moving. Was he talking to me? Whatever he was saying was lost in the roar in my ears.

Another time, I would wonder why this was my power: darkness and shadows. I never considered myself a "dark" person before, but right now, I could only lash out. My shadows turned to spears, and I hurled them at him. Poseidon used his own abilities to deflect, but where the shadows landed, they exploded, turning everything around them to darkness.

41

I formed more shadow spears, aiming them at my brother. They were responding to my unspoken desire to fight. To rage. To wail. To soothe this hole inside me.

I didn't even have to tell them to fly at my brother. They did so on their own. My attention faltered when the world shook again, the concentration and ultimate manifestation of my power vanishing as easily as it had come.

Poseidon cursed soundly, releasing his hold on his power as well. "Now what?"

I looked out to where that boulder sat, expecting to find another with it, but there was nothing. I frowned at Poseidon, but he didn't look at me. His gaze was focused on the trees, horror suffusing his face.

When I followed his focus, I gasped. The trees were vanishing. Not just vanishing, they were being sucked into the sky, along with the lake and creatures. Everything was hurtling back into the sky from where we once came.

I glanced at Poseidon. "The realm..."

Poseidon whispered shakily, "It's vanishing."

"How do we stop it?"

Poseidon looked at me sadly. "We don't."

"What?" I demanded, trying to pull the shadows back into me, even as the massive boulder was lifted from the ground, sailing back into the sky. Just as I had wished it would earlier. The blue blanket fluttered like a flag, finally freed from beneath the rock.

Poseidon grabbed my arms, shaking me. "Hades! Summon your armor! Now!"

Poseidon's own armor, created from the water he must have stolen before the lake vanished, appeared like scales over his chest and arms. The water had solidified, becoming as hard as steel on his skin. I closed my eyes, trying to focus on the emotions that had brought my power to me a moment ago, but I couldn't focus past the sound of the only world I'd ever known being sucked into the sky.

I opened my eyes and looked at my brother. "I-I can't."

Poseidon's eyes frantically took in my face, then back to the world vanishing around us. "You must!"

42

I locked my eyes on his. "I can't! What's happening?"

Poseidon glanced at the world and then back at me. "Hades, war is coming. We have to fight."

I shook my head. "I'm not a warrior."

Poseidon chuckled shakily. "We never had any choice in our futures, Brother. Fate picked them out for us long ago."

I tried to ask what he meant by that, but the realm continued crumbling around us until there was nothing but Void. The only remaining piece of our home was beneath our feet. Then, for a moment, it stopped.

An eye of a storm. A moment of peace.

Poseidon gripped my hand tightly. "Summon your armor. Fate is inescapable."

The moment of peace was shattered. Our feet left the ground, and the shadows finally obeyed me. They clung to me, creating the helm of darkness as we ascended. We flew back through the never-ending tunnel that we once descended from, toward a fate I didn't want.

Chapter Eight
Hades

IGRITTED MY TEETH, STRUGGLING TO KEEP
MY SHADOWS FROM FALLING DURING THE
ASCENT. *The rise was nothing like the never-ending
fall. The fall was peaceful in a way. This was agonizing pain.
It felt like my body was crumpling in on itself, the pressure
making me feel like my skull was being crushed into my
spine. My skin was on the verge of ripping, the force pulling
me up too fast for my body to tolerate. My skin, bones, and
muscles all want to go in different directions. Poseidon
looked at me, his face contorted with pain. I tried to keep
my eyes open, even as we careened higher. Maybe I should
stop fighting to keep my body in one piece and just let the
overwhelming pain rip me apart.*

*A flash of agony, even more intense, made me look down,
expecting to see half of my body had been left behind. But I
was whole, and my armor was still in place, the pressure still
there, crushing me. It felt like each of my bones was too heavy
for my body. Maybe my mind was finally snapping, and I
was feeling things that didn't exist. Even as we ascended, a
scent filled my nose.*

Roses.

*It was soothing, and familiar, allowing me to keep it
together as we continued moving higher. My mind was
definitely snapping. The light above us was becoming so*

bright it was blinding. It was so much like the sun of our pocket realm. The one that had taken me weeks to adjust to.

Fate. That was what Poseidon said waited at the end of this rise. It was an inescapable fate and one I had no say in.

Poseidon locked eyes with me again, his mouth moving, but I heard nothing past the pressure tearing my body apart. I couldn't keep my eyes open, the lids too heavy to stay up. This was it. The end. What did it matter if it was? No one would care.

I saw a pair of eyes, blue with a burst of sun around the pupils. A set of red lips curving into a knowing smirk. The scent of roses clouded my nose. My eyes snapped open, and resolve filled me. I had to survive.

The pressure slowly eased, my lungs filling fully. I focused on my brother. Poseidon looked even paler, but his armor was still intact, as was mine. We held on. Somehow.

We landed, my teeth slamming against each other. My knees buckled, and I hit the ground. Poseidon fell next to me, both of us barely conscious but clinging to the ground beneath us. Before we could fully adjust, someone grabbed our arms, yanking us to our feet.

I panted, my legs still a little weak from the ascent. I turned and locked eyes with a pair identical to mine. The same blue that Poseidon and I shared, but set in a new face.

Brother.

I didn't have time to speak before our new brother threw us behind him, using his golden shield to stop the new bolt of power that hurtled toward us. When I hit my shoulder against Poseidon's, the lingering nausea cleared, and I took in my surroundings. The remains of our pocket realm were littered around us like trash. I saw the corner of that crooked cabinet I was destroying earlier cast off to the side, the pieces strewn across the floor, golden smears of blood staining the blinding white marble. How long had this fight been going on?

There were numerous divine beings around us, their skin glowing ethereally, all armed and prepared for war. Several of them looked worn from the still-raging battle. My gaze collided with Poseidon's, and a wordless exchange took place between us.

Together we moved, flanking our youngest brother. My shadows formed spears, and I looked at our enemy. He hurled another bolt of power and vibrated the ground hard enough to make my teeth clatter. I locked eyes with the towering force across from us. His eyes were just like mine, like my brothers', but there was a cruel glint to them that none of us had.

Father.

"Poseidon," our youngest brother called, a smirk echoing in his voice, "Hades. Welcome to Olympus. My name is Zeus. I freed you."

Zeus. Our youngest brother.

"Why don't we wait for introductions after the battle?" I mused, more shadow spears preparing at my sides. Right now was hardly the time.

"We'll have plenty of time to bond," Poseidon added.

Zeus laughed. "I suppose we will."

My power rose in me as we faced our father. Poseidon's power felt like a crashing wave against the shore, a torrent of salty brine. Zeus was the crackle in the air, the spark in the storm cloud. My power was the unknowing darkness, the void of oblivion. Their powers complimented mine as if we were three parts of the same whole. Apart, we were strong, but together we could face anything.

As one, we attacked our father. Our captor. The Titan. Kronos.

I knew his name as I knew my own, and the way he laughed as he fended off our attacks with ease made my stomach roil. He was toying with us. His eyes glowed with maniacal glee, moving closer to us as he continued. Each time one of us launched an attack, he twirled his hand, encased in a green glow, and our blows turned to dust, having no effect.

As I focused on my father, trying to figure out how we were going to defeat him, my gaze darted over his shoulder. There was a shape looming behind him, something that didn't belong. My brows furrowed as I tried to bring the hovering *shape into focus, but my inattention cost me. Atlas, Titan of Strength, threw a spear at me, and I was too slow to dodge. I let out a shout of agony when the spear embedded in my stomach, dropping me to my knees. This pain was nothing compared to the ascent. I could take it. I grabbed the weapon, preparing to pull it out, gritting my teeth, and looking at the ground beneath me.*

Flowers?

Beneath my knees were flowers. Roses. When I looked back up, Atlas was on me, his fist pulled back, ready to throw a blow that I knew would shatter my arm.

Wait, this wasn't how it happened.

Atlas continued moving, but the blow never landed. When my eyes locked on the towering Titan, the memory of his face and form flickered. Everything was moving around me in disjointed order, a haze of shapes and colors with no definition.

This wasn't how it happened.

When I stood, Atlas fell through me, taking the injury with him, leaving nothing but a remembered wound, an ache from long ago.

My eyes swept over the battle, but it was a blend of gold and white, a clash of colors and bodies with no defining shapes. Except for one: the looming shape that hovered behind my father.

It was a tree.

I moved through the battle, gods and Titans falling through me, reliving the battle from memory. But it didn't hurt. I felt nothing.

I paused when I passed my father, looking over his harsh face. We all shared the same eyes, but I bore the most resemblance to our monstrous sire. The scar that bisected his eyebrow flickered in and out, appearing and disappearing. That was right. He didn't have that scar yet. Zeus would give it to him soon.

I looked back at the tree, stepping past my father, and the moment of clarity vanished as he joined the blur of color, movement, and memory. I didn't bother avoiding the other

Titans who fought at his side, even as they lunged against us. My focus was on the tree.

When I finally reached it, I stared, taking in the black trunk and watching as the golden sap dripped from the cracks in the wood. Tiny rivulets of gold soaked into the roots, then rose through the bark to the branches, the twisted tree veined with it, gilding it with gold.

I touched the trunk, and a tortured scream echoed all around me. Only when I fell to my knees did I realize it was my own.

"You're fighting the dream," a voice called. My eyes landed on the figure standing next to the tree.

It took a moment for me to place his face, those fathomless eyes, and the voice of both nightmares and dreams. "Morpheus."

Morpheus moved closer to me, dropping to one knee. "This is all I can do, my king."

I scanned his face. "You've trapped me in a dream?"

He shook his head, his midnight hair swaying against the movement as if of its own accord. "I came when you called."

I glanced back at the tree, studying the gold rivulets. "I'm in this tree, aren't I?"

Morpheus nodded, reaching out to touch my forehead. "Go back to the dream, my king. Don't ask questions you don't want answered."

Morpheus's touch pushed me back into the dream, into the memories. I fought, but only for a moment, just enough time to send an echo through the world of dreams.

"Come to me, my spring. Find me."

Chapter Nine

Persephone

IT CAN'T BE...
I try to gasp, but there is no air, nothing to breathe in, no way to find my voice to reply. I hear my name again, and I try to focus on it, but I realize I'm not hearing my name. His voice is projecting directly into my mind. I mentally grasp at the bond, sending my reply down it.

"Hades?"

No reply. I send it again and again, but the bond has gone eerily silent. I try to breathe again, but nothing happens. Faintly, I hear him again and try to strengthen our mind-to-mind connection.

"Come to me, my spring. Find me."

My spring? It is Hades.

"Hades, where are you?"

I wake with a start, the words still on my lips. I pant, looking around, orienting myself to my surroundings. My heart races, hearing his echoing words in my head, haunting me.

"Come find me, my spring. Find me."

I look at Cerberus and gently wake him, all three of his heads yawning.

"I need you to take me to Hekate. Now."

Cerberus sniffs the air, two of his heads howling. He paws the pillow, almost as if he's scenting Hades. I nod, petting him.

"I think he's in trouble. Take me to Hekate."

49

Cerberus growls, not at me, but at the threat to Hades. He jumps off the bed and hurries to the door. He paws at it, growing more anxious by the second. I climb out of bed. My heart pounds in my chest, and I try to breathe, to tell myself it was only a dream, but I've been feeling more and more uneasy about Hades' disappearance. I look at my broken phone on the bedside table and grab it, hoping Hekate may be able to fix it. Clambering out of bed, I rush into the closet and pull on the yoga pants from yesterday and another of Hades' shirts, this time going for an old band t-shirt.

Cerberus huffs from the door, wiggling his butt, impatiently waiting for me. I hurry out of the closet, pull my Converse on, and open the door for him. He bolts, hurtling down the corridor to the main foyer. I rush out of the bedroom, trying to keep up with him, but he dashes out of sight as he travels the maze-like halls.

"Wait! I only have two legs!" I call after my three-headed marshmallow.

I keep running, hoping Cerberus hears me. A moment later, the floor below me groans, and I feel a tingling in my hips. Noticing my increasing speed, I look down and gasp when I see two additional legs protruding from my hips. I stop running, blinking down at my additional appendages in horror, hearing Thanatos's voice echoing in my head.

I'm sure the palace would be honored to supply whatever you require, my queen.

I growl, "I didn't want four legs! I only wanted two. A horse would have sufficed."

In the blink of an eye, my two additional legs disappear, and a two-legged horse appears in front of me.

My eyes go wide. *Fuck, this building takes things extremely literally.*

"A *four*-legged horse... please."

The horse grows two more legs and huffs at me,

bumping my arm with its nose. I place my hand on its muzzle, patting it gently. "Take me to Cerberus?"

The horse whinnies, and I shove my foot into the stirrup before pulling myself onto the mare.

"Thank you. Though I don't love the horse being in the house," I mumble.

I squeeze my thighs and urge the horse forward, her heavy hooves loud against the wood. As we turn the corner, I see Cerberus far in the distance, the disturbed mist curling in his wake, leaving a trail for us to follow. I shake the reins, pushing the horse faster as we hasten our pursuit of Cerberus. Before long, I can clearly see him, his loud, excited barks finally audible. I lift my head, noticing the sun is only now beginning to rise, the watery light illuminating the vast planes of the realm, of my realm.

The sun rises, but I know the luxury of light won't last long as we barrel into the thick woodland. The mist falls heavier here. While it was wispy like clouds in the garden, here it is like molasses. The only sounds are Cerberus's distant bark and the muted pounding of the mare's hooves against the dense forest floor. The large, thick trees cast unsettling shadows, and a sense of foreboding sits heavily in my stomach.

"This is my realm. This is my realm. This is my realm," I whisper as the horse slows, almost as if to prevent making excess noise. A twig snap in the distance, and my head snaps toward it. I lean in, trying to focus my eyes in the almost pitch-black forest. The mare huffs, unsettled, and sidesteps uneasily. I hear another twig snap, and I gasp. Cerberus has long since stopped barking, and my heart pounds in my chest.

"You're okay. You're okay. You're okay," I whisper as I look around, patting the horse's neck. I swallow as another twig snaps, this one closer than the last. The mare shuffles her feet uneasily, and I tighten my hands on the reins, my breaths shallow. A bush rustles beside us, and an angry snarl rips through the silence. The horse bucks, and I struggle to stay on her. My scream catches in my throat as the bush rustles again and out jumps... Cerberus.

I glare at him, clenching my fists. "You little..."

He barks happily and playfully jumps from side to side. My horse huffs, obviously just as angry at the three-headed goofball as I am.

"Bad boy. Take me to Hekate now."

Cerberus looks up at me. His faces fall, and his heads droop as he slowly leads the way up a hill.

My eyes catch on various signs on the way up the steep forest slope. *Entering Propylaia. Turn Back Now. Enter At Your Peril. Hades Free Zone.* I frown but continue, following a very sad Cerberus. The trees thin as we reach the top of the hill, yet there is barely more light here than there was in the thick of the woods. It's as if the sun also feels uncomfortable shining here.

In the distance, I can see a manor perched right on the very edge of the cliff. The large house spans almost the length of the cliff, and the dark clouds behind it don't match the day it looked like it was going to be before we journeyed into the forest. The clouds sit low behind the manor and flash intermittently, although there is no thunder. I tug the reins once and jump off the horse,

Cerberus looks up at me hopefully. I roll my eyes and scratch each of his heads. "You're a good boy." I look at the manor again. Every light in the house seems to be on, the windows bright with fiery orange light.

"Is this where Hekate lives, Cerberus?" I ask, stepping forward.

Cerberus whimpers and takes a step back. I glance at him over my shoulder. "You okay, boy?"

He shuffles back, moving behind the happily grazing horse.

I look back at the manor. "Well, looks like it's just me then." I take another step forward but pause when I hear a blood-curdling scream coming from within.

I look back at Cerberus. He whines, backing up even more.

"Come with me?" I ask Cerberus hopefully. He backs up again, his whole body shaking.

"You have got to be kidding me. You are literally a humongous dog with three heads."

He peeks around the horse, fear clear in his eyes.

I roll my eyes. "Fine. I'll go myself, coward." Cerberus whines again, and the sound pierces my heart. I sigh heavily and walk over to him, kneeling in front of him.

"Will you stay here and look after the horse?" I scratch behind one of his ears. He pants, and I swear he smiles with all of his mouths. The horse gives me an exasperated look before going back to grazing.

I grin at Cerberus. "Okay, you be my brave boy out here?"

Cerberus lifts and drops his paws excitedly, wriggling his butt as he licks my face.

"Berry! Stop!" I laugh, wiping my face. I take a steadying breath and stand, starting toward the house.

"You can do this. You've been on the Haunted Mansion ride at Disneyland. This'll be just like that." Another scream echoes from the building, and my sure steps falter. I clench my fists and keep walking. I am doing this for Hades. Hades needs me. Potentially. Not that he deserves my help. Abandoning prick.

My anger at Hades makes my next steps easier, and soon, I'm fully stomping up the derelict path. My skin prickles with the feeling that I'm being watched, but I can't find the source.

Approaching the door, I knock. The painted dark purple wood looks like it's seen better days, like much of the outside of the building. I knock again, louder this time, and the door creaks loudly as it slowly opens for me. I frown, certain it was closed the first time I knocked.

"Hekate?" I curse under my breath at the shakiness

of my voice. As I step inside the manor, I shiver, the sharp coolness prickling against my skin.

"Hekate?" I call louder this time. I take in my surroundings, the sconces casting light on the hallway. A grand staircase sits in the middle of the room, the brass banisters dully glinting under at least an inch of dust. In fact, everything I look at is covered in dust, cobwebs, and grime. I grimace, already feeling like the filth is clinging to me... *just like in my dreams.*

Dirt, rotting bark, moldy autumn leaves.

No air, no power, no hope.

A loud clatter from somewhere toward the back of the house pulls me from the memory, and I hurry through, hoping to find Hekate. The farther into the manor I go, the more the rotting smell is overtaken by the overwhelming scent of freshly baked cookies. I follow the smell, my brows furrowing. The contrast between the aesthetics of the manor and the smell of the baking makes my head spin a little.

My eyes prick as I hear a haunting melody being sung from behind an old-fashioned swing door. Tentatively, I push it open, the words to the eerie song becoming louder. It sends a chill down my spine. I peer around the door, seeing Hekate pulling a tray out of the oven and slamming the door closed with her foot.

I clear my throat, trying not to startle her.

"My queen." Her voice even. She doesn't look up from her cookies, her long, sleek black hair neatly braided down her back. Her dark horns peeking through her hair. Her porcelain skin is so white it looks almost chalk-like. Once again, she is in her Morticia Addams form.

The mother.

I push through the door and step into the kitchen. "Hekate." I glance at the cookies, noting the intricate gothic designs on each one. "Sorry to just drop in. I knocked, but..."

"You are always welcome, my queen." She finally lifts

her eyes to me. Once again, I'm struck by how black they are. She looks down at her bakes again, admiring them. She picks one up, her critical gaze analyzing every inch. It is as if she is looking for imperfections, and she will be furious if there is even one crumb out of place. Her lips pull into a sharp smile, her painted purple lips making her look even more menacing. "Cookie?"

I smile uneasily and glance at the sweet, the spindly design perfect. "Oh, uh… no, thank you. I actually came here to talk to you about something."

She tilts her head, her long nails drumming against the marble countertop. "How can I be of service, my queen?"

"I'm worried about Hades."

Hekate all but rolls her eyes, her interest in the subject dropping to next to zero. She lifts her hand, examining her blood-red nails. "What about him?"

I take a breath. "I don't know where he is, and I—"

"Hades is not due back in the Underworld for another three weeks," she replies dismissively.

I blink. "Well, yes. I understand that, but that doesn't mean he *can't* come to the Underworld, does it?"

Hekate's gaze flicks to mine. "No, he is the ruler of this realm. He can visit at his leisure."

I nod. "Right, so where is he?"

"It is not my job to keep tabs on Hades, my queen, as I told you when I came to collect you. This is his time upstairs, so I would assume he is there."

"There is something wrong, Hekate. I know it." I pause. "There is no way he would curse me and then abandon me down here."

"Have you considered the possibility that he is giving you this time as a gift? To get to know your realm without the distraction of… *him?*" She practically spits the last word.

"No. He wouldn't do that. He'd want to be here with me."

55

Hekate purses her lips, assessing me, her eyes narrowed slightly. When she doesn't reply, I continue. "I've been having dreams recently… well, nightmares. They happen every night. I can't breathe. I'm powerless and alone. Every time, I wake up retching and gasping for air. Hekate, it's been happening since the last time I saw Hades."

She lifts her chin, her eyes sparkling with interest. Finally.

"Last night, I *heard* him."

"Heard him?" She frowns.

I nod. "He said, 'Come to me, my spring. Find me.' I-I think he's in danger," I say, trying to swallow the lump in my throat.

"And you can only hear him when you are asleep?" She holds a cookie up to the light, assessing it as if it holds the answers. I nod, looking at the cookie hopefully. "Then you need a dream god," she mumbles, nodding at the cookie before looking at me expectantly. "Even better if it's someone who specializes in nightmares."

I lift my eyebrows, waiting for her to continue. She smiles at me vaguely for several moments, unblinking.

"Heka—"

"You will need to get a ghost to send a message topside." She places the cookie back on the plate. "The Goddess of Nightmares works for IT at Plutus Industries."

I tip my head to the side. "You mean Mellie?"

Hekate's eyes meet mine. "You know Melinoë?"

I nod. "How do I get topside?"

She chuckles darkly. "My queen should work on her listening skills. I did not tell *you* to go topside. You are bound to the Underworld until Hades' next time to go upstairs. You must send a ghost to fetch her for you."

I frown, pulling my phone from my pocket. "Couldn't I just send a text?"

Hekate glares at my phone. Obviously, she's not

56

a fan of modern human technology. "While usually, you would be able to use... cellular devices in the Underworld, they must be working, which yours appears to be failing at."

"You don't know any spells to fix it?"

She gives me a searing look. "My magic is not for fixing silly human toys, my queen."

I sigh heavily. "A ghost then." I look around the otherwise empty room, searching for a ghost. The second I look away from Hekate, she sings her haunting shanty again, clearly done with the conversation. I glare at the back of her head and set about finding a ghost.

Chapter Ten

Hades

THE BLOW THAT ATLAS LANDED SHOOK ME TO MY CORE. *I could feel my entire body recoil from the force, and I shouted as the sound of my arm crumpling rang out. I thought the pain was nothing compared to the ascent, but my vision blurred when Atlas started grinding my broken bones against each other.*

Zeus slammed into Atlas, throwing him from me. The sound of their bodies clashing was like a landslide of boulders. Zeus watched the Titan slam against the far wall before turning back to me. He offered me his hand, his golden armor almost blinding, even covered in blood, and his white hair and beard matted with entrails and gore. I grabbed it, allowing my brother to help me up.

The clash of gods and Titans was a cacophony of power and strength around us, creating a whirlpool of death with my brothers and me at the center.

Poseidon let out a roar of delight as he swiped the Titans with a tidal wave, at one with his abilities. My eyes raked the battlefield. How could we win? Were we destined only to taste this single breath of freedom?

Zeus grabbed my face, dragging my focus to him. "Hades! You need to fight."

"I'm not... I'm not a warrior," *I whispered, even as the battle raged around us. Despite Poseidon forcing me to* roughhouse with him, I had no training, no ability. I was nothing. I was... weak.

Zeus's eyes crackled with power, his words ringing with authority. "None of us are. Poseidon's power is limited to the amount of water that's present. He'll run out soon. My power requires storms and skies. Soon Kronos will realize that and stop me. But you, Hades, you are limitless."

I opened my mouth to deny his words, but Zeus kept speaking. The deafening sounds of the battle dimmed as if fleeing from his voice. "Darkness is the other side of light, my brother. Each of our enemies possesses darkness. Turn it against them."

Zeus lifted his arm as another Titan attacked, blasting my brother from me. His body hit the wall hard, cracking the marble. I threw my arm up to block the Titan who landed the hit against Zeus, and my shadows formed a shield along my forearm, throwing him away from me. I tried to conjure the shadow spears again, hoping to hurl them into our enemies, but there was nothing, not even a tremble of power. Fuck, where was the anger and rage? The loneliness and desperation? The emotions I needed to fuel my power. Zeus was wrong. I was nothing.

I shouldn't be here.

I was not a warrior. I ducked behind an intact wall to avoid a bolt of power someone had thrown. My chest heaved with my ragged breaths, my vision blurring. The pain from my arm was shooting up into my shoulder. It was healing, but slowly. Atlas must have shattered the bone. The pieces would take a while to knit, and I would feel every second. I dared a look from my hiding space, my breath catching as I locked on my father. He moved disjointedly. Every step he took destroyed the surrounding time. The marble beneath his feet turned to dust, and the gods who came close enough disintegrated into ash, not even their bones remaining.

I shouldn't be—

Kronos grabbed Zeus by the throat, and my breath froze in my lungs. I watched as my father lifted my youngest brother off his feet.

59

"I'll enjoy killing you, little boy," Kronos mocked, grabbing Zeus's face and pressing his thumb into one of my brother's eyes with a sickening squelch. Our father crumpled half of Zeus's face with his grip as if my little brother was nothing more than a bug to be crushed beneath his hand. Zeus's eyeball fell between us, rolling on the bloodied marble. For a moment, I could feel Zeus watching me.

"Everybody has darkness. Turn it against them."

Slowly, I stepped from behind the wall. Something had changed in me. It was proven in how some stepped back from me, instinctively sensing a new threat on the field of battle. My armor flickered on my skin, not dropping or vanishing but preparing for what was to come. For what I was about to become.

When I'd summoned the shadows in our prison, I'd called upon all the dejected feelings, hatred, and rage I felt but denied, pretending they didn't matter.

Kronos pulled back his hand to take Zeus's other eyeball, my brother screaming in agony. Zeus struggled harder against Kronos but to no avail. My eyes narrowed dangerously, the power rising in me like an abyss of never-ending void.

My father imprisoned me. I grew up in the fall. Poseidon and I were swallowed. Prisoners. We lived inside a realm outside of time, alone and forgotten.

I would no longer accept the choices of others.

I would make my own fucking fate.

Like a wordless order, the shadows of everyone, Titans, gods, Cyclops, the hundred armed Hecatoncheires, even the shadows of the buildings, broke from their owners and fled to me. A black abyss surrounded me, my armor repairing itself from the hit I'd taken from Atlas as I stared at the army in front of me.

I would make my own fucking fate.

The shadows exploded from me, launching at our enemies. They manifested to strangle the Titans, forcing them to their knees, unable to fight what they couldn't touch or feel.

"Everybody has darkness."

"Turn it against them."

"Poseidon!" I shouted, and my brother turned toward me, following my gaze to Zeus. Absently, I noticed my older brother was missing a hand.

After a lifetime of hunting and living together, Poseidon and I were used to moving as one. Poseidon crossed the battlefield, slamming his foot into our father's knees from behind. My shadows collared Kronos, struggling to keep him from standing.

Zeus coughed but grabbed his dagger and slashed upward, slicing Kronos's face. The wound bisected one eyebrow but left his eyes. Zeus held the dagger to Kronos's throat, his ruined eye dripping blood down his cheek. Zeus's voice rang out across the battlefield. "Surrender!"

Kronos looked at us, then Zeus, blood turning his smirk gold. "Never."

I struggled to keep my hold on Kronos. He was too strong. I could see the strain on Poseidon's face as well. We had only moments before he broke free and killed us.

Kronos glared at us, but then his face paled. "Miteras?"

I glanced around, searching for who he spoke to. The ground rumbled, and as we held him, the earth opened beneath his knees. Kronos screamed and struggled as he sank, the world swallowing him. Poseidon and I released him and stepped back to flank Zeus, looking down at our father.

"This isn't over, whelps," Kronos hissed, even as his torso was consumed.

"It's really hard to take your threat seriously when you are being sucked into the earth," Poseidon mused. Even Zeus snickered at that.

I looked down as our father's chest vanished. "Enjoy your prison, Father."

Zeus put a hand on my shoulder and another on Poseidon's. "And should you even think of escaping, we'll be waiting."

Kronos's shoulders are sucked below, leaving only his head visible. "My present will be your future." His words rang like a warning, even as he disappeared, the ground closing over him as if he had never been.

Screams of terror echoed across the battlefield as the earth swallowed the Titans. I looked at Zeus. "What's happening?"

Zeus smiled at me, even as golden ichor dripped down his face. "Gaia."

Poseidon shrugged at me, as lost as I was.

Zeus dropped to one knee, yanking our arms to force us to do the same. I lowered my eyes as I felt the approaching deity.

"My grandsons," Gaia whispered, and I barely kept my shock from showing.

"Earth Mother," Zeus responded. He didn't move to stand, so neither did I.

"Stand," she commanded.

Slowly, the three of us rose. I lifted my eyes to meet Gaia's, but her face was... wrong. It wasn't kind or soft, but harsh, her eyes cold and cruel.

Blue eyes with sunbursts.

This wasn't right.

I took a step back from Gaia. The second I moved, the memory immediately spun out of sync. My brothers turned, vague impressions of themselves, the battlefield hazy. The only thing in focus was her face, made of harsh angles and lines, framed by long, dark hair.

I took another step back, and her form sharpened, stepping out of the disguise she wore.

"Demeter," I snarled.

Demeter laughed. "Pathetic. As if I would ever give her to you. Weak. Worthless."

"What have you done?" I snapped, reaching for my powers, but there was only an echo. No shadows formed and launched.

"I have done what is necessary," Demeter snapped, her body vibrating with rage. Even in the dream, everything around her began to die.

"She'll hate you for this," I hissed.

Demeter only laughed, and the world went dark again.

Chapter Eleven

Persephone

IF I WERE A GHOST, WHERE WOULD I HIDE? I push the heavy swing door into the hallway, the squeaking hinges almost in harmony with Hekate's wailing. Stepping back into the derelict hallway after being in the immaculate kitchen makes it seem even more desolate. The dust sticks to every available surface, making the brass and gold look dull, the sconces and banister are rusted, and the hardwood floor is scuffed and worn with threadbare rugs strewn haphazardly throughout.

It wouldn't surprise me if the rugs were actually strategically placed to cover up large holes. Bearing this in mind, I only walk on the visible hardwood, but every groan from the floor has me on edge that my foot will go right through and I'll be plunged into some mystical abyss.

I peer into each room on the ground floor, hoping to spot a ghost and cursing myself for dropping my phone on that first day. I would need Mellie to bring me a new one.

I do a lap of the floor, trying to avoid visiting the upstairs. I have some major concerns regarding the structural integrity of this house, and going higher seems like an endlessly bad plan. After another lap,

I am slowly accepting that I'll probably have to take the plunge and head to the upper floor when my eye catches something white and glowing passing the library window. The being slides easily through the wall into the library a moment later.

He appears to be male, a little taller than me, and dressed in clothing I'd seen in a book about the Victorian era. His bright white aura surrounds him, making his finer features more difficult to distinguish. But from what I can tell, he is an older gentleman with a bushy handlebar mustache, glasses, and a top hat. He hovers before a shelf and peruses the books.

I take a breath and walk over to him. Instinctively, I reach out to tap him on the shoulder, not even considering the fact that he's most definitely translucent. I gasp and jump back with a jolt at the feeling of the coarse fabric beneath my fingers.

The ghost whirls on me, his face contorted with fury. "Harlot! How dare you touch me? Don't you know who I am?"

My eyes go wide, not just from his rage but because the spot on his shoulder that I touched is no longer the bright white of his ectoplasmic light but now the light brown of his suit jacket. The area spreads, and his glow recedes completely. His skin is no longer bright but pallid and sickly. His hair is not a shock of ethereal white but limp, dark gray.

I blink, his words only now sinking in as he continues his verbal assault on me.

"… just staring at me, bloody har—"

"Enough!"

His mouth hangs open as he gapes at me, and it's obvious that his face would be beetroot red if he were alive.

"You slattern! You trollop! You accosted me! I shall—"

I bring my palm to his cheek, slapping him hard.

"I said, enough." I try not to flinch at the sound of my

64

own voice, so deep, so sure, so commanding. The ghost cradles his cheek, his dead eyes sparking with fury, but he wisely stays silent. I lift my chin, staring him down. My jaw ticks, my fury simmering nicely under the surface.

"I need you to deliver a message to Melinoë. Urgently."

The command ripples through him as though he is powerless to do anything but comply. Immediately, all rage drops from his face, and he bows his head in submission.

"Tell her that Persephone requires her downstairs at once. It is extremely important. She must drop everything and find me at the palace as soon as possible. Also, tell her I need her to bring me a new cell phone."

The ghost bows his head lower and fades out of sight. I roll my shoulders and neck, the strain like I've exercised a muscle I've never used before. I sigh heavily and leave the decaying manor.

"If I never have to come back here again, it'll be too soon," I murmur, stepping onto the crooked path. Even out here, the air doesn't feel fresh or clean. It weighs heavily on me, an oppressive being.

I smile when I see Cerberus still cowering behind the horse. My lips twitch, and I walk over to him, bending to kiss all three of his heads. "I can see why you don't like it here. The ghosts are a piece of work."

Cerberus sniffs me, whining softly, almost as though he's checking me for injuries.

"I'm okay, Berry," I reassure him as I scratch him beneath his chin on his right and left head before moving to the middle one. He wiggles happily, content in his inspection of me.

"You like my nickname for you?"

He barks, wriggling more, his tail wagging so fast that dust and dirt lift from the ground.

"My Berry."

He licks me, his wide tongue almost covering half of

my face. I grimace, wiping my cheek on Hades' shirt.

"Gross!" I chuckle. Cerberus looks as though he's grinning. "Let's go meet Aunt Mellie at the palace?"

Cerberus nuzzles me and barks happily before I jump onto the horse and squeeze my thighs, urging the mare forward and down the hill, back to somewhere less… *Addams Family*.

We emerge from the forest, and the second the sun hits my skin, I feel less haunted and more at ease. The feeling of relief only intensifies when I see the palace in the distance. I smile brightly. The dark brickwork covered with dark green vines would probably look daunting to most. The formidable pointed turrets pierce the sky. My heart swells at this incredible place, even as my concern for Hades intensifies, everything here reminding me of him and his darkness. I dig my heels into the horse's flanks, pushing her on, desperate to see Mellie. To see something familiar in this world of unfamiliar.

When we reach the gardens, I practically leap off the mare, running as fast as my legs will carry me into the palace. I can sense someone here, and I *know* it's Mellie, that she's here already. Relief floods me. She'll do whatever she can to help me, to help Hades.

I run straight to the throne room, Cerberus hot on my tail, happily chasing me through the palace. The second those heavy doors to the throne room open, I see her. Her half-black, half-white hair is in space buns. She is wearing bright red fishnet tights beneath a pair of corduroy short-shorts, an oversized white formal shirt almost covering them. She's tense, nervously chewing on her nails, shifting from foot to foot. My eyes are drawn to the right side of her face, completely covered in burn scars, angry, red welts vivid against her previously unmarred skin. The horn on one side of her head is broken, the other is a swirl of black and white. The other side is as I remember her. The scars are ancient, like they may have happened centuries ago, yet the way she moves, it's still fresh to her.

Part of me yearns to know what happened, to know if someone hurt her, but the other is just so fucking relieved to see my friend.

I fly to her, my body colliding with hers as I pull her into a hug.

She chuckles, relaxing into me.

"I'm so glad you're here," I whisper and pull back, my hands gripping her shoulders. "I need your help. Hades needs your help."

Mellie nods, her eyebrows pulling into a concerned frown. The burned one barely moves. "How can I help?"

I squeeze her shoulders, smiling. "Hades is missing," I pause, unsure where to start. "I've been having these nightmares. I think he's in trouble."

"Missing?" Her eyebrows furrow even more.

"You've got to believe me, Mel." My eyes sting with tears. No one is listening, but I *know* there is something wrong.

"I believe you, but I've not seen Hades in days. I assumed he'd activated the curse and had come down here with you." She nervously pulls on her fingers, her eyes going distant, the shadows of her demons playing in their depths.

"Mellie?" I squeeze her shoulder again.

She blinks, coming back into herself. "Right. Sorry. Tell me about the nightmare."

I take a deep breath, already feeling my throat closing up and the earth sticking to my skin. "I..." My heart thumps in my chest, and my stomach rolls with nausea.

There is no room for fear, Persephone. Hades needs you.

I open my mouth to explain, to push through it, but Mellie smiles at me kindly and steps forward. She presses two fingers to her temple, and the grand walls of the throne room bleed away, leaving Mellie and me standing in complete darkness. My eyes strain as I hear a small whimpering noise. The more I try to tune into it, the more I can hear a pained cry of something. A whisper of agony in the aching blackness.

Mellie squeezes her eyes closed tighter. "Hm…"

"Persephone."

I gasp, my head whipping around. "Hades?" I can only see darkness, only the void Mellie has brought us to. Mellie grabs my hand, pulling my attention back to her. Her eyes are open, milky white, and glowing as she concentrates.

"Focus on his voice, Persephone." A shiver rolls down my spine. She doesn't sound like Mellie. Her voice is hoarser, more strained, and distant.

I nod and close my eyes, waiting for his call again.

"Per…sephone…"

I whimper and a warm tear rolls down my cheek as I hear the distress in his call.

"My Spring."

I tilt my head toward his voice. He sounds so weak, so broken.

My eyes snap open, and I look at Mellie, her eyes still milky and glassy.

"We need to find him."

She nods. "Reach out to him mentally. You should be able to sense him enough for me to locate him."

I close my eyes again, the pull in my chest aching more than it ever has. I try to yank on it mentally. "Hades? I'm here. Where are you?"

Mellie gasps, and my eyes snap open once again, but this time the outline of a tree illuminates the darkness with an inner glow. A glow of viciousness, insidious nature. I look at Mellie, and cautiously we move toward it, the pull in my chest dragging me forward.

I reach out to touch it, and suddenly the tree looms above, the darkness gone. Soft grass cushions our feet, and rolling hills stretch as far as the eye can see. I look up, following the line of the trunk, my eyes going wide with terror when I see Hades. His head droops from the branch, his eyes gone, roots penetrating his body.

I release a blood-curdling scream, pressing my hands to the bark. "Hades!" There's a faint groan from him, but he isn't moving.

He's not dead. He can't be dead. I can feel him.

My thumb drags over the bark, my mind racing. *Who would do this? Who could do this? Who would be this mad at—*

My breath hitches.

"Demeter," I murmur. I look over my shoulder at Mellie. "My mother."

Mellie nods solemnly. "She has him. I can sense it."

I turn back to Hades, stroking his cheek. "What do I do? I can't leave him here."

Mellie paces behind me, trying to think of a way to save him, to save my Hades. She softly mutters. I don't hear most of it, only parts of sentences.

"... but you can travel in dreams... Ah-ha!" she exclaims. I whirl around to look at her, hope warming me.

"Break the tree."

I frown. "What?"

"You can do anything in your dreams, Persephone. Break the tree." She looks at me impatiently.

"But that won't help him in reality, right?"

"No," she admits. "But you will be able to speak with him. It is something until we can figure out how to free him."

I turn back to look at Hades. "I really hope this doesn't hurt you," I whisper, shuffling back slightly. My hands tremble as I twist them, palms up, summoning my new and improved purple vines. I turn my hands to face the tree trunk and thrust my arms forward. The deep purple vines get to work immediately, breaking the trunk apart piece by piece. I growl when they're not working fast enough. Standing up, I summon more vines with thicker stalks and will them to attack the trunk too. A bead of sweat trails down my temple with the exertion of pushing all my power into it. I will

69

burn myself out for him. I will keep going until the last ember of my power is extinguished.

I am his. As he is mine.

Chapter Twelve

Hades

THE OVERWHELMING PRESSURE ON MY CHEST LESSENS, Persephone's vines tearing at the tree, shattering it with the force of her power. I crumple forward, blood spilling from my legs and arms where the roots had pierced me. I don't know how long it will take me to heal or how long I've been here. Not that it matters anymore. My queen is here. I can't see her, but I recognize her scent. I'd know it even if I was deprived of all senses but one.

Roses blanketed in a dense fog.

Wait, I smelled roses before, in the dream. This is just the distracting allure of safety wrapped in the one scent I need to keep fighting. I tell myself I'm not out, even as my body hits the ground and pain shoots through me when I land on my injuries. I need to stand, but my body is so weak, and every inch is raw, flayed to the bone. How many times have I needed to regrow my skin and muscle?

I can't see. *Why can't I see?*

Hands are cupping my cheeks, the fingers so achingly familiar. I know every tiny dip and bend in them better than I know my own. They've traced every part of my body. I know them. Fuck, it is cruel to give me this hope. The scent of the roses should have vanished by now. I only had a flash before. It should be lessening, not getting stronger. I shiver as cold air sweeps over me, and I can see again, looking up into the face of my savior. My eyes slowly focus on her familiar features, and my chest aches with relief. It's her.

It's *Persephone*.

"Hades?" she asks, her thumbs stroking my cheeks. Her fingers are soft, just like I remember.

I lock eyes with her and fall into the sunburst at the center of the blue. "My spring. You found me," I croak.

Is this real?

Her eyes scan mine before she presses her forehead to mine. It is such a familiar movement, one full of the love we share. The bond pulses between us, and her scent surrounds me. "I will always find you, demon."

Are you real?

I focus on her hands on my cheeks, trying to root myself in this moment, clinging to the hope that this is reality. I desperately need to believe that she has come for me, and those memories can stay where they belong, buried and forgotten, but the initial relief has worn off. Her hands are on me, but the warmth of her touch is absent. "I can't…" I see Mellie standing behind Persephone, her mismatched eyes sad. My heart plummets. "Oh. This is a dream."

Persephone glances over her shoulder at Mellie, her eyes filled with worry when she looks back at me. "Can't what?"

I reach up to touch her cheek, feeling the barest glimpse of her soft skin. "I can't really feel you." Not really. Only a whisper of a touch. No warmth because this isn't real. It's a dream.

Another fucking dream.

I try to keep the pain from my face when Persephone looks back at me. Her voice is determined but still carries a hint of panic. "You will soon, baby. Just as soon as I work out how to get out of the Underworld to come find you."

My stomach roils for a new reason. Persephone can't leave the Underworld. I cursed her to remain. Her term started the second the curse did. "I'll be brought to you in less than a month. You only have to wait."

Three weeks trapped in dreams. In memories. Every painful moment and thought I've gone through the last two thousand years. These were the memories I stripped from my mind when I first became king.

I keep my face from betraying my thoughts or what I'm enduring. I know Persephone. She will act if she thinks I'm being hurt. Nothing would stand in her way to get to me. I can't risk that. I can't risk her, and so I'll endure.

"In the meantime, you'll be able to talk here," Mellie adds, her face contorted, her eyes more vacant than normal. She plays with sanity like a jump rope, and it takes me a moment to realize why.

Mellie came to the Underworld because Persephone called. She hadn't stepped foot in her home since I found her. I have no idea how long she wandered around the Underworld before then, and I wasn't sure if Mellie herself knew. I never asked her to come back, never forced her. So, she never came back. Not once. I know she hates it there, but she came back for Persephone.

Persephone shakes her head, her eyes filled with frustrated tears. "You don't have a few weeks, Hades. You're losing power by the second."

She doesn't know the half of what I'm losing. I kiss her softly, wishing I could feel the warmth of her lips. "I can hold out for you."

She whimpers, her eyes as broken as I feel. "I am so sorry. I am so, so, so sorry."

I kiss her again, the phantom touch of her lips making me ache even more. "You're worth it. You're not mad at me?"

Free from my memory prison, I remember exactly what happened before I was taken. Crippled by the fear of losing her, I'd cursed her.

She wipes a tear from her cheek, chuckling slightly. "Oh, I'm furious. I can't wait to fight about it when you're home."

Home. With Persephone. No more empty halls reminding me of my own isolation, my responsibilities, and a fated queen whose throne sat empty.

Persephone's eyes darken, and all my musing about a home with her fall away. I kiss her hard as if the pressure will make up for the fact that I can't really feel her. "Did you meet the dog?"

She smiles, nodding, wiping away her tears. "He's a good boy."

I snort. The three-headed dog is most definitely not a good boy. "He's a menace. Just like you."

She cups my cheek. "I'm your menace."

My chest aches with every touch. I wish to be at her side, to feel her touch fully, her kiss, but in dreams, it's only a whisper.

"I'll be with you soon. Demeter won't be able to stop the pull of the Underworld."

No one can stop the pull. Even me. Especially me.

She sighs. "Is there a way to get to you sooner?"

I cover my wince with a smirk. "Impatient, hm?"

She glares at me. "Hades. I can't bear to think of you suffering for a full month."

Treacherous waters.

I kiss her nose. "There's nothing we can do unless you can get your mother to release me."

She sags, nodding. I hiss out a relieved exhale. I smile, kissing her head. Even unable to feel her, I can't stop touching her. "Tell me everything while you're here." *Don't ask about freeing me. I can't keep this smile on my face for long.*

Persephone shuffles closer to me, and the look of longing on her face lances me in the chest. She misses my touch as much as I miss hers. "Everything?"

I nod. "You're mad at me."

That should distract her.

"I am."

I brush her cheek softly. "I couldn't tell you."

She exhales deeply, and I can see the anger lingering in her eyes. "I know."

"I thought you might like it better than the Mountain."

I couldn't lose you.

She shrugs. "I'll like it better when you're here."

I smirk at her, masking my pain. "Oh? You haven't been there with me yet. I could be unbearable."

She laughs, and the sound fills me with warmth. "I don't doubt it."

I kiss down her neck, trying to supply what I can't really feel. Her scent is an echo now as well. "You hog the blankets."

She pulls back, frowning. "I do not!"

"You do, and you snore."

She shakes her head slowly, her lips twitching, both amused and annoyed. My heart aches for her. "Oh, demon. Be glad you're not here right now."

I snicker, my eyes taking her in. "What would you do, fuck me?"

Mellie groans, reminding us both of her presence. "Please. I'm still here."

Chapter Thirteen

Persephone

I KEEP MY EYES LOCKED ON HADES, the sapphire blue never failing to captivate me. My gaze searches his face, taking in the hard line of his jaw, the soft curve of his lips, and how perfectly straight his nose is. His jaw is covered with stubble, and I graze my fingers over it, cursing under my breath when I remember I can't feel him, and he can't feel me. There is just the whisper of a touch, taunting and mocking us.

"Can you give us a minute?" I say to Mellie, my eyes still taking in every inch of Hades, hungrily roaming over his face.

The only sign that Mellie has left is a slight shift in the power surrounding us, but it's enough for me. I lean in, hovering my lips over his. "You think I'd fuck you after you just told me I hog the bedsheets and snore?"

"Yes," he growls, and I swear the sound vibrates through my bones, to my core.

I pull back slightly, his darkening eyes sending a shiver down my spine. I know mine reveal the same deep need for him.

"Oh? What makes you think that?" My voice is deeper, desire-addled.

His signature maddening smirk graces his perfect

lips. "Because you love me."

Cocky dickhead.

I place my hand on his thigh, holding back a growl of frustration. It feels like there's a barrier between us, and technically, there is. In fact, there are two: distance and consciousness. But we're talking, and we're together. I just need to touch him, to comfort him.

"I want to touch you."

His heavy sigh makes my heart squeeze. "I know."

I sit back on my heels, smiling as an idea pops into my head. I hold out my hand and slowly open it, the small black flower growing from its center. "Do you like my flower?"

He cups my hand, his phantom touch sliding gently over the petals. "I do. The darkness becomes you. As does the Underworld."

I close my fist, disappearing the flower before touching the collar of his shirt I am still wearing. "Do you like my new shirt?"

His eyes darken even more. "I do. It looks rather familiar."

"Oh?"

"It looks far better on you than it ever did on me." He shamelessly lets his gaze wander to my covered breasts.

I slide my fingers over the fabric of the collar to the buttons of the shirt and pop one open. "If you could touch me, this is what you'd be doing." I open another button, then another, the shirt gaping, showing the valley between my breasts.

My head snaps up as the ground quakes beneath us. Hades' eyes go wide, and his hands fly to his throat as he retches. I move in closer, cupping his cheeks. "What's going on?"

Hades' hand moves to his mouth, and he pales. "I think something's happening." He pulls away from me, bending and vomiting. I gasp when I see that it's not regular stomach contents, he's bringing up but debris, dirt, and roots. The ground shifts once again, and the

77

tree that I just tore to shreds with my vines repairs itself. The thick, lumpy trunk reforms and the hole where Hades was bound waits ominously for him to return to his prison. The hungry, angry power rushes through the dream, demanding Hades return to his jail.

I turn and shout for Mellie, my voice tight and panicked. She reappears instantly, concern etched on her face.

"What is happening to him?" I demand.

"It's nothing to do with me. It's him. He must be fighting in reality." Her brows furrow, and she moves closer to Hades. To my horror, she inspects his vomit.

I blink, watching as she sifts through it, and Hades continues to retch. Mellie's eyes go wide, and she picks up a small leaf. It looks like most others except it's completely see-through, the midnight black veins stark against the transparent membrane.

"The Underworld…" Mellie murmurs. Her eyes go wide, and she looks at me in alarm. "Persephone, he is in the Underworld."

I shake my head, continuing to stroke Hades' arm, trying to comfort him. "What? He can't be."

Mellie looks back at the leaf. "He's in the deepest part of…" Her eyes go distant, the blood draining from her face. "Tartarus."

I tilt my head. "Tartarus?"

Mellie's gaze is fixed on the leaf, but her mind is somewhere far away, somewhere that shakes her to her very core. "He is in the heart of a dying Primordial." Her voice is quiet, far away, haunted.

I grab the leaf from her. "Take me there. Now."

Mellie looks at me, her eyes wide, petrified. In the blink of an eye, the meadow dissipates, and I am no longer kneeling next to Hades but in the middle of the throne room. The cool marble is hard against my knees, drawing my attention to the contrast between where we are and where we have just come from. The leaf I was holding is completely gone, with no trace of its existence left. Mellie kneels next to me. She swallows thickly, her gaze fixed on the floor.

"I can't go there." She braces her hands on her thighs. "Only you can." She moves her hand to take mine, interlocking our fingers. "It *wants* you too. It wants to feed on you until you go mad, and it will not give up Hades willingly."

Chapter Fourteen

Hades

I THOUGHT BEING TRAPPED IN DREAMS WAS AGONY. Oh, what a fool I am.

I am yanked out of the Oneiroi realm and slammed into my body, into consciousness. The roots living inside me are torn from my throat, allowing me to breathe normally for the first time... in however long I had been trapped here.

The air is damp and moist, but that could be from the earth still inside my lungs. My body is healing my throat, mouth, and lungs, but each pinprick of regeneration feels like a dagger.

A gulp of air gives me a taste of the environment, hoping to use my senses to give me a hint of where I am. There's heavy fog and the stench of sulfur, but nothing truly distinguishable. Maybe... lilies? That could be anywhere.

The roots twist, burrowing deeper under my skin, breaking bones and tearing muscles. My body is forced to heal around the intrusions, trying to fight through them, breaking them off. When I was in the dreams, I didn't feel the torture, but now I do. I can feel them *feed*. I can't see them, but I feel them with every pull from my power, each agonizing part of me being torn by the roots. My eyes weren't just dark in the dreams. It is a reflection of reality. The roots are still pulsing behind my eyes, but the branch that shoved its way down my throat is gone.

I thought it was my strength that had allowed me to break free from the hold of the carnivorous plant, but I should have known better. It isn't because of me. It is because she wants an audience.

A captive audience.

A captive, blind audience.

What a bitch.

"I would offer you some refreshments or snacks," I croak slyly. "But my hands seem to be occupied."

The roots dig deeper into my wrist. I can't muffle my moan of pain, but I keep it short, not wanting to give her the satisfaction. She already has enough of an advantage at the moment. I won't give her more.

"You will release her from this curse," Demeter hisses. I can hear her walking around the tree, and I listen harder, trying to get a sense of where I am. Her feet land in water, the splash slight, but there. Maybe a swamp? What swamp has god-devouring trees?

The only thing I can smell is the overwhelming scent of rot and clinging moss. Even as Demeter circles me, disturbing the air, I can't pinpoint a single identifiable scent. I need my sight. I observe. That's what I'm best at. Right now, I'm stumbling through the void, hoping to find a ladder from this pit of despair. I grit my teeth, forcing a laugh through my throat, filling it with every ounce of haughty disdain I possess. "It doesn't work like that."

Demeter snarls, and even without my eyes, I can imagine her baring her teeth at me. "You cursed her to live with you. You will break the curse, and she'll come home where she belongs."

I laugh mockingly, even as the roots feed. Every little wiggle of my limbs causes them to dig even deeper, ripping more muscle. "She'll never go back to you."

Demeter screeches in rage, and I can imagine her

body vibrating with it. From that moment in my dreams, inside my memories, I can see the similarities between her and Persephone. They have the same dark hair streaked with red and the same eyes, but that's where the similarities end. An almost brutal shift from mother to daughter. Persephone is softened by curves, her face striking and alluring. Her strength and confidence radiate from her. Demeter is harsh angles, barely a wisp of body and form, a shell. I can tell she takes care with her appearance, every inch picked and plucked in the extreme.

Demeter is a shadow of her daughter, everything Persephone isn't while daring to share some of the same features. Just the reminder of what she had done to Persephone makes my powers flicker, fueled by the anger at her trapping me, taking me so off guard, and rage at how she treated Persephone as a child. I had seen the way Persephone braced herself for my rejection when she showed me her true form. That flicker of unease haunts me.

Rage and anger feed the darkness, and if I'm not careful, I'll slip into my power and never see the light again. I grind my teeth, focusing my mind. I won't let this bitch beat me.

I spoke to Persephone, but I couldn't feel her. It was another dream. Those dreams are a worse prison than anything this monster can conjure, and she doesn't even know. I can't let her find out.

What if Persephone gets trapped in the same dreamscape when she reaches out to me? What if… she sees?

My power flares again in response, alarm shivering through me. No, I can't think about that. Persephone's safe. She's in the Underworld. I hiss out steadying breaths through clenched teeth, stabilizing my power.

"You think you can keep me from my daughter?" Demeter hisses, and I can feel her breath on my face.

I recoil as if her breath is foul. I know I hit the

mark when the roots dig deeper into my neck and slither past my collarbone, fracturing one of my ribs. Grinding my teeth, I hiss, "You can't break her tie to the Underworld." I smirk even as blood drips from my lips. "Or to me. She's *mine.*"

My queen. My wife.

Another screech of rage, and I take a long inhale of clean air before the branch shoots down my throat again. I choke, and my body jolts inside the tree, trying to fight as my air is cut off again.

No. Not the memories.

Not again.

Come find me, my spring.

Chapter Fifteen

Persephone

WHAT DOES IT WANT FROM US?" I ask although I fear I know the answer. Mellie looks at me, her face equal parts hopeless and terrified. Her eyes are still distant, and the scars on her face seem more pronounced, redder, and angrier. Her eyes are shadowed, and I wonder what torturous memories have trapped her in the past.

The guilt of putting her through this and making her think about such a harrowing time squeezes like a band around my heart. But I need her if I'm going to try to find Hades.

"To feed from you. From your power." Her voice is distant, like her gaze, her eyes glazed over. I can almost see the horrors playing out across her face.

I place my hand on her arm, hoping the contact will bring her back. She blinks, her breath hitching as she looks at me. Her memories still haunt her eyes, eyes sparkling with gratitude that I'd pulled her from whatever nightmare she was living through.

I stand and help her up. "I need to try, Mellie."

She looks away, wrapping her arms around her waist protectively.

"I won't ask you to come with me."

Her eyes snap to mine. "But—"

I shake my head. "No, Mellie. I will never ask that of you. All I need from you is information."

Her shoulders visibly relax, but she searches my face, looking for any inclination of disappointment toward her. She won't find any. All she will find is love for her, concern for Hades, and unease with my new position in the Underworld.

"I need to... Fuck. I don't know what I need to do." I turn and start walking toward my bedroom, Mellie hurrying behind me. I don't even notice how easily I navigate the corridors. It's as if this has always been my home, and I have lived here for years. I walk into the room and straight to the closet, barely registering that half of it is now filled with garments meant for me, the Queen of the Underworld. I glide my fingers over the expensive fabrics but pull back.

No time, P.

I open a drawer and pull out what looks like a pair of battle leathers. Confusion fills me as I slide my fingers over them. The black leather is soft beneath my fingertips, the dark material drawing attention to how pale my skin is against it. The palace must have known this was coming, and Thanatos's words echo in my mind.

The palace will provide.

The Underworld knows what I'm about to go up against. Why else would a queen of a realm at peace require battle attire? I push off my yoga pants and pull the leathers on, along with a matching long-sleeved shirt. When I look back down at the drawer, a blood-red dagger glints at me from where it rests on a black silk cushion. I pick it up, and the blade glows as I rotate it, taking in the small carvings etched into the steel and the handle. I return the blade to the cushion and fasten the holster around my thigh before picking the dagger up again.

"P?" Mellie's shaky voice carries from my bedroom.

I stow the dagger in the thigh holster banded around

85

my leg and grab the black combat boots neatly placed next to countless pairs of high-heeled shoes before returning to the bedroom. The boots look comically out of place, yet I know they will be needed. Mellie sits on the edge of the bed, Cerberus next to her, one of his heads on her lap. My heart squeezes. My huge, fearsome marshmallow is providing comfort to my best friend.

Cerberus lifts his other two heads when I enter the room, his concerned eyes locking on me. He whines and lifts his third head before standing and padding toward me. He can tell I need comfort too, but I also get the sense that he needs the feeling of safety he knows I can provide. I don't know why this canine and I have the bond that we do, but it's so strong and undeniable, not unlike my tie to Hades and my tie to the Underworld.

I stand in front of Cerberus and nuzzle all three of his heads. "You're a good Berry."

Mellie looks up, her lips twitching. "What did you just call him?" I glance at her. Humor dances around her eyes, breaking through the terror that she previously wore.

I blink, thinking about my words to Cerberus. "Berry?"

Mellie bursts out laughing. "Please, *please*, let me be there the first time you call him that in front of Hades."

I blink again. "Why?"

Mellie continues to laugh, struggling to breathe. "You're calling… his terrifying, three-headed, monster guard dog, *Berry!*"

My brow furrows as I look at Cerberus, his sweet faces and wide eyes full of love. I don't have any doubt that he would be a fierce protector, but to me, he will always be my sweet berry marshmallow who enjoys cuddling on the bed and misses his daddy.

I scratch each of Cerberus's heads before standing. Mellie finally gets control of herself as I sit on the bed next to her.

"Where is Tartarus?"

She tenses, all humor evaporating into thin air.

"I…" She hesitates, and I turn to look at her. That haunted look slowly floods her eyes, burying the joy that had suffused her features. When she was laughing, her scars faded, but now, they are angry and red again.

"Mel?"

She looks at me and swallows. "I'm not the best person to ask about this."

I frown, and Cerberus nudges my hand with his nose, wanting attention. I scratch behind one of his many ears.

"Then who is?" I ask, my eyes still on Mellie.

"Have you met…Thanatos?" I can't help but notice the slightly pink blush that creeps up her neck when she says his name. It is even more obvious by the paler complexion her fear has provided.

I nod.

She blushes more. "Oh, well… you should talk to him."

"About Tartarus?"

Mellie nods. "He is the God of Death. Sometimes he has to escort souls there."

"All right." I hesitate. "Only problem is, I don't know how to—"

As if on cue, there is a knock at the door. Cerberus goes wild, barking and charging for the door. He stands on his hind legs, his enormous paws pressed against the door as he waits for me to open it. He wags his large tail, creating a draft.

I walk to the door and look at Cerberus. "Okay, Berry. Down."

Cerberus moves away from the door, his tongues lolling from each of his mouths.

"Good boy."

He barks happily and starts running around excitedly. I open the door and am greeted by the now familiar sight of a tall, robed male, his face completely covered save for a sliver of visible skin where the light catches his jaw and the top of his heavily tattooed neck.

"Thanatos! I was just thinking about you!"

"My queen, I felt you summon me," he states, his voice even.

"Summon you?"

He nods solemnly. "How can I be of service?"

I open the door wider, welcoming him into my room, and I can sense Mellie tense behind me. Thanatos looks deeply uncomfortable and makes no move to enter the room.

"My queen, your private chambers are—"

"Oh, just get in here." I grab his arm and pull him into the room. He only walks into the space enough that the door closes. Cerberus runs madly around the room, and I look between him and Thanatos.

"When my king is in the mortal realm, I walk and feed Cerberus for him," he says, replying to my silent question.

I nod, my lips twitching.

"How can I be of service, my queen?" Thanatos asks, clearly trying to spend as little time in mine and Hades' bedroom as possible.

"I need you to take me to Tartarus."

All the air seems to leave the room, and I swear the temperature drops by a couple of degrees. Even Cerberus stops his zoomies, skidding to a halt.

Thanatos turns to face me fully, his intense stare searing me, even though I can't see his eyes.

"Tartarus is not a place you visit lightly, my queen—"

"Hades is there," I interrupt. "He's trapped there, and I... I need to save him, Thanatos." My voice cracks, and I exhale shakily.

"My king has more—"

"It's true," Mellie says, pushing to her feet. She walks to my side and links her arm through mine. "I was able to find him through a dream."

Thanatos seems to assess us both, clearly skeptical. "My king has never entered the Underworld a second before his time on the mortal realm has ended." He pauses and glances at me. "But then again, never has his queen been here," Thanatos says before returning his attention to Mellie. "You spoke with him?"

Mellie looks down nervously, but to her credit, her voice doesn't waver. "We both did. He is in peril, Thanatos."

"Please, Thanatos," a tear slides down my cheek, "I need him."

Thanatos regards us for a long moment before nodding once. "Tartarus is vast. Did you narrow down his location?"

Mellie squeezes my arm. "He's in the heart."

Thanatos clenches his fists, and the room seems to shift once again. The silent curse Thanatos doesn't utter, vibrating in the air.

"I don't know what you know of Tartarus, my queen. Forgive me if I am giving you information you already know." He pauses. "Tartarus is made from the carcass of a Primordial. Certain areas are more treacherous than others. The heart is... the most so."

I wipe the tear from my cheek. "I need to get him back, Thanatos."

Thanatos looks away. Every second he doesn't reply is like an eternity. Finally, he answers, "If you wish to venture there. We will need to make a stop first."

I frown. "A stop?"

He nods. "You will need arms stronger than your dagger."

I glance down at the dagger sitting proudly in the sheath.

"We will need to visit my mother and father, my queen."

Chapter Sixteen

Persephone

YOUR MOTHER AND FATHER?"

Thanatos nods, Mellie still tense beside me. I turn and squeeze her arm.

"You should go back," I say, smiling.

Mellie looks at me, visibly relaxing. "Call me if you need anything." She smiles. "Oh! I almost forgot!" She pulls a brand new phone out of her back pocket and hands it to me. "It has all the important numbers already programmed into it."

I pull her into a hug and squeeze her. "Thank you, Mel."

She hugs me tightly and slowly disappears, leaving the Underworld to her own place of safety in the mortal realm. I take a minute to hope that Helios is waiting for her, ready to give her the support she needs.

I face Thanatos, who is doing his best to ignore an affectionate Cerberus.

"Lead the way," I say.

Thanatos holds out his hand, and a scythe appears as if summoned from thin air. He steps away from me a little and spins it, slicing reality. The rip in the fabric of time looks exactly as I'd expect, the ominous hole appearing to suck at the blue and green light surrounding it. Thanatos waits patiently, holding his other hand up, gesturing for me to step through first. I take an unsteady step toward the portal, the blackness of the abyss doing nothing to ease my misgivings.

Thanatos steps closer, sensing my trepidation. "After you, my queen." He lowers his voice a little. "You have nothing to fear."

I glance at him and nod before stepping through the portal into the unknown. Thanatos steps through right behind me, the presence of death making a chill run down my spine. I don't know why I've never felt it when I've been around him. Maybe it's because he's never used such potent power in my presence.

Between one breath and the next, our surroundings change. We are no longer in my chambers, and I'm surprised to notice the loss of comfort that I didn't realize I felt.

This room is large, the walls formed of windows on all sides. I look up, seeing that they extend to the ceiling. The entire room looks like a cross between a greenhouse and an observatory, but the most elegant of either I have ever seen. There is no scenery outside, only the expanse of the universe. Bright star constellations twinkle against the midnight background of the sky. I walk closer, looking out into eternity, my eyes wide. My footsteps echo on the black marble floors. The solid gold window frames contrast beautifully against the velvet darkness outside.

The portal closes and Thanatos brushes some lint from his cloak. I glance at him and am surprised to see him nervously shuffling from foot to foot.

"Miteras? Pater?"

The sound of heels clicking against the marble pulls my attention from the view, and I glance up as a stunning woman seems to glide through the room, her dark hair flowing behind her as she walks. Her alabaster skin starkly contrasts the ebony black hair flowing down her back. I can see faint lines covering her bare arms. One of which looks exactly like a constellation just outside the window. She smiles broadly when she sees Thanatos, her purple-painted lips pulling to show her dazzling white teeth. She quickens her pace, and only then do I notice someone following behind her. An extremely handsome man with dark skin trails her. His hair is jet black, and his face is equally perfect as the woman's. His skin doesn't have constellations, but something swirls and moves over it, enticing me to look deeper, step closer.

"My son," the woman says, pulling Thanatos into a tight hug.

Thanatos remains tense, pulling away after a moment. I can almost feel the embarrassment seeping from him.

"My queen, this is my mother and father." He gestures to them. "Nyx and Erebus."

Erebus pats his son on the shoulder and moves back to his wife's side, wrapping an arm protectively around her waist.

"My queen," Nyx bows, stardust littering the floor as she moves. "An honor."

I smile, still not used to the bowing thing. "The honor is mine. Your son has been very kind."

Erebus glances at Thanatos, uncertainty plain on his face. "Though it is an honor, your majesty, this visit is… unusual." Nyx gives him a scathing look, but he continues. "We rarely have visits from the monarchs since we handed over control of the realm."

I tense a little. Thanatos takes a step closer. I lift my chin and look at Erebus. "I understand, but I am here because I need your help. This is not about matters regarding the Underworld. This would be a personal favor for myself and the king."

Erebus tilts his head slightly and waits for me to continue.

"Hades is trapped."

Nyx lifts her eyebrows, and Erebus watches me

carefully.

"I believe he has been trapped by my... mother." Even saying my suspicion out loud makes my stomach twist with anger and hurt.

"Are you certain? Hades isn't due back in the Underworld for..." Nyx glances out of the window, studying the constellations.

"Weeks yet. I know. But he is trapped. Melinoë confirmed it."

If one more person tells me that Hades isn't due back in the Underworld for weeks...

Erebus lifts his eyebrows. "Oh?"

I nod. "We searched for him in a dream because I have been experiencing nightmares."

Nyx regards me, her head slightly tilted, her silken hair swaying from the movement. "Nightmares?"

I meet her gaze. "The same every night. I can't see. I can't breathe. All I feel is pain and panic. All I smell is soil and rotting leaves. Every night it's the same." I hesitate for a moment, trying not to slip back into the panic. "Sometimes... I hear someone calling my name and..." I pause again, my stomach rolling.

"I believe my queen is right, Miteras, Pater," Thanatos adds, stepping forward in a show of support. "I have been doing my own searching. Nobody has seen Hades in the mortal realm for many days."

I glance at him, my heart speeding up. This isn't news to me, but something about the confirmation that he is missing yanks the rug from under me. The last flicker of hope that this is all just one huge misunderstanding is completely doused.

Nyx's melodic voice pulls me from my thoughts. "And how are we to help you?"

Thanatos turns toward his mother. "My king is in Tartarus."

Nyx and Erebus exchange a look, a secret conversation taking place between them. I briefly wonder if Hades and I will ever be allowed enough time together to get to this point.

"He is believed to be in the heart," Thanatos continues.

Erebus tightens his hold on his wife. "How would Demeter get to the heart of Tartarus?"

My eyes flash, the anger surging at the mere mention of her name. "I don't know. She is not to be underestimated. She shows no one the extent of her powers, not even me."

Nyx glides forward, reaching her slender hand out to me and cupping my cheek. "The heart is the most perilous of lands, my queen. You will need protection if you hope to find and save our king. We will help you." Her hand glows, and a rush of power surrounds me. It seeps into my skin and mingles with my own power, embracing it. A slight burning sensation on my forehead makes me wince a little, but another surge of power follows and my whole body trembles.

Nyx regards me, then steps back as if admiring a piece of art, she has worked on for months. Erebus glances lovingly at his wife and holds his hands out, palms raised. A longsword appears, the black steel so dark it seems to swallow the light surrounding it. A single large ruby sits at the hilt, seamlessly flowing into the handle. He steps forward again, looking from the sword to me.

"This will only strike what is not real."

I hold my hand out to accept the sword. I try to steady my nerves but can't stop the slight shake of my arm as I lift it. The blade doesn't feel unbearably heavy, but it has a comforting weight to it. Nyx's power hums happily as I adjust my grip on the hilt. Their power bonded just like their souls.

"How can I ever repay you for your kindness?" I ask.

Nyx and Erebus glance at one another, sharing secret smiles. "Maybe a visit every once in a while? We like to provide our insight," Erebus says.

"And we miss our son," Nyx adds, laughing.

I smile and nod before glancing at Thanatos as he turns to face me. "I cannot escort you any further, my queen."

My brows furrow. "Why?"

"I am only permitted entry with a soul. I would only be cast away again," Thanatos replies, the regret clear in his voice.

"Oh." I frown. "How am I supposed to find him?"

"You are the Queen of the Underworld. Be the queen. The realm will obey," Nyx replies, her chin raised.

I nod, grateful for the advice but unsure it is as helpful as she thinks it will be. Thanatos nods once and swipes the air with his scythe, creating another portal. If I thought the last one was terrifying, this one makes it look like Disneyland. The light surrounding the portal is completely black, and every so often, flashes of red lightning angrily surge across the rip in reality.

"Good luck, my queen," Thanatos says.

I look into the black chasm of the void, and my heart races. Can I do this? Enter the heart of Tartarus alone? Can I find him? What if I'm wrong? What if I am also lost? The air I'm taking in doesn't seem to fill my lungs the same.

Hades needs you. Hades needs you. Hades needs you.

I swallow, accepting that I would do absolutely anything for my king, even go to the very depths of hell.

I take a deep breath and step into the unknown.

Chapter Seventeen

Hades

COME FIND ME, MY SPRING.

"You don't belong here," Hekate hissed at me, even as I took a seat on my throne. The entire palace was cut from darkness, with white veins accentuating the pillars surrounding the spacious room. Zeus had joked that we should throw a party to celebrate our new stations. There wouldn't be a party because we'd been torn apart again. I'd gone from prison to battlefield to my new home, my realm. Alone. With Gaia's decree, we were sent to become the new kings of a new age of gods.

Three brothers. Three kings. Three realms.

Yet I was the only one trapped for half the year in mine. The realm of the dead was different, Gaia told me. Unlike my brothers, my crown was weighed down like lead with responsibilities. My realm would take more of me and give more to me. With all things, there was a price, and this was mine. Gaia's words echoed in my head. "If your realm dies, so do you." What if I didn't want this realm? This crown? This throne? But I'd be damned twice if I let myself break in front of Hekate.

I had my moment of cowardice. A single moment, and I'd emerged from the other side, a man unwilling to buckle even before the Prime of Witchcraft.

"You speak to your king," I snapped at her, shifting in the throne, faking a casual arrogance I didn't feel. How could I feel comfortable in a room I'd never been in? In a throne I didn't belong in?

Thanatos raised a hand to stop his older sister from lunging for my throat. His entire face was shadowed within his cloak, only his hands visible. Each finger was inked with different tattoos, swirling depictions of death.

Hekate was in her matron form. Her two midnight black braids were shot through with grey and wrapped around her small horns, making them appear more prominent. Her face was supposed to be lined with wisdom, but instead, it looked as if she contained nothing but bitterness. She hated me. It was etched into her expression.

Under Thanatos's hood, I knew he had horns as well, a ghostly white pair to match his hair.

My fingers curled to stop myself from touching my bare head.

I didn't belong here.

Only Gods of the Underworld had horns. That I had none was a glaring weakness and a difference they were quick to point out.

Intruder. Usurper. Outsider.

"Not my king," Hekate hissed.

I tilted my head, and my new connection to the Underworld roared to life inside me. I had just discovered my power, and now it felt like a never-ending abyss, a well with no bottom. The connection only made me feel more out of control, more out of sorts. Thanatos glanced around at the shadows dancing on the walls, and I rolled my shoulders, trying to restrain my abilities.

"I could make you bow," I warned. Hekate's eyes flashed with defiance and a tiny bit of uncertainty. Here, with this new bond to my realm, we both knew I could force her to the ground with little effort if I chose to. She bristled, waiting for me to do it. "But I won't."

Hekate blinked, and her form shifted to the maiden, a young woman in place of the crone. Surprised at my choice?

97

Thanatos's fingers flexed slightly. Did he wish for his scythe? Was he hoping to fight his new king?

I stood slowly from the throne and descended the steps to the dais, leaving the two of them standing there. They were the first to come to see the new king, but there would be more seeking to test me, break me. Hekate and Thanatos were formidable, but their parents were another matter. It would be the same for my brothers.

Zeus in Olympus.

Poseidon in Atlantis.

At the top of the steps, I stopped and turned to face them, the weight of the crown on my head an ever-present reminder. It was as heavy as lead, each of the pointed spikes atop wrapped in shadows, no jewels or adornments, just like the realm I'd been given. It was a blank metaphysical plane, souls experiencing their own various versions of the afterlife. I was given a blank slate, all this power and subjects. I could submit them to my will or try to build something in this realm forced upon me.

"Propylaia is yours," I stated clearly. Propylaia, the realm of lost souls, where I knew Hekate felt the most at home. Along with the realm and the power had come knowledge, and I seemed to know every being who called the Underworld home. They were all a part of the Underworld, and now they were a part of me.

Hekate gasped a little in surprise before pressing her lips closed.

"I didn't ask for this. But neither did you." I looked at them both.

"Come find me, my spring."

I glanced over my shoulder, trying to find the source of this other voice. But there was no one.

I turned back to Hekate and Thanatos, pinning the reaper with a stare. "I understand you maintain a modest cottage. It is yours. I have no intention of stripping your homes from you. Inside your homes, you may do as you please. With no interference from me."

Brother and sister glanced at each other warily.

98

Mistrustfully.

Why wouldn't they be? I did not belong here.

I let my eyes travel around the barren throne room. It was so big. So... empty.

"We can be allies or enemies," I said plainly.

"Come to me, my spring. Find me."

I whipped around completely to find the speaker, but only the two thrones sat there.

Wait, two?

There was an identical throne sitting next to mine, the same size and shape. A queen's throne, but she was equal. I stepped closer to it, my hand outstretched. "Where did this come from?"

Neither Thanatos nor Hekate answered.

"I expect an answer when I ask a question," I snapped, turning back to them. But there was nothing.

Instead, there was a massive rip in reality, and I had only a breath before the tear became a vortex, sucking the world around me inside. My feet slipped on the smooth floor, terror holding me by the throat. No, not again. Don't make me go through it again. *I slid against the marble, moving ever closer to the gaping void, the carnivorous beast waiting to be fed.*

No, not again. I can't live through it another time. Please. Not again.

I struggled against the call, the sucking vacuum of space. It took my legs out from under me, and I flashed my claws, digging them into the marble, barely holding myself from its open mouth.

The pull became stronger, almost as if it enjoyed watching me struggle. I tried to lunge, to embed my claws higher, but they slipped on the smooth marble. The force yanked my hand back, and again, I looked down into the open abyss. I gritted my teeth, my fingers bleeding from the hold. A distant laugh echoed, and agony ripped through my hands as it tried to pull me back into the darkness of the never-ending void of the fall. My claws ripped the marble as it pulled at me, refusing to surrender its prize. Every move I made was agony, blood streaking the smooth floor.

I couldn't give up. Each tortured inch forward I counted as a success, a tiny bit of distance between me and the howling abyss—one more step from the fall, the prison, the war.

Don't make me do it all again.

My claws missed, and I slid back. I couldn't get any traction to stop myself. No! My hands slipped, and my body lifted. My tears were ripped from me as the abyss swallowed me.

Back to the fall.

Chapter Eighteen

Persephone

THE PORTAL CLOSES BEHIND ME, and I'm plunged into complete darkness. The only sound is my heart thudding in my chest, and the only sensation is the ground under my feet. Is it ground? I am standing on *something*. The blackness surrounding me makes me uneasy.

Where am I?

I take another step forward and tentatively reach my arm out, feeling for something, anything, something to prove I'm not stuck in a void. My hand meets vacant air. The hair on the back of my neck stands straight. Did Thanatos's portal take me to the wrong place? If it did, where am I, and how do I get back?

Fuck.

I close my eyes and take a breath, trying to calm my racing heart. "Think P. Think." I open my eyes.

Be the queen.

"Tartarus."

Nothing happens. I take a steadying breath and clench my fists.

"Tartarus," I say again, stronger this time.

Still, nothing but the fear previously knotting in my stomach melts into fury as my mind goes to Hades. My Hades, trapped somewhere in our realm. In our kingdom. In our home.

"Tartarus!" I yell, panting in my rage. The anger heating me from within, and I'm about to scream when I notice a blip of light in the distance.

I reach my hand out again and step toward it. The darkness retreats, the hard ground beneath my feet giving way to lush grass. Rolling hills form from the complete darkness. The familiar landscape makes my heart squeeze in recognition, and my stomach drops at the memory of this place.

"Olympus," I mutter under my breath, taking in the place I'd called home for centuries. Already I can feel the imaginary shackles wrapping around my ankles.

"I knew you'd come to your senses." The voice sends a chill down my spine, and I whip around, gasping as I come eye-to-eye with my mother. "Welcome home, Persephone." Her voice is trained into the one she used to use when she wanted something from me. This is not her true voice. It is a manipulation, like everything she does.

I shake my head, taking a step back. "No…"

Demeter moves like a viper, wrapping me in her lithe arms, so fragile looking but as strong as an ox. She pulls me close, holding me like a vise, her licorice and cotton scent enveloping me.

"My daughter." That voice makes my whole body recoil. I remember how she used it to lull me into a false sense of security, only to be met with pain if I failed or refused to do whatever she asked.

I remain tense, careful not to move in her arms. "Mother?"

She squeezes me tighter and tighter until the embrace becomes close to bone-crushing. I can hear her wicked smile, her lips at my ear. "You should have listened to me, Daughter." She tightens her hold on me again, her voice twisting, sharpening. "Now, you will pay for it."

Nyx's powers weave inside me and the weight of

Erebus's sword increases in my hand, reminding me of its presence. I don't hesitate for another second, groaning as I try to wiggle enough to free my arm.

"No, Mother. You shouldn't have kept me prisoner for centuries. You should have been a mother and cared more about me than my potential and power."

I pull back the blade and shove it into her side. Her scream of pain is cut off as the illusion of her and Olympus completely collapses.

Darkness presses in on me again, but this time, I know it won't last. I have woken Tartarus, and it wants me. I can feel it. The air shakes around me, and I grasp the sword tighter. Another beam of light in the distance is my only warning before another memory encapsulates me.

The terracotta and burnt oranges of Helios's apartment take shape right before my eyes. I smell the scent of jasmine and bergamot, the comfort of my friend. I turn, taking in the large open-plan space. The kitchen tiles provide the pop of green color that ties the whole apartment together so beautifully. I step forward, the feeling of my bare feet brushing over the rug drawing my attention. No longer am I wearing my leathers, but a pink sundress, the soft cotton whispering against my skin. I frown, noticing that the sword Erebus gave me is no longer in my hand, replaced by a long-stemmed sunflower.

My brows draw as I look at the vibrant petals of the sunflower. The center is darker than usual, resembling the light-consuming black of the blade. I move farther into the apartment, my anger and terror melting away with every step.

Why am I here again?

I look down at one newspaper sitting on the kitchen island.

"Olympus Today," *I murmur, reading the name of the paper. That is strange. Wait... is that strange? I'm not in Olympus. Or am I? What is—*

103

"Persephone!" Helios's deep voice vibrates through me, and I look up, his happy, glowing face drawing me in. I smile brightly back at him.

He glides toward me, his arms open. My feet move of their own accord.

"Helios." I try to stop myself from moving toward him, but I'm not sure why.

Why wouldn't I want to embrace my friend?

Helios cups my cheeks, staring at me. "I have always loved you, Persephone."

Something twists in my stomach, and I look in horror as he moves his face closer to mine.

"Helios... No..." He can't be feeling this for me. It's not right. I have Hades. He's waiting for me at home.

He presses his lips against mine.

No. This is wrong. I don't want to kiss Helios.

I push away but to no avail. Helios deepens the kiss, his fingers gripping either side of my face, turning into claws. They dig into my skull, the excruciating pain making me cry out against his lips. Warm, thick blood slides down the side of my face.

I once again feel Nyx's power jolt within me, trying to warn me. A memory flashes through my mind, a rush of power, a weapon grows heavy in my hand. But I don't have a weapon. The stalk of the flower dangles harmlessly in my grip.

Helios digs his claws in more. The pain is unbearable, and I try to push him away, to free myself, but I can't. Completely out of options, I lift the flower to his face, pushing the petals against his cheek. He howls in agony, releasing me. I step back, panting. Helios falls to his knees before me, the sword piercing through his right eye. The second I step back, my memories return. Tartarus. The heart. Hades.

He looks up at me helplessly, blood pouring from his face. I release a sob, seeing my friend slowly dying in agony, knowing I did this to him. I stumble back, my hand going to my head, feeling the gashes where his

104

claws pierced me.

Unlike with my mother, the illusion holds for a little longer. It's as though Tartarus knows that this is breaking me but holding a broken illusion must take great power.

I keep my eyes on Helios, not able to bear to see him but also not able to bear looking away. Even if it is an illusion, the thought of letting him die alone shatters my heart completely. This doesn't feel like an illusion, but I know it is. I'm certain that Mellie is in the mortal realm with him right now, yet my heart breaks as if I really have plunged my sword into his eye. My friend. Helios. The embodiment of sunshine.

Eventually, the illusion unravels, one element at a time. The last thing to disappear is Helios's dying body slumped against the kitchen island. Before it fades completely, I pull the blade from him and stagger back, unshed tears burning my eyes, my throat aching from unreleased sobs.

Hold it together, P. Hold it together.

My hands shake, and I clench my fists, trying to steady myself for whatever this hellhole throws at me next.

The next scene forms, and I immediately know what's about to happen. The beige walls, the navy leather couch, the scent of expensive cologne.

Oh, no. Please... not this. Anything but this.

"Hello, Persephone." Jackson leans against the wall. His face pulls into the cruel smirk still so foreign to me, so unlike the Jackson I thought I knew.

"Jackson." I step toward him, but his face changes, all signs of the cruelty gone. His smile drops, and his eyes change from glinting maliciously to shining with genuine sorrow.

"I've been dead for months, and you didn't even notice." His voice is so raw, carrying so much emotion. This is the familiar, kind lilt of the Jackson I'd met in the club all those months ago. How hadn't I noticed the change? I'd been so lost in the excitement of being in the human realm, of being free, that I hadn't noticed him change. I hadn't cared enough.

I shake my head, my brows furrowing. "Dead?"

He looks away, and his pain is almost unbearable to witness. "You never cared for me." He looks at me, his eyes fierce, but not in the cruel way of Hermes. This is devastation. "You are heartless."

I shake my head, the tears I have been holding back streaming down my cheeks. "I didn't know. Jackson, I-I'm so sorry."

"I had a family, parents, a life. I could have found love." His words are hard, but I can hear his heartbreak. "And you didn't even notice."

I move in closer, a small sob escaping me. "Jackson, please."

"I thought you were kind and gentle." His lips form a thin line, his own tears falling. "But you are the worst of them all, Persephone." He hisses my name like it tastes sour. "A beautiful rose, with pretty enticing petals," his hard eyes find mine, "covering the lethal, poisonous thorns beneath."

I sob again. The sword in my hand practically vibrates, desperate to be used to pull me from this nightmare, but how can I do this to Jackson? I've hurt him so much already. He deserved better. He deserved for me to notice.

"A nightmare disguised like a dream." He pushes off the wall and moves toward me.

I am frozen in place, and my heart aches as I see how broken he is, and I know without a shadow of a doubt that there is an ounce of truth to his words. Because where else could Jackson be?

"I am so, so sorry, Jackson."

He steps in closer, his face twisting into the hateful expression I'd seen from him for so long. I try to lift the sword, but I can't move my arm. I glance down, noticing that my own vines are restraining me.

Jackson laughs evilly, and I pull at the vines. "See that, Persephone? There is so much poison inside you it's turning against you."

I pull on my vine again, but it only tightens on my wrist. I groan and pull harder.

"You should have listened to your mother. The darkness was never yours to harness." Jackson's voice changes, dropping another octave, morphing into a sound that would make anyone want to run in the other direction. No longer does he sound like himself. He doesn't even sound human. I glance back at him, his eyes completely black save for a dark red rim that lines the lid. "It is mine."

I pull at the vines again, my breath coming in sobs as I stare at the being in front of me. The darkness inside me swirls, caressing the light, and then melding. Together, they fight against the foreign forces, trying to obscure my powers. I look into his eyes. "You are wrong."

The two halves of my powers, along with Nyx's, push at the compulsion, and the vines around my wrist retreat. Before the beast can reply, I drive my sword through his heart.

The second the steel pierces him, everything disappears, everything except Jackson. He collapses to the ground, panting. "Seph?"

I crumble to my knees. "Jackson?"

He reaches to cup my cheek, but before he makes contact, he fades away.

I cover my face, sobbing, but once again, this time is different. There is no darkness, no reprieve. I vaguely notice the smell of woodland. The ground is soft beneath my knees, and I hear birdsong.

"My spring?"

My whole body tenses, and I hold my breath.

It can't be. It can't be.

"My spring?" He's closer this time, and the air seems to shift as it always has when he's near.

107

Could I have defeated him? Did I... win?

I slowly drop my hands and look at the ground, scared to hope, scared to dream.

Slowly, I lift my eyes. First, I see his shined-to-perfection shoes, then his tailored-black pants. His black shirt fits him perfectly, tightly hugging his biceps. I stand and run to him, jumping into his arms, sobbing. His sandalwood and citrus scent surrounds me, and I inhale him deeply. "Hades," I whisper, my voice thick from crying.

"You found me. You saved me, my spring." He squeezes me tight.

Home. Hades is home.

"You are so brave." His voice is low, his soft words spoken against the top of my head. I love the way he buries his nose into my hair. There's a sharp tug in my chest, the pull trying to separate us, but we are together. He is safe.

"I'm so relieved you're okay." My words are breathless as I cling to him.

Hades pulls back, cupping my cheeks. "My spring." He smiles and slowly lowers me to my feet. He glances around uncertainly before looking back at me. "Let's go home."

He tries to take my hand, but my arm lurches away from his touch. I frown, trying to reach for his hand. Hades steps toward me, and I instinctively step back, something in my chest tugging me away from him. It feels similar to the bond that usually pulls me in his direction.

"What's wrong, my spring?" He tilts his head. "Don't you want to go home?"

Wrong, wrong, wrong.

I look at him, my brow furrowing. "Hades. What do you call Cerberus and I?"

He frowns. "What?"

"You called us a really cute name before, and I can't remember it. What was it again?"

He crosses his arms, narrowing his eyes at me. "Don't you love me?"

I step closer. "Of course, I do. It was just so sweet, and I can't remember it for the life of me."

Hades shakes his head. "You don't love me. You've forgotten about me."

Not Hades.

I quirk a brow. "Funny, Jackson said something similar."

Hades' face morphs into one of boredom. "I shouldn't have made you my queen. It was a grave mistake."

"You know," I lift my chin, "you almost had me with this one."

Hades scoffs. "What are you talking about, gardener?"

I smirk. "It wasn't until you said, 'You've forgotten about me.' That's what ruined it for you. If only you hadn't been recycling lines, you could have been consuming my power right now, Tartarus."

Hades hisses, lunging for me. "You bitch!"

I lift the sword and bury it in Hades' chest. My heart cracks at the sight; knowing it's an illusion makes it no easier.

Hades roars in fury, pain, and surprise. The illusion created by his power surrounds us. Tree branches fly, many almost hitting me, and soon we're in the center of a tornado. My power surges to the surface, ready to combat Hades', if necessary, even though it hurts my very soul to consider it. I have no idea how illusions work. No idea if this Hades also has immense power.

I push the sword in even deeper and look at Hades, but the eyes looking back at me belong to Tartarus. The wind roars around us, and we both pant with exertion.

"You cannot have him!" I scream, twisting the blade. He roars again, and the illusion crumbles. I fall forward, my head slamming against the ground, my body, mind, and power completely drained.

Finally summoning the energy, I roll onto my back and open my eyes. I blink, frowning at the sight above me. I'm still in the forest. The birds still chirp, the trees swaying harmlessly above.

"What now?" I pant, sitting up. My hand goes to my chest, the aching pull there intensifying. I catch my breath and try to center myself, trying to figure out what I'm being drawn toward. I slowly stand and look around.

My gaze snags on one tree. It is thick, lumpy, and darker than the others, with gold veins traveling through the bark. Dark smoke cascades off the bottom, and I notice lights within the trunk. The orbs seem to shoot down the trunk to the roots and disappear into the ground. I move closer, noticing that the other trees have left a perimeter around this tree like it might infect them if they get too close.

I take a step closer and gasp when I see what looks like a face covered in mud, so covered, I would have missed it had I not been drawn to this tree. I take another step, and my breath hitches.

Hades.

His face is contorted in pain, and he's making soft groaning noises, his throat completely occluded by a branch. I run to him, standing just in front of the tree.

"Fuck, fuck, fuck."

I look around, trying to find the answer to releasing him on the forest floor. I lift my palms, trying to summon a vine. It grows around three inches, then falls limp.

"No, no, no, no, no," I sob. I lift my palms again, groaning at the effort. "Fuck!" I step forward and cup his cheek. "I'm going to get you out of here, demon."

I step back again and pace. I shake my hands and close my eyes, thinking of every memory with Hades, how it feels when he touches me, the taste of his lips against mine, his scent, the sound of his voice, his hands.

I look back at him and step closer again. I lift my palms and grunt with effort. Vines emerge from the ground beside me. I keep pushing power into them, making them longer and thicker, knowing I'll need them to be as strong as possible to free him.

I pant, keeping my eyes on him, and I scream as I push my palms forward. The purple vines strike like vipers, pulling the bark from the tree. I feel a trickle of blood slide down the side of my face, but I keep pushing. I cry out again, my vines working harder to free him.

My power has almost completely bottomed out when Hades falls from the trunk, his body limp. I collapse onto my knees and crawl to him, panting as I struggle to roll him onto his back. I look down at his face and can tell he's weak. Even covered in dirt, I can tell how pale he is. I pull the branch from his mouth, freeing his airway, and throw it away in anger. I cup his cheeks, needing to hear his voice, to hear him groan, anything to show he's alive.

I stroke his cheeks with my thumbs as I look down at him. "Hades?" My voice is barely a whisper.

He groans softly, and his eyes flicker. "You… found…" His voice is so strained.

"Shhh, don't talk."

He opens his eyelids, and I whimper when I see his eyes are gone. "Y-your eyes!"

"Home… heal…"

I nod, looking around helplessly. I try to sit him up, but between his limp body and my weakened one, I feel so helpless. After a few failed attempts, I stand and pull him to his feet, his full weight resting on me.

I groan and summon some vines to support him. They are weak, but it's enough to help.

"How… did… you…?" he croaks.

"Later. We'll talk later," I pant, struggling to support us both.

"Are… you… real?"

I stop walking, knowing he needs proof that this isn't some dream. My stomach lurches as I think about the hell he's gone through. I press my lips softly to his. "I'm here. I'm real. We're going home."

His lips twitch. "My... menace..."

I smile, a tear escaping and tracking down my cheek. "My demon."

I walk again, having no idea where we are or if I'm going in the right direction. All I know is we need to keep moving. I groan in pain and tighten my hold on Hades, pushing more magic into my vines.

After walking for what feels like forever, I lose hope. Hades isn't healing here. My power isn't regenerating anywhere near as quickly as I need it to. My steps have slowed dramatically, and nothing looks familiar. I stop walking, raise my face to the sky, and close my eyes.

My eyes snap open, and I look ahead, seeing another tear in reality. This time, Thanatos stands in the throne room, his body tense.

"Than... Thanatos?" Hades asks in a gravelly voice.

"Yes, baby, it's Thanatos!"

I walk faster now, pushing through the exhaustion. We are almost there. Almost—

Hades is yanked to the ground hard, pulling me down with him. I grip Hades tight and look back, seeing his ankles wrapped in darkness. Tartarus wails as it pulls him back.

I scream, twisting my hands as I struggle to my feet. I grab Hades' wrists and pull him closer to the portal. The shadows resist. Tartarus has replenished its power. I tighten my hold on him, summoning vines to wrap around Hades, pulling him harder toward the portal.

I scream as I completely empty the well of my power into Hades, into protecting him. I will bring him home. "You! Cannot! Have! Him!"

Chapter Nineteen

Hades

THE AIR BITES AS MY LUNGS FILL FOR THE FIRST TIME IN WHAT FEELS LIKE YEARS. Did that moment with Demeter happen months ago? Years? It's cold and harsh. My body aches, my skin is sensitive, and my muscles are weakened. Am I actually healing? *Truly* healing? When my lungs refill, there's no dirt or branches impeding my breath. The bond that connects me to the Underworld shoots through my body, allowing my muscles, eyes, and skin to regenerate.

My vision is blurry for only a moment before my eyes focus, and I take in the open chasm in the throne room—a tear inside my realm. I was here? The whole time? Why does that fact feel like it will break me when nothing else has come close? To know I was home but trapped in the place I am supposed to rule. A king trapped in his own kingdom. What a joke.

Persephone stands between the rift and me. What breath I gained when I could finally see her is lost as I take her in.

This. This is the Destroyer of Worlds.

Dressed in battle leathers that mold to her luscious body, a tiara made of stardust rests on her brow. As my eyes sharpen, I can see the glittering stardust shift with every slight movement of her body, images of the night sky dancing over her leathers before vanishing.

She is wearing armor from the First of Chaos. Nyx's armor from the last Titan War. *How did Persephone get it?*

The gash is closing, and Persephone's still got one foot in that place. She straddles the barrier between our palace and the Heart of Tartarus. That's where I was. My stomach churns with that realization. Tartarus isn't just a place. It is the last remnants of a dying Primordial who gave up his form to create the Underworld. Parts of him lingered, and over time, the half-existence had driven him mad and cruel. Through the flickering fog, I can see the dark outline of the tree, the light from the throne room reflecting off the golden veins. The veins which I'd fed, my blood pulsing through them.

My eyes, still so sensitive, flicker over the tree, and for a terrifying moment, Persephone is the one in the tree, enduring all her most horrible memories as her limbs are torn apart, and her skin flayed.

Never.

My shadows awaken as if from a long slumber and reach out to grab Persephone around the waist, pulling her through just before the portal closes. I won't let her be trapped. She won't experience that. *Never.*

She lands on top of me, and the fresh air whooshes from my lips as her elbow hits me hard in the chest. I cup her cheek, my fresh eyes scanning her face. I can barely keep the sound of relief from leaving my lips when I *feel* her.

Real. This is real.

My eyes scan over her features and those dark curls with hidden fire in them. Her blue eyes, with a circle of gold around the pupil, like the sun on a clear day, stare into mine. Her face softened by gentleness and kindness rather than violence. Persephone. My Persephone.

I don't move my eyes away from her face, still committing each part of her to memory. I hear

114

Thanatos's rough voice. "W-Welcome home."

He must have been responsible for the rip in reality. Neither Persephone nor I look at him, and I can feel the puff of air as he leaves.

Persephone's hands shake, touching my face. I whisper shakily, "My spring."

I try to wrap my arms around her, but she pushes up, scanning me, searching for more wounds. There's so much for her to find. How long have I been there? How many times had the tree ripped open my skin, flayed my muscles, and broken my bones before allowing me to heal, only to do it again? Morpheus let me escape reality, but dreams and memories were not the solaces they should be.

I growl softly, "Persephone."

She doesn't hear me or ignores me.

"I started healing once you got me through the tear," I remind her, my voice hoarse. When I try to swallow, a flash of the root shoving its way down my throat plays through my mind, the memory throwing me back into the pain and helplessness.

Persephone finally makes a sound, a small broken sob that pulls me back to the present. Her eyes fill with tears, and I wrap my arms around her tightly, keeping her on top of me as we lie on the floor of the throne room.

She kisses my cheek softly, her hand resting on my chest. "I'm not hurting you, am I?"

I shake my head, the slight movement reminding me how very weak I am. "Never."

She pulls back almost immediately and scans my face. "I want to check your injuries."

I tighten my arms on her, and with a thought, I shadow us to our bed. My stomach drops when we fall a few feet, the bed no longer the height I'm used to. I glance around in surprise. What happened to the bed? It is lower than it was before.

Persephone's fingers trail over my face, distracting

me, tracing every healing cut and bruise, cataloging them all. With every touch, she solidifies our bond as king and queen. I'm more connected to my realm with her here touching me. With her near, I feel more powerful than I ever have, even in this weakened state.

My wounds are tugging closed faster than ever, but Persephone works faster. She rips my tattered shirt, running her hands over my chest.

I tuck a lock of her hair behind her ear. "I'm fine."

I'm really not, but I can see the bags under her eyes, and the lines of worry etched into her face. How long have I been gone? How long has she searched?

She pulls back, gesturing for me to sit up so she can see my back. I sit up slowly, humoring her. Why does she need to see it all? She moves behind me, and I tense when she's out of my sight. Was she even real? Is this another dream? Her lips touch my back, rooting me in reality again. She grazes each cut with her lips, keeping me present, keeping me here.

I sigh softly. "Believe me now?"

Chapter Twenty

Persephone

BELIEVE ME NOW?" His voice makes my skin tingle. I brush my lips over his back, my hands gliding over his skin, needing to feel, see, and touch every part of him because, no, I don't believe this is real. Tartarus tricked me one too many times, and every time it learned and adapted.

I move around him, my eyes roaming over every inch of his body, cataloging every cut, every bruise, every freshly healed scar. I feel his gaze trained on me, assessing me. Deep down, I think I know it's Hades, and he's worried about me. He is probably trying to work out how long I searched for him and what I went through to get him back. But what if I'm wrong?

What if this is Tartarus watching me, learning my weaknesses and insecurities? What if I'm being fed upon right now? What if we didn't make it out, and we're both in that tree?

My chest aches at the sight of his torn-up skin. He's healing quickly, so quickly I can barely believe it, but I keep seeing him fall from the tree trunk, completely broken, his eyes gone, his skin raw.

"Pants." I don't even realize I've said it, my instincts taking over, desperate to make sure he is definitely healing. All the while, I'm assessing him, trying to catch any inconsistency, trying to catch out Tartarus.

When he doesn't move to remove his pants, I look up, the sight of his face taking my breath away. How can anyone still look so incredibly handsome while covered in mud? His sapphire blue eyes are trained on me, and they're hard with concern. I have no idea what my face is conveying or if I'm covered in mud or blood. There is grime against my skin, but it feels no different from the phantom filth that has coated my skin following every nightmare since Hades was taken.

"I told you, I'm fine," he says finally.

I glare at him, waiting for him to remove his pants. Hades rolls his eyes, the gesture so normal, so perfectly Hades, that my uncertainty about the reality of this situation slowly starts to melt away. He pulls his ripped pants off, discarding them on the ground, keeping his intense gaze on me. He's looking at me with the same suspicion I feel. I'm unsure if he's also concerned that this might be an elaborate illusion created by his captor or if he's worried I'll lose my shit in the next second.

I shuffle closer, placing my hands on his legs. They're as cut and bruised as the rest of him, but he's healing so quickly. The angry red scars are already fading to a docile pink, standing out against his tanned skin.

After completing my inspection, I pull my hands away and climb off the bed. Hades makes no move to stop or follow me, but my skin seems to scorch beneath his gaze. I stand at the side of the bed, hesitating. I start to turn my head to look back but stop myself.

What if he's not there?

"Persephone…"

I whimper at the sound of his voice. My whole body sags in relief that he is, in fact, still there. I walk through to the bathroom. Everything in me seems to be in conflict. I need to stay with him. I need to be touching him at all times to prove to myself that he's really here and won't be taken again. But another part of me needs some space, some time to think about what I went

118

through and what Tartarus threw at me.

I focus on my breathing as I step into the bathroom. Even the quiet click of the door as it closes sets me on edge. I walk straight to the tub and turn on the hot water. If I focus on taking care of Hades, I'll feel better. He's been through hell. I don't know how long I was in Tartarus, but I know it wasn't as long as he was. What did he go through? What did he see?

I reach for the tub of bath salts on the shelf, trying to stay in the moment of the small tasks I'm completing, focusing on one thing at a time and taking deep, regular breaths. I concentrate on the pop of the bottle as I pull the cork from the container of bath salts. The smell of the sea and lavender fills the room as I pour them into the tub, steam clouding the room.

The bath is almost full when Hades enters the bathroom. His presence both steals the air and allows me to breathe easier.

I hear the door close and he does not coming any closer to me.

"Persephone?" His voice is barely above a whisper, almost inaudible over the sound of the scalding water cascading from the tap, but a shiver runs down my spine all the same, my body reacting the way it always has with him.

I dip my fingers in the water, making sure the temperature is perfect for him. "In." The word comes out as a command, and I think I sound angry. It couldn't be further from what I'm feeling, but I don't trust my voice enough to explain, and I don't want him to worry any more than he already is.

I hear him sigh heavily and then his surefooted steps come toward me. My skin tingles even at that, and the closer he gets, the more normal I feel. I glance up at him when he stops beside me, lines of concern etched on his face. He manages to crack a small smile, but I know it's more for my benefit than his. He pushes down his boxers, and I blush, looking away. I'm acutely aware of how ridiculous I'm being, but everything feels strange and uncomfortable.

He steps into the bath, and I turn away from him, my blush deepening when he groans, no doubt at the way the hot water eases his tense muscles.

I swallow and grab a towel from the cupboard. Setting it out for him, I do not look back before leaving the bathroom.

"Persephone???" I hear him sputter from the bathroom as I leave. The pull in my chest urges me to go back to him, but I don't know what to say to him. I don't know how to act. So, I will care for him.

What else will he need?

Food. He'll need food.

I light the fire in the bedroom and go to the kitchen to make him something to eat. He can't have eaten since he was taken, and I assume it's hungry work being consumed by a power-devouring asshole.

The mahogany cabinets in the kitchen seem to mock me as I start to look through them. They are fully stocked with food, ingredients, cookware, and utensils, but I am no chef.

Why couldn't I be the Goddess of Michelin-star restaurants?

I glance at the pantry and pull out a box of pasta. Pasta is comforting, hearty, carbohydrates. Is it what I would want if I were sick?

If only my mother had ever cared for me, maybe I would be better at this. I'd always looked after myself. Plus, if a goddess gets sick, it can only really mean two things, they're dying or pregnant. I have no idea what to do with a god in this situation.

I think back to my time among mortals, trying to remember when one of my human friends was sick. My brows furrow as I try to pull on any memories from before my time in the Underworld, but with every memory, I'm taken back to Tartarus.

Fuck.

Wait. I'm sure once, when Sarah was sick, Jackson had suggested taking her soup. That sounds right. Soup is very comforting and warm!

I grab a heap of vegetables and carry them to the counter. I decide it's best to separate them into types before considering how to make the soup. Three potatoes, four carrots, an onion, and an eggplant, this will be fine, right? You can't fuck up soup.

I shrug and start chopping the vegetables, once again focusing on each task, not letting my mind wander for a moment. When everything is diced, I grab a large pot and fill it with water before dumping all the vegetables in. When the water starts to boil, I stir the soup, grimacing at the look of the eggplant. That may have been a bad call, but surely, nothing some salt and pepper can't fix.

I add salt, pepper, and some other random spices I've never heard of into the concoction. I stir it again and lean over to sniff, wincing at the smell of the soup.

"Well… this might not be all that comforting," I murmur.

As the soup boils, I cut up some bread for Hades. I ladle the soup into a bowl, place it and the bread on a tray along with some water and head back to the bedroom. My stomach flips. What if he's not there? What if he's been taken? What if he's gone?

I step into the bedroom just as Hades is exiting the bathroom, the fluffy white towel hanging low around his hips. I quickly avert my eyes to the very excited Cerberus, who is jumping around Hades. My lips twitch at how unaware Berry is of his size. He acts like he's as small as a cocker spaniel when, in reality, many fully-grown bears are smaller than him.

I walk to the bed and place the tray down before patting my thigh, beckoning Cerberus to come to me and allow Hades safe passage to the bed. Cerberus bounds to me, all of his tongues lolling out of his mouths, his eyes brighter than I've ever seen them with the return of his daddy.

"There's my good boy!" I say as Cerberus skids to a halt just in front of me. I scratch behind all of his ears, giving all of his heads their own attention. Cerberus looks excitedly between me and Hades.

"Did you find Daddy?" I smile warmly at him. "Oh, what a good boy you are!" I glance up at Hades, who is frowning down at the bowl of soup on the tray. "I made you soup."

He glances at me, quickly schooling his face into a grateful expression, though I caught the surprise in his face when I said it was soup.

Should I have blended it?

Cerberus's whole body wriggles in excitement as he runs circles around the room. I smile, watching him.

"Why are you coddling me?" Hades asks, pulling me from my marshmallow observations. He sits on the bed and dips the spoon in the bowl. I watch as he eats the spoonful, and to his credit, he hides his wince pretty well.

"Coddling?" I ask, returning my attention to Cerberus as he runs back to me.

I glance back at Hades when he doesn't reply, and he looks pointedly at the soup.

"I…" I hesitate, not knowing how to start this conversation, not even sure I'm ready to have it yet. "How are you feeling?"

Good one, P. Historically, we know repression is the healthiest option.

Hades lifts another spoonful of soup to his lips. I can see the hint of reluctance, but like a trooper, he eats it.

Fuck, this is painful to watch. It would be kinder to starve him.

"Persephone," he says, his voice hard and unbending. "Tell me."

I look down at Cerberus and kiss all three of his heads. "Are you hungry? You want Uncle Thanatos to feed you?"

122

Cerberus barks and bolts from the room, and a moment later, there is a large clatter of what sounds like pots and pans, followed by the muffled sounds of Thanatos cursing.

I close the bedroom door and sit by the fireplace in one of the armchairs. "How's the soup?"

Hades hesitates, looking at me intently. "What is it?"

"Vegetable… I guess," I say with a grimace.

He sighs heavily. "Not the soup, my spring. What's wrong?"

I look down at my hands in my lap, nervously pulling on my fingers. "What do you mean?"

Hades stands from the bed and walks to me. My stomach flutters as he gets closer. He kneels in front of me and takes my hands in his. Slowly, he brings my hands to his face, cupping his cheeks with them.

"I'm here." His voice is soft and reassuring. I lift my gaze to lock with his, the piercing blue eyes bringing me home. This feels so real. But what if it's not? I can't do that again. I try to pull my hands away and look away. The eyes that were once so comforting to me now bring memories of how it felt when the steel pierced his heart, the way his skin tore so easily. All I can see is how thick his gold ichor was as it spilled from the fatal wound that I'd inflicted on him.

I feel Hades flinch, his body recoiling from my rejection. This is it. This is where he tells me that he is Tartarus, and I have been fooled again.

I can't do it again. I can't harm him again.

I hear him walk away and the sound of clothes ruffling in the distance. I can't bear to look, can't bear to watch him leave me, to turn against me.

The feeling of the sword, heavy in my hand, the way my arm shook as I raised it, the sound as I pierced the muscle of his heart, feeling it beat around the steel.

My chest feels tight, my whole body shaking at the memory, the pain of my heart breaking almost unbearable. A tear escapes, leaving a cold trail in its

123

wake as it slides down my cheek.

"I should get to work," Hades says, his voice distant.

Don't leave, don't leave, don't leave.

Fear twists in my stomach, and I feel another tear slide down my cheek. "You c-can't leave me," I whisper. "Y-you won't come back. I-I was alone. She took you." The tears start to fall unchecked, and my heart aches so badly that I'm sure it's going to shatter into a million pieces. "She took you. She hurt you. And I—"

My words are interrupted by his lips crushing mine, his perfect soft lips. His large hands cup my cheeks, his warmth seeping into me, his comfort easing me.

He pulls back, pressing his forehead to mine. "I'm here."

"Please don't leave me," I sob, clutching his shirt.

Hades sweeps me into his arms, his hard chest providing the safety I need. I don't open my eyes, just bury my face into his neck and inhale him over and over, holding onto him tightly, not letting go even when he lays us down in the bed, not letting go when he wraps me in his arms, not letting go when he pulls the blanket over us.

I am never letting go again.

Chapter Twenty One

Hades

DON'T LEAVE ME. PLEASE DON'T LEAVE ME. The words echo in my skull like a curse, reverberating in painful vibrations, reminding me of what I endured, of my howls of agony, rage, and hopelessness. My mind goes back there for a moment, to the fall, to the war. Persephone buries her face into my chest, weeping openly, the great Queen of the Underworld, sobbing into her king's chest. The cries aren't of relief or happiness but of *anguish*. The wrongness of it is enough to snap me into the present and out of the past. I thought the captivity broke me, but I didn't think it through. I didn't realize she was broken, too.

I stroke her hair softly, kissing her head, whispering comfortingly, "I'm here, my spring."

She doesn't stop, her body shaking as she sobs. I've never seen her cry, and for her to break like this... *What happened to her? What did she go through to save me?* I want to soothe her and take away all her pain. But how can I when my pain is overflowing? I am a cup that has spent the last two thousand years being filled with tragedy, and now it's leaking down the sides. I can't handle it anymore, and I know I am failing her already.

I brush her hair softly, keeping her close as if I could weld her back together with my arms. Maybe if I could do it for her, I could do the same for myself. It's all I can offer both of us. I'm supposed to be this feared king, but right now, this is the extent of my power.

"I'm not going anywhere."

Fate knows we'd paid enough. It needs to leave us alone. I squeeze her tighter to me. I won't let this happen again. It cannot happen again. The slightest ember of my power awakens inside me, responding to my emotions. The darker my thoughts, the more it returns to me in slow bursts.

I don't know how long we sit like that before she starts to fall asleep. No doubt she's barely slept since she arrived in the Underworld. I hum softly, trying to lure her deeper into sleep, but she keeps forcing her eyes back open, pushing it off. It takes a moment for me to realize why.

The last time she slept, I was taken.

My chest aches. My broken queen, shattered and shaken by what she'd seen. Fuck. How do we piece our souls back together when neither of us knows where to start? The wounds on my skin have healed at least, but the memories, those haunting, tortuous moments of my life. How many times had I relived each one before Persephone freed me?

I kiss her softly, reassuring her and myself. Once I can think clearly, after I rest, I'll devise a plan to heal our minds. "No one can take me from the Underworld. I'll be here when you wake up."

Here, I'm at my strongest. With Persephone with me, the bond with my realm is deeper, as if I'd only had a portion of its unknowable power before. It's the great abyss of my domain of death, yet I'm too weak to access even a fraction of it now. Maybe I just need rest, but what if I dream? My body tenses at that. No, I can't dream. I can't go back there. I'll find another way to restore my power without sleeping.

She looks up at me, her eyelids drooping. "I love you."

"I love you too, my spring." My chest aches with the realization that it was the first time I'd said the words out loud to her.

I don't sleep, so I stroke her hair, watching each inhale and exhale from her, counting each one, using them to tether me to reality. I won't go back to my dreams. Not yet. Not for a while.

Barely an hour passes before Persephone thrashes against me, frantically mumbling, "Mother, Helios, Jackson, Hades… No. Please, no!"

I cup her cheeks. "My spring, wake up. It's just a dream."

It's just a dream. The words taste like acid on my tongue. It is never just a dream.

She keeps thrashing against me. "No."

I shake her, careful not to hurt her. "Persephone?"

I gasp when thorns thrust from her skin and pierce my hands, several slicing through muscle and bone and appearing on the other side. I look at the thorns for a single terrifying moment. They look like branches. Persephone thrashes, bringing me back. I shake her harder, not releasing her, even as more thorns tear through my hands.

She bolts up a second later, her chest heaving, thorns forming a layer of armor made from sharp points over her skin. Each thorn is black, tipped with a violet edge. Poisonous?

I brush her cheek. "My spring." She lifts her arm, frowning at the thorns. I touch one lightly. "These are new."

She takes a few stuttering breaths before nodding. "There are a few new things."

I brush a lock of her hair back, my palms healing from the wounds left by her thorns. "Tell me."

The thorns retract back into her skin, vanishing. She twists her hand, and it is such an achingly familiar movement that my heart beats a little faster just seeing it.

Real.

The vines she summons aren't the verdant green that I remember. They're sinister in appearance, deep purple, almost black, with pulsing red veins. Persephone wraps her hand around the vine, handing it to me.

"Your powers are morphing," I remark, looking at the vine. Is she adapting to the Underworld? Or are her abilities growing with her surroundings, becoming what they were always meant to be?

She releases the vine, and it wraps around my wrist almost lovingly. Sinister in appearance but docile to the touch, like most things in the Underworld. She opens her palm. The bright white daisy that used to grow there is no longer soft and curved but black, severe, and sharp. Deadly.

I touch the petal gently, unsurprised that it's closer to silk, even with how jagged the edges are. Persephone shivers in response. "Beautiful and deadly. My dark spring." *My queen.* Pride makes my chest swell. Has there ever been a more awe-inspiring queen? She would fill that empty throne at my side and rule over our kingdom with an iron fist and a kind touch.

Her eyes search my face, the slightest bit of surprise betrayed in her eyes. I focus back on the flower. "Does it upset you?"

After a moment, she shakes her head, and I fondly stroke the petal. "Good."

The longer she was in the Underworld, the more she could experience these shifts in her power. With her here, I'm able to access more raw power than before, and I've been king for two millennia.

"She killed him," she whispers.

My brows furrow, still focused on the flower. "Who?"

She closes her fist around the flower, cutting off my

sight of it, the sharp petals cutting her skin. "Jackson."

I recoil slightly at the name of my old rival and grind my teeth. *I'm not really that petty, am I?* Clearly, I won. Wait, did she say he was killed?

"How do you know?" I ask, my voice a little strained.

Blood trickles down Persephone's wrist, and her eyes are unfocused. "Tartarus."

What did the darkness show her? What horrific visions did she endure to free me? I don't know how many times I relieved the worst moments of my life, but I hadn't thought about what could have been shown to her at the same time.

"Tartarus lies," I add. Eons in the half-alive state had driven the Primordial to the edge and far over. Madness twined with cruelness, and Persephone had been at his mercy.

She shakes her head, and I cover her closed hand with mine. I force her palm open, watching the black flower retreat into her skin and her wound heal. "No. This was the truth. She killed him, and she tried to kill you."

I grab her hand. "Look at me."

She blinks at me, her eyes still red from sobbing. Oh, Persephone. What had she endured in my absence?

I kiss her softly, inhaling her scent. "You found me." *You saved me.*

She pulls back from me, pulling her legs to her chest. "Not quick enough."

I pull her into my lap, wrapping my arms around her. "You found me. The time doesn't matter." The time doesn't matter. It can't.

Chapter Twenty-Two

Persephone

I HUG MY KNEES TO MY CHEST, my head a mess. His arms around me are grounding, but they aren't piecing me back together as I expected, and I don't know why. I feel sick when I think of Hades being fed on for so long. I feel sick thinking about Jackson being dead, and I feel sick at the thought that I didn't fucking notice.

Hades nuzzles his nose into my hair, and I hold my knees closer. Maybe between us, we can hold each other tight enough that we'll heal.

I'm so acutely aware of the bond in my chest, finally humming happily to be near him. My whole body feels wrong, like I've finally got back the other half of my soul, but the price was my sanity. I pull back from him. "I think I'm going to go take a shower."

Hades observes me but nods once, his arms still around me, like he's as unwilling to be parted from me as I am him. When he doesn't release me, I look up at him and our gazes meet. His piercing blue eyes search mine for a moment before he releases me slowly. I look away and slide off the bed. Every step I take away from him makes me feel uneasy. I grab some pajamas and walk to the bathroom, hesitating with my hand on the bathroom door to glance back at him over my shoulder.

"Will you… just… be in the bathroom with me?" I ask shakily.

Hades doesn't hesitate. He climbs off the bed and follows me into the bathroom. I turn my back to him as I slowly remove my fighting leathers, and once again, I can feel Hades' gaze on me. I quickly step into the shower, unsure why I'm so self-conscious of him looking at me.

The water sluices over me, and I close my eyes. With every drop that falls on my body, I feel a little of myself returning to me. The nightmares are retreating, not completely gone, but enough that I'm feeling more myself. Hades' presence in the bathroom strengthens me and though I don't look at him, I can practically see him leaning against the vanity, his arms crossed and his powerful body tense.

I take my time washing my hair, the strawberry and rose scent filling the room. When I wash my face, I feel for the cuts Tartarus Helios left on me, but there is nothing there. Whatever wounds Tartarus left on me have healed, the external ones, anyway. I exhale heavily as I feel clean again, and now that the water has soothed me as much as it can, my chest aches for Hades again. Even though he is just through the shower door, I need his hands on me.

I stop the shower and wrap a towel around my body, finally glancing at Hades. His concerned gaze is still locked on my face. I step out of the shower and dry myself wordlessly before pulling on my clean pajamas. I try to smile at Hades, but I'm certain I'm unsuccessful when his face doesn't change.

Looking away, I head back to the bedroom, Hades following close behind. We both climb back into bed, and it hurts my heart how awkward we are.

After a moment, Hades pulls me closer and nuzzles into my neck, inhaling deeply. "Persephone…"

I close my eyes, relaxing a little, a small sob escaping. "Persephone?"

"Hm?"

"Would you like to see him?" His voice is gentle, but I don't miss the slight edge. "Jackson?"

My entire body tenses, and I pull back to look at him.

"If she killed him, his spirit will be here," Hades says, his eyes roaming over my face.

I swallow. "You can find him?"

Hades nods. "After I rest for a bit."

I look away, thinking. "I want to see him."

Hades' lips pull into a smile, and he nods before laying down on the bed and pulling me with him. Instinctively, I relax into him. My head rests in the crook of his arm, and I place my hand on his chest, feeling his even heartbeat.

The feeling of my blade plunging into his heart, feeling the vibrations slow beneath my hands.

I close my eyes and grasp his shirt, my stomach twisting. "You won't leave?"

Hades tightens his arms around me and buries his nose in my hair, kissing the top of my head. "Never, my spring."

I swallow thickly and grasp his shirt tighter.

"Would you like to wrap me in your vines as we sleep? You know I can't escape them." I hear a slight smile in his voice, and I glance up at him, seeing that his lips have tilted in a genuine smile.

The corners of my lips pull a little, but they quiver, and I feel more tears burning my eyes.

"Wrap us, Persephone. We'll sleep together."

I keep my eyes on his, not moving, but my vines slip around us, starting at our legs and then wrapping around our bodies, pressing us closer together, the large pillowy leaves brushing against our skin. When we are completely covered in purple vines, Hades presses his lips softly to mine and whispers against them, "Tighter, my spring. You have to know I'm going nowhere. Not without you. Never again."

A tear slides down my cheek, and I tighten the vines, our bodies pressed together but still comfortable.

"You got me," he whispers.

I loosen the vines ever so slightly to reach up and cup his cheek before brushing my lips over his.

I feel the power shift, and his shadows blanket us, filling in the small gaps in my vines. "Okay?"

I exhale heavily. "Okay."

"Sleep, my love," Hades says, kissing the top of my head. I fight it initially, not wanting the nightmares, not wanting to wake up without Hades, but I feel his shadows brushing against my skin. The warmth of his body soothes me. I eventually fall into a heavy sleep, and for the first time since Hades was taken, it is completely dreamless.

Chapter Twenty-Three
Hades

I DON'T SLEEP. I CAN'T. Shakespeare clearly didn't know what the fuck he was talking about when he wrote *to sleep, perchance to dream.* Dreams were a prison, and having grown up inside one, I would never willingly enter another. Not again. My eyes trail over Persephone's features, memorizing every slope and lush line. Would I have experienced those memories differently if I could remember what awaited me once I broke free? What if I could have remembered that Persephone waited, and one day, I'd hold her in my arms as she slept? My queen. My spring. My Persephone.

I hold her as she dozes off, my arms tightening around her every so often, reassuring myself that she's real. I focus on the warmth of her skin, the scent of roses in my every breath. It's real. It has to be real.

This has to be real.

But… what if it isn't? No. The dreams or memories were of the past, not the present. Not a single one featured Persephone. If they had, they wouldn't have been torture. Even when we were at odds, Persephone was paradise, and I should be completely at ease lying here with her. Yet, I still don't close my eyes. I barely blink. I know Morpheus meant well when he sent

134

me into my memories, into my dreams. The fall. The rise. The war. The crown. The loneliness that spanned decades and was broken only by a handful of years growing up in a prison. He'd reopened wounds I thought long healed.

Torture was one thing. I could have lived with those roots if it meant keeping Persephone safe. I would have become one with that dark tree. If I was conscious, I would have relished in each branch, each drop of blood it consumed. I'd gather all the vitriol in my blood to hurl at Demeter, daring her to do her worst. Torture I could withstand. I could pile on wounds until I was nothing but a husk, so long as I had my mind. My mind is my haven, my retreat, but then Morpheus made it my prison, and it ripped open the scar of my past with relish.

Normally, I could heal, but this is a different wound. A wound I'd buried so deep I thought it was gone. Foolish of me to think anything is truly gone. Even the gods ache and scar. We live long lives, accumulating scars like badges of honor, but some wounds of the soul never quite heal.

I stroke Persephone's hair absently. She saw something. I can see it in her eyes, a terror that seeped into her, haunting those perfect sunburst eyes. I need to help her, but I have no fucking idea how. How does the broken help the broken? How does the wounded heal the wounded?

What can I do?

Her vines tighten on me a bit more, my shadows a comforting presence around us. Vines and shadows entwined into a single entity like we were. King and Queen. Death and life. I pull her closer, fitting her against me.

Fucking bitch. We won't let her win. I won't let that haggard crone break us.

I take a shaky breath, letting my eyelids close. *"Leave me be tonight, Morpheus."*

As I drift off, I hear him answer, *"As you wish, my king."*

My eyes snap open when light filters into the room. Thankfully, the few moments of sleep I'd managed were dreamless. I stretch slightly beneath her vines and my shadows, Persephone's hand tightening on me at the slight movement, keeping me close. Her vines respond to their mistress's unconscious demand and squeeze me tighter.

I smile and kiss her gently. *Real.* "My spring, wake up."

She groans, nuzzling into me. *Real.* I release the shadows that had wrapped us in warmth all night, but her vines only tighten. Can I really blame them for protecting their mistress as she sleeps?

"My love," I whisper, kissing her head.

It takes a long moment before she slowly blinks her eyes open and looks up at me. "Hi," I whisper to her. My heart thunders in my chest. *Real.* "I'm still here."

Her lower lip trembles for a moment before she wraps her arms around my neck, kissing me hard. Without words, she tells me what she is thinking as her lips press urgently to mine. She needs to reaffirm that I'm still here, that she didn't lose me again.

I pull back after a moment, but my lips linger over hers, our breaths mixing. "How did you sleep?"

She slides her hands over my chest, pausing where my injuries were the worst. Even though there are no lingering wounds, she is checking. "Better," she says, the warmth of her breath another caress.

I glance at the vines still binding us, raising a brow at her. She pulls back more to look at me. "What?"

My lips twitch. "I need to eat and use the restroom."

She blushes and slowly lets the vines lower and

retreat. I shift a little, lifting her into my arms to carry her to the adjoining bathroom. Her weight in my arms is a comforting familiarity, the curves of her body reassuring me. Maybe we can put ourselves back together. I put her on the counter next to the sink, leaving the door open as I use the restroom so she can see my back the whole time.

I hear her cover a laugh as I relieve my bladder and glance at her. "What?"

She lowers her hand from her mouth, shaking her head. "Nothing."

I finish and wash my hands in the sink next to her. She watches me, her lips twitching. I dry my hands and ask, "Are you laughing at me?"

She widens her eyes, the picture of innocence. "Would I do that?"

I lean over, kissing her hard, bruising her lips with the force. "Yes."

She wraps her arms around my neck, deepening the kiss. Her fingers tunnel into my hair, pulling me closer with every part of her as if I would ever be far away from her by choice.

After a moment, I press my forehead to hers, my voice husky and still hoarse. "I thought you wouldn't want me out of sight for a moment."

She kisses me again, a quick peck of her lips, whispering, "I don't want you to stop kissing me either."

I kiss her again. "Breakfast?"

She pulls back and shrugs. "I guess."

I wrap the shadows around us and take us to the kitchen. Persephone's ass lands on the counter. "What would you like, my queen?"

She shrugs again. "Coffee."

My eyes narrow on her. "What else?"

She smiles, but I can see it's forced. "Just coffee."

I growl at her. "Persephone."

She jumps down from the counter and pours herself a cup of coffee. I watch her out of the corner of my eye as I make crepes for us, adding all her favorite fruit. I prepare strawberries, raspberries, chocolate chips, whipped cream, and a little bit of Nutella. Persephone takes a seat at the island, and I slide the crepe in front of her as I make my own.

She sips the coffee, ignoring the crepe. I growl, "Persephone. Eat."

She glares at me but takes a begrudging bite as she does. I relax a bit but say, "You're concerning me." She takes another bite as I watch. "Thank you."

I finish my crepe and lean against the island across from her so I can watch her as she clears her own plate. I keep my eyes on her. "Finished?"

Chapter Twenty-Four

Persephone

I LOOK UP AT HIM, AND MY LIPS PULL INTO A SMILE. I cradle my mug in my hands and nod, sipping the coffee. Last night was exactly what I needed. I'm not completely healed, but after a night pressed against my Hades, I'm more at ease. The doubt that this is all an illusion has almost completely melted away and continues to do so with every touch, chaste kiss, and look of longing he gives me.

I slip off my chair and move to place my cup in the sink. Before I can set it down, Hades is on me, slamming his lips to mine. His kiss is intoxicating and insistent. His tongue slides along the seam of my lips, and I open eagerly to him.

His hands wrap around the mug, and he moves to the side, aiming to put it on the counter, but in his fervor, he misses, and it smashes loudly against the kitchen tiles. I don't even have time to react before his hands wander up my body and tangle into my hair. I grasp onto his shirt, my body responding as quickly to him as it ever has, and fuck, have I missed him.

His hands move again like he can't decide where he wants to touch me, and they wander back down my body to my ass. His low groan sends a jolt of electricity through me, and I wrap my arms around his neck, pulling his body closer to mine until we're flush.

Hades lifts me from my feet, wrapping my legs around his hips and sitting me on the kitchen island. I feel every hard inch of him pressed against me and moan into his lips. Like a starved animal, he growls, deepening the kiss.

He curls his fingers into my shorts and yanks at them, desperate for the clothing separating us to be gone. I am scarcely less eager as my hands find his sweatpants and push them down.

"Hades..." I moan, my voice low. If it weren't Hades, I'd be embarrassed by how desperate I sound for him.

Hades discards my shorts to the side and wriggles out of his pants. He pulls back, looking at me. His eyes are black, and his gaze makes my stomach twist deliciously. "Yes?"

I wrap my hand around his shaft, squeezing his heavy length. "I need you."

"Fuck. You'll have me." His words are a heady mixture of a groan and a growl, and the sound sends a pang of desire straight between my legs.

I lean forward, kissing him deeply, and he growls again, sending a shiver down my spine. Hades brushes my hand away and wraps his own hand around his cock, lining it up with my pussy. His swollen crown just touching my opening makes me practically feral for him.

Without hesitation, Hades slams inside me, my dripping pussy stretching to accept his incredible size. I dig my nails into his shoulders, and his lips swallow my cries as he pulls his hips back before slamming them back into me.

"Mine," he growls into my mouth.

"Fuck." I pant, dragging my nails down his chest. He ups his pace, slamming his cock inside me over and over. His fingers dig into my sides, and he moves his mouth to my neck. I tilt my head for him, giving him

140

the access he demands as he kisses, nips, and bites at the sensitive skin there.

"Found me…" He moans, and I move my fingers to tunnel into his hair, keeping his head pressed into my neck.

He slams into me harder, our worries, desperation, and longing fueling us. He bites my neck, and I moan, my body arching as he continues to plunge into me hard and fast.

"Need this. Need you," Hades grunts, his fingers digging into my hips so hard that I'm sure I'll have his handprints marked into me, and I hope I do. I need to be marked by him.

My cunt throbs as he thrusts his length into me over and over, my whole body tensing as I near my release.

"Hades," I moan, my husky voice in his ear, making him shiver.

He brings his lips back to mine and kisses me searingly. His tongue flicks mine, and I almost come at the taste of him.

"Can't live without you…" The words are muffled against his lips before I deepen the kiss.

"You're so wet for me, baby," he groans, his hips still pistoning, and I can sense he's getting closer too. I try to rock my hips as much as I can, needing more of him, chasing the pleasure only he can bring me.

"Persephone," he groans. "Close…"

"Come for me." I moan, panting.

He roars with his release, and in the next moment, I find mine, too. I scream his name, my body writhing in his grip, completely at his mercy.

I feel him fill me, and my whole body shudders.

He presses his forehead to mine, panting, and I close my eyes, basking in our closeness, connection, and bond.

"Perfect." He cups my cheek and tilts his head, pressing his lips against mine.

"This feels so real," I whisper.

"It is real." His arms tighten around me as if he needs to feel me to convince himself that his words are true.

I nod. "I finally feel like you're right."

He pulls back, assessing me. "What?"

"I was... worried it wasn't real." I glide my hands over his chest, needing to be touching him constantly.

"Is there anything I can do to convince you further?" He strokes my cheek with his thumb.

"Just exactly what you're already doing, demon."

Hades exhales, closing his eyes, his lips pulling into a smile. "Hearing you call me that is just..." He opens his eyes, his gaze meeting mine. "Home."

I wrap my arms around his neck, pulling him closer again.

"We can sleep in your vines for as long as you need."

I kiss along his collarbone. "And you'll touch me constantly?"

He nods. "Every moment."

I lean in and bite his neck. "And kiss me?"

His deep chuckle sends a warmth to my very core. "Every chance I get..."

I feel him tense, and I pull back, tilting my head as I study him. "Baby?"

He smiles, but it doesn't reach his eyes. A haunted look passes over his face. "Hm?"

"What's wrong?" I ask, my brows furrowing. "Nothing, my love" He shakes his head and kisses my cheek. He's lying. I know he is, and I am stuck in between not wanting to push him and also wanting to fix everything Tartarus broke. I want to give him back everything that was taken from him, but how can I fix my soulmate when my soul is in ruins?

Chapter Twenty-Five

Hades

I DON'T BELIEVE YOU," SHE WHISPERS, her
eyes narrowing dangerously. *Treacherous waters.*
She'd seen the tree and freed me, but what I am
dealing with isn't about being trapped in the tree. I am
struggling to process the healed-over scars that were
ripped open in my dreams. The memories I relived:
growing up in a prison, being snatched from my only
home into a battle to be used as a weapon. They are
memories I buried, froze in ice, and forced myself to
forget.

"What?" I ask her, but even I hear the edge in my
voice. I tense, prepared for her to snap at me for the
sharpness in my voice.

She sighs, her eyes flickering even as she kisses my
jaw and turns away. I preferred if she had snapped at
me. The quiet defeat in her eyes is worse. I grab her
hand before she gets far enough away, pleading with
her, "Talk to me."

She turns to face me, and the sadness lining her face
tears at me, and I want to howl. "I never know what
you're thinking," she says.

If I give her a little, maybe it will help.

Lie.

I lift her hands and press them to my cheeks,

needing her to keep me centered in reality. "I'm worried about you."

"I know." She rubs her thumbs along my cheeks soothingly, as if it is more important to keep me rooted than for me to focus on her. "I know you're worried. And I know you want to talk about things at length. But I... I can't right now." She drops her hands from my cheeks, rubbing her arm absently. "I'm going to take another shower. I still feel grimy. And then you're going to take me to Jackson."

She's pulling back from me, retreating behind the wall surrounding her heart. I can't let her do that. I won't. "Do you truly wish to know what I'm thinking?" I ask, scanning her eyes, willing to do anything to keep her here with me, even this.

"Yes," she whispers. Her eyes flicker with warmth, and I cling to that.

I close my eyes and press my forehead to hers, establishing the mental link between our minds, speaking to her through it. *"I worry you'll never forget what Tartarus showed you."*

My eyes open to analyze her face. She tilts her head from mine as if rolling my voice around her head before replying the same way. *"I won't."*

I cover my flinch. *"You freed me from there, but now you're trapped."*

She cups my cheek, speaking out loud. "I want us to talk about this. Tonight. After."

"Maybe you shouldn't have freed me," I whisper.
Did I say that out loud?

She clenches her jaw, stepping closer to me, erasing any lingering space between us. She places a hand on my chest. "Hades, look at me."

I slowly look into her eyes. "It broke you, and you won't let me help."

Don't leave me in the dark with my own thoughts.

She tunnels her fingers into my hair, anchoring me in that moment. "I need to do this, Hades, and then you

144

and I will talk. All night if you want. Please."

I glance away. "Fine."

She shakes her head, releasing me and walking away from me. I follow her silently to the bedroom, and she heads for the shower while I dress for the trip. I keep focusing on the sound of the shower running and her footsteps on the ground. *Real.*

When I step into the closet, the one so familiar to me, my breath catches in my throat. The side that had always stood empty is filled with clothes. I look at what the Underworld has provided for her. Gowns of every dark shade hang on the racks, and heels and boots are placed neatly on shelves. When I open the drawers, I smile softly, seeing that it's trying to replicate some of the clothes she often wore on the surface.

It's still learning her habits and proclivities. The longer she's here, the more it will anticipate exactly what she wants and needs. I can't imagine Persephone walking down to breakfast with me in one of these gowns. She needs more comfortable clothes to feel at home. I smile as the very clothes I'm remembering her wearing appear.

Yoga pants and a comfy sweater. Sneakers. Fuzzy socks. I feel her eyes on me, even as I stroke a finger over one sock.

"It's still learning you," I whisper.

"What is?" she asks, and I look back at her.

I gesture with my hand as I reach for a pair of black slacks, turning my back to her as I pull them on. "The Underworld."

I hear the towel drop and stop myself from turning to look at her. It is not the time, very not the time. Though I can hear the elastic of her underwear as she slides it into place.

"Am I not the queen?" she asks as she dresses.

My chest aches hearing her say that. "It's nice to share it with someone." To share with you the burdens, the responsibilities, the joys, the pain, the wonders, the

145

terrors, and the tiny places that only I see.

I finish dressing and lean in the doorway as she pulls on jeans and her shirt. My queen. Gods, she's beautiful.

She pulls her sweater on, fiddling with the end. "I wouldn't want to have this responsibility alone."

I step closer to her, closing the distance, waiting for her to look up at me. It takes an agonizing moment, but she does, her eyes shimmering with vulnerability. I press my forehead to hers, needing that small connection to solidify what I always knew.

I am hers, and she is mine.

She turns to me fully, wrapping her arms around me.

"He's in the Elysian Fields," I whisper, not releasing her as I shadow us to the golden plains. It is paradise incarnate, where the spirits of the righteous dead are reunited with their loved ones. Golden wheat sprouts from the ground, and the orchard is full of perfect fruit that never grows old. The place is beautiful and peaceful, full of meadows, groves, and sunlight. The life after death that all souls wish for but not all deserve.

Chapter Twenty-Six

Persephone

HEAVEN. THIS MUST BE HEAVEN. The breath seems to whoosh out of me as I take in the landscape. It's everything my home should have been and everything it isn't.

The grass beneath my feet seems lusher, and the trees stand prouder, the fruit growing on them plumper and shinier. The small, delicate flowers on the meadow floor are far more beautiful than the carefully cultivated and landscaped ones in my mother's garden.

The difference? This place was obviously designed with love. Hades' heart beats within it, in the small details. It's in the way the breeze is warm and gentle, in the way the leaves rustle as the branches of the trees sway. I can hear the faint sound of birdsong, but I can't see any birds in the crystal clear sky.

I pull my gaze from the cloudless sky to look at Hades. He is so breathtakingly beautiful, mind, body, and soul. Only someone truly good could have created such a space. He glances at me, and our eyes meet. I cup his face, sliding my thumb over his cheek, the stubble deliciously abrasive.

"What do you think?" he asks. I can hear the slight unease in his voice. It's important to him that I like this place.

Who'd have thought the God of the Underworld needed validation?

I smile. "I love it."

His body seems to relax slightly, but I feel him immediately tense again, his attention on something over my shoulder. He places his hand over mine on his cheek, and his eyes search mine as if he's waiting for me to break into a million pieces at any moment.

His lips part like he's about to speak, but no words come out. Instead, he moves his hands to my waist and slowly, gently turns me around.

I frown, not understanding until my gaze locks with Jackson's golden brown eyes, a relaxed smile on his face. I lean back into Hades, remembering the illusion of Jackson in Tartarus. Hades tightens his grip around my waist, and I know he is ready to shadow me out if needed.

Jackson lifts his hand and waves as he steps forward. I study his eyes and take a deep breath. This is the *real* Jackson. Tartarus missed so many details about his face, like the slight laughter lines in the corners of his eyes and the sparkle in them, the unfiltered kindness. How his dirty blond hair glints in the sun.

Hades must feel me relax a little as he loosens his grip on my waist and bends to whisper in my ear, "I'll be right here, my spring." He nuzzles my ear. "If you need me."

I nod, brushing my cheek against Hades' nose. I walk toward Jackson. The second I take my first step, my vision goes blurry as my eyes fill with tears.

Jackson takes a few steps to meet me.

"Hi." His deep, kind voice makes my heart ache, and the tears flow freely down my cheeks.

"Jackson," I whisper.

We stop just in front of each other, and he smiles. "I've been expecting you."

"You have?" I smile, wiping the tears from my cheeks, but they keep coming like a never-ending

148

fountain. They are the tears he deserved a long time ago. The tears I should have given him when he died. How could I not have noticed?

He nods, his face still relaxed into an amiable smile, but his eyes gleam with the pain of seeing me hurt. "You're a sweet girl. I knew you'd feel guilty about what happened."

"What happened, Jackson?" I ask, my voice shaking.

The question is pointless. I already know what happened to this poor, sweet guy, but I need to hear it from him. I need to feel that rage again.

Jackson reaches forward, wiping my tears. "That you are here means you already know." Jackson pauses, looking me over. "I'm happy now, Seph. I never told you about my grandparents. Didn't get the chance." He drops his hand, but the serene smile stays on his face. "They raised me. My parents weren't around all that much. I missed them."

I release a sob and take a step forward to wrap my arms around his neck. "I am so, so sorry, Jackson."

Jackson wraps his arms around my waist and squeezes me. How had I not noticed the difference?

"It's not your fault." He squeezes me again, and I cry into his shoulder. "I never blamed you, Persephone, and I cherished our time together."

There is so much I want to say, so much I have to say, but I just continue to cry.

"I'm happy now, Persephone. And you," he pauses, "you have the chance to be happy."

I pull back to look up at him, but his eyes are focused on Hades over my shoulder. "He's really trying not to storm over here." I can hear the humor in his voice, his smile easy, his eyes peaceful—such gentle humor.

How didn't I notice?

I glance over my shoulder, my heart swelling when I lock eyes with Hades. His body is racked with tension, his fists clenched, and his face is contorted in a look of genuine concern for me. There's no jealousy there, no anger, just worry.

My god. My king. My demon. Mine.

I give him a small, warm smile, and I see a little of his tension melt away. I look back at Jackson.

"Thank you for being in my life. You were a good person, a good man. You deserve to be happy."

Jackson cups my cheek again. "There's a future for me in the next life if I want it. If I decide to be reborn, I hope I find something close to what you two have."

I cover his hand with mine on my cheek. "I hope so, too."

Jackson brushes more of my tears away. "Don't waste tears on the dead, Persephone. The living need them more."

Another small sob escapes. "But you are such an enormous loss to the world. And to me."

Jackson laughs, and it's such a joyous sound that I can't help but smile through the heartache. "I was so committed to rising up the ladder that I forgot to appreciate what was happening in the moment. Like you."

I shake my head. "No—"

"Yes, Seph," he interrupts. "Plus, you've not lost me. I'll be here, in your realm, Queen Persephone."

I glance over his shoulder, noticing an older couple sitting under one of the apple trees. They're looking at each other with such love, but every so often, they glance at Jackson, checking in on him. I realize that he'll be looked after. He'll be happy here.

I cup his cheek. "You should go back to your family, Jackson, and be happy."

Jackson leans in, kissing my cheek softly. "Go back to yours and do the same."

I pull him into another tight hug. "Goodbye, Jackson."

Jackson laughs again, and the sound knits the part of my heart that shattered into pieces when I found out he was dead. "Go," he says with a smile, gently pulling away from me. I step back, smiling at him once more before turning and walking back to Hades.

Hades watches me carefully, his body seeming to thrum with concern. "My spring?"

I run the last few steps and jump into his arms, burying my face in his neck. It doesn't matter how okay or not okay I am. I will always breathe easier with Hades holding me. The second he catches me against him, the second his powerful arms wrap around me, my body relaxes.

"I've got you," he says soothingly, his lips against my shoulder grounding me, reminding me I'm home. I'm finally home.

Chapter Twenty-Seven

Hades

FOR AS LONG AS I LIVE, I'll never forget the look on Persephone's face when she sprinted those last few steps back into my arms. I'll never forget how her eyes were dim with sorrow, but the slightest bit of hope shone in them. A light in the darkness that seems to surround us now. Maybe, just maybe, we can both heal from this and become stronger.

Ghosts surround us in our home, we rule them, but pain won't turn us into ghosts of our former selves. Her scent anchors me to reality, and her arms around my neck keep me in the present, not lost to memories or dreams.

Real.

She pulls back after a moment and kisses me deeply as if to reassure me. Or herself. "Thank you. Thank you. Thank you."

What is she thanking me for? I'm the one who should thank her.

"For what?" I ask between her kisses.

She cups my cheek. "Bringing me here. Creating this place. Being mine."

How could I have not brought her here? When I took over the Underworld, this place existed in a more metaphorical sense. Souls could be at peace, but they couldn't truly feel or see the others around them. When I became king, I made it a field, a garden.

I made it for Persephone without knowing it. I knew my queen would love this place, so I made it for her without even realizing it. She was always destined to be mine, just like I was always destined to be hers. Two souls wrapped around each other, performing an intricate dance with fate.

I scan her eyes, searching for something. Maybe I am looking for a sign of healing, of letting go of the recent painful past. "Home?"

She presses her forehead to mine, the slightest bit of a genuine smile on her face, giving me a bit of hope. "Home."

If she can move forward, so can I.

Lie.

Shadows wrap around us, taking us back to the palace. I don't release her when we arrive. I can't even if I tried. She tips her head back to look up at me as I hold on to her longer than I should, scanning my eyes for some glimmer of my thoughts. As if that would help, my thoughts are so muddled it would be easier to see through a storm cloud.

"He can be reborn," I whisper. "If he wants to be."

She stares at me as if she needs to re-memorize my face. My chest aches at the clear pain in her eyes. Seeing Jackson's spirit may have helped, but it didn't heal the wound. It only put pressure on it for a moment, but it still hemorrhages behind my hand.

Persephone strokes my cheek, and I lean forward to kiss her softly. The kiss is full of unanswered questions and unspoken truths of a love shared that feels lost and slightly out of reach.

She presses her lips more insistently against mine, her tongue darting and teasing. I open my mouth, allowing her entrance. Urgency crawls through me. My need for her is always barely held in check, but I gentle

153

myself and slowly lower her back to her feet. I keep my forehead pressed against hers, whispering, "Are you all right?"

She nods but doesn't move away. "Are you?"

Lie.

I nod back. "Did it help? Seeing him?"

Persephone steps out of my arms to sit on the bed, her shoulders slightly less burdened. "It did. Jackson's at peace."

I sit next to her, the bed dipping from my weight, and pull her closer to my side. The scent of her keeps me steady. "And you? Are you at peace?"

She sighs, that small defeated sound so full of anguish. "I'm getting there."

I wrap my arm around her back, and she leans her head on my shoulder. She reaches out to put her hand on my thigh but then pauses, pulling her hand back. "I feel like there's something on your mind," she whispers. "I need to ask you something, and I need you to be honest with me."

Lie.

I nod. "Ask."

She pulls away from me, shifting on the bed so no part of us is touching. This can't be good.

"When I was in Tartarus, you were one of the illusions, and you said you regretted choosing me. I feel you're pulling away from me a little, and I guess I'm just wondering if that's actually how you feel. "

I blink. Then again. "Persephone!" I manage, my voice ringing with shock. "I could not be more honored to have you as my queen. My only fear is that I am not worthy of being your king."

She nods, looking down at her lap, and I realize *she's* not hearing me.

I kneel in front of her, taking her hands in mine. "When I thought you were lost to me, I panicked." I drag my thumb along her palm, debating how much to tell her. "And if you're sensing me pulling away, it's not what you think." I exhale sharply. "I'm waiting for you to remember you are furious with me."

Thankfully, she lifts her gaze to mine, her eyes narrowing. "Oh, yeah…" I wince, but it is better she remembers her anger rather than her pain. She leans in, brushing her soft lips against mine. "Later."

I relax into her kiss, knowing we can endure this, but as she touches and kisses me, the wall that keeps me together cracks a little. Fuck. I pull back to stare into her eyes, stroking her hair back from her face and rubbing a lock under my fingers.

Real.

I can feel her warmth, her scent. This is real. It has to be, and if I keep my eyes on her face, I can remain rooted in place. For some reason, when I kiss her… I'm back there.

Fuck. I open myself up to her when I touch her, and everything in my head and heart becomes jumbled. I took her frantically in the kitchen earlier, needing to feel and touch her, but now, slowly and steadily, I'm being thrown back into the past.

I grind my teeth and whisper softly, "Real."

Chapter Twenty-Eight

Persephone

REAL."

In his faint whisper, I can hear the strain and his anguish. My heart aches to make this better for him and make him whole again, but how can I when I'm not whole myself?

Tartarus took a part of both of us. I can only hope there is enough left of me to salvage so I can help him. The nightmares, the struggles, and the torment must have been so much worse for him. I have no idea how long I was in Tartarus, but not one part of my soul does not feel like it's been savaged, chewed up, ripped, torn, and thrown back at me.

Along with that, I know I should be furious with Hades. Hell, I *am* furious with Hades, but the part of me that's relieved to be reunited with him, that's thankful that he's safe and beside me again, outweighs any other feelings I might have for him except one. The overwhelming, consuming, unadulterated love I feel for him.

I focus on his eyes, so blue and clear but so haunted. Not unlike how Mellie's were when she visited, not unlike how I'm sure mine look. I lean in, kissing his neck, needing to feel close to him, needing his hands on me to ground me and make me feel sane.

He moans softly, his hands moving slowly up my thighs, the wide span of his fingers completely covering the tops of my legs. I wrap my arms around his neck and kiss him deeply, my tongue flicking, sliding against his, and I groan at his taste.

Fuck, I've missed him.

I move my hands to his shoulders before sliding them to the buttons of his shirt, slowly opening them. The last time was so rushed, so frantic, and so hot. This time is going to be slow and passionate. His body over mine, his hands roaming my skin.

I move my lips to his neck again, biting at the sensitive flesh. The rewarding growl that comes from him sends a shiver down my spine and a surge of desire straight between my thighs.

"Tell me what you want, demon." I moan into his neck, sucking on his skin.

This time, his reaction is not one I'd expect. His entire body tenses, and he moves his hands to my arms, pushing me away from him.

"My spring."

I frown, tensing. *Does he not want me?*

"I need… I need to know you're okay with being my queen."

I try to lean in again, to kiss him again, but he holds me tighter.

"Hades, as long as I'm yours and as long as we're together," I say, trying to reassure him.

He visibly relaxes but doesn't move to get closer to me. "You're mine?"

I nod, but a thought crosses my mind. "That doesn't mean we're not going to talk about what happened, Hades."

He frowns, looking down as if he's trying to work out what I'm saying, trying to make sense of it. The desire in his expression melts away, and I know he understands. There is a fight coming.

"Then no sex," he says firmly.

157

What?

Irritation and frustration fill me. How could he have come to that conclusion? We've just been reunited. We're both broken and fragile and hurting. How could he take an act so intimate away? Something that will help us feel closer and bonded.

"What?" I ask, though the question is ridiculous. His statement was perfectly clear.

"Until we fight," he adds as if that makes the situation any better.

"Hades—"

"I can't, Persephone. Until everything is aired." He clenches his jaw, obviously frustrated.

"But I don't want to fight with you," I reply, my brows furrowed in confusion. "I… I need you to touch me and hold me."

"I will touch you." He rubs his thumb over my tricep. "And I will hold you, my spring."

"You know that's not what I mean."

"We need to fight this out. I will not be intimate with you until we do." Hades sits back on his heels, his hardened gaze locking on mine.

I stare at him, my heart and mind battling it out. One screams at me to stay, fight with him, do whatever he asks of me, and bring him whatever peace he needs. The other tells me to stand my ground, that my heart and soul are not ready for this fight, and I'm not ready to face the fact that my options were taken from me. Hades made my choice for me, not dissimilar from my mother, and it doesn't matter if I would have chosen this life for myself. But more than all of that, I don't think Hades is ready for this fight. He isn't ready to hear how betrayed I feel, how coerced I feel. I have not had time to come to terms with it, and if I talk about it now, all I will do is rage. I was so lost in being down here and then trying to find Hades that I had no chance to feel anything else.

I stand from the bed and move to the door. Hades

glances over his shoulder at me.

"Where are you going?" he asks, his voice soft. The worry in it makes my chest ache.

"To walk Cerberus."

I don't turn, knowing that if I see him kneeling on the floor, I'll turn back and go to him, and we both need this space to think. I leave the bedroom and force my feet to carry me down the halls, calling for Berry as I go.

After a moment, the crystals of the chandeliers tinkle. Another moment passes, and the ground shakes slightly. He's coming.

My Berry.

Cerberus bounds around the corner, his tongues lolling from his mouths as he clumsily runs down the hall, the rug bunching each time he pushes his legs forward. I plaster myself against the wall, hoping not to be taken out by my sweet but heavy marshmallow.

He slides as he tries to come to a halt in front of me, the rug slipping and pushing him forward, the sound of his claws against the marble-like chalk on a board. I grimace when I realize that at the speed he's going, he's going to crash right into the priceless-looking vase in the corner. I wave my hand, and the purple vines appear to catch him just in time. The vase wobbles a little, and both Cerberus and I look at it, holding our breath.

The vase steadies, and I wave my hand again, ridding Berry of the vines. He trots over to me happily, all three of his heads smiling as they pant. I kiss the top of each of them.

"Want to go for walkies?"

He shuffles excitedly from paw to paw, and I smile at him. Cerberus tilts his left head as if he's looking for Hades and whines when he realizes he won't be joining us on the walk.

"Let's go then. Daddy's being unreasonable."

We leave the palace, and the second I get into my

garden, I feel as if I can breathe again. I stand, looking at my red rose in the sea of black.

You cannot dictate to me when we fight, Hades. This is a choice I get to make for myself.

Chapter Twenty-Nine

Hades

FUCK. I could hardly bear the look on Persephone's face when I told her I didn't want to be intimate. It took all my strength not to buckle under her confusion and pain. But I can't kiss her until I know why my head is still returning to those haunting dreams and memories. I thought I'd left them behind. In the fight that followed, I lashed out to keep her from looking closer, from seeing the absolute coward I am.

Lie.

She exposes me. Two thousand years alone, and I'm falling back on old habits, becoming the man who iced everyone out. It is as if I was never thawed by the Goddess of Spring. I slam my fist into the ground beside my knee, shattering the black marble and breaking my knuckles. For a moment, my golden blood flows along the cracks, reminding me of a different marble, another's blood.

The ascent was worse than the fall.

I slam my fist into the floor again and again. The blood on my knuckles spills over the floor, but the pain keeps me here. Each time my skin splits, the discomfort pushes the memories of the war further away.

I finally stop breaking my fists against the ground

when the palace gives up on fixing it, letting me cut my skin more on the shattered marble. I raise my head, focusing on the present, keeping myself here and out of the past. The memories pound at me, but I can control this. I'm the fucking God of the Dead, King of the Underworld. There is nothing I cannot overcome.

Lie.

I push to my feet, touching the indent on the bed that still smells like her. I pull myself from the memory. If I wasn't such a coward, I would have tried to talk through the past with Persephone. To be the man she deserves, I need to face it, to face everything. I leave the bedroom and walk down the hall to the painting I constantly avoid.

The echoes of my heavy footsteps are my only companion on the long walk. My eyes remain downcast, tracing the lines of the floor I'd memorized long ago, but there is something different this time. I can see the slightest hint of purple threading among the normal veins in the marble. It is so dark it is nearly imperceptible. Hidden and darting among the lines, ready to flourish. With a pang, I immediately know the source.

Persephone.

When I get to my destination, I drag my eyes from the floor. It takes me longer than it should to focus on the painting and the swirling vortex of pain and anguish laid bare in front of me. I can almost feel the sensation of the endless falling as I stare at it, transfixed by the memory. It is the void of emptiness I'd ripped from my mind and thrown onto the wall. I felt the memory wrap around me, pulling me into it.

"I warned you once, my king," a voice intones next to me, stopping it from taking me completely, "about pulling your memories from your mind and putting them into a canvas."

I am not surprised by Morpheus's presence. The God of Dreams can go where he is needed. He shares the trait with a few other gods, Eros, the God of Love, being one of them. However, the latter enjoys that ability too much for my liking.

Fucking tricksters.

"You said that if I took them from my mind, I would never truly come to terms with what happened," I add in a monotone. "If I remember correctly, I told you to fuck off."

Morpheus's laugh is an echo from a forgotten dream. "Not your exact words, but the meaning was close."

I drag my eyes from the painting to look at him. "Why did you put me inside them? Why not send me to memories I enjoyed?"

Why did Morpheus trap me in the most painful moments of my life? Was there any kind of sympathy in him? Empathy? Was getting tortured not enough punishment? I relived the fall, the rise, the war, and even more painful memories I can't even think about, much less speak aloud.

Morpheus doesn't retreat from my tone or my eyes, which betray my anger and sorrow. Many gods would have stepped back, even trembled. I am unpredictable like this, but the son of Nyx and leader of the Oneiroi only stares back at me, his fathomless eyes peering at me unblinking.

"Because those were the memories you needed to see." His voice is the same fantastical tone of dreams, nightmares, hope, and despair.

"Why?" I whisper, wishing I could call upon the arrogant facade I usually wore around the Underworld and its denizens. But Morpheus has seen inside my mind. There is no hiding from him, and a part of me hates him for that.

Morpheus tilts his head, his hair moving in the opposite direction as if it is its own entity, floating on an unseen wind. "When you're ready, my king, I'll be waiting."

I growl, reaching out to grab him and make him

explain further, but he vanishes. He doesn't shadow or collapse into himself as Hekate does. Morpheus appears to dissolve, leaving behind a trail of iridescent sand.

I look down at the sand, kicking it, muttering to myself, "Fucking gods, always leaving a mess for me to clean."

Look. See. Remember.

I slowly drag my eyes back to the canvas, trying to put myself back into the body that fell and fell and fell. I try to remember the voice of my mother, Rhea, who whispered the knowledge to me in the dark, sparking my thirst for learning. The beginning of my life was spent in the never-ending drop, my bones breaking as they grew, agony my constant companion.

How long have I kept these memories hung on the castle wall to be admired and looked at but never remembered? I've kept this part of me locked up so firmly that I can barely look at it. While I stare at the painting depicting my fall, the magic that keeps it pinned to the canvas fades. The oils drip, merging into a blob of darkness, swirling in the center of the canvas. More of the endless abyss, the memories of the fall waiting to return.

I reach out slowly, knowing what comes next. I carefully press a finger to the middle of the paint, watching it change from oils to the spell I once cast. The magic slides along my finger and onto my arm, swirling as it crawls up my skin. I want to fling it off, throw it away, but I can't. I'd cast the spell to bind the memories of my past. Now, the past must return to where it came from.

Me.

The magic climbs up the side of my neck, along my cheek, and into my eyes. It blinds me for a moment before it settles. When it clears enough, I can see the blank white canvas in front of me. A tear slides down my cheek before I can stop it. I won't be able to put that memory back on the canvas again. I take a slow breath, wiping the tear away, and my eyes drift to the portrait hall hidden around the corner from this painting. It is filled with painful memories I refused to keep. I lost count of how many I made over the years. It was a bittersweet moment to pull a memory from my head. The emotions remained, but the cause was gone, and eventually, the emotions faded as well.

Now every feeling of abandonment, isolation, and staring into the abyss slams into me at once. I refuse to let the tears that gathered in my eyes fall this time. I need to escape to the one thing that consumes my mind completely.

Persephone.

Chapter Thirty

Persephone

I LOOK OVER MY GARDEN, planning the landscaping I want to do. The roses are in the perfect location, but I would love a pop of pink in front of the large, dark hedges. The entire garden needs some color. I bend, feeling the soil. It's dark, full of nutrients, and I'm certain I could have a thriving garden down here. I wonder if it was always like this. The garden was vast when I arrived here, but everything seems healthier now. On my first walk-through, I remember noting the flora looked sickly, stunning and dark, but not flourishing like they are now.

I wonder if my mother's garden is suffering without me. Probably not. The Goddess of the Harvest would never need the Goddess of Spring to ensure her flowers bloomed year-round. I stroke the petal of a black rose, watching as it turns purple under my touch. I lift my eyebrows, looking down at it. My powers are growing. Every second I'm down here, with every passing moment, I feel the darkness consuming me, wrapping around me. It is not muting my light but mingling with it like a lover. I tilt my head, staring at the now partially purple petal, and my lips twitch.

I am meant to be here.

Cerberus nudges me with his head and whines

softly, pulling me from my musing.

"What's wrong, Berry?"

He pointedly looks back at the palace with his left head, whining again.

"Missing Daddy?"

Cerberus nudges me again.

"If you want Daddy to come on walks with us, you'll need to tell him to stop making decisions for me. You'll need to tell him he needs to give me time." I look at the palace. Most would consider it daunting and terrifying, but it already feels like home to me. I could go back inside to Hades, to nuzzle into him and hold him until we are both whole again, but I can't, not yet. I look at Cerberus, sniffing the rose with the purple splodge on the petal. He tilts his middle head, and I move closer, scratching him behind the ears. "Let's go, marshmallow."

Cerberus barks, jumping up and down like a puppy. There's no way he's aware of his size. I open the gate, and he bounds off, running in large circles around me. I laugh, watching him. His joy is so pure and complete. In his world, he's got everything he needs. His daddy is back. He's got all of this room to run and play. I like to think he enjoys me being here, too. We seem to have bonded.

Cerberus runs over to me, all three of his heads nuzzling against me before he pulls away and runs ahead. This time when he stops, he turns to check I'm following.

I stroll after him, enjoying the heat of the sun on my skin. We walk for a while before Cerberus stops at the edge of a grove of tall trees. These differ from the others I've seen. The bark is almost bronze, metallic-looking, and while some leaves are vibrant green, others are the shiniest of gold. I gasp as I walk toward them, noticing plump apples hanging from the branches, some satin red and others gold. I brush my fingers over one trunk, surprised it doesn't feel like metal. The coarse, hard bark nips at my fingertips. I reach up, touching a gilded leaf. The membrane feels delicate and soft, but it's cool to the touch, like gold would be.

Cerberus barks, urging me on. I stroll through the grove, looking at every tree as I pass. My mouth drops open when we leave the orchard, and a wide expanse of rolling hills greets me, the grass the most lush I've ever seen. Cerberus nudges me, and I continue on, walking up one of the hills. The sun seems even brighter here, and the baby blue sky is completely cloudless.

Cerberus lays down when we reach the top of the hill, and I drop next to him, the soft grass feeling more luxurious than a plump cushion. The green blades seem to hum happily beneath me, and I lay down, closing my eyes, the heat from the sun soaking into my skin.

My eyes open as Cerberus stands. I push up on my elbows to watch him bound away, happily chasing pink and purple butterflies through the fields. One of the beautiful insects lands on Cerberus's left nose, and he stops. Confused, he tilts his head, and the small bug shifts. Cerberus sneezes, falling back onto his butt, and the butterfly flies off into the distance. Berry stands to chase it but stumbles over his huge feet, hitting the ground hard.

I sit up. "Berry! Are you okay?"

Cerberus looks at me, his enormous eyes wide and sad. I stand and rush over to him, kneeling in front of him. "Let me see, good boy," I say, taking the paw he holds out for me.

I lift his paw to check the underside, searching for the source of his pain. Cerberus shuffles closer, sadly placing his right head in my lap. I hiss in sympathy when I find a large thorn protruding from the pad. I glance at him and pull it out quickly. He yelps, but as soon as it's out, his discomfort seems to disappear, and he licks my face with his left head.

"You had a thorn in your tiny baby paw!"

He licks me again before turning to chase butterflies again. I stand up, also wanting to explore this paradise.

"You can only avoid me for so long, my spring."

I jump slightly at Hades' voice and turn my head to face him, but he's not there. I spin completely and frown when I realize he's nowhere in sight.

"Mental link, remember?" Hades says.

I sigh, closing my eyes. I don't even know what to say to him. This whole walk, I've thought about gardening and landscaping, not even beginning to think about the things I need to.

"I could walk with you. Stroll hand in hand." Even through the mental link, the timbre of his voice sends a shiver of awareness right down my spine.

"I think we both need some time alone," I reply along the mental bond.

"You have this terrible habit of running from me," he responds.

Anger sparks within me. Then it hits me. This is his plan. I'm not ready to fight with him yet, so he's going to push me, make me angry so it will all come out. But what he doesn't understand is that if I give into it right now, I won't have any control over what I say to him. Everything in me is angry, frustrated, hurt, and broken, and I'm not ready to feel it yet. Why is he pushing this?

"I know what you're doing," I say.

"What am I doing?"

"Trying to get me angry. It's not fair, Hades."

There's a pause at the other end of the bond, and I can almost hear him considering his next words. I know he doesn't understand me. He doesn't get that I *can't* feel these things right now because I'm barely holding myself together.

"I love you, Persephone. I can't bear you being upset with me." His reply comes, and I can hear his anguish.

"Hades, I need you to let me deal with this in my own way. I need you to stop being the one who rules every aspect of our relationship." I pause. *"There are certain emotions I*

am not ready to deal with, and I need you to respect that."

"Persephone—"

"And to take sex off the table when we both need intimacy is cruel, to be honest," I interrupt.

"You... tend to use sex to prevent yourself from feeling things."

I can hear the hesitation in his voice. He didn't want to say that. But it's been said, and now it's out there. My frustration bubbles under my skin, mingling with my stubbornness. The pain, rejection, heartache, and anger all combine to create a foul stew of vitriol.

You don't want sex until we've aired everything, Hades? Fine.

Chapter Thirty-One

Hades

I WINCE AS I SEND THE WORDS TO HER, knowing I'm simplifying things and making a mess of it. I'm so used to cleaning up after others, but I don't know how to clean up my own messes. Is this how these things happen? Do we find ourselves in these situations because gods act like fools and have trouble expressing their emotions?

I know Persephone. She's trying to use the consuming physical bond we have to forget, and I want to give in, but she deserves a husband who's whole, not this fractured piece of god I am now.

Persephone needs to feel the anger lurking under her skin, even when directed at me. We won't move forward when we're trapped in the past. Air everything and move forward. That's my new motto.

I kept a secret from her before. Even though I was mystically bound, I learned my lesson.

"Do you love me?" I ask her, needing confirmation at that moment. Being at odds with her makes my skin too tight, even more so since I reabsorbed my memories of the fall. The memories gnaw at me, refusing to stay buried. The protective shield is down, and without my queen, I'm lost.

Finally, the truth.

Fuck, I need the intimacy as much as she. I need to seal Persephone to me, and I need to push her away. We need to face the past to move forward. That's what healthy, functioning couples do, right?

"Yes," she affirms, and I let out a hissed breath of relief.

"Even when I infuriate you?"

When you know about my past, will you still love me, Persephone? The man you love, your king, is a coward, but I can be better if you let me. Let me be better for you.

"Yes," she growls in my head. I can nearly see her jaw clenched tight in annoyance. I know she didn't want to admit that, but could not reject me.

"Come home to me." Accept me, despite my faults.

I pause, holding my breath as I wait for her response.

"I will soon." Her voice is a little gentler, less angry.

No, don't leave me alone with the memories, my spring. I'm grappling with a past I so desperately wanted to forget that I'd yanked it from my mind and pretended it didn't exist. Now those ancient memories are tearing at me, along with the new ones, and I'm floating in a world untethered. Without my anchor, without my spring, I'm—

The shadows around me flicker, and my control on them slips. I flinch as the lamp next to the bed shatters. The palace replaces it before I can even assess the damage.

"May I join you?" I ask Persephone, working to keep the panicked edge out of my voice. I feel something drip down my cheek. When I brush at my face, my fingers come away stained with gold ichor. I rub the blood over my thumb, staring at it. I know I should be strong enough to do this on my own, but I need her.

"If you want," she says. I wipe the blood off my cheek before shadowing to her side in the Fields of Asphodel. She stands among the beautiful rolling hills, Cerberus unsurprisingly with her.

I take her hand, releasing a shaky exhale, more rooted in the moment just by touching her.

She looks up at me, her eyes searing me. "Hi."

I cup her cheeks, gazing at her, my power and my very essence solidifying. "My spring, do you understand why it's difficult for me when you... when I know you're mad at me? You want to yell at me. You're planning to, but instead, you try to ride me into the sunset?"

That's an excellent plan, Hades. Pretend you had no ulterior motive for postponing intimacy with her. That's how you got into this mess. Fate may have prevented me from warning her about the consequences of sealing our union, but I could have found a way. I'm renowned for my good counsel, for fuck's sake.

She yanks away from me, her eyes flashing with her anger. I said the wrong thing again. Fuck.

"I'm not ready to yell, Hades." Each syllable of my name is deliberately enunciated, telling me how much I just fucked up. "I'm just barely hanging on, and I can't even feel the anger I know I should be feeling because I am so fucking relieved you are here, so fucking relieved that you're safe." Her voice grows louder, and the hole I dug for myself grows deeper. "And yes, I wanted sex. I make no apologies for that. I missed you so much, and I... When you touch me, I feel less broken."

My heart breaks in my chest hearing her say that, but then why did she leave me alone if she ached to feel close to me?

"But you left me to go on a walk," I mumble, the fight with Persephone making my mind whirl.

She gives me a look before turning and walking away.

Don't leave. Please.

"I've... I've never been in a relationship," I admit. My ears burn at the admission. Two thousand years old, and I'd never been in any kind of serious commitment with another person. How could I when I knew I was fated to find and curse my queen?

She stops walking, her back to me. The words flood from my lips, unstoppable now. "Never. You're... the only one."

I do not know what I'm doing. I'm completely inept when it comes to things that mortals do with ease.

She turns to face me, and some of the tightness in my chest eases seeing her face. "Why didn't you tell me?"

I groan, my neck feeling heated. "I thought it was obvious."

She focuses on me, then gestures at me as if in explanation. I look down at myself. "What does that mean?"

She blinks, smiling softly. "You're the sexiest man that has ever walked in any realm."

I roll my eyes. "That's not true."

There are gods renowned for their beauty, and that moniker had never been attached to my name. I am too serious and withdrawn, too isolated from everyone else.

Persephone crosses her arms over her chest. "Please, Hades."

Why are we still talking about this? It was embarrassing enough to admit it out loud. Did we have to keep focusing on it? I'm a bit out of my depth when it comes to dealing with relationships. It probably doesn't help that the only one I've ever been in is with someone like Persephone. Someone who's comfortable in every room, able to talk to anyone. She draws everyone's gaze like a magnet. Even mine.

Especially mine.

Chapter Thirty-Two

Persephone

I'VE NEVER BEEN IN A RELATIONSHIP."
I have trouble processing his admission. It cannot be true. While I know now that the confident arrogance is a front that conceals his depth, anxieties, and fears, surely people have been drawn to him in the past. Every part of him is just so… irresistible to me. It's a challenge to believe that no one else has ever won his heart. Selfishly, it's also a relief. I like having him all to myself. I like knowing there's no one else out there who has even the smallest claim on his heart.

The more I think about his behaviors and quirks, the more it makes sense. Not that I'm going to excuse him for being an asshole because of his inexperience.

I can't imagine how difficult it would be to date if I knew I had a fated mate out there in the ether. Before Hades, I was free to see whomever I wanted without the burden of knowing that at some point, fate would intervene, and I would be ripped from the arms of another. Not that I had to be *ripped* from anyone's arms, not for Hades. After the initial shock of my undeniable draw to Hades and once I worked through my own insecurities and fears regarding allowing myself to open up to him, I would have jumped headfirst into the

175

relationship, regardless of my situation.

Meeting him was a supernova. Nothing made sense until that moment. Nothing mattered.

"Why?" I ask, tilting my head.

Hades shuffles his feet, clearly uncomfortable. "I don't have the," he pauses, "charm my brothers have."

Without thinking, I roll my eyes. Hades is in a completely different league from his brothers, not only in charm but also in looks, personality, work ethic, humor, and ability to not cheat on his partners.

"You charmed me with little effort," I reply, biting back the words I actually want to say.

You charmed me out of my panties easily enough.

Hades charmed me even when he was actively trying not to when he was also feeling completely flummoxed by the position fate forced onto him. Not that he's unhappy that I'm the one that was chosen for him, but he is also a victim of being pushed into a situation he did not ask for.

"I seduced you," he says matter-of-factly. "That's different. It's not a relationship."

"That's interesting. I thought we were in a relationship, but I must have misinterpreted your signals," I reply dryly.

"Persephone," he warns, the deep domineering tone sending a wave of desire through my body to pool in my lower stomach.

I quirk a brow, waiting for a fuller explanation, my brattiness coming out to play. *Gods, I love provoking the Dom in him.*

He sighs heavily. "We are in a relationship now, and I'm out of my depth."

He's not playing. Noted. It's not that he's not good at it. Truthfully, he's a wonderful boyfriend… partner… husband? Fuck, is he my husband now that we have been bound by the curse? I shake my head to get rid of that thought. Hades and I haven't even been together six months, but does that matter when fate has tied you to someone?

"Did you want a relationship before?" I ask.

"No," he replies pensively. "Once I knew I had a fated queen, it seemed a waste of time."

My lips twitch at his blasé tone. Only Hades could talk about fate in such a casual way. When he speaks of fate and the future, the edge of bitterness no longer sharpens his voice. Instead, he sounds… positive about it.

I nod, my eyes going to Cerberus, who is still harassing butterflies, his tail wagging so fast he's creating a draft. I walk over to him, the grass softening my steps as I walk. Hades keeps pace alongside me, brushing the back of my hand with his knuckles.

"Only you, my spring."

I look up at him to find his gaze locked on mine with such intensity my cheeks heat.

"Perhaps that's why I'm so bad at it."

I sigh heavily. "You're not *that* bad at it."

He slips his hand around mine and lifts it to his lips, kissing my knuckles softly.

"Oh?" he asks, a small smile playing at the corners of his lips.

"Not great, but not terrible," I tease.

He smiles, playfully nipping at my knuckles with his teeth. "I don't know what you mean. It has been such smooth sailing for us."

"Relationships aren't easy, demon."

Something passes over Hades' eyes, and his smile dims. My brows furrow, and I tilt my head.

"What's wrong?"

"I hate it when you're upset with me," he replies.

"Do you understand why I'm upset?"

He nods, rubbing his hand over his stubble. "I do. That's why I'm finding this so difficult. Because I understand why you're upset with me."

I frown. "Well, now I don't understand. Why are you pushing this?"

"Because I…" He rubs a hand over his face. "Because for the first part of our relationship, I felt like time was slipping through my fingers like grains of sand. I was constantly trying to stem the flood and mitigate the feeling of doom. Now, you're here. My queen." He closes his eyes. "I find I'm impatient to finally have the life we are fated to."

I move closer to him, placing my hands on his chest. "I love you."

Hades opens his eyes, raw emotion shining in them. "I love you, too."

"You need to let me do this in my own time."

Hades closes his eyes again, resigned. I lean up on my tiptoes and kiss the corner of his lips. A low groan escapes him, and he wraps his arms around my waist, pulling me in close.

Chapter Thirty-Three

Hades

MY CHAOTIC BRAIN GOES QUIET AS SHE WRAPS HER ARMS AROUND MY NECK, her warmth keeping me grounded in the moment. I want to cling to her words. *I love you.* But I can see the anger lurking in her eyes, not yet unleashed. What if when her mind clears, and the lust fades, she realizes I wasn't worth loving? What if she remembers I took her choice, bound her to me eternally, to a man she never truly loved? What if—

Cerberus's barking stops my spiral from continuing. Most of the time, my own mind is my worst enemy and my greatest asset. I frown, looking in the giant dog's direction, but he's too far for me to see what he's barking at. "What's he doing?"

Persephone follows my gaze, not releasing her hold on me. "Playing with the butterflies. I don't think they're playing back."

My chest aches, hearing the affection in her voice for Cerberus. For a long time, Cerberus and I were a team. Yet he couldn't come with me for half the year, and I had to rely on others to care for him. I could visit the Underworld outside of that time, but I couldn't remain. There needed to be balance.

Cerberus's next bark breaks off on a yelp of pain.

Persephone and I snap straight, and I grab her hand, sprinting toward our boy. Coming closer to him, I can see one of his legs has completely vanished into the meadow, swallowed whole by the ground. Persephone rushes to him. "What's happened, Berry?"

The giant three-headed dog looks at Persephone for comfort. I look over the situation. "He's stepped in a sinkhole and got stuck."

A sinkhole in the Underworld. It sounds like an oxymoron.

"Why is there a sinkhole here?" Persephone asks, wrapping her vines around Cerberus, forming a harness.

I study the edges of the hole before glancing at her. "There shouldn't be."

There is nowhere to sink to, really. This is the *Underworld*. You can't get much lower than that.

Cerberus whimpers as Persephone hoists him out of the hole, putting him gently on the ground. I move to pat his side. "I know that was scary, huh, boy?"

With Cerberus out of the hole, I can see it clearly. It, and the area around it, is blackened and dead, completely devoid of any kind of life. It is as if someone took hold of the earth in a single spot and sucked it dry.

My jaw twitches, and my vision turns red. I was willing to let the whole kidnapping and torturing me for weeks thing slide. What are a few weeks of agony when you live thousands of years? I got the prize. I got Persephone. So I was going to overlook Demeter's antics, but this fucking *bitch*.

Persephone places her hand on my arm. "What do you think happened?"

"A patch of dead earth," I growl, moving closer to the sinkhole. Within the hole is nothing but the Void from which the Primordials themselves were cut. With Persephone's hand on my arm, I tug on the bond with the Underworld, forcing the hole to close, but the mark of black and brittle earth remains.

Persephone bends, touching the soil at our feet. "This is healthy soil, Hades. Look at the grass. It's perfect."

I glance away from the dead spot. "Can you feel if there are any other weak spots in the meadows?"

Persephone nods and plants both palms on the ground. As she harnesses her power, the markings of her immortal form glow, signaling her call for magic.

"Hm… There are no other weak spots. I'm not even registering this as a weak spot, but…"

I frown when she trails off. "But?"

She looks up at me, her eyes uncertain. "There's a slight residue of power, barely a glimmer."

I fucking bet there is. Oh, I am going to enjoy torturing this bitch.

My jaw ticks again. "Do you recognize it?"

She shakes her head. "There's not enough left for me to know."

"But you can guess, and so can I," I growl.

She sighs. "If it is her, her power feels off. I'd recognize my mother. Could it be the realm masking her?"

That's a good point. I pace for a moment. "Demeter shouldn't even be able to do this. The power to interfere with the Underworld should be beyond her."

She might be the daughter of a Primordial, but she does not have the abilities of one.

Persephone slowly stands. "Unless she has help."

Unless she has help… But who would dare? To strike against me is to enrage not just me but my brothers. They wouldn't walk away from a conflict like that.

I take Persephone's hand. "We'll need to have my brothers come here." I pause. "Fuck, that's going to let her know we're suspicious. We need another reason for them to come here." I lock eyes on Persephone. "Like the crowning of a new queen."

Persephone blinks. "You want to… hold a coronation?"

I stare at her, and that her head is not wearing the matching crown to mine at the moment is aggravating. She's my queen, and everyone should acknowledge her place at my side.

"Zeus is closely monitored on Olympus. People will notice if he's gone for even a couple of hours." And by people, I mean his wife.

She swallows audibly. "Can I be crowned before we're… married?"

I blink. Then blink again. "We are married."

Isn't that the reason she's upset with me?

Her brows shoot up. "We absolutely are not."

I drop her hand, crossing my arms over my chest. "Once the curse was activated, you became my wife."

"There was no engagement or a wedding."

"Ancient curses rarely allow for that," I point out.

Her eye twitches, and she purses her lips. Fuck. She's pissed. "I'll start making plans for the coronation." She spins on her heel, walking back towards the palace. She calls over her shoulder, "Cerberus, heel!"

The three-headed monster trots to her side, only the slightest of limps in his gait. Taking the dog with her was a low blow. I walk to catch up with her. "We will make plans."

She doesn't look at me or even stop walking back toward the palace. "Do you want an engagement?" I snap.

"I want to make my own fucking decisions," she snarls.

Her anger only escalates my own. "I asked you a question."

She takes a deep breath, no doubt attempting to stop herself from lunging at me. "The coronation will happen next week."

I grab her hand, putting it on my chest, right over my heart. I need her to keep me rooted and focused on the moment. She looks up at me, tense.

"I didn't get a choice either, my spring," I whisper.

"I'm trying to make the best of what has happened to us."

She winces, pulling back and nodding once. Fuck, this is what I meant when I said I didn't have charm!

I scramble to fix it. "Because I got what I wanted, I suppose."

She takes another step back, flinching this time. "I'm going to go feed Berry."

Fuck!

"I mean… I got you!" I blurt out, "That's all that matters to me."

I need to just stop talking and let the Underworld open into the Void beneath and swallow me whole.

She puts on a smile, but it doesn't reach her eyes. "We have a coronation to plan."

She walks away from me and back toward the palace, Cerberus, the traitor, dutifully at her side.

This time I don't follow. I know I'm not wanted.

Chapter Thirty-Four

Persephone

I DIDN'T GET A CHOICE EITHER, MY SPRING."
"I'm trying to make the best of it."
"I got what I wanted, I suppose."
I suppose... I suppose... I suppose.

The words circle my brain, and my heart thunders in my chest. I walk faster, swallowing the ground to the palace with my quickening footsteps. I need space, time, and I need not to think. But most especially, I need not to feel.

Cerberus pads beside me, keeping pace easily with his large strides. He whines and nudges me every few beats with his left head. I clench my fists and plow on, needing as much space between Hades and me as possible. Fuck, my whole body is radiating tension.

I hope I'll find some semblance of peace when I step into my garden. That being surrounded by flowers will bring me some clarity, but it doesn't. I glance at my roses. The red rose and the rose with the swell of purple seem to taunt me, screaming at me to go back to Hades and give him what he wants so that we are okay. Maybe if we are okay, I will be, too.

The whole Underworld seems to be affected by our tension. The sky is a little more ominous, the air slightly more humid and unsettled. I growl at the roses, forcing my feet further away from Hades.

I need a task. Having something to do will help. I will feed Cerberus.

My mother's voice echoes in my head, the shrill sound like nails on a chalkboard, the memory just as vile as the reality.

My mother entered my room, finding a five-year-old me sitting on the floor, holding my favorite doll. Raven was my only doll. I had fallen, and her arm had come off. I was too young to know how to repair her using my powers, and I knew my mother would never do it for me. She hated Raven, hated her black hair, hated that her clothes were not pink and purple with florals and buttons but black and gothic. I loved her.

Demeter walked over to my vanity and sat on the chair in front of it, turning to face me. She picked up my hairbrush and gestured for me to kneel in front of her. I was confused. My mother never brushed my hair.

"Goddesses do not cry, Persephone. Falling apart is for the weak, and you are not weak, daughter," my mother said as I sobbed.

Raven was my only toy and the only comfort I was ever allowed except for books. Apparently, goddesses also didn't play. My mother tugged my hair harder as I continued to sob silently, her movements growing rougher until she was hurting me. The way she pulled my hair and pressed the bristles into my scalp, I knew she wanted it to hurt. I cried more, but she just brushed harder.

"Are you weak, Daughter?"

I whimpered, the shame from her words weighing heavily on my five-year-old shoulders. "N-No, Mama, but you're hurting me."

My mother yanked my head back painfully, some strands of my hair coming loose. "Are. You. Weak. Persephone?" she hissed in my ear.

I closed my eyes tight, trying to stop the tears, trying to stop the pain, trying to shut down. When I didn't reply, she slapped me hard across the face.

My hand goes to my cheek, the phantom pain of her slap still there. Her words haunt me but keep me from losing my grip on my emotions. *Falling apart is for the weak, and you are not weak.*

I step into the kitchen and grab Cerberus's bowl. He shuffles from foot to foot, excited to get his breakfast. I step into the pantry and start scooping the kibble into his bowl.

"So, you're getting a crown?" I hear a familiar voice call from the kitchen, Mellie's lyrical voice traveling through to me. I finish filling Cerberus's bowl before heading back to the kitchen, not looking at Mellie as I walk to the feeding mat.

"Cerberus. Sit."

He sits, his butt shuffling on the floor as his tail wags excitedly.

"Stay," I say, slowly bending to place the bowl down. Cerberus waits patiently, but all of his tongues loll out of his mouths. "Okay, go." Cerberus's paws slide on the marble floor as he rushes to dig in, the bowl big enough to fit all of his heads.

I watch him for a moment before turning to face Mellie. She sits on the counter, watching me, the usual mischievous glint missing from her eyes. My chest swells a little with how comfortable she is showing me her unglamored self now.

"I guess." I shrug, leaning against the counter.

"You guess?" Mellie replies, tilting her head, her eyes trained on me.

I sigh heavily, glancing at Cerberus, who is getting kibble all over the floor in his haste to eat, but grateful to look away from Mellie's scrutiny. "I mean, yeah."

Mellie frowns. "You don't want the crown?"

"It's not that, Mel."

"We could convince them to do a vajazzling, maybe?" She ponders, and if I didn't know Mellie, I'd assume she was joking to lighten the mood. However, I know Mellie, and I know she considers that a genuine

186

suggestion.

I close my eyes, the threads that are holding me together are rapidly snapping under the pressure. "Mellie, please... I can't do this right now."

I hear Mellie's feet collide with the marble of the floor, and before I can even open my eyes, she pulls me into a hug. Some of the tightness in my chest eases slightly. The embrace of a friend is so stress-relieving, and while it's only temporary, I'm going to enjoy any peace I can get. I bury my face against her shoulder, and she strokes my back soothingly.

"Do you want to go someplace? Just us?" Mellie asks softly. I almost decline, wanting to stay in this moment for a little longer, but I'm also aware that Hades will return soon, and I'm not ready to fight with him yet. He's only going to keep pushing at me. I pull back and nod, smiling gratefully.

"It's the one place I actually like down here." She smiles, taking my hand.

Mellie and I walk in companionable silence as we leave the palace grounds, traveling through the Underworld. There's still so much of this realm I've not seen, but every corner captivates me. Every square inch feels like home.

We arrive at a body of water, and Mellie brings her fingers to her lips before whistling loudly. For a moment, nothing happens, and I look at Mellie with an eyebrow raised.

Mellie whistles a happy tune and just waits. I'm about to ask her what we're waiting for when, in the distance, I see a boat making its way to us. It looks to be made of wood and appears old, with two smokestacks standing in the middle, dark gray smoke billowing from them. The front of the boat is primarily taken up by a large red paddlewheel, with propellers churning the near-black water below.

Mellie is practically vibrating next to me as we wait. When the boat docks, I see a skeletal being standing

187

on the deck, ushering people onto the dock. They look human, but they are noncorporeal.

"Who are they, Mel?" I whisper.

She grins. "Your new subjects!" She glances at me and notices my frown. "That's Charon." She points to the skeletal being. "He ferries souls across the treacherous river Styx."

I lift my eyebrows.

"After they arrive, there's a bunch of boring stuff that happens. You can ask Hades about it," Mellie continues.

"And we're going to…?"

Mellie takes my hand as the last soul departs the boat, and we walk along the dock before boarding.

"Charon, your queen wishes to go to the Oneiroi!"

Charon wordlessly bows his head in acknowledgment and respect before he leaves to take his place at the controls of the boat. He wears a pristine waistcoat and black slacks with a captain's hat perched on his head. I watch him, noting the paleness of the bones showing through what is left of the skin covering him.

I look at Mellie. "Using my position to get what you want?" I ask wryly.

"Pfft. He'd have taken me, anyway. Charry and I go *way* back," she replies, looking out at the Styx.

I follow her gaze, my eyes locking onto the inky black of the water. It's almost opaque, but… I instinctively reach out, drawn to it, bending over the side of the boat. I'm pulled from my trance as bleached bones wrap around my forearm, and I look up to see Charon, his sightless eyes staring right into my soul. Mellie places her hand on my other shoulder, and Charon releases me, wordlessly returning to the wheel.

"Shit, yeah. Should have warned you. The Styx doesn't care who or what you are. It just wants to feed. You need to keep your wits about you." Mellie shudders, looking at the water. "Even Hades doesn't fully control it. It is its own entity."

I nod, frowning at the water before turning my back to it. My brows furrowed.

I swear I saw something move down there...

The loud chugging of the boat becomes background noise as we move down the river, and it is some time before another dock comes into view. We continue toward it, and I shiver as we pass through something. It's not exactly a portal, but the air suddenly becomes stiller here, and the sky turns an inky black. The stars sparkle, but they don't look right. The boat pulls up to the dock. This one isn't like the one where we boarded the boat. Its dark wood almost blends into the water beneath it, and it shines like it has been covered in black lacquer. I look at the beach on the other side of it to see black sand and an eerie mist.

Mellie grins, squeezing my arm. "Welcome to the land of dreams!" She grabs my hand and pulls me off the boat. I say a quick thank you to Charon, who bows his head silently before pulling away from the dock.

Mellie leads the way, chatting excitedly about something. I have been looking around and not truly listening. This place sets me a bit on edge, but Mellie seems unphased by our surroundings, so I follow her into the unknown.

Chapter Thirty-Five

Persephone

SO, THEN I SAID TO HER, 'Please. As if he'd be interested in an ass-sucking leech like you!' You should have seen her face, P!" Mellie buckles over, laughing. "She was *furious*! I thought she was going to hit me!" Mellie laughs harder.

"Right," I reply, looking around warily, only half listening to Mellie. The mist is thicker now, swallowing up the distance in front of us until we can barely see our own feet. My ears are sensitive to the smallest sound, and I gasp every time Mellie or I step on a branch.

Mellie stops walking, and I turn to face her, alarmed.

"What? Did you see something?"

"You're not listening." Mellie pouts, crossing her arms over her chest as her eyes narrow at me.

"I am!" I reply.

"Oh, yeah? What was the last thing I said?" she asks smugly.

"I…" I grimace. "Okay, I wasn't fully paying attention. I'm sorry, Mel, but have you brought me here to off me?"

Mellie laughs again. "You are fated to be with the scariest and most powerful dude in all the realms, but you're scared of a little fog?"

I glare at her, about to reply, when my head snaps up as I hear footsteps approaching. Through the mist, I see a large silhouette approaching. From what I can tell, it's a man, around the same height as Hades, if not a little smaller, and a hair narrower in build.

"Your Majesty." His deep, rumbling voice carries through the fog. "Welcome to Oneiroi, the land of dreams."

"Wow, no welcome for me?" Mellie lets out a low whistle. "That's hurtful."

The man doesn't even acknowledge her. "I am Morpheus." The mist seems to retreat slightly in his presence, and his face becomes clear. His dark features suit his demeanor, and his near-black eyes seem to lack any light at all. He bows his head in respect. His horns are similar to Hekate's, vanishing when his hair moves a certain way.

"And I am invisible," Mellie grumbles.

I smile at him, taking Mellie's hand. "Persephone."

"It is an honor to welcome the queen to the Land of Dreams. Is there a particular dream you wish to visit, Your Majesty?"

"This was my idea, Morphy. We want the one I used to come here for," Mellie replies.

I see a flicker of irritation in his otherwise emotionless eyes. He nods at me and bows his head again, receding into the mist.

I glance at Mellie, waiting for whatever is supposed to be coming next. She squeezes my hand and glances at me. "Ready?"

I lift my eyebrows. "Ready for what?"

Mellie's lips twitch, and she pulls me between two trees. The second we walk through them, the misty forest recedes. Before me, a scene unravels, and slowly, the landscape morphs, growing into the dream. The uneven forest floor becomes soft grass, and the pitch-black sky transforms into a picture-perfect sunset, the reds, pinks, and oranges creating the most romantic of

191

backdrops.

The landscape is first, and then the smaller details perfectly form as if on a 3D canvas in front of us. A couple appears. They are sitting on a blanket, a wicker basket propped open beside them.

Mellie grabs my hand again. "Come on, the fireworks will start soon!" she whispers, pulling me to an old pickup truck that has just appeared about fifteen feet away from the couple.

Mellie hops up into the bed of the truck, and I sit next to her, watching the couple. They are looking at each other with such tenderness, such love. Every second we are here, details become more pronounced, and after a moment, it's clear from their attire and general style that this moment is from decades ago.

The sun sets, leaving the sky almost purple, and the first firework shoots into the sky, illuminating the field with pink and purple light when it explodes. The woman claps, her face glowing, and I imagine it is from both the thrill of the display and being with her love.

"I used to come here all the time," Mellie says, her voice hushed and wistful. I turn to look at her, seeing her gaze locked on the couple as another firework is set off, the brilliant orange lighting the entire sky.

"Where are we?" I ask, looking back at the couple, my heart aching as I watch the man leaning in to kiss his love on the cheek.

"His name is Arnold Spencer," she replies, her head tilted as she watches them almost dreamily. "He lives in Milwaukee. He's almost 104 now."

I look back at Mellie. "Why this dream, Mel?"

She pauses, thinking for a moment. "Because it's… perfect. The perfect moment frozen in time." She pauses again. "That's his high school sweetheart, Margaret Jane." Mellie looks up at the fireworks, her face lighting with the different colors as they explode above us. "A month from now, he'll be drafted and sent to France. But right now… right now, he's just a boy in love with a girl, staring up at the sky." Mellie looks at me, noticing my gaze on her. "What?"

I look back at Margaret Jane and Arnold. She leans in, kissing him sweetly. "I don't think I've ever felt that kind of peace."

"Me neither," Mellie replies. "That's why I come here. Sometimes I…" Mellie drops her voice to barely a whisper. "Sometimes I feel like the madness will take me, and I'll descend so deeply and quickly that I'll never return."

I close my eyes, my heart aching not just for the young and in love couple, not just because my best friend has never known any semblance of peace, but also because I have never felt peace.

My mother intentionally made my life difficult, always keeping me on the edge of fear. With my mother, it's her fault. While fate has matched Hades and me, it has also made things very fucking difficult, setting obstacle after obstacle in our path.

I glance at Mellie, the pain she's feeling so apparent on her face that I link my pinkie finger with hers, not wanting to cause her any more discomfort but to give her the smallest reminder that I'm here for her and always will be.

"He doesn't understand me, Mel," I whisper, the admission tasting like acid on my tongue. I don't know if it's strictly true or if I'm just hurting so deeply that I can't see clearly, but Mellie told me her truth, so I owe her the same.

Mellie hesitates for a moment before replying, "Hades is an old god, Persephone."

I sigh, squeezing my eyes closed. *No, Mellie, don't make excuses for him, please…*

"Which makes him a dumbass, unfortunately."

I relax a little. She understands. My best friend is on my side.

I lie back in the truck's bed and look up at the fireworks. "He just… He wants me to get angry with him, to fight with him. But I can't. Not yet."

Mellie lays back beside me. "Because he was hurt?" she asks.

"Because…" It surprises me how long it takes me to wade through my thought process. As if this isn't the only thing I've been thinking of since we got back from Tartarus. "Because I know the hell I went through to get him back, and he went through *weeks* of that." I take a breath, trying to steady myself. I can feel myself losing that tight grip on my emotions, the one my mother brutishly enforced on me. But maybe it's okay this time. I can trust Mellie, and gods, I need to get this out. "And I still feel like I'm barely keeping it together. If I lose it now, I'm worried I'll never get it back." My words come out in a rush.

Mellie glances at me, her multicolored eyebrows furrowed. "What is 'it'?"

I exhale heavily. "Myself."

Mellie tips her head. "P, have you ever actually let yourself fall apart before? Like properly?"

"I've cried before," I reply.

"Not the same thing," Mellie states, shaking her head. She looks back up at the sky. "When you let yourself fall apart and *feel* all those things you've been repressing, you realize they're nothing to fear."

"Falling apart is for the weak, and you are not weak, Daughter."

I push my mother's voice from my mind, unease churning in my stomach. "What if… What if I can never put myself back together?"

"But what if you can? What if you've built yourself on broken foundations, ready to crumble?"

I close my eyes again, a tear sliding down my cheek. "Mellie, I can't. I'm not ready," I whisper, the words barely audible.

Mellie's warm hand squeezes mine. "No one ever is, P. Good thing you're not alone."

I discreetly wipe away a tear and squeeze her hand

back.

Maybe my mother was wrong, and falling apart doesn't show weakness. Maybe repressing emotions is the weak thing to do, cowardly, foolish, and unhealthy.

"You always seem so strong and confident and comfortable in who you are. You don't have to be those things with people who love you, P."

My lips twitch. "You can thank my mother for my inability to fall apart."

I feel Mellie's gaze on me. "Have you spoken to her? After what happened to Hades?"

I shake my head. "She can't know that we know she was involved."

"You know that if you're holding yourself together because of some bullshit she said to you, you're still giving her control."

Is Mellie right?

I sigh. "I need to get through this coronation, Mel. Everything else can wait."

"Can it?"

"It needs to," I reply firmly.

"You think you can be at odds with Hades for that long?" Mellie asks.

I tense. "Hades cannot dictate to me when I feel things, Mellie. Whether or not it needs to happen, these are my emotions, and I get to choose."

I can practically hear Mellie's smirk. "That's my queen."

I keep my gaze up at the sky. The fireworks are over, but the stars twinkle overhead. "I am done with others making decisions for me."

"So, what are you going to do next?"

"Plan my coronation," I pause for a beat, "and my mother's downfall."

Mellie squeals. "How can I help?"

I think for a moment. "Initially, I only need help planning the coronation." I sigh, not wanting to request this from her but knowing it would help me greatly.

"Also, will you stay with us for a day or two?"

I can practically feel Mellie's body clench as my request lands. "Yeah," she replies through gritted teeth.

"No, it's fine. I'm sorry. That was selfish of me. I know you hate it here." I glance at Mellie, seeing her face tense in a grimace.

She shakes her head. "If you need me, I'm here. I'll get over it."

"Mellie—"

"Persephone. I'm staying." She visibly forces herself to relax.

"Helios will manage without you for a few days?" I ask, trying to lighten the mood a little.

Mellie rolls her eyes. "Please. We are *not* dating."

"Does he know that?" I snort.

"Well, I may or may not have emptied his bank account. So maybe he'll take the hint this time." She laughs.

I roll my eyes at her. "Mellie, the first time you fucked him, you knocked him out after. I doubt an empty bank account will do much to deter him." I search her face. "You don't like him?"

Mellie pouts. "He's too…" I wait for the end of her sentence. "Sunny. It's unnatural."

I scoff. "Whatever, Mel," I reply, rolling my eyes.

Holy fuck, is this what denial looks like? This is what I must have looked like my whole time at Plutus Industries. Wow, how embarrassing.

"Totally not changing the subject, but," Mellie begins, "should we shop around dreams for some coronation inspo?"

I roll my eyes again. "If my relationship wasn't in such shambles, I'd be meddling more in yours."

Mellie sits up and pulls me with her. "Let's go dream shopping!"

I give one more look to Arnold and Margaret Jane, still embracing and whispering sweet nothings in each other's ears, living in such bliss.

196

"They got married before he left, and had kids, grandkids, and great-grandkids. He was there when she died at the old age of ninety-six after seventy-six years of blissful marriage," Mellie says, squeezing my hand. I smile, watching them as Mellie pulls me to the portal and into another dream.

Mellie and I visit countless dream coronations, many of them completely ridiculous. Some are tacky. Some had obviously been thought up by an eight-year-old girl, a pink balloon crown in an even pinker bounce house. The last one we visit is familiar to me. A blond woman with pointed ears walks down an aisle in an almost completely destroyed throne room.

"Mel?" I interrupt. "I think I've seen enough. I'd quite like to just plan it myself. In my own style."

"What's your style?" Mellie asks, a note of suspicion underlining her tone.

She doesn't think I can plan a coronation. Dick.

"Let's go back to the palace."

Mellie shrugs, and we head back through the portal toward the dock. To my surprise, Charron is already there waiting for us. We step onto the boat as Mellie continues to express her concerns about my design skills. I take extra care not to look at the blacker-than-black water of the river Styx as we cross it, not wanting to feel the seductive pull of whatever nightmare calls it home.

"I'm just saying, you've never planned a coronation before," she states matter-of-factly.

"Well, neither have any of those people! They're just dreams!"

"I don't know, the bounce house and flying pigs had potential," Mellie says.

"I have a vision."

Mellie considers me, narrowing her eyes. "Regale me."

"The throne room covered with my vines and flowers. The flowers are bright and vibrant at the door, but the farther into the throne room you walk, the flowers get darker, paying homage to my background and his."

Mellie's eyes go wide. "That's genius! Much better than anything in those dreams," she says as if she had been telling me the dreams had been mostly giving trash ideas.

We spend the trip back discussing the coronation, and when we arrive at the palace, we go straight to the library to continue our planning. I feel lighter and more myself. My time with Mellie, the distraction of planning, and seeing that couple in Oneiroi have helped clear some of the storm clouds sitting atop my head.

Chapter Thirty-Six

Hades

DAMN MY TONGUE and my inability to give voice to my thoughts and feelings without coming off as a complete ass. *I suppose?* What the fuck was that? I was ready to do anything to ensure that Persephone remained mine. There is nothing unsure about the way I feel about her. I'd do more than just kill for her. I'd tear this world and the next down to its barest bones if it meant she would look at me with love in her eyes for a single second. Even my loyal companion, my bound sentry, has tossed me aside for her. I should be upset by such a betrayal, yet the only thought that crossed my mind was, *Good, he'll choose to protect her even if it meant losing me.*

I once prided myself on the world I created. I knew every blade of black grass, every blooming orchid, and every being that called this place home. They were all a part of me, and I, a part of them.

All except for one.

The one being I want bound to me in every way is the same one that perplexes me and turns my silver tongue to lead in my mouth. I never stumble over my words or blurt things out. Only around her.

Fuck. All the skills and abilities I'd honed for millennia were useless when pitted against my queen. I once thought of life as a game of chess. Each move causes another, then another. Persephone doesn't follow any of my predictions. She took one look at the chessboard and flipped the thing over.

My head jerks up when I hear their voices. My feet move toward the sound without conscious effort, in constant search of the goddess who makes me feel whole, calm, content, and relaxed yet makes my heart race and cock harden. I'm a mess of contradictions, and the only thing I can think is how much I need Persephone.

I find them in the library, my favorite spot in the palace, my dragon trove of history and fantasy, including scrolls from the Library at Alexandria to a signed edition of *Fire and Blood*. My brothers collect weapons and power. I collect knowledge. In the end, the weapons that always stood the test of time were between the pages of a book.

It is fitting she should choose here to plan. It might just be a facade to bring my brothers here, but it still means she will completely accept her role as queen and be mine.

I lean against the doorway, crossing my arms. "Where have you two been?"

Persephone glances at me, and for a moment, she looks happy to see me, but then her eyes become guarded. "Mellie was showing me some of the Underworld."

I grind my teeth. That is my job. I should be the one showing her the world she would call home for half the year.

"Morpheus hates when you go there," I admonish Mellie. There is only one place Mellie would choose to visit. There is a good reason that Morpheus couldn't stand the sight of Mellie. She is a goddess of nightmares, and she should be under his rule, but

200

unlike the other Oneiroi, even Morpheus himself, Mellie is not bound to the world of dreams. She can make nightmares *real* so they can affect the physical world outside of the dream.

Mellie scoffs. "For a son of Nyx, I don't understand why he's such a bitch about it."

Persephone looks back at her list, studying it. I wave my hand, adding the numerous Underworld gods to her growing guest list.

Persephone glances at me. "Aphrodite?"

I raise a brow. This is the problem with her coronation. There is extensive history with each god. "We can have her or her husband. Which would you prefer?"

She frowns. "She's married? Helios never mentioned a husband when he spoke of her."

Most didn't.

"They were married almost two thousand years ago. I don't think they've been in the same room for centuries." I sit in a chair and stretch slightly. "They hate each other, I suppose."

There is that phrase again. What is wrong with me?

"Just out of the blue?" Persephone looks back at her list, writing Aphrodite's name in her flowery script.

"They're only married in name now."

Mellie winces, reminding me of her presence. I am too focused on Persephone's minute expressions. "That sucks."

"What's his name?"

"Hephaestus." Persephone focuses on her list, adding his name directly below Aphrodite's. "My spring…"

"He can come or not. Who are we to only invite one and not the other?"

I scoff. Her motives are so transparent. "If you're inviting them, we need to leave Ares and Eros off the list. One less trickster."

There is no doubt Eros is a menace, but he is a lesser trickster than other gods, like Eris and Hermes.

201

"You're becoming an old grouch," Mellie says.

I'm old, but I'm not that old.

"Why would we leave them off?" Persephone asks.

"Eros's father is Ares, Hephaestus's older brother. Eros's mother is Aphrodite."

Mellie hisses. "Oh, shit."

Persephone's eyes snap to mine, and I wince. Nothing like being betrayed by your own brother and your wife, and this is just one god. Imagine the entire pantheon.

She keeps her eyes on me. "It's been a long time. Surely we can invite them all."

She has such a kind heart.

"There's a very high chance Hephaestus will not come. He's extremely isolated."

I'm not going to discuss that he works as an inventor for Plutus. His mind is full of creations, and steering him toward a single project is a bit challenging at times. He is the real reclusive grouch who hates being bothered by anyone. Even me.

"Also, can we not invite Helios?" Mellie adds.

My eyes snap to her. What is wrong with Helios?

"Mellie," Persephone says, a warning in her tone.

What am I missing?

"I was just asking." Mellie crosses her arms, sulking down into her chair.

I blink at Mellie. "You and Helios?"

When did that happen?

"I'm saying this as your best friend. Fix your shit with Helios."

I open my mouth, but Mellie snaps, "Mind your business, Dad."

Persephone shudders. "Don't call him that."

"He's acting like he's my father."

I sigh, rubbing a hand down my face. Some things I am better off not knowing.

"We need to invite my mother, right?" Persephone asks, and my entire body snaps tight.

"I doubt she'll attend," I bite out. I'll kill her if she does, not just for me or my realm, but for my queen.

"She might come."

I growl. "Oh, I hope she does."

Persephone adds her name to the list. "If she does, we need to act unaffected."

I roll my shoulders, aggression seeping from me. "Are you going to be able to?"

She looks over her shoulder at me. "I was able to hide my resentment and anger at her for over two hundred years. I think I can do one more day."

I stand, and Persephone frowns at me. "What?"

How can I say all the ways it kills me to know that Demeter abused her? All the ways I'm plotting to make her mother suffer for what she's done?

Instead, I say, "Nothing."

Persephone bristles, turning her back to me in a clear dismissal. I'd be lying if I said that small movement didn't bruise my heart.

"I'll leave you to it then." I pause, hoping she'll ask me to stay and tell me she doesn't want me gone.

"Hades?" Persephone whispers, and I freeze.

"Yes?"

She doesn't look at me. "We could use your help."

My smile splits my face, and I step toward her. "Oh? I wouldn't want to be in the way."

She finally looks at me, searing me with those eyes. "Stay."

I step closer to her again, ignoring Mellie and putting my hand on her hip. "You want me here?"

She turns to face me, placing a hand on my chest. "Always, demon."

I hear Mellie wisely leave the room, but I never take my eyes off my queen.

Chapter Thirty-Seven

Persephone

I DON'T KNOW WHY I ASKED HIM TO STAY.
Lie. We're not doing this again, P.
I keep my eyes locked on his as my heart beats in my chest for him, always for him. I asked him to stay because the thought of him leaving and being apart from him made me ache. I asked him to stay because fucking Mellie just took me to Arnold and Margaret Jane's dream, and it made me sentimental. It softened me to Hades. She probably knew what she was doing.

Bitch.

Then, when he walked over to me, placed his hand on my hip, and his warmth seeped into me, I found myself softening more. We had our issues, and we had things to talk about, but I needed him near.

He pulls me closer until I have to crane my neck to look up at him. His piercing eyes lock on mine, beautiful orbs hiding his inner turmoil from everyone but me. I can see past them to the stress he hides behind the sapphire blue.

"It didn't seem like you did earlier." The low timbre of his voice soothes me.

I sigh heavily. "I always want you around, Hades, even when I'm frustrated with you."

Hades studies my face for another moment before I reluctantly pull away from him and reach for the marker, returning my attention to the list of invitees. I feel him shift behind me, his hands sliding around my waist as he pulls me back against him and wraps himself around me. Instinctively, I relax into his embrace, the heat of his chest soothing me as I study my list. His lips brush over my hair, and he absentmindedly strokes my stomach with his thumb as if it's something we've been doing for years.

"Who else?" he asks.

"I don't know. This is everyone I know of. I'll need to study up before the big day."

Hades kisses my head again, nuzzling into my hair. "The only ones that matter will be those wearing crowns."

"Which will be your brothers and their wives, right?"

Hades chuckles. "Only the ones wearing these crowns." Hades pulls his hands from me and holds them palm up. At first, it looks like he is simply summoning shadows, but after a moment, the solid gold coronet takes shape, the diamonds and rubies sparkling as they catch the light streaming in from the library window. I reach out, my finger brushing over the cool metal as if greeting an old friend.

Hades lifts the crown over my head and steps back. I turn to face him, my eyes going wide when I see him wearing his crown, mine still in his hands. They are of similar design, but his is not as delicate, and it has no diamonds. Instead, black stones rest alongside the rubies, and it seems to be shrouded in a cloud of shadow, making it even more devastatingly beautiful.

"May I?" he asks, his eyes roving over me.

I finally pull my gaze away from his crown, the sight of him wearing it stoking the flames of desire deep in my stomach.

My king.

I nod, my eyes trained on his lips as he slowly lifts

the crown and places it on my head. He trails the back of his hand down my cheek and neck, along my collarbone, before resting it on my hip again. His eyes darken as he takes me in.

"Perfect." The word is a lustful growl.

I place my hands on his chest, moving into him, my gaze locked with his.

"May I have this first dance, my dark spring?" he asks, cloaking us in shadows. A heartbeat later, we appear in the throne room, and the ghost of a melody plays, the hauntingly beautiful tune echoing in the large empty space. My outfit changes to the black silk dress from that first day, the material clinging to my skin. Hades' own outfit morphs into a perfectly tailored black suit.

Fuck.

I nod and slide my hands to his shoulders. He leads us in a slow dance, and I follow him as if we have been doing this for centuries. My heart thunders in my chest, completely entranced by my God of the Underworld. His scent surrounds me, his eyes captivating me, his body molded to mine.

The room seems to spin around us, and I can practically feel our bond, the way it vibrates in contentment as we dance. Nothing matters in this moment but him and me.

A bright light illuminates Hades' crown. A thin, laser-like line of light moves, leaving an engraving in its wake, and I realize that it now has tiny delicate roses and vines etched into the metal, cementing my tie to him. I wonder briefly if my crown is also changing to show my tie to him. I see his gaze focus on my crown, his eyes sparkling with joy and all but confirming my theory. The second his eyes meet mine, his power washes into me, combining with my own. Every one of my nerves and cells seems to be jolted by it, and from the look on Hades' face, he feels it too. Above us, black flowers and vines entwined with gold leaves grow, covering the vast ceiling. It is a manifestation of our power, union, and fate.

I look back at Hades and tangle my fingers in his hair, needing to be closer to him, my breaths shallowing as I stare at his lips. With the next turn of the dance, Hades lifts me off my feet until my eyes are level with his.

I feel my cheeks heat as I flush. The music slows, becoming even quieter and leaving the sounds of my heartbeat almost deafening. Hades slowly lowers me to the ground, my body sliding against his as he sets me on my feet, but our gazes remain locked, his eyes a black so deep I could get lost in them.

The silence is thick with tension, and we both stand still, his hands still on my hips, mine still on his shoulders, my body still pressed against his.

"I didn't get to welcome you," he says, breaking the silence, but his voice does nothing to ease the ache between my legs. "When you arrived." He strokes his thumb over the silk of my dress at my hips. "Welcome home, Persephone."

"Thank you, Hades," I reply, suppressing a shiver of desire as he continues sliding his thumb in maddening circles.

He moves his other hand to tuck a loose strand of hair behind my ear. "We've been waiting for you." His knuckles brush along the curve of my cheek.

I close my eyes and lean into his touch.

"*I've* been waiting for you." He strokes my cheek again, his voice a mixture of desire and vulnerability.

My breath hitches at the admission, and I push to my tiptoes at the same time I feel him lean down. Our breath mingles as his lips hover over mine.

I'm about to close the distance when a large crash comes from down the hall, followed by Cerberus barking. I open my eyes, pull back, and glance at the door.

"This dog..." Hades curses under his breath, but

207

there is a note of humor in his voice. I laugh and take a step back.

"I should check if he's okay."

Hades slides his hand into mine, interlinking our fingers. "We'll go together. He's our baby."

I smile at him, my heart lighter. As we pass out of the ballroom, our crowns vanish, and we're back in our everyday clothes.

Still a king and queen, but for the moment, simply Hades and Persephone. A couple who are struggling but are deeply in love.

Chapter Thirty-Eight

Hades

CERBERUS SEEMS TO ENJOY FINDING the most expensive thing in my collection and breaking it at the most inopportune time. This time the fatality is the Pinner Qing Dynasty vase gifted to me by Yanlou Wang. The gods of every pantheon's underworlds met every couple of centuries to discuss the division of souls to each of our realms. Though the Judeo-Christian pantheon felt they were *above* such a meeting. They are another constant pain in my side and another mess for me to clean up.

Cerberus looks at me, wagging his tail. I sigh at him. "What am I going to do with you?"

Persephone runs to him, kissing each of Cerberus's three noses. "Who's my marshmallow?"

She already has him hopelessly spoiled. He's become even more of a menace with Persephone enabling him. Cerberus barks happily, not even the slightest bit contrite, but then he never is. He's never understood how big his body is. He wags his tail so hard it is moving his entire body, creating a draft, and making another vase teeter dangerously. I put my hand out to stop it from falling.

I shoot Persephone a mock glare. "You are spoiling him."

"He's just a baby!" Persephone insists, kissing his noses again.

I pick up the broken pieces of the vase, though my eyes are locked on my queen and my mischievous, destructive dog. "He's older than you."

Cerberus was bonded to me almost fifteen hundred years ago as a tiny three-headed puppy. He used to sleep on the pillow next to me until he was too big to fit, but even then, he always sleeps near me. I can feel Cerberus's restlessness when I'm not in the Underworld at night. Even when he infuriates me, I can never bring myself to discipline him.

Persephone nuzzles his middle head, cooing, "My baby Berry."

I snicker softly to myself. Only Persephone would find such a harmless nickname for what most others fear. As I dispose of the broken shards of the priceless vase, I hear Persephone speaking nonsense to him. I glance back in alarm when I hear the sound of another loud crash but relax when I see Cerberus has merely rolled onto his back, exposing his stomach.

Persephone scratches his stomach. "Who's a good boy?"

"He's already a menace, and you are emboldening him!"

There's no heat in my words, and all three of us know it. I press the heel of my palm into my chest, watching Persephone and Cerberus. They're so at ease with each other. It is as if he knew the second he beheld her that she was the thing he'd been missing.

We have that in common.

I drop my hand and step forward to wrap my arms around her waist, lifting her off the ground and away from Cerberus. "I'm keeping you two menaces apart for my sanity."

Persephone squeals as I lift her high. "Cerberus! Save me!"

Cerberus gets to his feet, but I lift her higher, out of

his reach. "No, she's mine! I don't share."

Persephone laughs, the sound suffusing my body. "Berry!"

Cerberus jumps at her. "No. Down! Bad dog."

Again, there is no heat in my words.

Persephone wiggles in my hold. "Berry, save me!"

Cerberus jumps, but I dart into our bedroom, locking the dog out. "Menace."

Persephone squeals, the sound making me feel lighter, less bogged down by the past and lost in my misery. "Hades!"

I put her down, keeping my hands on her hips, wanting to freeze the moment and stay here in this softness, free of everything weighing down our minds and hearts. "Trying to get the dog to turn traitor!"

Not that there's any chance she hasn't already achieved that. When the numerous Underworld gods arrive, will she win their hearts as easily as she won our dog's? As easily as she won mine?

I fake a growl at her. Cerberus paws at the door, the wood bowing slightly under the pressure.

"Please tell me you're not jealous of our dog."

Our dog. Ours. Our palace. Our bedroom. Our realm.

Ours.

I wrap my arm around her, pulling her against me. Her eyes keeping me here and focused on her. Only her. She's all that matters. "I'm jealous of anything that gets attention from you." I want to turn anything that gets her focus into dust.

Persephone bites her lip, muffling a soft moan, the sound intoxicating. It is such a simple movement, but it has me spellbound. I press my lips to hers, reveling in her familiar taste: pomegranates and a hint of cherry. I pull back enough to mumble against her mouth, "How did the rest of the planning go?"

"We had just started."

We covered the guest list. I can't imagine there is

much more needed. Then again, the last time I held a party in the Underworld was... Surely I had thrown one. I must have.

"What else is left to plan?"

"The ball." Persephone pulls back a little. "I'll need to plan the decor, the catering, the dress."

Did it used to be so complicated? It must have been simpler at this last party I had in the Underworld. Which happened. I can't have lived here for two millennia without ever having some kind of event. Surely.

"We can choose a dress right now." I gesture to our closet lazily. "The Underworld provides."

Persephone purses her lips. "Wait. Maybe you shouldn't see it."

"Why?"

She shrugs, and I hear Cerberus slump and lie down outside our door. "It might be nice to surprise you."

I lean back against the door, crossing my arms over my chest. "You don't want to model them for me?"

"You want me to?"

I smirk wickedly. "I need to match."

King and Queen. It would be our first official introduction to our realm and all the gods.

Persephone's eyes darken before she turns away, disappearing into the closet. I sit on the settee, stretching my long legs out in front of me.

I don't have to wait long. All the breath leaves my lungs in an unsteady whoosh. The midnight black silk drapes her curves sinfully, every perfect inch of her body barely concealed. The plunging neckline accentuates her breasts, the slit high on her leg showing glimpses of her tan thigh.

"Fuck."

She moves her hair over one of her shoulders, sending a wave of her scent in my direction.

I stand and close the distance between us, stopping only a breath away. "You can't wear that."

She blinks, rubbing a hand down the side of the dress. "You don't like it?"

I growl, putting my hands on her hips, my eyes trailing up and down her body. "This dress, my spring, you wear only for me."

I want my tongue to travel over every inch of skin that the dress is touching. Fuck, am I jealous of a dress? I look her over again. Fuck yes, I am. She looks up at me through hooded lashes, her eyes dark. My claws flex a little, wanting to dig in, to cling.

"Any other who saw you in this would soon call me their king after I made them join the dead."

Her cheeks flush, and she grasps my shirt.

Mine.

I look her over again, my claws digging into her dress. "For me. Alone."

She pants, "Hades."

There's something reminding me about resolutions and intimacy, but at the moment, I don't care.

"Fuck it," I growl and yank her up, pinning her to the wall before slamming my lips to hers.

Chapter Thirty-Nine

Persephone

FUCK IT." His words, his voice, his growl send a shiver down my spine. My body readies itself the second he grabs my hips and slams me against the wall. His lips are insistent on mine, his tongue desperately pushing into my mouth, and when it brushes against mine, I'm completely lost to him.

His large, rough hands skim up my sides to my breasts, and he cups them for the briefest of moments before curling his fingers into the silk of my new dress and tearing it as easily as if it were construction paper. The silk parts for him like it is as entranced by him as I am.

The material slides against my skin as what remains of the dress slips off me and pools on the floor beneath us. Hades' hands follow the path of the ruined dress, and the contrast between the slippery coolness of the fabric and the rough caress of his touch is nearly overwhelming. His hands do not whisper against my skin like the silk. They leave a scorching trail in their wake, his rough calluses brushing against my skin, igniting the fire in me that only he can.

I moan into his mouth as he bites my lip hard. His responding groan makes the low heat curling in my stomach spark and flicker. I trail my fingers up his chest, hating the feel of his crisp shirt and not the softness of his skin. I rip the shirt open, buttons flying everywhere in my haste.

Hades' sinful touch explores every inch of my chest as he moves his lips to my neck and bites down hard. I instinctively tilt my head for him, giving him the access we both desperately need. I feel the sharp sting of his claws sink into the flesh of my ass, pulling my hips closer. His hard cock presses against my stomach, turning the heat pooled between my thighs molten.

"Fuck… Hades."

Hades' answering growl sounds so much more savage than the one before, and he practically bursts free from his glamor. His wings spread wide, casting a shadow over us, and I reach forward to drag my nails down the main body of his left wing. His shudder is the encouragement I need to do it again, and he moves his head to bite the other side of my neck, sinking his teeth in just as hard.

Before I've considered it, I feel my own glamor slipping. I groan as my wings stretch out, but I only have a moment to bask in the relief before Hades' lips are on mine again, insistent and urgent.

I fumble with the buckle and button of his pants before I end up just tearing at them, freeing his hard length. His hands grip my thighs, and he lifts me, pushing my back against the wall before thrusting inside me so hard that I scream, his girth filling me with such a bittersweet, delicious ache. The bite of pain as his cock stretches me quickly morphs into a deep, undeniable pleasure that has me greedily rocking my hips, demanding more of him. His deep, pleasure-addled groan only adds to the arousal bathing his cock.

My nails dig into his shoulders as he moves, pulling his hips back until his cock is almost completely out of me before plunging back in. His claws dig deeper into my ass as he thrusts over and over, his lips still against mine as we swallow each other's pants, growls, and moans of pleasure. His tail wraps around my thigh possessively, the familiar action making my heart squeeze with affection for him.

"Hades!" I cry out, his hips slamming into me with such force that I swear the wall behind me shudders with the impact.

"Shit, Persephone," he growls, his wings pinning mine to the wall above my head. He pulls back to look at me, his eyes wild, shining with desire and savagery, showing me his beast, my demon.

I try to move, to push against his thrusts, wanting it even harder, deeper, needing us to be even closer than we currently are, but his body has complete control of mine. He has my submission, and all I can do is rock my hips in time with his brutal rhythm. I drag my nails down his back, feeling the warm stickiness of his golden ichor as I break the skin.

His nostrils flare, and he slams into me even harder. "Scream for me," he growls before bringing his lips to my neck and sinking his demonic fangs deep into the soft flesh there.

My body arches and my vision blurs as my orgasm shatters through me. I scream his name as I tremble and quake, riding out my release. Hades' roar of pleasure picks up where mine left off, and I feel him filling me with his scorching release, his body going rigid as he empties inside me.

I moan, my whole body feeling boneless. Hades slows his thrusts, panting against my neck.

"Fuck," I whisper, breathless.

Hades chuckles, the sound so dirty it sends a shock of awareness through me. "You said it."

Slowly, our glamors return, and we just stand there, basking in the bliss of our releases. I run my fingers through his hair and press a soft kiss to his shoulder, neck, then jaw.

"I'm not… I'm not sleeping," Hades whispers after I don't know how long of just holding each other.

I tense a little but wait for him to continue.

He keeps his face buried in the crook of my neck, inhaling me. "I'm… not sleeping. I don't want to go back to… My dreams are…" His voice is so quiet, and his vulnerability makes my heart ache. I run my fingers through his hair again and kiss his head.

"When I was… there. It wasn't the torture. That was nothing." Even the mention of the torture he experienced in Tartarus makes my blood surge with rage. Tartarus tortured both of us, but Hades was my whole life. I would go through it endlessly if it meant I could protect him from ever going through it again.

"I-I called to Morpheus…" he continues, gulping. "And he sent me to dreams. But they weren't dreams. They were memories. Memories I'd long since buried. Or at least I thought I had…"

I slowly untangle myself from him and slide my hand into his, looking up at him for a moment before leading him to the bed.

"What are you doing?" Hades asks.

I don't reply, simply pull back the sheets and climb in, pulling him in after me. I lie down and rest his head on my chest. He tenses, and my heart breaks for him.

"Persephone."

I kiss his head, and with a wave of my hand, my purple vines wrap around us, binding us together.

"Persephone, please. I don't…" He exhales shakily.

I kiss his head. "You are safe. You are with me."

"I don't want to go back there," he whispers, tightening his arms around me.

"Then dream of me. Of our life. Of our future," I whisper back, nuzzling his hair. "I'll stay with you." I feel him tense more, and I bring my hand to his chin and tilt his head up so I can softly press my lips to his. "Close your eyes, baby. Sleep."

I can see his exhaustion now that he has told me about it. Maybe saying the words is what he needed to succumb to it because Hades slowly closes his eyes.

"Don't leave me," he whispers, his voice already far away.

I tighten my vines around us, just like he told me to do last night. "I'm not going anywhere, demon," I whisper into his hair. "Think of the first time you saw me, the first time you touched me, the first time you kissed me."

His body relaxes, but I continue to stroke his hair and kiss his head. I stay awake the whole night, desperate to give him the comfort he needs.

Chapter Forty

Hades

ISLOWLY COME TO CONSCIOUSNESS. I hadn't dreamed. Thankfully. My bones finally feel at peace, relaxation seeping in. Some of my power has returned, a slow trickle rising to a puddle inside me. A small part of me is starting to heal from such a simple thing as sleep. I suppose the old adage is partly true. *A long sleep can be one of the best cures.*

I reach for Persephone without opening my eyes, reality slamming into me, stealing my breath. Where is she? I slept. She could be taken—

She cups my cheeks, and my eyes flash open. "I'm here, baby. I'm here."

My vision is still blurry, and it takes a moment to focus on her face. I struggle to pull myself from the torturous in between of awake and sleep, where nightmares are real, and reality is a dream. My breath is still unsteady, coming out in shaken pants.

"Are you all right?"

She nods, stroking my cheek, soothing me. "I'm fine. I'm here."

Her skin is warm against mine, her scent clouding my nose. She is so soft and supple, her curves so fucking addictive. Her vines twine along our legs, keeping me pressed to her, bound together by her

219

powers. I search her heart-shaped face, with its flushed cheeks and bow-shaped lips that remain that constant shade of red. Her eyes are a sun shining in a clear sky, piercing through the darkness of my mind. They are a lifeline in the stormy sea.

A moment passes, then another, and my breathing steadies. "I'm sorry."

Her calming eyes search my face, unknowingly easing more of my panic. It feels so familiar, as if she's done the same thing a thousand times. "For what?"

I brush my hair back from my face, the locks damp from sweat. Even when I didn't dream, panic still came. "For being… like this." For being unable to face my dreams. My past. For being a mess when she needs stability. I try to sit up in bed, and she slowly retracts her vines. A chill licks at me without her warmth, the sweat cooling on my skin. "I don't know why it's affecting me so much. I lived through these things firsthand, but reliving them…" It is different.

Persephone takes my hand, and like always with her, the words tumble from my lips. "I grew up in a prison."

Just like you did. Just like the one I put you in when I bound you to the realm of the dead for half the year.

Persephone's eyes are soft, her focus wholly on me as she silently waits for me to continue. Her patience makes my guilt even worse. My Goddess of Spring, trapped in a world where flowers only grow black.

"I was put there by my father," I whisper. "So was Poseidon. Zeus saved us." I close my eyes. "We went from a prison to a battlefield in the blink of an eye. I was never a warrior."

Persephone squeezes my hand, silently asking me to continue. Does she know I might falter if I hear her voice? That I can't bear to admit to her that the man she loves is a coward? The man who cursed her. She wears the sun in her eyes, yet she won't see the sun for half the year.

"When I became king, Morpheus showed me I

could… remove memories from my mind if I wished. I pulled them all." My voice is turning emotionless, a coldness seeping over me.

Morpheus cautioned against this, telling me it was a temporary solution. I didn't care. Didn't listen, and now I'm paying the price.

Persephone crawls into my lap. I love when she does that. It's a simple action, yet it brings me such comfort and warmth. I wrap my arms around her, absorbing the strength to continue, to keep from shutting down completely. "But when I was… where I was, I relived them all. Every moment of loneliness and pain."

Persephone whimpers softly, wrapping her arms around my neck. Her tears scald me where they drop onto my chest. "I should have saved you sooner."

I shake my head, lifting her chin to wipe away her tears. "No, that's not… I didn't want you to feel guilty."

She presses her forehead to mine, our breath mingling. "I am so sorry you had to go through that."

I never addressed the memories that created the emotions, trying to heal the symptoms but not the cause.

Persephone places her hand on my chest, over my heart. "Let me help you with it."

I cover her hand. "You're the only thing that helps."

Persephone kisses me softly, and the gentle movement makes my chest ache. She has her own problems to deal with, and she doesn't need to worry after mine. She cups my cheek, her eyes shining with tears. "We are bound. Your troubles are mine, just as mine are yours."

I press my cheek into her hand. "I'm sorry I didn't warn you about the curse."

"We're not talking about that."

I shake my head. "But we need to."

We can't keep avoiding it. That's how we got here in the first place.

She strokes my cheek with her thumb. "In my own

221

time."

She won't be rushed by anyone, even me. One of the reasons I fell for her was her strong independence.

"All right."

Don't push. Don't push.

She kisses me again, the worst of my nerves lessening. How does she do that?

"I love you."

"I love you, too." She pulls back. "Before we deal with that stuff, we're going to work on you. I need you to be okay, and I don't know how it will go if we try to deal with all of that right now."

I tense, my stomach churning. She's sheltering my feelings like I'm a child or a coward. "You don't know if you'll ever forgive me."

She pulls back. "Hades."

"That's what you truly mean, isn't it?" I try to keep the sharpness from my voice, but I know I failed. "You don't know if you'll ever forgive me."

That panic I thought gone was only lying in wait, and it rises to seize control. Never have Persephone in truth? To have her despise looking at me? No. I can't do it. I won't.

Persephone closes her eyes as if searching for patience. "No, it's not."

My teeth grind. "Then what are you saying? That you'll want to leave?" Never. I'll never let her go.

Her fists clench. "No."

"You don't want to be with me?"

She climbs out of my lap, bristling. "Are you fucking kidding me?"

I growl, standing from the bed. "What else am I supposed to think?"

She growls back, standing on the other side of the bed, the massive expanse between us. It might as well be an ocean.

"That I need time. That I'm not ready to have this conversation with you."

I roll my shoulders, facing off with her. "Not ready to leave me, you mean."

Persephone's eyes flash with temper, and she snarls, "I'm not going to leave you."

Why would she want to stay? I grab my pants and yank them on. I give her my back as I find my shirt and pull it on.

Her voice is lethally quiet. "How fucking dare you."

I whirl on her, barely noting the thorns breaking through her skin. "How dare I?"

She hisses, and the world around us seems to take a deep inhale as if preparing for a storm. "You curse me. You make decisions for me, irreversible decisions, and you have the fucking nerve to guilt me into expressing my feelings. I told you I wasn't ready, Hades, yet here we fucking are!"

My anger rises to match hers. "And I more than paid for taking away your choice!"

The second the words leave my lips, I want to call them back. But it's too late.

"I paid, too. I'm still paying," she hisses. "You think I just forgot what I endured in Tartarus?"

I scan her eyes, searching for something. "How would I know? You don't share things with me."

She pulls on her clothes, each movement jerky and unnatural. "I share what I can. You are not entitled to my every thought and feeling."

I flinch. "Right, I don't get to know anything about you."

I share my deepest fears and vulnerabilities, but she won't do the same.

"You are being so… incredibly unfair."

I feel unfair, but I can't stop. "You want to leave me alone again. I suppose that's all I've ever really known."

I turn to leave because if I stay, I'll beg, and there's the slightest bit of pride left inside me.

"You're the one leaving me," she whispers, and her voice is so shattered it takes my breath.

I stop in the doorway, my back to her. "You don't want me here."

Don't beg.

"Nothing I'm saying is getting through to you. I'll move my things out today."

I let out a strangled sound. "You want to sleep apart?"

Have her close but not in my arms? I'd rather go back to the tree.

A small sob escapes her, and I still don't turn to look at her.

Coward.

"I can't stay here while you're not listening to me. I can't sleep here when I know that I will never have the power to make my own choices. I am Persephone. Goddess of Spring. Queen of the Underworld. And I am my own ruler."

I feel the Underworld respond to her, and a tear slides down my cheek. "If you cannot bear to be near me. Then the castle will provide."

Take it back. Take it back.

But she walks past me, leaving the room, and I stay silent.

Coward.

Chapter Forty-One

Persephone

TEARS BURN MY EYES. I try to hold them back, but a few rogue ones leave fiery, salty trails as they slowly roll down my cheeks.

"I am Persephone. Goddess of Spring. Queen of the Underworld. And I am my own ruler."

The words are true, but why does the memory of them taste like ash on my tongue? They are bitter and harsh. It's not because I don't believe them. I do. This has been my reality since I escaped Olympus over two years ago, from the moment I finally stole my life back from my mother's clutches. Yet, having to say those words to Hades, having to find a way to vocalize my right to freedom, my right to rule myself and my destiny, tears at the fabric of my soul, of my very being.

Hades is my fated mate. Surely, a mate does not have to be told these things. Surely, he should know how I need to be treated. He opened up to me, telling me of his past and the imprisonment he endured. How can he not understand my need to rule myself?

I walk down the endless corridors, each blending into the next, the black, gold, and red colors morphing into blobs through my tear-filled eyes.

I feel the Underworld beneath my feet, the tension between Hades and me resonating in a feeling of unease throughout the realm. I've felt the tie between Hades, the Underworld, and myself strengthening every second I'm here, but to feel the realm shift following our fight only proves that the bond is becoming stronger.

My attention is drawn to a door on my right. It appears before my very eyes, and I have to blink to clear the tears away. I wipe my cheeks and reach for the handle, pushing the door open.

Coming from the darkly lit and decorated corridors, it takes a moment for my eyes to adjust to the brightness in the room. The walls are cream apart from the back wall, which is a deep shade of maroon. Small delicate roses are painted under the crown molding, creating a stunning border around the room. A large, white, four-poster bed sits against the middle of the maroon wall. Gossamer curtains hang from the tops of the posts, flowing in a phantom breeze. The large windows are closed, and the room appears still otherwise. A large red and gold rug in the shape of a rose mostly covers the light marble floor, the outside petals flaring gently.

I notice that the room layout is similar to that of our... *No*, of Hades' room. The walk-in closet and large bathroom are in the same place. I walk into the wardrobe and find it filled with clothes of my size. Some I recognize from the other room, and some are new. The bathroom layout is familiar, but the decor is much more feminine, the shelves stocked with all my favorite products and succulents flourishing in the bright room. The bath mat before the white tub is shaped like a potted plant with a cartoon face.

With a heavy heart, I move back into the bedroom. *The palace will provide.*

But it won't provide what I truly need. *An understanding Hades.*

The door opens, and I look up hopefully. My heart sinks a little when Mellie enters.

"Did I hear shouting?" she asks. She looks around the room and whistles. "Sweet digs." Mellie's eyes land on me, and her face falls, obviously seeing my pain. "P? Are you okay?"

The second that question leaves her mouth, I crumble. My knees buckle, and I crash to the floor before falling completely apart.

Everything from the past few weeks seems to crash down on me, and I feel like I can barely breathe, smothered by grief for my old life, the trauma Tartarus inflicted, Hades pushing me to *feel* things I wasn't ready to feel, things I'm *still* not ready to feel. But it's too late. The dam has burst, and there's no going back now. My lungs burn as I try to pull in oxygen, but no matter how hard I try to breathe, it isn't enough. My vision blurs with tears, and my throat grows raw with sob after sob.

Mellie is at my side in moments, her scarred hands cupping my cheeks. The coolness of her touch grounds me only the slightest amount, not enough to stop this. She wraps her arms around me, and I feel her stroking my hair, whispering soothingly to me, but I can barely hear her over the roar of my emotions.

The tears don't relent, and I can't breathe. Every wall, every defense I have crumbles to dust as I lose my grip on my emotional stability. Mellie kisses my head and just holds me. Doesn't she know I can't breathe? Doesn't she know I'm dying in her arms? I want to push her away. I need the space so that my lungs can finally expand, and I can feel oxygen finally filling my chest, but I cling to her, my fingers wrapped around her forearm as I hold her to me, anchoring me.

I have no idea how long we sit there or how long I cry. The tears never seem to end, but eventually, I realize I'm not dying. I'm just *feeling* everything all at once, and it is *excruciating.*

Finally, everything goes quiet, and I feel Mellie helping me to my feet. My body feels weak, boneless, and broken. I don't know where she's taking me until I feel the soft mattress beneath me, and my head hits the down pillow.

The tears continue to flow, and I continue to fall into the well of my pain, hoping to find the bottom, but it never comes. I just fall and fall, deeper and deeper.

I feel the bed dip, but it's not Hades' weight. There is no comfort to the way the mattress shifts under my new bedmate. Mellie shuffles closer and wipes my face with a warm damp flannel. She places it to the side and shifts until she's holding me, kissing the top of my head again.

My only indication of time passing is that the sun no longer casts light into the room. Instead, the eerie silver of the moon reflects against the marble of the floor.

"Mel?" My voice is raspy and broken from my sobs.

"Yeah?" Mellie continues stroking my hair.

"Can you check on Hades?"

Mellie's body stiffens, and I can nearly hear her outrage. "But—"

"Please?" I ask with a whimper.

I feel Mellie nod against the top of my head before she climbs out of bed. I grab her arm, and she glances back at me.

"Don't tell him which room I'm in." I pause. "Just for now."

Mellie nods again, her eyes filled with concern. She gives me a small smile and leaves my room.

Without Mellie anchoring me, I continue to fall. I close my eyes, hoping that this isn't the thing that breaks me forever.

Chapter Forty-Two
Hades

I CAN'T MOVE FROM THE DOORWAY. I just stand there, staring at the last place Persephone stood. My feet are rooted to the floor as if her vines have crawled up my calves and shackled me. I feel torn in two. One part of me wants to crawl and beg for Persephone. The other part is too proud to do so. When did pride take such control over me? My brothers are prideful fools. My nephews. My... *my father.* Disgust fills me at the comparison. I am nothing like him and would never do what he did. I will never be like him. *Never.* If I thought for a second—

Her face flashes through my mind, her beloved features imprinted there. The agony in her eyes is, no doubt, mirrored in my own. I should go after her. I should stay.

Fuck.

Instead, I stand and stare uselessly, wondering why this happened. I just shoved away my queen with both hands for something as foolish as pride. What did pride matter if I had her? The black marble wavers in front of my eyes.

A booted foot hits me mid-back, sending me to the floor. I catch myself on my hands and spin toward my attacker, prepared to fight, but when I look up, I am staring into Mellie's dual-colored eyes.

My eyes narrow, and I bristle as I snarl, "Why are you kicking me?"

I lift myself onto my elbows, glaring at her. She closes the distance and kicks me hard in the ribs. My breath leaves me on a pained exhale.

"Your queen has hit rock bottom. What did you do?" Mellie snarls.

I catch her foot before she stomps on my balls. "She made her choice." I release her to stand, and she pulls back her arm as if to punch me in the face. My shadows coil around her wrist. "Enough."

Mellie lets out an annoyed huff and lowers her arms, and I allow the shadows to release her. "She won't stop crying. She begged for me to check on you."

I flinch. Even broken, she sent Mellie to check on me.

"She doesn't want to stay," I whisper brokenly.

She doesn't want me. She doesn't want the ties that come with being mine.

I don't see the next hit coming, but it lands in my solar plexuses, making me bend over and wheeze.

"The woman who's sobbing her fucking heart out? Yeah, she obviously doesn't want to stay," Mellie mocks.

"Don't make me ban you from the Underworld," I hiss, wishing to call the words back the moment they fly. For the second time in an hour, I've wished for that. As much as Mellie hates the Underworld, it's her home. The place she came from.

Mellie recoils, and any familiarity or kindness in her face drains away, leaving only disappointment and disdain. "I don't even recognize you."

Direct hit. What have I become? I'm not the person who snaps at others. I'm calm, serious, and rational. Yet, since I met Persephone, I've lost the traits that made me renowned for good counsel over the last two thousand years.

"I..." What can I say?

Mellie looks me over from head to toe, her dual-colored eyes locking on mine. "Pathetic. Get your shit together."

She spins on her boot and leaves the room, leaving me alone.

I wish she'd kept hitting me. When I look back over the room, my stomach churns, remembering the fight. I need to get out of here. I need to... face the past.

I don't think twice before shadowing to the cave. The thick wet air, the darkness, and the cold are exactly as I remember. The cell is formed from the bedrock, made from the Underworld itself. I would never risk keeping him imprisoned with the other Titans. For him, I crafted a cell made from the ribs of Tartarus, strong enough to keep him contained for eternity.

His fingers curl around the bars, coming closer to the light. "If it isn't my jailor. To what do I owe the honor of your visit?"

I keep my face blank, sitting at the chess table placed right outside his cell so he can move the pieces.

I don't know why I do this every year.

I place the pieces in precise order, leaning back in the chair and crossing an ankle over my knee. "Your move."

My father looks at the board, making his first move of the white pawn. "You're four months early for your normal visit. Something must be wrong."

I move the black piece without responding. I learned my lesson long ago about sharing anything when I come here.

Kronos flicks his next piece into the same place he always does. "Must have to do with the disturbances I've been hearing about. Holes in the Underworld, tsk, tsk."

My eyes snap to his. How the fuck does he know about that? His lips twist into a cruel smile. No doubt he enjoyed invoking that small reaction from me. It's more than he's gotten in the last two thousand years.

231

I force my face to go blank again, focusing on the game.

"I don't know why I expected you to have some backbone," Kronos continues. "You're a coward."

I grind my teeth. Why do I keep coming back here? Just to hear him insult me?

"How does your new queen feel about being fated to such a coward?" Kronos provokes.

My body moves before my mind can rationalize, grabbing my father's throat in my hand. Persephone. He knows about her.

Kill. Destroy. Protect.

Kronos smirks and grabs my arm. Belatedly, I remember why I'm not supposed to touch him.

I try to pull back, but he's got me in his grip. I look into his eyes, the same eyes as mine, his hold unwavering as time passes around me.

Clarity rings through my head, as clear as a bell. I'm turning into him. It is more than how we look so alike or the blood we share. Kronos let his paranoia rule him to the point he attempted to subvert fate by swallowing his sons whole. He let his fear control him until he lost everyone he cared for.

The world spins, and time whirls.

If I continue to feed my anxiety and anger, I will lose Persephone, and then I will turn into my father.

No.

I summon my shadows to slam into him, throwing him away from me. I fall back, hitting the side of the cave.

I can't be him. I can't break what I've been given. But what if the damage is already done?

"How much did you take?" I snarl.

Kronos smirks, his eyes glowing an eerie green before returning to the sapphire blue we share.

"Three days. I'm not as strong as I used to be," Kronos says and pushes to his feet.

Fuck, how could I be so fucking careless?

Kronos is more than just my father and former King of the Titans. He is the destroyer of time. With just a touch, he can steal it from you, taking the hair from your head, the breath from your lungs, the beat of your heart.

Chapter Forty-Three

Persephone

EVENTUALLY, THE TEARS DRY UP, and the headache that follows sits heavy behind my eyes. The door closes quietly, Mellie doing one of her four daily checks on me. I blink my eyes open and glance at the door. She didn't leave a tray this time, so it must be the afternoon visit.

Mellie's checks have been the easiest way to keep track of the days passing. The days in which the agony has continued to permeate every fiber of my body, days that I've felt as if my soul has been torn in two, days when I have not seen Hades.

She comes in the morning, not long after the sun has risen, with a variation of toast, coffee, fruit, pancakes, granola, and yogurt, anything to get me to eat. Then she returns at lunch and sighs at the full tray, replacing it with a new one full of assorted lunch foods. My least favorite visit is the afternoon one because when she sees I haven't eaten, she gets frustrated with me and sometimes cries. Then in the evening, along with bringing my dinner, she crawls into bed and lies with me for a while.

The sun is spilling into the room, sitting high in the sky. It must be around 2:30. I stare at the ceiling, wondering at what point this will get better. Surely, I'll be able to breathe again soon.

Is Hades okay?

Mellie said she hadn't seen him since I'd last asked her to check in on him, and my heart aches at the thought that he could be in as much pain as I am.

One thing's for sure, laying in bed is doing nothing to pull me from the never-ending abyss of my emotions. I reluctantly climb out of bed and head to the bathroom to shower. The near-scalding water does wonders to ease the aches in my body from having lain in bed for so long, and as I wash my hair, I feel more myself. The sadness is still rife beneath the surface but not as all-consuming as it was.

I pull on shorts and a crop top before deciding to head to the kitchen to see if I can find anything that might intrigue my appetite enough to end its strike.

I walk down the corridors, half dreading and half longing to see Hades. Will he be in the kitchen, waiting for me to emerge from hiding? Will he pull me into his arms and kiss me until I forgive him? Does he hate me now? I shake my head, trying to push my hopes and anxieties out. There is no use in dwelling on what might happen.

I wander to the fridge, the cool air blasting me as I open it. I should have dried my hair. The selection before me is overwhelming, offering literally anything I could want, yet nothing looks appetizing.

"You've caused quite a stir, you know?" The voice behind me is deep, like Hades', powerful, but with an undertone of cunning and amusement.

My entire body tenses, and I turn around. A large man with white hair and a beard perches on one of the bar stools. He tilts his head to the side, studying me, an amused smile playing on his lips. Deep blue sapphire eyes meet mine, and I know exactly who he is.

Zeus.

He lifts the mug to his lips and sips his coffee. The cup is light pink with roses all over it.

My mug.

"Zeus, right?"

Zeus grins, almost all of his white teeth on display. "Aren't you the smart one?"

Arrogant, mother fu—

"Aren't you... exactly what I expected?" I roll my eyes and turn away, grabbing another mug from the cabinet and pouring myself some coffee.

His lips twitch. "The guppy will be here soon. You'll have all three of us under one roof. That hasn't happened since..." Zeus pauses, thinking. "Ever, really."

I sip my coffee. "Plutus Industries, last year. Someone got pissy and rocked the building."

Zeus laughs. "That would be the guppy, but I meant actually staying together in one place."

I consider him for a moment. He stares back, and I can't help but feel as if I'm being studied like he is searching for any areas of weakness. I stand my ground, my gaze hardening.

"If we're to have more guests, I should change. If you'll excuse me." I place my cup on the breakfast bar and turn to leave.

"Your mother has been quite insistent on meeting with me." I can practically hear the smirk in his voice, as if he knows he has something over me.

I pause and turn back to face him. "Lucky you. She's a delight."

Something passes through Zeus's eyes, and the air fills with powerful static. I can tell my mother has not been passively requesting a meeting with her king. She's definitely been a thorn in his side, probably since the moment I left.

I lift my chin again, not backing down. Zeus means to intimidate me, but I won't let him. Not in my home, in my realm.

The air shifts again, and I feel Hades shadow in behind me. He slips his hand around my hip to rest on my stomach.

236

"Zeus, I was just told you had arrived." His smooth voice dances over me, even sweeter since it has been so long since I last heard it. His touch is even more electrifying than usual, and my whole body becomes hyper-aware of every place we touch.

The static calms slightly, and Zeus's smile returns. "Brother. I was just talking to your new queen."

I resist the urge to lean back into Hades, to press my body into his.

"I was actually just going to change. I'll leave you both to it."

Hades moves his hands and places them on my shoulders, squeezing gently. "Let me formally introduce you, my spring. Brother, this is Persephone Plutus, Queen of the Underworld. Persephone, Zeus Jupiter Maximus, King of the Gods."

His hands on my shoulders send tingles of awareness through me, making my body come alive for the first time in days. I want to turn around and slam my lips to his, fit my soft curves to the harder planes of his body, but I school my face into a bland smile.

As far as Zeus knows, we are as happy as can be with zero issues, and we need to keep it like that. We must present a united front as rulers of the Underworld, in spite of the fact that behind closed doors, we're crumbling like millennia-old walls hit by a tsunami.

Zeus stands and circles the island. He takes my hand and kisses the top of it.

"King of the Gods is such an impressive title," I state, keeping the bored smile on my face.

"My title is the *least* impressive thing about me," Zeus purrs.

Hades tenses behind me, his hands tightening on my shoulders.

I tilt my head. My bored, unimpressed smile etched on my face. "Let me make something very clear, Zeus." I pull my hands from his hand and place it over Hades' on my shoulder. "My only king is the one standing behind me."

Hades squeezes my shoulder again, but there is no tension to it this time.

Is that pride I feel coming from him?

"And on that note, I'll help my queen change." Hades holds out his hand for me. I keep my gaze locked on Zeus, a silent challenge as I take Hades' hand. "Shall we, my spring?"

"Yes, let's."

Hades lifts my hand, kissing the exact spot where Zeus did, as if erasing the memory of his lips from my skin, and we leave the kitchen together, an unfaltering unit. We walk in silence until we're up the stairs and out of earshot.

"He wasn't supposed to be here for another couple of hours," Hades says, and I finally lift my gaze to look at him. There are dark circles below his eyes, and they seem dull and broken, just like mine looked in the mirror earlier.

"Yes, well, I get the sense he doesn't follow anyone's schedule but his own."

Hades sighs heavily. "He knows how to get under my skin." He searches my face. "What did he say?"

I pull my hand from his, the small contact making my heart and body ache for more, and knowing I can't have it is unbearable.

"Nothing much. My mother has asked for a meeting."

Hades looks down at his hand, stretching his fingers. "Not surprising."

I shake my head. "I should change," I say, turning to head back to my room, but Hades clears his throat, stopping me.

"They're staying until after the coronation, so you should," he pauses, "probably stay with me while they're here."

My whole body goes rigid, but I know he's right. It would be very suspicious if we're putting all of this

238

effort into showing a united front and then are caught out when we go to separate rooms to sleep. It's only for a night, and it changes nothing.

"I can sleep on the couch in our... my room," he adds, obviously seeing my discomfort at the idea, but there will be no sleeping on couches. Hades and I are still... married, I guess. We've shared a bed before, many times. It'll be fine.

"That won't be necessary." I feel the all too familiar sting behind my eyes, and I clench my fists, trying to stop them. "Excuse me." I walk toward my room and almost whimper when I feel his hand wrap around mine, stopping me.

"I..." he starts.

I look at his hold on my wrist and then up at him. His devastated eyes are trained on where our skin touches.

"I..." he whispers again.

I wait, barely breathing, tears pooling in my eyes, readying to escape down my cheeks.

He strokes his thumb along the inside of my wrist, his eyes finally meeting mine. He just stares at me as I stare at him, desperately trying to memorize everything about him. My breaths come in shallow gasps, my chest squeezing, not from pain but from deep longing.

"Fuck, I've missed you," he whispers.

I close my eyes, and a tear falls, sliding down my cheek. "Hades."

I feel his hand cupping my face as he wipes away the tear. His tenderness is my undoing and more fall. I whimper, my heart feeling like it's ripping. "Hades, don't. Please. I can't." I pull away from him and leave, hurrying to my room.

The second the door closes, I fall to my knees again, dissolving into my heartbreak, knowing I need to get this out before I pull myself together to jump headfirst into the lion's den.

Chapter Forty-Four

Hades

ISTAND THERE WITH MY HAND UP for longer than I should have. This is my life now. Standing ineffectually in moments where I should have said more, trapped in moments of should have been and could have been. The silver tongue that made me known for giving good counsel had abandoned me in my time of greatest need.

There is devastation in her eyes, and I can't even explain where I've been. I can't tell her my father had trapped me in suspended animation for three days. I can't explain that I was wrong and want to fix it. She doesn't want to hear it, and this isn't the time.

My brothers. Fuck. I invited them, but I don't know why I continue to seek their company. Every single time I underestimate how much of an actual pain in the ass they are. It's probably the same reason that I visit my father every year: I hate being alone. I crave the family I never had and try to make do with the one I was born into, as absolutely fucked up as it is. So, I repeat the same mistake over and over, hoping for a different result. There's a reason my method is found under the definition of insanity.

I walk downstairs to the living room, sighing when I see Zeus has his feet on my coffee table, a glass of what is no doubt the most expensive liquor in my collection in his hand.

"Feet down," I growl. I know he won't listen. He may be my youngest brother, but he acts as if he's the oldest. And wisest. And strongest. When in truth, he's only one of those things, and even that depends on the day.

Instead of removing his feet, Zeus summons a cloud between his feet and the coffee table. He gestures to it as if I should be so honored by this concession. I suppose that is the best I could expect from him.

I glance up when I hear Persephone descending the stairs, my heart slamming against my ribs. She's dressed in a velvet maroon gown with a high slit that gives me glimpses of her thigh with each step. Each of her heart-racing curves are on display, her figure enough to hold and never let go. My queen.

Persephone's eyes narrow on Zeus, and I follow her gaze, watching as purple vines wrap around Zeus's feet and yank them to the floor. He fumbles his glass in surprise, barely managing to save his drink. Poseidon hides his smirk behind his glass.

I cover a laugh within a cough as Persephone glides across the room to pour two tumblers of brandy. She hands one to me and stands at my side, every inch the queen.

Fuck, I love her.

I wrap my free hand around her waist, pulling her into my side. "My spring, this is my older brother, Poseidon, King of the Seas."

Poseidon comes closer, the golden beads in his curls clinking. He takes a long look at Persephone, his gaze sliding from head to toe. My smile turns forced, and my hand tightens on Persephone's hip before I force myself to relax it.

Poseidon smirks. "Little brothers have all the luck."

I lift the drink to my mouth to cover my snarl. Fuck, where is this coming from? These are my brothers. Why do I feel like throwing my fist into Poseidon's face?

Persephone tilts her head. "I'm sure your wife would be disheartened to know you don't put her in the same category as Hera and I, but maybe if you were to ask Zeus very nicely, he'd share Hera with you."

I smirk. That's my girl.

Zeus smiles sharply at Persephone. "Bold of you to think we haven't already. Loving brothers and all that."

My hand tightens even more on Persephone's hip. "Only if you want a war, Brother."

She was mine, and I didn't give a fuck if Zeus was technically the king of all gods. I'd find a way to tear him to pieces.

Woah, where did that come from?

Zeus's eyes flash with lightning. "Maybe."

My shadows gather, but Persephone's voice rings out, eerily quiet. "Are you threatening my husband? In our realm?"

Persephone's vines wrap around Zeus's forearms, restraining him. He raises a brow and smiles. "I like her."

"So do I," I murmur, my eyes on her.

Poseidon sits and leans back into a chair. "Better tell her the truth, Sparky, before she tries to kill you."

Zeus smiles even wider. "Sorry. I wanted to see what you'd do."

I kiss Persephone's head. "He enjoys provoking people." Me, especially.

Persephone tenses and tosses back her drink before going to refill it. I follow her, even though I've barely touched my drink.

"Arrogant prick," Persephone mutters.

"I don't disagree," I say.

"I heard that," Zeus says, zapping the vines to ash and sitting back in his seat.

"Good." I turn to face them. "Where are your wives?"

Poseidon shrugs. "No idea."

Zeus smirks. "I knocked her out before I left."

Persephone looks at me, lifting her refilled glass to her lips.

I lean down and kiss her softly. "He's kidding. I think." With Zeus, you never really know.

I start to pull back, but Persephone deepens the kiss, and I wrap my arm around her back. Her taste. How had I gone even a few moments without tasting her?

"Do you mind?" Zeus asks, and I flip him off as I bite her lower lip.

Persephone shivers and pulls back, licking her lips before clearing her throat. I immediately want to draw her back against me. She takes my hand and leads me to the vacant sofa. We sit, and I wrap my arm around her back, tugging her against my side.

"Will your wives attend the coronation?" she asks, leaning into me. "Or will they be indisposed?"

Zeus relaxes back in his chair. "Hera will be here."

I muffle a groan at that. The only person more volatile than Zeus is his wife.

"Amphitrite might be. Not sure." Poseidon shrugs again.

Persephone glances at Poseidon. "Do you put effort into not giving a fuck about your wife, or does it just come naturally?"

I smother a laugh into Persephone's hair. When has dinner with my brothers ever been this *fun*?

"Amphitrite is flighty. She changes her mind like the sea."

Now that I am sitting next to her and I have her back in my arms, I'm realizing how much of a fucking idiot I am. Why was I pushing for more? Why couldn't I rejoice in the fact that this incredible fucking goddess loves me?

She nods, having no idea I'm rethinking my entire life sitting at her side. "Between your inability or unwillingness to keep track of your wife and Zeus's renowned infidelity, neither of you are giving Hades much of a challenge for husband of the year."

I want to tell her I am sorry for everything. I can work on it. Give me another chance. Stay with me.

Zeus lifts his drink. "I really like her."

"What you mean is the most boring." Poseidon snorts.

I roll my eyes. "Having a job does not make me boring."

"Neither does being loyal to his queen," Persephone quips, grabbing my face and brushing her lips over mine.

Fuck.

I growl into her mouth, wanting to pull her into my lap, but I force myself to resist and return my attention to the business at hand. "There is something we should discuss with you both."

Persephone places her hand on my thigh, and I cover it with my own, pretending we're not just putting on a show of unity for my brothers. If only this was the truth of us.

"We have reason to believe someone has poisoned the Underworld."

Zeus's glass shatters in his hand.

Poseidon lowers his drink slowly. "How?"

"We don't know."

I focus on Zeus, seeing his jaw click as I continue. "Our realms are vulnerable."

"And so are we," Poseidon finishes for me. We used to finish each other's sentences when we were young, but that was long ago.

"We think Demeter has formed a sort of sinkhole in the Asphodel Meadows," I say, tightening my hand on Persephone's.

"She can't have this power," Poseidon insists. "She's the Goddess of the Harvest, her powers inconsequential."

"You should not underestimate my mother or her allies." Persephone's eyes focus on my younger brother. "When did you find out about my existence?"

Zeus doesn't even bother to clean up the shattered glass, only wiping the golden blood from his hand onto my couch. "The moment you were born. I knew you were his queen within the first year."

I leap to my feet. "You knew?!" For two hundred years?!

"And you didn't share that because..." Persephone prompts.

"You told me she wasn't into me and to leave her alone!" I shout, sitting back on the couch. "Fucking dick."

Zeus shrugs, completely unrepentant.

Persephone puts her hand on my thigh. "Given that divine offspring are so rare, it's strange that so few knew of me."

Zeus tilts his head, clearly just considering this for the first time.

"It didn't occur to you that maybe my mother might have done something to make you disinterested in me?" Persephone adds, and I can see Zeus's mind working. "The fated queen of your brother."

"Something besides your need to be a prick," I growl.

Zeus ignores me. "You think she's played with my mind?"

Poseidon tenses. "She'd need allies on another level to accomplish that."

To alter the three of us in any kind of permanent way, you needed to change our bond to our realms. Which she's already proven herself capable of.

Zeus's jaw clicks the more he considers, the electricity in the room rising. I growl, summoning my shadows.

Poseidon frowns. "Z..."

Persephone hisses. "We can't move on her yet. So behave like a fucking king, and don't blow this or my drawing room."

I don't know if he's listening anymore, and I shift, gathering my shadows to block any bolt that might

245

head for Persephone.

Zeus stands slowly, his electric eyes pinning me with his glare, a silent communication between us.

"I checked, Brother. Locked in tight," I assure him.

"You're sure?" Zeus insists.

I nod.

I can practically feel his need to confirm my claim, and I sigh. "If you want to investigate for yourselves, do so."

Zeus doesn't wait, and neither does Poseidon. The first vanishes in a crack of thunder, and the latter in a shake of earth.

Chapter Forty-Five

Persephone

THE TENSION IN THE ROOM RISES to an uncomfortable degree the second Hades and I are alone. I curse myself yet again for kissing him. My body has been burning since the second my lips touched his, but I couldn't help myself. I told myself it was part of the show for his brothers, to convince them that Hades and I are perfect and a strong pairing leading our realm, but it was a lie. I kissed him because I wanted to, because I was desperate to.

I turn from him and start heading toward the door, needing distance and room to stop thinking about his hand on me, the way his lips tasted. But my stomach twists as I reach for the door, my very soul begging me to stay with him.

"I can leave. You don't have to."

His words make me hesitate further, and my control shatters. "We should probably both stay," I say, turning to look at him. "To keep up appearances." I see the light of hope in his eyes dim slightly.

I am an asshole.

Hades pours himself another drink. "Right, appearances."

I walk back to the couch and sit down, looking at my lap and doing everything in my power to keep from

247

throwing myself at him.

Hades walks back over to me and hands me a tumbler. I look up at him and take the glass, my fingertips brushing his. It's the briefest of touches, but my whole body tingles from it.

Hades takes a deep drink before asking, "How have you been?"

I sip my drink, shrugging. *How have I been?* Why is that question so incredibly complex?

"Yeah, me too," he says, taking another deep drink.

I gulp the amber liquid, welcoming the warmth as it slides down my throat, dulling the ache of this painful need. Unable to stand the silence, I stand and walk to the record player. I turn it on and carefully set the needle to the disc, smiling as the music fills the room. As I sway to the melody, I hear Hades place his glass down. I feel him come up behind me, his presence intoxicating and my body exquisitely attuned to him.

"Dance?" The deep timbre of his voice sends a surge of desire between my legs. I look up at him and nod before considering the implications. I slip my hand into his, and he walks us to the center of the room, pulling me in close and placing his hand on my waist.

His heat seeps into me, and I can't help but melt into him. I crane my neck to look up at him, and our gazes meet. His eyes are bleak, but I can tell he's not unaffected by the contact.

"I love you." He sounds so sad when he says it, but the love is so clear in his voice.

"Do you?" It's an unfair question, but if he truly loves me, would he not trust me to know when I am ready to discuss what we went through?

He nods. "Yes. Very much."

I search his eyes, looking for any sign that he might be lying, but there is none. I only see pain, love, and the smallest glimmer of regret.

"I love you, too."

Relief floods his face. My poor, wonderful God of

248

the Underworld still can't see how deeply I cherish him.

"Kiss me," he says, leaning down, our breaths mingling.

I close my eyes, my breaths shallow. "Hades..."

My body is screaming at me to give in, to give him everything, but my mind is so conflicted. If we kiss, everything else will melt away, and I will completely lose myself to him. All the things we were fighting about will flutter away into nothing, but the issues will still be there. Our relationship will still be fraught with tension and misunderstanding. All intimacy will do is blur the edges of the pain, not eradicate it.

"We have tonight," he whispers, and I can feel the tension radiate from his body.

"What?" I open my eyes, meeting his gaze.

"To pretend," he replies, searching my eyes.

My heart breaks at his words, and I cup his cheek. "With us. It's never pretending."

It's all the allowance he needs before he leans in more, brushing his lips over mine. It's the faintest of touches, but my whole body ignites for him. I open for him, my tongue sliding along the seam of his lips, and he grants me entry with an eager groan.

Hades lifts me, wrapping my legs around his waist, and we fall back onto the couch, deepening the kiss, consuming each other. He growls into my mouth, and I tangle my fingers in his hair, moaning into his lips.

Fuck, this man wrecks me.

Hades pins me beneath him, and his sinful tongue flicks mine. I can taste his need, his desperation, and it drives me wild. I move my hands to his arms and drag my nails down his powerful muscles, needing him closer. Needing him to consume me fully. We shift positions. The sofa is too small for us to roll, but we are so in sync that we wordlessly move until I'm on top, straddling him. I rock my hips, grinding against his hardening cock, my eyes rolling back and closing at the feel of him. His hands go to my ass, squeezing, rocking me harder against him.

"Fuck, Hades," I moan almost incoherently, but I can tell he's heard it by his answering growl.

His fingers move to my skirt, and I shiver as he curls them under the material, inching it up.

"Oh, yes, Hades! Fuck me with your tiny cock!" A fake falsetto voice comes from behind us. We still, and Hades growls before sending a wall of power toward the voice.

I turn my head just in time to see Poseidon slam into the brick wall. He groans in pain as I let out a low curse and move off Hades, trying to fix my skirt.

"Why are you back?" Hades growls, sitting up on the couch.

Poseidon stands and stretches with a wince. "Talked to your river nymphs. You know, they are rather upset about you having a queen."

River nymphs?

My blood surges with jealousy, and I try to push down the need to pounce on Hades and smother him in my scent.

You are not an animal, P.

I move to the mirror and fix my lipstick, turning back to them when my hair and makeup are once again pristine.

"What did they say?" Hades asks, his eyes locked on me, possessive hunger shining in them.

"They said they've seen rumblings and cracks in the river beds that lead to the Void," he replies as he pours himself another drink.

"Cracks?" I ask, my brow furrowing.

Poseidon nods. "Whatever is happening, it's affecting the entire Underworld, not just the fields."

"We need Zeus to get information out of her." I look at Hades, meeting his gaze.

In a flash of lightning, Zeus appears, his face tense with fury. "There's no sign of a break-in," he states, commanding the room.

"Like I told you, Brother," Hades replies dryly.

I sit on the couch next to Hades, trying to think of a plan.

How discrete can Zeus be?

"I'll be sticking around to be sure," Zeus declares.

Arrogant prick.

"No. You'll alert Hera and, by extension, Demeter," Hades says. I can't help the flutter in my stomach as he speaks against his brother.

I glance at Hades. "I agree. You need to go along as always."

Zeus's electric gaze studies us. "Hm."

"We can only prepare for the coronation. Everything must go on as if we suspect nothing," Hades says, standing and holding out his hand for me. I take it and look up at him, nodding.

"The coronation is in two days. You're both welcome to stay should you wish, but please don't feed scraps to Cerberus. He has a sensitive stomach."

Zeus blinks at me. "He's a beast! How does he have a sensitive stomach?"

"He has a kinder heart than you could ever have," I snarl.

Hades squeezes my hand soothingly. "He's her child now." Hades pauses, kissing my hand softly before continuing, a wicked smile gracing his lips. "Speaking of children, you should know that both of your favorite children will be in attendance. And Aphrodite."

Zeus narrows his eyes but blanches when he hears about his sons both attending the coronation.

I smile at Zeus. "And your grandson."

A maniacal laugh bursts from Poseidon, but I'm distracted when Hades tugs me to my feet.

I look up at him, tilting my head.

"We should go check on Cerberus. He's been penned up," he says.

Penned? My son?! Absolutely fucking not.

Hades' lips twitch, obviously reading the anger on

my face. He kisses my hand again and leads me from the room. Poseidon's cackle can be heard all the way along the corridor, and I realize that Zeus's discomfort has been the first win I've had in a while.

Chapter Forty-Six

Hades

EACH GROOVE AND LINE OF HER HANDS is imprinted in mine. Have I ever wondered about the softness of her hands? How it feels when I hold it in my larger one?

We walk through the halls of our palace to the west wing, where I've formed my shadows into a pen to contain Cerberus. The giant three-headed dog sees us approach and paws sadly at the shadow walls. I roll my eyes at his dramatics and release him.

Persephone lets go of my hand and claps. "There's my good boy."

He doesn't even look at me before running to her to lick her face. I smile, rubbing his side. "I know you hate when they're here."

Persephone kisses each of his noses. "It's not fair that he's locked up when they're in his house."

I scratch his side. "I know."

Cerberus whines and Persephone nuzzles her face against all three noses. She never neglects one head for another, making sure to give each of them affection. I would never tell her that each head feels what the others do. So kissing one nose is kissing all three.

"No more cage while they're here," Persephone purses her lips. "But, Berry, if they try to feed you, do not eat it. Got it?"

"They're not going to poison him."

I am not sure poison would actually have any effect on Cerberus, and anyway, my brothers give Cerberus a wide berth, especially Zeus. I swear I catch him rubbing his legs each time he sees Cerberus.

Persephone cups Cerberus's middle head. "He's not good with pork."

I laugh softly at the idea of Zeus or Poseidon slipping the three-headed dog a piece of pork from their plates. Of all the things my brothers would feed him, pork would definitely not be on the list.

The bell rings for dinner, echoing through the halls.

Persephone nuzzles each of his heads one last time before taking my hand again. Together, we head downstairs and enter the dining room. I see Zeus sitting at the head of the table with Poseidon seated at his left and sigh. I swear he can't help himself.

I pull out Persephone's chair and frown when I realize she's no longer next to me. I scan the room in a panic, blinking when I find her hovering next to Zeus, glaring down her nose at him.

"You're in the wrong chair." Her tone leaves no room for argument, her eyes sparking with annoyance.

"Persephone, it's all right. He's a guest," I assure her, trying to smother my smile.

Zeus looks at Persephone, unmoving, his eyes crackling. A silent battle of wills takes place between the two of them. Persephone puts her hand on the table, leaning closer to Zeus's face.

"Move. Before I move you."

I hold my breath, waiting to see who will break first. Poseidon's eyes ping between Persephone and Zeus. I can't take my eyes off my queen. I know Persephone won't break, even in a battle of wills with Zeus. But I have no idea how my brother will react.

Zeus slowly stands and moves to the seat on the right.

I slide into the chair at the head of the table and pull Persephone onto my lap. "That was not necessary, my spring." Unnecessary but highly entertaining.

"She's got a mouth on her," Zeus says with a glare as Poseidon muffles a laugh.

Persephone brushes her lips over mine, whispering, "It was absolutely necessary."

I snicker, waving my hand for the ghosts to serve the appetizers.

"I have to say," Poseidon laughs, "this is the most entertaining dinner I've attended in millennia, and it's just started."

Persephone wraps an arm around my neck, winking at Poseidon. "Wait until the coronation."

Poseidon laughs, and I can hear Zeus's teeth grind as he dips his spoon into the soup.

Persephone takes my spoon and lifts it to my lips. Carefully, I accept the bite, savoring the taste before smiling at her.

"How's the soup, Z?" Persephone asks, but her eyes are on me. She continues feeding me, and I nudge her to take a couple of spoonfuls for herself.

Zeus leans back in his chair, his bowl already clean. "I have a theory about why Hera kept you a secret."

I frown. He's right. If Zeus knew about Persephone, so did Hera. As the Goddess of Marriage and Childbirth, she would have felt it was her duty to celebrate the new divine offspring. She had always done so in the past. So why hadn't she done so for Persephone?

Persephone remains focused on me. "Oh?"

"She's quite the jealous queen," Zeus says, and I bite the spoon she just slipped into my mouth. It takes a moment for me to relax my jaw.

Persephone finally turns to look at Zeus, raising a brow. "Why would she be jealous of me?"

Zeus smirks. "She's jealous of any pretty young thing that I might look at twice."

I tense. Zeus looking twice. At my queen. At Persephone. Darkness roils in the corners, and Poseidon catches my eye, raising a brow. I force myself to calm, and the shadows disperse.

"That doesn't explain why she kept me a secret when I was a baby," Persephone points out blandly.

Zeus snickers. "You're underestimating her paranoia."

"Is it really paranoia when she's right?" Poseidon points out.

Zeus laughs as the salad is served.

"At least she seems as exhausting as you," Persephone says.

I chuckle, using my fork to feed the salad to Persephone.

"Are you always this sharp-tongued?"

She swallows. "Why do you think your brother fell for me?"

I smile wide and open my mouth as she offers me a bite.

"You're definitely not what we expected for him," Poseidon says, making short work of his food.

"No, not at all," Zeus agrees.

Persephone settles into me more. "What did you expect?"

I spear the salad, feeding Persephone.

"Someone like him," Poseidon answers.

"The serious, no-fun type."

I roll my eyes. They are obsessed with the fact that I'm not their brand of *fun*.

Persephone nuzzles into my neck. "He is very fun."

I kiss her forehead. "I'm just not your type of fun," I say to my brothers.

"What's *our* type of fun?" Poseidon asks, a smile in his voice.

"Adultery," Persephone answers, and all three of us laugh.

The salad is taken away, and the entrée served. I kiss

Persephone's head again. "My hands are full with you."

Zeus rolls his eyes. "We all say that."

Persephone releases a growl, and beneath the table, I can feel her vines wrapping around my ankles possessively.

I want to beam. This means I still have a chance. She wouldn't be possessive of me if she didn't care.

"All yours," I assure her.

She tangles her fingers in my hair and lowers her lips over mine. I can't help but take a bite of that plump lower lip.

"Please, no PDA unless we're all allowed to participate," Zeus states.

I growl at the idea.

Persephone grimaces. "We'll pick this up later. I've dried up at your brother's words."

I groan. Perfect. Zeus ruining my night with his big mouth.

Persephone leans in, whispering in my ear, "I lied. When can we be alone?"

Chapter Forty-Seven

Hades

I DON'T BOTHER WITH NICETIES before wrapping the shadows around us and moving us back to our bed. I can't risk breaking the fragile truce we have. Persephone doesn't move out of my arms when we land, and I take that as a good sign. Maybe this wasn't just for show, not an act in front of my brothers, a facade of strength and security.

Our eyes lock, both of us waiting for the other to make a move and break the silent battle of wills that's created this rift between us. The one my pride formed.

"Kiss me," one of us says. The voice strangely sounds like mine.

She hesitates for a second before slamming her lips to mine. The taste of her is even more heady than it was earlier. I shift her to straddle me, my hands splaying over her ass, rocking her against me. I can already feel her heat soaking through my pants.

She is such a liar. She gets so wet for me.

I fist her dress, shoving it up her thighs until it bunches at her hips. Her hands go to my pants, yanking at the belt and buttons. I find her panties and rip them off her, not daring to move even a little from this position, afraid I might break this moment of need between us. I might let everything back in if I even toss her onto her back on the bed.

She frees my cock, and I grab her hips, slamming her down on me. I watch her face as I stretch her pussy, wanting to see every moment of her feeling me inside her, every slight change in expression, every way she changes as I fuck her. It's more than meeting each other in pleasure. It's a meeting of souls. Hearts. Fates.

Our fates have always been entangled.

My hand slides up her back. I fist her hair and yank her head back. With that bite of pain wrapped in pleasure, her cunt bathes my cock in molten heat. She arches against me, kissing me hard, her tongue flicking against mine as I move her up and down on my cock.

Her nails dig into my back, and she writhes against me. I make her bounce faster on me, taking me deeper, and I can feel her pussy soaking my pants, which are only open enough to free my cock.

Her nails rip my shirt, and I widen her legs so she takes more of me. My shadows free themselves, wrapping around us. I need to take her higher and make sure she remembers how good we are together.

"Hades," she moans into my mouth, her nails drawing my blood as the shadows touch every inch of her. I will make sure she knows that every part of her belongs to me.

I growl, "My spring."

She bites my lower lip. "Don't stop."

I move her faster, nearly frantic now. I thrust deep and grind her down against me. Her body stiffens, and she stops breathing as she comes. Her pussy clenches hard, squeezing my cock to near pain, demanding her due. Unable to resist any longer, I come, muffling my roar against her neck.

There's a moment of silence, only broken by the sound of us panting. I don't want to move, not even an inch. She shivers against me, and I kiss along her neck and shoulder, soaking up all the affection I'd missed in our time apart. Even in suspended time, I'd felt it pass

259

and been unable to do anything about it. So I've felt the seventy-two hours without Persephone, without her touch, her kiss, the sound of her voice.

"I've missed you so much," I blurt out.

And the moment ends as Persephone tenses. "Hades."

I don't release her, even as I apologize. "I'm sorry."

"For?"

I sigh, lying down on the bed with her. I keep her on top of me, careful not to pull out of her. "Ruining the moment."

Persephone looks away. "I miss you too."

I nuzzle her ear, unable to stop touching her. "You do?"

She doesn't look at me, even when she whispers, "So much that I can't breathe."

I kiss her ear, tightening my arms around her.

She swallows audibly, her entire demeanor changing. "But nothing's changed."

She rolls off me, and I exhale, fighting back the exclamation of pain that I feel at her withdrawal.

"We have this time… to pretend," I whisper, trying to keep the agony of having her so close yet feeling worlds apart.

"Can you stop calling it pretending?" she asks.

I tense, wanting to reach out and touch her, pulling her back into me. "What should I call it?"

"A truce."

I look over her profile, studying it. "A truce, then."

I scan her body language, unable to stop from pressing a kiss to her cheek and jaw. "You called me your husband."

She nods. "That's what you are, aren't you?"

I give her a small smile. "You seem to love clashing with Zeus."

"He's an asshole," she says, her lips twitching, "who expected me to be the demure Goddess of Spring, stolen away by the big, bad God of the Underworld. I'm enjoying showing him just how wrong he is."

I kiss her softly, unable to stop myself. "You should be careful. Zeus isn't used to being challenged."

She growls, "I do not take kindly to people disrespecting my king. Family or not."

I smirk. I suppose she has a point. If someone disrespects Persephone, I will be ruthless. "You making him move seats is a memory I'll always cherish."

His face, waiting for her to back down, and her unwillingness to relent. It was perfect.

She shifts to stare at me. "Oh?"

I nod, moving closer to her. "And holding you in my lap, letting you feed me."

She pauses before kissing me softly. "We shouldn't be doing this... should we?"

"We have a truce." I kiss her again.

"But will it just hurt more when it's over?"

"Will it?"

"I don't know," she says as I brush her hair back from her face.

I lean closer. "Then what should we do?"

She moves closer too. "The smart thing to do would be to have the truce while we're in company only."

I shake my head. I've been smart my whole life, and I don't want to be smart now. She is my queen, and I want more of Persephone, of having her in every way and not just in front of my family.

She brushes her lips over mine. "Why don't we forget about being smart and deal with the consequences later?"

I pull her against me, deepening the kiss.

Later. There will always be later.

Chapter Forty-Eight

Persephone

MY BODY STILL HUMS FROM MY release and being close to Hades. His words play over and over in my mind.

I've missed you so much.

Gods, the pain in his eyes when he admitted that to me. I deepen the kiss, my tongue flicking his, savoring his taste. We're both excruciatingly aware that nothing has been fixed, but we need this truce. It's about far more than being a united front to his brothers. It's about Hades and me, what we've been through, what we continue to go through. But the love between us is still there and always will be.

Hades pulls me into him, and I wrap my arms around his neck, my body molding to his like it was made to do so.

He lazily circles his thumb over the small of my back as we kiss, our mouths locked in a passionate embrace. Hades moves his hands to my hips and pulls me on top of him, biting my bottom lip.

"Missed you," he says, his voice filled with deep contentment.

I kiss his lips, his cheeks, and along his jaw before burying my face into his neck, inhaling his citrus and sandalwood scent. "I should show your brothers to their rooms," I say, not moving to pull away.

"No. Stay here," Hades growls, his hand wrapping around my back possessively.

I bite his neck playfully. "You want them wandering around the palace?"

"They're going to do that, anyway."

"Maybe Cerberus will eat them." I nuzzle into Hades but grimace at the thought of my perfect Berry eating Zeus and Poseidon. No doubt they would be tough, and Cerberus has a more refined palate.

Hades snorts. "What about his delicate stomach?" He kisses my cheek lovingly.

"I'm sure he'd survive." I contemplate the pros and cons of having Berry eat my brothers-in-law.

Hades pulls back, cupping my cheek. "He does have a strong stomach when he wants."

I laugh and brace myself against his chest, smiling down at him.

My perfect Hades.

"I forgot how much I can..." he considers for a moment, "relax around you."

I smile and lean in to kiss him. I've never been able to relax as much as I can around Hades. The world could be going to shit, but I feel safe as long as I'm in his arms. Ever since Tartarus, just being in the same room as him eases some of the fraught energy buzzing through me. It's one of the reasons those three days were so unbearable.

Hades deepens the kiss, but suddenly, his body completely relaxes beneath me. I pull back to find him completely unconscious.

My poor king probably hasn't been sleeping.

His face is completely relaxed, and I gently glide my finger along the hard lines of his jaw. My heart squeezes and thrashes as I look down at this man who owns me, body and soul.

I nuzzle into him, my own eyes growing heavy as I slip into a deep sleep.

263

I blink my eyes open, the bright morning sun streaming through the windows. The yellow glow stings my eyes, and I groan. I reach out for Hades, but my hand only meets the too-soft cotton of my sheets. I frown and lift my head.

The Underworld is never this bright.

The haze of sleep clears as I look around the room. This is not our chamber in the Underworld. Gone are the dark details, the deep red walls, and the dark wood of the bed. In their place are a wash of pastels, cotton candy and lavender walls. The sheets are not the rumpled white of those I had gone to sleep in, but champagne pink and baby blue with finely embroidered daisies along the border. I push the duvet back and look down at my nightdress. The white cotton reaches mid-calf. I'd worn something similar every night for over 200 years.

I sit on the edge of the bed, my feet pushing into my satin slippers on muscle memory. They are in the exact place they always were... are...

What is happening? Is this a dream?

I stand and walk to the mirror, studying my reflection. My brows are furrowed, and while I feel like I look the same, there is something different. My eyes are dull, my skin pale, and my heart is... yearning. I look around my bedroom, but nothing is different. Walking out onto the balcony, I look at the rolling hills of Olympus, trying to find one inconsistency to prove that this is a dream, and I will wake up in my home, but the longer I'm here, the more this feels like my reality.

Did I dream that my mother let me go to the human realm? Did I dream up my relationship with Hades? Did I—

"Persephone."

My body goes tense at my mother's curt tone. She's unhappy with me. I can always tell. I slowly turn to face her, and any warmth that I feel turns to bitter cold with her icy gaze.

"Mother?" I swallow, watching her with uncertainty.

"You've misbehaved, Persephone," my mother says, walking farther into the room.

I frown, the memories of... What was his name?

My mother snaps her fingers, drawing my attention. She hates when I daydream. I can't even count how many times I've been punished for it.

"Listen, Daughter," she snaps. "You have misbehaved." Her lips pull into a wicked smile, full of malice. "And now you will be punished."

I look away, trying to control my heartbeat so she doesn't see my fear.

"Mother, I—"

"Do not think to apologize now, Daughter." She moves closer, grabbing my chin and forcing me to look at her. "I look forward to seeing you again." The cruel smile still twists her face. She snaps her fingers again, and the scene melts away until only she and I are left, surrounded by darkness.

She steps back, and her body seems to dissolve into nothing, the memory of my dream fading along with her. Everything turns to black as Hades' scent surrounds me once again, and I know I'm safe.

Chapter Forty Nine

Hades

BY THE TIME MORNING COMES, I'm more rested than I've felt since before I was trapped in the tree. I even dreamed, but these were peaceful dreams, weightless and fleeting. I stretch and yawn, luxuriating in how the heavy scent of roses clouds my nose.

She nuzzles into me, stirring slightly, and I take a moment to look at her. I memorize her heart-shaped face and slightly upturned nose. Those maddening plump lips, slightly parted in sleep, beg for my kisses. Her cheeks are rosy with sleep. Gods, she's stunning.

I need to fix the divide between us, but where do I start?

I lean forward, dragging my lips along her cheek to her ear. The soft skin feels like silk under my mouth.

I smile as she scrunches her nose, trying to bat me away. "Time to get up, my spring."

She groans, opening her eyes, still half asleep. My breath catches seeing the love contained in those eyes.

I press my lips to hers, trying to keep her in the suspended world where nothing has kept us apart. In this moment, she doesn't have to get ready for her coronation today, and she hasn't been sleeping in another room. I know the moment she remembers. It's the slightest of stiffness in her body, the minute tension where there was only softness before.

I pull back. "Shower with me?" Stay with me in the moment, my spring.

She brightens immediately, and I laugh. "I knew that would get you up, menace."

She jumps out of bed, heading for the shower. "Come on!"

I laugh again, following her. "I'm coming."

Under the hot water of the shower, I press my chest against her back and slide my hands around her waist, pulling her ass against me. She looks up at me, biting her lip, her eyes turning black with need. It's a need I'm more than willing to satisfy.

"You need me?" I growl, pressing her against the shower wall, my hand fisting her hair.

"Always, demon," she moans.

I rub my fangs against her throat, reaching down to lift her leg over my arm, spreading her enough for me to slam myself inside her. I thought the frantic energy might have dimmed after last night, but it hasn't. With each thrust, I press her face against the glass. I keep her pinned, her body clearing the fog on the shower door, and I can see our reflection in the mirror. Persephone reaches up and wipes the remaining mist from the shower glass, so we can look at our bodies in the mirror as we fuck.

"Look how perfectly you take me, how you take your king," I growl, watching her in the mirror, her ruby nipples crushed against the glass.

"My king," she whimpers, reaching her hand back to tangle into my hair.

I thrust faster but continue to clear the glass to watch as I take her lush, curvaceous body.

"I'm going to fill you up, my spring," I warn, my cock swelling.

267

She squeezes me, her own orgasm close, and nods frantically. I come with a roar at the same time her cunt squeezes me like a vise.

Both of us pant, our breaths mingling together after the frantic coupling. Persephone pulls back after a moment, and I try not to tense when she scans my eyes. Instead of waiting for the awkwardness to seep into this moment, I grab her shampoo, lathering it into her hair and then into mine. It doesn't matter to me that the scent is a delicate rose. I will wear anything that smells like my wife. I smile as I rinse us off, then squeeze the conditioner into her long, dark hair. She looks at me, her eyes seeking.

I shrug at her unspoken question. "I like doing this."

I like proving that I can be the husband she deserves, proving to her and myself that I can break the cycle of the past.

She cups my cheek, and I'm flayed open by her gaze. She sees through me. Every artifice and mask is useless against her, and I'm a fool to think I could ever pretend otherwise.

"Should I stop?" I whisper.

She shakes her head, and I continue to work the conditioner into her hair, then scrub us both with her body wash. We're both silent, but it's not an uncomfortable silence. It's the silence of long friends, of people comfortable enough with each other that they don't feel the compulsion to fill the quiet.

I turn off the water and grab a towel to wrap her in before reaching for my own.

She smiles up at me as I secure the towel at my hips. "What are you thinking?"

I scan her eyes and whisper, "How I don't want this to end."

She presses her lips to mine, smiling softly. "Our shower?"

I shake my head. "Our truce."

She tenses and turns away to sit at her vanity. I

268

follow and stand behind her, picking up the ivory-handled hairbrush before she can reach for it. Slowly, I brush her hair, and her eyes lock on mine in the mirror. A sense of longing connects us, an understanding.

This is a glimmer of the life we want. A silent agreement that we are going to figure it out. I keep brushing her long hair, feeling lighter than I have since this tension between us began.

We can do this.

She stands when I finish, wrapping her arms around my neck. I rest my hands on her waist and say, "I would love to send them all away." If she agrees, I might just do it. I would love to pretend that my brothers and all the gods of our pantheon are not gathering in our hall below. We could stay in this bubble of happiness together and pretend our realm isn't threatened.

She smiles. "But what about the coronation?"

I fake a pout. "We could have one with just the two of us. Naked."

We would wear nothing but our crowns. I add to my mental to-do list: fuck Persephone in nothing but her crown on my throne.

She shakes her head, laughing. "But then I wouldn't be able to wear the new dress I designed."

I frown, pretending to weigh my options. "Hmm..."

She leans into me, kissing me softly before whispering against my lips, "I can be naked after."

I lean down to wrap my arms around the bottom of her ass, lifting her against me. "That is acceptable."

She looks down at me, the love shining in her eyes nearly luminescent. "I should start getting ready."

I smirk up at her and walk toward the closet.

Chapter Fifty

Persephone

THERE'S A GNAWING FEELING IN MY GUT as I walk into the closet, and I find myself unable to identify it. Could it be because Hades and I feel more healed even though we've simply put a Band-Aid over a bullet wound? Truthfully, I felt a little uneasy when I woke up this morning, but the second my gaze met Hades', all my worries melted into nothing, his sapphire eyes grounding me as they always have. But now that I'm alone again, without him here to keep my mind from overthinking and over-analyzing, that feeling of unease is back like a flutter of foreboding in my chest.

My eyes go to my dress bag, hooked on the mirror, and I push the unease down. *I need to concentrate on one thing at a time.*

I unzip the bag, and my lips tilt up at the sight of my dress. It's similar to the one I tried on last week but more modest. Made from the same midnight black silk, perfectly tailored to my body, it fits me like a glove. The neckline doesn't drop to my midriff but swoops around my chest, allowing cleavage but in a more timeless fashion. However, the dress does still have a thigh slit, but this one does not go so high that I'll need to worry about people getting an eyeful.

This dress is also more detailed, incorporating some elements from the gown the Underworld provided to me. I added a fine lace train imbued with intricate skulls and roses, matching the ones decorating the neckline. Black diamonds encrust the bodice, subtly sparkling in the light.

I drop the towel and slip into some black panties before pulling on the dress, using my vines to help me with the corset. Hades comes up behind me and places a soft kiss on my head. I look at us in the mirror. The Underworld has altered his suit slightly, adding matching skulls and roses to the lapels of his jacket to match my dress. Hades kisses the sensitive spot just under my ear and then moves away wordlessly, allowing me to finish getting ready.

I finish applying my makeup, a more drastic look than I'm used to, but I need to look the part. My eyes are dark and smoky, and I'd painted my lips a deep purple, almost black. My hair tumbles down my back in loose curls, except for two braids I pull back in a clip, keeping it off my face.

I feel Hades' searing gaze on me and turn to face him, trailing my fingers over the silk at my thigh.

"Do I look okay?" I ask nervously.

Hades leans in the doorway, the suit fitting him exquisitely. The material hugs his muscles in a way that makes my mouth water, and the nervous flutters in my stomach turn into swirls of desire. My eyes trail over his body, and then...

Fuck, he's wearing his crown.

My king. My sexy, wonderful king. I'll get on my knees—
No, P.

Hades' eyes glow as he takes me in. "You look stunning, my queen."

My queen. Fuck, that's so hot.

I exhale shakily and keep my eyes on him, using him once again to ground me.

Hades holds his hand out, offering it to me,

271

somehow knowing I need his touch. "What is it, my spring?"

I slide my hand into his and move closer. "You're sure I'm right for this?" I ask. "What if fate made a mistake?"

I'm yanked into Hades' arms, and he wraps me in a tight embrace. "Fate has never been more correct than when it chose you to be my queen."

I keep my gaze locked on him, dropping my voice to a whisper. "You can't kiss me." Hades' brows furrow, a flash of hurt crossing his eyes. I point to my lips. "Lipstick."

Hades smirks and releases me before stepping back. "Since I can't kiss you..." He looks at me with such adoration in his eyes and drops to one knee before me, bowing his head. "My queen."

I gasp, looking down at him. Hades, God of the Underworld, King of the Dead, who bows to no one, is on his knees for... me.

"Hades."

He looks up at me, love shining in his eyes. "I know it's not traditional, and I know you're still..." He pauses, trying to word whatever he's trying to say. "Our truce is still in effect, but..." He pauses again, but this time, he lifts my left hand, and a sliver of shadow dances over my skin, moving to my ring finger and encircling it. The shadows dissipate, and a ring remains in their place. It is breathtaking. The gold band supports a rose made of rubies flanked by two small diamonds pressed into the band. "You are my fate, Persephone."

I look at the ring, my eyes filling with tears. I try to blink them away, thinking that if I lose sight of the ring and Hades for even a second, they will be snatched away from me.

"Hades." It's all I can say. It's all I can think. Every other word has gone missing from my brain except the one that matters: his name, only ever his name.

"Yes?" Hades asks, slowly standing.

I slam my lips to his, not caring that we're probably already late for the coronation, uncaring about the smudged lipstick, not caring about anything other than this moment with my fated.

Hades deepens the kiss, his fingers tunneling into my hair, holding me closer. Too quickly, he pulls away, pressing his forehead to mine, both of us breathless and smiling.

"Pretty sure my lips are purple now," He says, his voice full of humor.

I laugh, tears spilling down my cheeks, the ring practically humming with happiness on my finger.

Hades pulls back, wiping my tears. "You're going to have to redo your makeup, my spring."

I shake my head. "I don't care. Kiss me again."

Hades smirks. "Persephone, as much as I want to kiss you and never stop. We have to go. They'll be waiting."

I sigh heavily and nod. Pulling away, I walk back to the mirror, my eyes never straying from the ring for too long. I grimace when I look at my reflection, mascara tracking down my cheeks, my lipstick smudged, and my lips swollen from our kiss. *I am a mess.*

I fix my makeup and walk over to him, wiping the lipstick from his lips.

"Leave a hint of it," Hades says, smirking wickedly.

I chuckle and wipe it off completely before pressing a kiss to his jaw, leaving a lipstick mark there.

"Perfect," Hades growls.

My body immediately reacts to that sound, but I force myself to pull back, slipping my hand into his and linking our fingers.

My Hades. My mate. My king. My husband.

Chapter Fifty-One

Persephone

THE HALLS SEEM LONGER AS WE MAKE THE JOURNEY from our bedroom to the throne room. Everything is silent, as if even the Underworld is holding its breath, anticipating the crowning of a new queen. The air feels… lighter, as if with acceptance of my fate, every realm is exhaling in relief.

My heels click against the marble, and Hades squeezes my hand in silent support as we reach the doors to the throne room. Fuck, have they always been so big and daunting?

Hades pulls me to a stop before we reach the doors and turns me to face him. He cups my cheek and smiles, his eyes shining with emotion. He nods, silently waiting for me to be ready. Keeping my gaze locked on his, I exhale and nod back.

I can do this. This is my fate, my destiny.

Hades strokes my cheek with his thumb before turning back to the doors. I follow suit and swallow hard, my heart feeling as if it's in my throat. He waves his hand, and the heavy double doors open slowly, the light from the candle-lit room bouncing off the marble floor in the hallway, illuminating us for our audience.

He squeezes my hand, my cue to walk, but my

feet feel planted to the ground as if they have been cemented there, never to move forward. "My spring?" Hades whispers, squeezing my hand again, and with something as simple as my pet name coming from the man I love, I find the courage to move forward.

The room is nearly silent, and I keep my gaze focused on the two vacant thrones sitting proudly on the dais. Power seems to radiate from them.

As it should.

The invited gods have formed a pathway from the door to the front of the room, but all their faces blend into one. My stomach flutters and knots, and my entire body is wracked with nerves. As we get closer, I see Zeus and Hera to the right of our thrones while Poseidon and Amphitrite stand to the right, their chins lifted as they watch us approach.

For the first time, every realm will have both a king and a queen. However, the Underworld will be the only realm whose rulers actually love one another, making for a stronger, more resilient realm.

The walk to the dais seems endless, but my hand in Hades' is the grounding I need. I think if he weren't holding my hand, I'd be running out the door. Not because I don't love him or want this, but because I'm still not confident that I'm up to the task.

I glance at Hades as we step onto the dais together. He turns to face me, my back to our captivated audience.

"Persephone Prosperina Plutus, kneel." His voice is deep and commanding, and I'm not sure if it's hearing my new surname or him telling me to kneel, but I have to work hard to suppress the shiver of desire running down my spine.

I glance down at the black marble where a plush black velvet cushion has appeared for me to kneel on. I slowly lower to my knees, looking up at my husband, my king, my fated one.

"Do you swear to protect the realm of the dead as

both queen and goddess?"

I keep my gaze locked on his, and I don't miss the vibrant sapphire blue of his irises being swallowed by the black of his pupils.

"I do," I reply. My voice seems to echo in the room even though it is filled with people.

"Do you so bind yourself to the Underworld, committing to living here six months of the year in service to the realm of the dead?" he asks, a glimmer of pride shining in his eyes.

"I do," I repeat.

Hades holds his hands out, and my crown appears on his palms. The dark beauty of it speaks to the newly awakened part of me, my darkness swirling in happiness.

Hades steps forward and slowly lowers the crown, placing it on my head. Once again, the pleasant weight of it makes my whole body thrum with rightness. He looks down at me, a ghost of a smile on his lips. "Then rise, Persephone Prosperina Plutus, Queen of the Underworld, Goddess of Dark Spring."

I slowly rise, and just like when I first arrived in the Underworld, I feel something within me changing, my power evolving and strengthening.

Hades takes my hand and turns me toward our audience. We sit in our respective thrones, the Queen and King of the Underworld, side by side, holding court.

The Underworld feels as if it's buzzing with power, overjoyed with its new queen. The strength that my bond with Hades brings will add to its already immense power.

"And now we stand three kings and queens!" Zeus's voice booms, filling the room, his tone jaunty but with a mildly threatening undertone.

I glance at Hades and squeeze his hand. He smiles and says to those gathered, "Please, enjoy the party."

Music swells in the room, and the sound of chatter

fills the silence as the gods mingle. Zeus, Poseidon, and their wives move into the masses, but Zeus remains visible due to his height.

One by one, gods approach us, and thanks to my research, I recognize all of them. There are some I am only able to put a name to the face, but for others, I can recount little facts I'd read. They comment on my dress, the decor, and my crown, but my eyes keep straying to one goddess who is waiting to speak with me.

She is breathtaking, her beauty almost otherworldly. Her long blond hair has a gentle curl and is artfully styled. The golden waves look as soft as the most luxurious silk and flow down the graceful curve of her back. Somehow her face appears perfectly made up while also looking as if she's wearing no makeup at all. Her eyes are the color of the morning sky, clear, blue, and surrounded by long thick lashes. A slight blush kisses her high cheekbones, and her lips are a nude color with the smallest hint of a shine. The closer she gets, the more I see of her dress, and it is almost as jaw-dropping as her. Light pink silk hugs her curves, and the corset cinches in her waist, allowing the dress to better showcase the flair of her delicate hips.

Aphrodite.

I sigh, trying to concentrate as I'm greeted by god after god, but my mind keeps going to Aphrodite, her beauty, her elegance, her grace.

Gods, why is she so perfect?

A mischievous voice chimes next to me, a new god leaning against my throne. "Yeah, I know. It takes a second to get used to looking at her."

Hades looks at the god leaning on my throne, his expression going hard. "Eros."

Eros winks at me before vanishing again, no doubt reappearing somewhere else in the party.

I blink and turn to Hades, my brows drawn in question.

Hades sighs heavily. "God of Love and Desire, and

trickster. His mother has a bit of an... enchanting presence."

"Oh?"

Hades nods, squeezing my hand. "You get used to it, and the longer you're with her, the easier it is to counteract with your own defenses."

"Persephone," a light, lyrical voice pulls my attention from Hades, and I look at Aphrodite standing in front of me, radiating light as if she has her own personal sun shining from within. Her smile is bright and kind.

"Aphrodite." I smile, drawing on my power to remain composed and not let myself be stunned by her power. The second I wrap myself in my power, not only do I feel less star-struck, but I notice that her presence is pleasant, and I feel completely at ease with her. "It's so lovely to finally meet you!"

Aphrodite seems to glow more, as if truly happy to be talking to me. "The honor is mine. I've been impatient to meet the goddess who finally locked down Hades."

I glance at Hades. He is looking at Aphrodite, amusement pulling at the corners of his mouth.

"Locked down?" I ask, looking back at Aphrodite.

Aphrodite glances at Hades, her eyes sparking with amusement. "You know that at least eighty percent of the single ladies in Olympus were vying for your love, affection, and attention." She waves her hand, rolling her eyes. "You get the idea."

My lips twitch, and I realize I like her. She seems so down to earth, and while she is completely stunning, she doesn't seem to care. She doesn't seem to see herself as any better than anyone, even though her beauty is without rival.

Hades squeezes my hand, and I feel his eyes on me. I turn my head to lock gazes with him. "I only wanted a goddess who wanted nothing to do with me." His smile is warm as he lifts my hand to his lips, kissing it softly.

I look back at Aphrodite, and just barely catch

278

the flash of pain that crosses her face, her bright smile dimming a little. It is so quick that it's almost imperceptible.

"I should stop stealing all of your attention, Persephone." Aphrodite plasters the smile back on her face, but this time, I can tell it's false. "I hope we can speak again later! I want to hear all about that dress. You look so beautiful!" Aphrodite steps back.

"Your husband is here." Hades' voice stops her in her tracks, and her entire body stiffens.

The ghost of a smile she'd donned like a mask completely vanishes from Aphrodite's face, and while still breathtaking, her bright, sunny disposition becomes a picture of beautiful devastation.

Aphrodite looks down and smooths out invisible creases in her silk dress.

"Aphrodite?" She looks up at me. Her lips are curled into a smile, but her eyes are awash in sadness and regret. "You look incredible."

Hades nods. "Perhaps tonight is this night for healing old wounds."

Aphrodite tries to hide her emotions, but the facade she built, maybe since the last time she saw him, has been torn to shreds. I admire the way she tries, lifting her chin and smiling.

"Too late for that. I've never been what he wants, but thank you both. Excuse me." Aphrodite leaves, and I know from experience that she will try to rebuild the defenses she has spent thousands of years developing.

Chapter Fifty-Two

Hades

I WATCH AS APHRODITE WALKS AWAY from Persephone, her glow dimmed. Even from this distance, I can see her fragility in the way she holds herself. Persephone stares after her, worry filling her eyes. I feel for the other goddess, but my queen holds all my attention. Even surrounded by the glowing divine, Persephone stands apart.

Her gown is exquisite, making my heart slam with need at the way it hugs her lush curves. I love how her crown sparkles, and that she wears it makes the one on my head feel lighter. Even her train makes her stand out, the dainty roses twisting around the skulls, matching the lapels on my suit. She is my queen, crowned and recognized before all.

She turns away from Aphrodite and heads back toward me, her eyes distant. I reach out to her mentally. It is comforting that even surrounded by people, I have this intimate way of reaching out to her. *"You can't help everyone."*

She locks eyes with me, crossing the throne room with effortless grace. *"But she's clearly in love with him."*

Sometimes that isn't enough. A chill shoots down my spine.

We're different. We have to be.

Persephone sits back down on her throne, situating her gown. The ebony thrones of the Underworld are filled. I reach for her hand and squeeze her fingers when I see the god approaching us.

He's taller and broader than his father and walks with a pronounced limp. His hair is dark and tied up in a knot tonight, but I know it reaches past his shoulders. At least he trimmed his beard. Slightly. Barely. Gods part for him, and though he pretends not to notice, I can see the way his eyes tighten.

I smother a smile when I see what he's wearing. Everyone arrived wearing the height of fashion, yet he's wearing dark jeans and a long sleeve shirt with heavy boots.

Hephaestus barely lowers his head to me. "Uncle."

Persephone glances at me, then back to Hephaestus. "Lovely to meet you, Hephaestus. I'm Persephone."

She must have studied up for tonight. I try not to beam with pride. He nods shortly at Persephone, and that's actually more than I expected from the reclusive god.

"We are honored that you made an appearance," I add, deliberately dragging my eyes over his attire. Most gods would blush or at least shift awkwardly. Hephaestus doesn't even react.

"It seemed impolite not to make an appearance," he responds gruffly.

He looks at his watch, not even trying to hide his eagerness to leave.

"I just met your lovely wife." Persephone smiles, squeezing my hand.

Hephaestus's entire body tenses, and though his expression doesn't change, a flame sparks in his eyes.

His jaw ticks beneath his beard. "She is lovely to all she meets."

I watch his reactions, studying them. "That she is."

"And that dress!" Persephone continues. "She looks stunning. I'll need to ask her where she got it."

Unsurprisingly, Persephone and I are of the same mind when it comes to Hephaestus and Aphrodite. *Meddlesome.*

"She likely custom-designed it. Excuse me." Without waiting for a nod from me, Heph turns and limps away.

"Was it something I said?" Persephone asks, a trace of humor hiding in her voice.

I lift her hand to my lips, kissing the back of it. "You were perfect."

She looks at me, her eyes narrowing on Hephaestus's retreating form. She stands and says, "Excuse me for a moment."

I nod, watching her follow him. A flash of emerald green catches my eye from across the room. My lips twitch when I see Mellie pressed back against the wall. Helios hovers over her with his hand braced above her head, pinning her in as they exchange heated words.

I shadow from my throne to reappear directly behind the Titan of the Sun, only catching the end of his words.

"... can run to the Underworld all you want, hellcat. I'll still find you," Helios warns.

"Is that right?" I ask, making the Titan jump.

Helios spins to face me, having to raise his head to meet my gaze. He's only a few inches shorter than me, but it's enough.

Mellie seizes the opportunity to try to slip away, but I shift to stop her from escaping. She roasted me over the coals about Persephone. It is time for payback.

"Hades," Helios sputters. "I was just explaining..."

I wrap an arm around Mellie's shoulders. "I see you've met my errant adopted daughter."

Helios's eyes practically bulge out of their sockets, and I smother a smirk. I knew Mellie hadn't told him about the connection between us.

Mellie elbows me hard in the side and grimaces. "I think you're overstating it, demon daddy."

I don't move away, but my fingers tighten at the

282

moniker she's chosen. Helios pales, his eyes pinging back and forth between Mellie and me.

"How do you know Mellie, Helios?" I drawl, enjoying watching the two of them squirm. Mellie presses a high heel into my foot, but I just pull her closer, squeezing her shoulder. "I don't suppose you're the reason she wore a color other than black today?"

Helios blinks at me, then looks at Mellie, taking in the emerald green dress with new eyes. I see a spark of satisfaction lighten his expression as he reads the Goddess of Nightmares like a book.

"I don't like you without Persephone. Speaking of, where is my bestie?" Mellie grits out through clenched teeth. Another traitor who tossed me over the second Persephone entered our lives.

I quirk my brow. "Do you really think Persephone needs my protection?"

Though I'd offer it to her, I knew you underestimated Persephone at your own peril—my dark and deadly spring.

"We're dating," Helios blurts out, bringing my attention back to him.

My smile turns lethal. "If you're talking about my queen..." You're about to die.

Helios blinks, shaking his head. "What?! No! Mellie and I."

I drop my arm from around Mellie, not even bothering to hide my smirk. Oh, the ammunition he'd just provided. "You are?"

"We are *not* dating. I'd rather spear out my own eyeballs and feed them to Berry," Mellie hisses, glaring at Helios.

I tsk. "Cerberus has a sensitive stomach. He's off eyeballs this week."

Helios crosses his arms over his chest, tilting his head, acting as if I hadn't spoken. "Yes, we are."

Mellie steps forward, getting right in Helios's face and slamming a finger into his chest. "You are

283

a delusional, UV carcinogenic fuck, and I'm always wearing factor fifty to repel your unevenly tanned ass. Fuck off."

Did she just compare him to skin cancer? Having been the target of Mellie's lethal tongue, it was refreshing to have her venom directed elsewhere for once.

Instead of shrinking back, Helios's smile widens, and he shifts closer to Mellie. The Titan of the Sun acts like her words just glanced off him, immune to her snark.

"Then you'd better grab your sunscreen, hellcat, because you're my girlfriend."

Mellie opens her mouth to respond, but Helios kisses her.

I smother a laugh before shadowing back to my throne.

Chapter Fifty-Three

Persephone

HEPHAESTUS! WAIT!" I call, hastening to catch up to the large, imposing presence that is the God of Fire and Forge.

His body is wracked with tension, as it has been since he approached us on the dais, but when he hears me call on him, he becomes even more rigid. He stops walking, allowing me to catch up, but he doesn't turn.

I gently place a hand on his shoulder. "Hephaestus?"

He finches a little, and I drop my hand, blushing at his reaction to my touch. He slowly turns to look at me.

While his stature is large, I do not fear him. This man has been deeply wounded, and it has nothing to do with his limp. This pain runs deeper, entwined with his soul.

"Lady Persephone," he says curtly, his voice a rough, deep bass.

"I apologize if I upset you."

Hephaestus crosses his arms, his gaze hardening. "Why would you have upset me?"

I shrug, feigning ignorance. "You seemed upset when I mentioned Aphrodite."

"There is nothing between us, no reason to be upset." His gruff voice is laced with a bitter hint of sorrow.

I clear my throat, sensing that he'd rather jump off

a cliff than continue with this particular conversation. "Right, well, I actually wanted to ask something of you."

"What?"

"I understand you work for Hades, making things for him?" I tilt my head.

"I do," he replies simply.

A man of few words, I see. I wonder why he and Aphrodite ever thought they would be a good match.

I nod, smiling. "I was wondering if you could make something for me to give to him. A wedding gift of sorts." Hephaestus seems to consider me, his stormy eyes searching my face. I think I see a glimmer of envy within them, but it is gone as quickly as it appears. "I would pay you separately, of course," I add.

Hephaestus nods. "Send me the details, and I'll get started."

"I'll call you in the next couple of d…" I trail off as a lyrical laugh floats over the chatter of the crowd. Hephaestus's head snaps up, zeroing in on the source. I follow his gaze and find Aphrodite at the end of it, speaking with Eros. Her face is once again relaxed into that serene, stunning facade as she laughs with her son. Her love for him is so apparent that seeing it makes my chest ache.

I glance back at Hephaestus. His whole body is vibrating with tension, but the storms have cleared from his eyes, and they are shining with longing. While I now know the hold Aphrodite's power has, this isn't from that. This is raw and true.

I watch Hephaestus as he silently watches her. As if a magnet is drawing them together, Aphrodite's head raises, and she turns toward him, their eyes locking. Even from this distance, I can tell her eyes darken with desire, and a flush fills her cheeks, making her even more stunning than before.

For long moments they just stare, as if the room is completely empty save for them. I glance at Eros. He winks at me and smiles smugly before disappearing into the crowd.

My lips twitch. *Eros really is tricksy.* "So I'll call you?" I ask, breaking the spell that has fallen over the two gods that seem destined to be apart.

Hephaestus keeps his gaze on Aphrodite for another beat before dragging his eyes away. Barely looking at me, he nods once, turns, and leaves. His limp seems even more pronounced and his shoulders more slumped than before.

Chapter Fifty-Four

Hades

PERSEPHONE STROLLS BACK THROUGH THE CROWD, but she keeps glancing back at the doorway where I saw the towering form of Hephaestus exit. He stayed far longer than I expected of him.

"How did that go?" I ask Persephone through our link.

She settles into her throne as if she's done so a thousand times. *"Unsure."*

I lift her hand to my lips, kissing it tenderly. *"You're being a menace."*

Not that I wasn't doing the exact same thing with Mellie and Helios only a moment earlier. Fate did not make blind matches. Now, I simply need to prove fate correct. It is an odd thing to realize for someone who hates fate. I can just imagine the Moirai smirking knowingly as they looked through the golden thread.

Ethereal music starts, a ghostly quartet playing instruments in the corner, each note hauntingly and beautiful. Our lives are half divine and half death. It is suitable for Persephone's coronation, a sign of her own duality as the Goddess of Spring and Queen of the Dead.

I stand and hold out my hand to her, torchlight glinting off the ring on my forefinger, the seal of the king. "Shall we?"

She nods, keeping her eyes on me as she slips her hand into mine. As we step down from the dais, the crowd parts for us, clearing the dance floor. The eyes follow us, but my only focus is the goddess in front of me and the haunting scent of my queen.

I turn to face her, sliding one hand around her back, and her hand lands delicately on my shoulder as if we've done this a thousand times at a hundred events.

Maybe it is a glimpse of our future. A future that hangs precariously in the balance, depending on the choices of our bruised and fearful hearts.

Our eyes don't leave each other even as we dance. Nothing matters but us. The gods turn into nothing but a blur of color as we turn and dance. It is just us, as it should be. Hades and Persephone. Persephone and Hades. Life and death.

"What happens when this ends?" I breathe, leading her through the dance. The words slipped from me, and a part of me hated I endangered our fragile moment.

"When what ends?"

I don't look away, nor does she, my soul attuning with hers. Every breath from her came from my lips. Every beat of her heart is echoed in my chest. My body moves more on instinct than anything else. "The truce."

Her lips twitch down for a second before she remembers our audience and schools her face back into the regal countenance she wore during the coronation. "I don't know."

Even as we dance, the bond between us strengthens. This is it.

"I don't want to go back to how it was," I whisper, even as the music slows, signaling the end of the dance.

"Me either," she says, her eyes shining with vulnerability.

"What do we do?" I ask as the music stops and the world around us comes back into focus, intruding on us.

She parts her lips to respond, but someone taps her shoulder, drawing her attention. I practically snarl and spill the blood of the god who thinks to take her away from me. I fist my hands but regain control of myself before nodding at Dionysus. He chuckles and spins her away. I turn to leave the dance floor, but a soft hand stops me, pulling me into the dance.

I know it's Aphrodite without having to look. She has a certain scent. Or rather, she smells different to each person. Aphrodite's scent is love personified. If someone has a deep love of books, she smells like crackling pages and ink. Or if they feel love in the outdoors, she will smell like a wind coursing through trees. To me, she smells like roses in a dense fog, but there's the lingering aftertaste of magic in my mouth. It is a pale imitation of my true love. I could pick Persephone's scent out in a rose garden.

Aphrodite starts the dance, forcing me to go along or look like a poor host. She glances at Persephone and says, "She's incredible."

I nod. I don't have to look at her to know that. "She's not what anyone expected." But she is exactly what I need. I just didn't know.

Her golden brows lift. "She is exactly what I expected."

I nearly stumble and hurry to cover my misstep, focusing completely on Aphrodite. She expected Persephone? How could *anyone* expect Persephone?

Aphrodite smiles at my slip. "She's a force, Hades. She's exactly what you need. Exactly what you've always needed."

This is getting a little too personal. Time to redirect and evade.

"And you?" I lock eyes with her. I know how intense my gaze becomes when I do that. "What do you need?"

Aphrodite holds my gaze for a moment before glancing away as usual. The only person who has ever held my gaze for a prolonged time is Persephone. I'm too *intense*, as many gods put it.

"To know my son is happy," she replies, but her voice betrays her emotions, the longing barely concealed.

My eyes dart to where Eros is leaning against a wall, spinning one of his golden arrows around his fingers. They have the same golden hair and sky-blue eyes. Both have a sort of effortless beauty, but that is where their similarities end. Aphrodite, beneath her exterior, yearns for love and acceptance. Eros is a complete enigma. I can never tell what he wants or even what he is thinking.

Right now, he looks like he's bored but amused. Yet his body is coiled tight, ready to spring. I have no doubt he could recount every movement of every god present. What I don't understand is why.

"Happiness for your son, but not yourself?" I ask Aphrodite, focusing back on her. Eros is a puzzle I have yet to figure out. That phone call weeks ago only piqued my curiosity.

"He's all I have."

But he's not. She could have more. "It's never too late to make amends," I say. "Only fear holds you back."

Her eyes dim, the clear blue becoming murky. "He didn't want me before I had Eros. Following my indiscretion, he wanted me even less. I doubt anything has changed in the last two thousand years."

There is no need to ask who *he* is.

"You'd be surprised what a stubborn man in love can forgive," I reply wistfully.

"Are you speaking from experience?" she counters. "Trouble in paradise?"

Damn it. I'm not usually so sloppy.

"Don't you already know?"

As the Goddess of Love, Aphrodite could sense the love and even the struggles between couples. Unfortunately, she refuses to use her abilities when it comes to those closest to her. Her husband especially.

"I try not to pry. You know that. It's rude." That's

291

only a recent development. She used to pry all the time. "But now that you've brought it up, yes. There is tension, not all of it is bad. What's going on?"

Not all of it bad? The fuck did that mean?

"I don't discuss these sorts of things," I reply stiffly. Thankfully, the dance is ending.

Aphrodite laughs. "But that's not the issue, is it? It's that she's not talking. We've been friends for a long time, Hades." Friends might be stretching it. "Trust her. Trust her with your heart, but trust her with hers, too."

My back straightens. "Thank you for the dance."

But Aphrodite isn't done. "She loves you. So much that she's overwhelming my power. Don't take this for granted."

She smiles sadly at me, leaving me on the dance floor, blending back into the crowd.

Chapter Fifty-Five

Persephone

RELUCTANTLY, I AM SWEPT AWAY FROM HADES BY DIONYSUS, God of Wine, Merriment, and Madness. I immediately recognize him from my research. He looks exactly like he did in the books I scoured over. His long, deep red hair almost looks purple when it catches the light just right, and it seemed to make it into every portrait, photograph, and written description. Tonight, tied into a messy bun, paired with his stubble, it makes his otherwise perfectly tailored appearance look casual and nonchalant. He is effortlessly handsome.

"Quite the party. Everyone was wondering about an event held in the Underworld." Dionysus chuckles. "Hades has never invited anyone to his illustrious palace before."

I laugh. "He's not big on social events."

"And to be invited to see his fated queen?" Dionysus dips me dramatically. "How could a god resist?"

I laugh again. "Hades said you were trouble." When he stands me again, I add, "And when paired with Eros, I hear carnage ensues."

Dionysus smirks. "Carnage is a bit strong. I prefer casual maiming, and it's always consensual."

"Well, unless you want my terrifying dog set on

you, you better behave," I reply, my eyes glinting with humor.

Dionysus looks around. "Surprised he's not in attendance, though I'm guessing dear old dad was insistent on that. He's never been fond of the pup. You know, the sinews and all."

"I may have already threatened him with Berry... a few times."

Dionysus laughs loudly, the sound infecting the gods and goddesses closest to him with mirth. "Now, that sounds like something I should see."

I laugh. "I'll be sure to invite you to the show when I inevitably reach the point where I tell Cerberus he can eat him."

Dionysus laughs again, his smile wide enough to light the room. "Oh, I doubt Hades will let any of us near you after tonight."

I tilt my head. "What makes you say that?"

"Because I know it's taking everything in him not to rip you away from me at the moment."

I roll my eyes. "That is a bit dramatic. He's dancing with Aphrodite."

Dion smirks. "Oh, you have no idea, sweet Persephone. You didn't know him before."

"What do you mean?"

He glances toward Hades. "He was very aloof, hard to get to know, intimidating as fuck."

I blink. "And now?"

"He's aloof, intimidating, and unapproachable." Dionysus snorts, "But he's completely different the second you touch him." The music slows and ends. "If I were him, I'd guard you jealously."

I turn my head to look at Hades, and our gazes lock. I notice the way his eyes soften the second they meet mine.

"Thank you for the dance, Dionysus," I say, not looking away from Hades.

"It was my pleasure, Persephone. And you can call

me Dion." I can hear the smirk in his voice, but I barely hear anything else he says as I walk toward Hades. My Hades.

The invisible string that ties us tugs at me, desperate to get back to him. My heart flutters when he slides his hand into mine and pulls me in close, brushing his knuckles along my cheekbone, his touch so achingly gentle I think I'm going to melt on the spot.

"One more dance?" he asks, his deep voice sending a shiver down my spine.

I chuckle. "You're over the celebration already?"

His lips twitch, and he moves his hand from my cheek to my waist, squeezing slightly. "I want to be alone with you."

I pull my hand from his and wrap my arms around his neck, our bodies flush. His warmth seeps into me like the silk of my dress is a conductor. I draw it in and bask in it, enjoying the feel of his hard body pressed against my softer one.

"Alone, huh?"

"Yes." Hades pauses for a moment, thinking. "You look like you belong."

I tilt my head up at him. "Of course I do. I'm with you."

Hades sways to the music with me, everyone in the room blurring into nothing. "Aphrodite said that I..." He hesitates, his brows furrowing a little. "That I should trust you with your own heart."

I tense a little, scanning his eyes and waiting for him to continue.

Hades doesn't back down from our intense eye contact. He squeezes my waist again and says, "I'm... I'm going to try to be patient. Try not to push."

Surprise steals my ability to speak. This is what I wanted. I've been trying to get him to understand this, and he seems to get it finally. Aphrodite very well may have saved my marriage with a single statement. Hades may not fully understand, and he may still try to get me to talk, but the admission that perhaps I know what I need better than he does means a lot.

Hades dips me over his arm as the music ends. Time seems to stand still at that moment, Hades and I in a position of trust, physically and emotionally. I trust him not to drop me, and I trust him with my heart because he is allowing me the chance to give him that trust instead of demanding it.

Hades straightens us and leads me back to the dais with my hand clasped in his. He clears his throat, and in an instant, the whole room stills and goes silent. The way he commands a room is so impressive and sexy that I can't bear to take my eyes off him.

"Thank you for attending this coronation. My queen and I will be taking our leave. Enjoy the rest of the night."

Hades turns his head to look at me, and all the air seems to whoosh out of my lungs. I rarely see this side of him. The commander, the ruler, but fuck if it isn't sexy as hell.

The crowd parts for us, and Hades leads me down the center of the room. I manage to pull my gaze from him and briefly lock eyes with Aphrodite. Her smile is both hauntingly beautiful and devastatingly heartbreaking as I see the ghost of regret dancing with the joy that she may have helped another couple avoid the reality she is living. I give her a grateful smile and silently send a hope into the universe that she will find happiness.

Hades and I walk in silence through the palace halls, the noise from the ballroom a memory as we move deeper into the palace. The only sounds are our feet against the marble and my heart pounding in my chest.

Hades slows his pace before we get to our bedroom and pulls my gaze. He stops completely, and I tilt my head.

"I don't want our truce to be just a truce."

I scan his eyes, my heart thundering in my chest.

Hades watches me intently. "Do... you?"

No. I don't. I want to scream it, to throw myself into his arms and wipe that anxious, uncertain look off his face. But what I need is for that statement to be *my* truth, and we still have so much to discuss and work through.

"I think we have a lot to talk about," I reply honestly, and my heart shatters when his face falls. We continue walking, and Hades hesitates briefly before opening the door.

Did he think I'd be going back to my bedroom? I squeeze his hand once before stepping into our room. Hades follows, and I turn to face him as he closes the door. He strokes my cheek again before removing my crown and placing it on the designated cushion on the vanity. As he removes his own, I reach behind me to unzip my dress, but his much larger hands brush mine aside. He deftly unzips my dress, leaning down to kiss my shoulder as he pushes the fabric aside. My eyes fall closed, and I moan softly at the feeling of his lips on me.

Hades pushes the straps from my shoulders and leans down to kiss the base of my neck. The silk glides down my body to pool around my feet, leaving me only in my matching black lace bra and panties.

"You commanded the room tonight. I could not have been more proud," Hades murmurs against my skin.

"Really?" My words are half moan half sigh as I lean back into him.

Hades nods and runs the tip of his nose to my ear as he gently pulls the pins from my hair, allowing it to fall down my back in loose curls.

"Yes. Every eye was on you. My queen. My dark spring," Hades growls in my ear. His hands move to my waist, squeezing. He sighs heavily and pulls away. I frown, looking over my shoulder to see him getting my silk robe. He returns to me, sliding it onto my shoulders.

"What are you doing?" I ask, confusion replacing

297

desire. Out of all the possibilities, I would have never guessed that he would put more clothes on me.

"You want to talk," Hades says. "I need you clothed for that."

I tie the robe tight. He's right. I did say we should talk. I hate it when he does that. Being right is my thing.

Hades kisses my neck again and then my jaw before pulling back. I walk to the couch in our bedroom as he disappears into the closet, emerging a moment later in sweatpants and a t-shirt. This is my favorite Hades.

That's what you say about every variation of Hades. Stop being an embarrassing simp, P.

Hades sits next to me, gently lifting my hand to his lips and kissing it softly before placing it on his thigh, still in his hand. He absentmindedly strokes the ring on my left finger.

Hades and I are inevitable, right? Well, this is it. Make or break.

Chapter Fifty-Six
Hades

THIS IS IT. I can feel it thrumming around us, a heaviness in the air. This is our chance to move forward or to break. A coin spins in the air, and I'm holding my breath, waiting for it to land. The golden thread between us squeezes the air from my lungs. Is it doing the same to her?

Trust her with your heart. And her own.

Don't be a part of the wheel. The cycle that began with my grandfather and was continued by my father. I need to break the wheel.

Why does that sound familiar?

I wasn't even aware of this cycle until recently. I suppose that's how it is. You never realize you've fallen into the repetitive cycle of tragedy until it's too late.

Please don't let it be too late.

Persephone strokes my cheek with her thumb, pulling me back into the moment. That soft touch is all that I need to stop my spiral. We lock eyes, neither of us wanting to begin. Trepidation vibrates around us, yanking those golden threads of fate tighter around my lungs. Does she feel it too? Is she scared to begin like I am?

"What do we do now?" I whisper shakily, taking the first step, the ground pitching beneath my feet.

She sighs, and my entire body tenses, my breath freezing in my lungs. I prepare for the blow that could easily render me the walking dead. Truly the God of the Dead, lifeless and cold, without a hint of life. That is what I would become without her.

"We either try to talk it out now, or we accept that we're never going to find a middle ground and have a marriage only in name."

The words drop like bombs in my head, explosions that leave debris and shrapnel behind. *No.* Most gods had marriages only in name, so many strayed from each other out of boredom or lack of affection. The idea that another would *touch* Persephone…

Destroy.

The breath hisses from me as I recoil violently at the suggestion. My claws come out. I want to bind her to me and mark her permanently so no one doubts my claim.

"Never," I snarl, "will we have a marriage only in name."

I won't be like my brothers or my father. I will break the cycle. Persephone and I will shatter the past and build a future from the remains. I will burn this world to the ground and put the heads of any person who'd dare attempt to take Persephone away from me on spikes outside the palace.

She watches my face, and it takes a few moments to calm my breathing, to rein the darkness inside me back under my control. Sometimes it's so easy to forget how my power can rage if I let it. It had never been such a problem until I met Persephone.

"Then we need to talk or fight it out," she says.

I exhale, trying to organize the thoughts that have been brewing inside me since I saw my father. Every time I need the cold, calculated side of me, it vanishes, especially when it comes to matters of the heart. The more I care, the less control I have. I take a deep breath, Aphrodite's words echoing in my head.

"My actions were..." I can't say that, so I restart. "I was desperate, but that's no excuse. I wanted you here with me. It didn't matter what it took for me to achieve that. Because I love you."

The banks of my kingdom are littered with those who died for love. It killed far more people than any war.

She stands and paces back and forth. With each step of her bare feet, my heart slams against my ribs. "It's so difficult for me, Hades, because..."

I want to leave you. I don't want to stay. Stop it.

"I know you couldn't tell me. But after a lifetime of being my mother's captive, of being hidden from the world and made to live in her home..." Demeter grew Persephone from her own tears of loneliness if the rumors are true. "My life seems to always belong to someone else."

I need a clear head to reason and not panic. I can't act the same way I did before. My claws dig into my thigh, keeping me in the present. The sharp bite of pain quiets the destructive thoughts slightly.

I shake my head. "It's not your fate to belong to me. It's mine to belong to you. You can walk away. I cannot."

She can walk away. She wants to. I dig my claws deeper into my thigh.

"What are you talking about?"

I scan her eyes, trying to read her thoughts. "If you wanted... you could leave."

It took everything in me to admit that to her and take this risk she would go. I wanted to tear the tongue from my head for even daring to offer it. Why give her a way to leave me?

"No. Hekate said..."

I look away. "There is a way. I don't want to be your jailor."

It would kill me to do it, but I would break the cycle.

She sits on the coffee table, and I look at her,

memorizing every detail of her face, preparing myself for the next words I need to say. This might be the last time I get to study her.

"Your fate should be yours to decide. Even if it's not me." I clear my throat, hoping to dislodge my heart.

"Tell me how."

My entire body wants to recoil, to lie. I want to be the coward and run from the room. No. My father was a coward. My grandfather was a coward. I will not be like them.

"Gaia," I manage. "She's the one who bound me to the Underworld. She'd be able to break the bond."

Gaia, the Primordial of the Earth, gave us the three worlds after the war and bound me to this realm. She could break Persephone's tie to the Underworld and free her, but not mine. I'd be alone again.

My stomach roils, and I look away, unable to look at her as the words fall like rocks between us.

"And then I would return to the human realm?" she asks.

My voice dies, and I can only nod. The only thing I can offer her is the opportunity for freedom and the choice she didn't have.

"All of my ties to the Underworld would be severed?"

I close my eyes, nodding tightly.

There's a pause, pregnant with her decision.

"Ask me," she whispers, and my eyes snap open to look at her. "Ask me to be your wife, your queen, to accept my fate."

I keep my eyes locked on her, needing to see her thoughts, but scared to the depths of my soul to hope.

"Will you take me as your king? Your husband? Your fate?"

She keeps her eyes on mine, and I hold my breath.

"Yes," she whispers. "I choose you, Hades. Always."

The sound that tears from my throat is both broken and joyful. She closes the distance, sliding into my lap, and I press my lips hard to hers, needing to reaffirm

302

that I hadn't lost her. I pull back after a moment and look at my hand. Fine, black vines are wrapping around my finger, weaving together to make a ring for me. They form a band, the pattern intricate and stronger than steel. The vines tighten, and the tiny leaves turn gold. I am bound. Persephone has marked me as hers.

"My spring..." I flex my fingers, looking at it.

"You needed a wedding ring, too."

For the first time since she freed me from the tree, I can breathe easily.

Chapter Fifty-Seven

Persephone

I KISS HIM AGAIN, my lips the slightest of whispers against his. Relief eases the pressure in my chest, and I have never felt stronger. For the first time in my life, I know I can trust someone. This man will catch me if I fall. He will hold me together if I break.

Even thinking he might lose me, Hades showed me my options and handed me the key to my freedom. He trusted me to make my own decisions and follow my heart. It was in that second that I knew for sure I could never give him up. I could never give up my home, which is what the Underworld has become to me. It is the only home I need.

When I left Olympus, something shifted, and I thought the mortal realm was it for me. I was happy, but now I realize while that realm will always have a place in my heart, and I'm happy that we will spend six months of the year there, it was merely a stepping stone to my true haven.

Home is the Underworld. No, home is wherever Hades is.

"It killed me to give you this choice, you know?" Hades whispers, pulling me from my musings.

I cup his cheek, searching his eyes. "I know, but you

did. You gave me the choice. That is something I've never experienced, and I can't tell you how much it means to me," I whisper, wondering how I got so lucky to be mated to Hades. "I chose you, Hades."

"After torturing me first," he growls, but I can hear the playful lilt in his voice.

I pull back to glare at him. "I wasn't torturing you."

He quirks a brow. "So, what would you call asking about Gaia?"

I bristle a little, impressed at how he can go from being irresistibly sweet to irritating as all hell in the space of three sentences.

That's one of the reasons you love him, P.

I glare at him and move off his lap. "Hekate told me there was no way I could leave the Underworld when I was trying to save you."

"Hekate has been foaming at the mouth for a queen for millennia." Hades snorts, but then his face falls a little. "And…" he hesitates, "if you had decided to break the bond, there would be no way for you to return." I can see the agony of that alternate reality cross his face, the unbearable pain I would have caused him by choosing to leave. But I can't help but retreat into my own hurt at the insinuation that I asked for more information only to prolong his pain.

"Yes, well, I'm sorry I took half a moment to think about my future before telling you my decision. As I have a history of emotionally tormenting you, of course, that's what your initial assumption would be." I clear my throat. "I'm going to take my makeup off."

Hades grabs my hands, looking up at me, his eyes shining with vulnerability. "No. The only torture was self-inflicted. I put you in this position in the first place."

I meet his gaze. "The only reason I asked about Gaia was so I could make an informed decision. I wanted you to know, without a shadow of a doubt, I will always pick you."

305

I gently tug my hands from his, frustration bubbling beneath my skin.

Hades grabs my hands again. "Persephone."

"What?" I growl.

Hades stands and places his hand on my cheek. "I love you. I'm sorry."

I exhale heavily, some of the tension releasing. I know I'm not being fair, but neither was he. We've both been through such a lot in the past few weeks, and things between us have been so tense. We're both bound to be fraught.

"This has been a rough day. Let's just go to bed."

Hades immediately swoops me into his arms, walking straight past the bed and sitting me down on my stool at the vanity in our bedroom. My brows furrow as I watch him take a makeup removal wipe from the pack and bring it to my face, softly wiping my skin.

His brows knit in concentration as he glides the cloth over my cheeks and lips. I watch him, taking advantage of this time to memorize his face. Every time I look at him, my heart reacts like it did the first time, but it feels fuller, whole. I know that every single inch of me belongs to him.

I tilt my head as Hades glances away before returning his focus to me. The third time this happens, I realize that he keeps looking at his new ring. His eyes sparkle every time as if he enjoys the physical sign of belonging to me as much as I belong to him.

After he has cleansed my skin, I smile warmly at him. "Thank you." It's funny how such a mundane task can be so intimate with him. My heart swells as he leans in, kissing both of my cheeks.

I sigh contently, grab my moisturizer, and apply it to my clean face. Hades takes over, his rough hands surprisingly soothing against my skin. I close my eyes, enjoying the feel of his touch.

"Anything else?" Hades asks as he finishes.

"Just pajamas," I reply, opening my eyes.

Hades lifts me again and walks to our closet.

"I can walk, you know?" I say, my lips twitching.

Hades shrugs, placing me down on the chaise and removing my robe before getting shorts and a cami for me. He kneels in front of me and places my feet in the holes of the shorts, one after the other. "I'm not allowed to spoil you?"

I roll my eyes, shifting to help him pull my shorts up, but my cheeks hurt from my wide smile. Hades unhooks my bra and slips it down my arms, freeing my breasts. His eyes darken, and he presses a kiss to each nipple before pulling the cami over my head, growling low in his throat as he covers me from his view.

Hades picks me up again and, this time, walks to the bed. Using his shadows to pull down the covers, he gently lays me down and kisses me sweetly.

I'm about to deepen the kiss, but he pulls away and slips off the bed.

"Hades?" I frown, watching him walk to the bedroom door. In a blink, Cerberus has leaped from the door into the bed, and all three of his heads are licking my face. I squeal.

"Berry!"

I hear Hades walk back to the bed. He sighs heavily. "Off the bed, Cerberus."

I nuzzle into Cerberus, wrapping my arms around his left head.

"Persephone, don't let him on the bed," Hades growls, and I shift slightly to see him. He wears a look of exasperation and love for both me and his *terrifying* three-headed marshmallow.

"But why?" I ask, my eyes wide and my lip pulling into an exaggerated pout.

Hades gives me a look. "Because he takes up the whole bed!"

I kiss each of Berry's noses, and he nuzzles into me, licking me again.

I sigh, scratching behind all of his ears. "Daddy is right, Berry. There isn't enough room for all of us."

Cerberus tilts his middle head and barks happily, jumping off the bed and padding over to the fireplace. He grabs his bed with his right head and heaves it over to my side. He sits heavily and looks at me expectantly, all three of his tongues lolling, making him look like he's smiling proudly.

I tilt my head at Berry. He paws his bed before climbing into it and barking again. I chuckle, understanding what he wants. I climb out of bed and lay in Cerberus's bed with him.

"Okay?"

Hades blinks at me. "What are you doing?"

Cerberus shifts, getting comfy, and I rest my head on his back. "Cerberus wants me to sleep here."

"Come here," Hades growls.

Cerberus puts his paw on me, not wanting me to leave. My lips twitch. "You're the one who let him into the bedroom, demon."

I feel Hades' scent surround me as he wraps me in the warmth of his shadows. Cerberus whines as I appear back in the bed with Hades.

I look at Berry, reaching out to scratch his head. "Daddy needs me to sleep here tonight because he missed me. Is that okay?"

I swear Cerberus pouts as he lays his heads down in defeat, huffing.

"We'll take you for a long walk tomorrow," I say, trying to sweeten the deal a little.

Cerberus whines again, but his tail flickers slightly—stubborn beast.

Hades looks at me. "You don't need to sleep with me, too?"

Great, now I have two pouting males.

"I do, but this way, he feels like he's doing something good for his dad, and his mom isn't picking his dad over him," I whisper so that Berry can't hear.

308

Hades wraps his arms around me and pulls me against him. His hand drifts down my side to cup my ass, squeezing once before sliding it to the back of my thigh. I shiver at the contact, my body humming for him. Hades digs his fingers into the soft flesh of my thigh, wrapping my leg over his hip to pull me even closer, fitting me against the hard planes of his body.

"You are picking me over him." His voice is so low it's practically a growl, and it turns my core molten.

"Shhh, he's my baby," I whisper, feigning outrage.

Hades raises a brow, his gaze trailing to my lips. "And what am I?"

I lick my bottom lip. "My husband. My love. My demon. My king."

"And I come before the dog," he growls.

Unbelievable. He can't possibly be jealous of a dog. His *dog, no less.*

I cup his cheek. "You come before everyone and everything, my fated."

Hades growls again, his eyes black. He digs his fingers harder into my thigh and slams his lips to mine, kissing me desperately. I moan into his mouth, his kiss dizzying.

"My fate," Hades murmurs against my lips before he deepens the kiss, his tongue flicking mine, his hands pulling me tighter into him.

"I love you," I whisper when he allows me a chance to gasp a breath of air.

Hades bites my bottom lip, sucking on it. "I love you too, my dark spring. My queen. My wife."

I moan again but pull back. Today has been so overwhelming, and Cerberus is in the room with us. We better not get carried away.

"We should sleep, my love."

Hades nods reluctantly. "Persephone?"

"Yes?"

He cups my cheeks, looking into my eyes with such intensity that I think I'm going to get lost in the sapphire pools. "Thank you for choosing me."

My heart squeezes, and I lean in, pressing my lips to his softly in a soft caress. "Thank you for choosing me, too."

Hades slips his hand beneath my cami, not wanting anything separating his hand from my skin. He draws shapes on my back as he searches my eyes.

"I'll choose you every day," he says. The words sound like a vow, and I shiver at the feeling of his whisper-light touch against my hip. "I don't ever want to be another prison for you."

My eyes sting at the reminder that he heard me, and I cup his cheeks. "I want to be here. I want to be with you. Wherever you are."

"I love you." His voice breaks slightly, and I can't help but kiss him again, needing to ease his pain.

What starts as a soft kiss builds, and Hades moves his hand to my ass, squeezing my flesh.

"We should get some cute sleepwear for us. Matching ones," Hades murmurs into my lips.

I blink, pulling back from our kiss. "What? That's what you're thinking about right now?"

"Well, I'm trying not to get too into it because you already said we should sleep, and then I just thought… matching pajamas!"

I have to bite the inside of my cheek to stop my laugh. "We mostly sleep naked, demon."

Hades smirks. "You don't want matching pajamas with me and Cerberus?"

My eyes go wide at the idea of getting Berry his own pair. "I definitely do!"

"They would be our morning pajamas." Hades laughs.

I nod enthusiastically and climb on top of him, straddling him and smothering his face in kisses. Hades' laugh washes over me like the sweetest of honey, and he tickles my sides, making me wriggle and squeal. I continue to kiss all over his face and neck. He tickles me until Cerberus starts barking, clearly concerned about what's going on in the bed. I kiss Hades deeply, joy radiating from me as I bask in the feeling of being with someone who loves me so completely that my heart can barely take it.

Chapter Fifty-Eight
Hades

PERSEPHONE LAUGHS AND ROLLS OFF ME. I frown, not liking that little bit of space between us. I'm still raw from everything, and I need her pressed to me, skin to skin, for at least the next decade. Maybe longer. "Where are you going?"

She glances at me, then down at the massive three-headed terror lying next to the bed, with an expression close to exasperation. "We can't while Cerberus is in the room."

I blink. Then blink again. Is she serious?

"Why not?"

She gives me a stern look. She can't be serious. He may be bonded to me, but he's still a dog. Granted, he is a gigantic three-headed dog that sometimes breathes fire, but he is still a dog.

I growl at her. The dog practically stalks Persephone. If this is her new rule, we'd never be intimate. "Persephone."

She crosses her arms. "We are not having..." She glances at the giant dog, "S-E-X while Cerberus is in the room."

My mouth gapes open. She did not just spell the word sex, so Cerberus would not understand like he's a toddler. I let out an astonished laugh, which makes her eyes narrow. I bite my lip to keep from laughing again. The things she worries about.

She rolls away from me, her body radiating annoyance.

"Goodnight, Hades." Each letter was pronounced with such force it sounded like she was trying to puncture the air with her words.

I pull her into me, kissing along her neck to her ear. Even though her reactions have helped level off some of my lingering anxiety, it wouldn't hurt to level it off more. And more. And more. It's been forever since I've been inside her. Years. Decades. I can barely wait a moment more.

She moans softly and presses back against me, her body fitting so sweetly against mine. "Hades, you can't do that."

I bite her jaw, licking along her skin, addicted to her taste of pomegranates, cherries, and strawberries. "I'm not doing anything."

She moans, shifting against me until there is not even a single breath of space between our bodies. "No?" I don't stop biting along her neck, and she tips her chin to give me better access. "My mistake," she says, tunneling her fingers into my hair. I love when she does that, constantly pulling me close.

I bite her ear. "I like when you wear these little shorts to bed."

They barely contain her perfect curves. Her life-changing ass stretches the fabric tight, making me imagine ripping each of those tiny stitches with my claws, one by one, slowly revealing her every dip and curve. She tightens her grip on my hair to keep me close as if I am going anywhere.

"Because I like the sound it makes when I rip them from you," I growl into her ear and pull hard on her shorts, ripping them from her body. I will have the castle replace them over and over, so I can enjoy her gasp.

313

She drags her nails down my arms. "Hades."

"Yes?"

She tilts her head more for me, and my lids lower, imagining how my fangs are going to sink into her shoulder, that perfect slope of skin just waiting to be marked by me.

She moans. "Not with Cerberus in the room."

I frown. Why is she so hung up on this?

"Cerberus, out."

Cerberus huffs, not moving a muscle.

I growl, "Cerberus."

Cerberus lifts his heads, looking at me, and I swear his eyes narrow on me. Is he challenging me?

Persephone looks at him. "Berry, go ask Uncle Thanatos for a treat and give Daddy and me some private time?"

Cerberus crosses one giant paw over the other, glaring at us.

My eyes narrow back at him. "He knows what he's doing."

"And what is he doing, demon?"

"Being a half-ton cockblock."

She laughs, and I growl at the dog. I try to avoid using my abilities on him. It didn't feel right, but sometimes, like now, it feels justified.

She trails her nails along my arms, making me shiver. "We could always go to one of the spare rooms."

I sigh and fall on my back in defeat. "He would follow."

This is just my luck. I finally feel like Persephone and I have made up, but of course, fate saddled me with a dog who has extreme attachment issues.

She leans over the bed, glaring at the giant three-headed hindrance. "Last chance. Get a treat from Uncle Thanatos, or you're going in a pen."

I smother a laugh at my wife negotiating with our dog.

"I love you, Berry," she adds, "but Daddy and I need

some alone time."

A lot of alone time. Years of it. I have an eternity of loneliness and isolation to make up for. Cerberus whines and stands, his heads hanging low as he heads for the door.

I reach out to grab Persephone, but she's already climbing out of bed. She pulls on some new shorts and asks Cerberus, "How about we both go for a treat?"

I fall back on the bed. "You're such a sucker."

Cerberus barks at his mom, bouncing around her. I shake my head. He's as enraptured with my wife as I am.

I watch her leave the room, my eyes trailing down her outline. That ass is as magnificent as it was when I saw it for the first time. I've traced every dip and curve with my tongue, worshipping, disciplining, and owning every part of her, but there's so much more I want to do to her luscious, fucking body. I can already see her struggling in my shadows as I tease her to a fever pitch. When I finally give in and fuck her, I'll use my shadows to fill every inch of her until she knows nothing but me. The door closes behind them, and I rub my stiff cock under the sheets.

Don't be impatient. We have an eternity. Nothing will keep us apart now that things are settled. We have time.

We have time.

Chapter Fifty-Nine

Persephone

I WALK THROUGH THE PALACE HALLS toward the kitchen, Cerberus happily padding beside me. There's almost a bounce in his step. He is excited to be hanging out with me... and to be getting a treat.

Asshole. He knows what he's doing.

I can't help smiling at my huge boy as we walk, his excitement palpable. The second the kitchen is in sight, Cerberus launches himself at the swing door, slamming through it. I laugh and run after him, trying to quell the chaos that will no doubt ensue when my marshmallow is as excited as he is.

Cerberus runs straight past the treat jar to the hooded figure standing at the kitchen island. His familiar tattooed fingers are braced on the counter, a steaming cup of coffee in front of him.

Cerberus barks and jumps excitedly around Thanatos, his tail wagging so much he's creating a soft breeze.

"Thanatos?" I tilt my head at him, walking farther into the kitchen.

Thanatos tilts his head slightly in my direction, his ever-present hood covering most of his face and casting the rest of it in shadow.

"Your Highness, I'm sorry for the intrusion." His voice gives nothing of his thoughts away. I've never considered the palace a place where Hades and I live alone, and while I've seen Thanatos a few times, I always just assumed he lived here, too.

"Intrusion?" I ask, my brows furrowed.

"Being here, Your Highness." He pauses for a moment. "Uninvited." I can feel the unease radiating from him, but there's also an underlying tension.

"You don't live here?"

I can tell he shakes his head from the small movement of his hood. "No, Your Highness." Thanatos straightens, and Cerberus wiggles excitedly as he moves. "I will take my leave. Apologies again." Thanatos bows and turns away.

I step forward, almost reaching out to touch him, but I stop myself. "Thanatos?"

He tenses, his fists clenching in unease.

"Are you... all right?" I'm not sure why I'm asking. I don't know him very well, but there's something about finding him here, the way he's holding himself, that compels me to check on him.

Thanatos turns back to me, the light catching him in a way that exposes some of the pale skin of his jaw. "The Underworld is not used to having living guests, nor am I. Especially divine ones." He clears his throat, obviously very uncomfortable. "It's just taking some getting used to, Your Highness." He bows his head again. "Somehow, the palace doesn't seem as unsettled by the change, even though the guests are here."

I nod, understanding. "Thanatos?"

"Your Highness?" He bows his head again.

"You're always welcome here."

Thanatos's body seems to relax ever so slightly, and although most of his face is still hidden in shadow, I swear I can see the ghost of a smile.

"Please, stay, and if you want to use one of the guest rooms tonight, you're more than welcome," I say before circling the island to get Cerberus a treat.

Thanatos picks up his coffee but remains standing. Probably because I'm here, I doubt he'll ever be able to relax in my presence.

I choose a large bone for Cerberus, one that will take him ages to eat. "Cerberus, sit."

Cerberus pants, wriggling his ass as he sits down, looking at the large curved bone, perfect for all three of his heads to enjoy.

"Stay," I say, stepping back from him. I slowly place the bone on the kitchen floor, and Cerberus lifts one of his heads, yelping at me impatiently.

"Now. Are you going to give Daddy and me some alone time?" I try to make my face stern, but it's difficult when I look at my adorable marshmallow boy. Cerberus shuffles his feet, his right head barking. "Berry," I say firmly. Cerberus tilts his head and sits up on his back legs, his paws in the air, begging. Sitting like this, he's much taller than me, but all I can see when I look at him is a tiny little baby. I sigh heavily and roll my eyes. "Take it," I say, and Cerberus leaps, the ground shaking as he dives on his treat. I smile warmly at him before looking back at Thanatos. "If you'll excuse me, I need to get back to my husband."

Thanatos bows his head again. As I leave the kitchen, I hear the faint scraping of a stool against the tile as he sits down, relaxing now that he's no longer in his queen's presence.

I walk back to our bedroom with a slight spring in my step, feeling lighter than I have for a long time. I don't dawdle, wanting to spend as much time with my husband as possible before we're interrupted by our hellhound again.

Hades sits up in bed when I step into the bedroom, and the sight of his naked chest and the sheets gathering at his hips has my breath leaving me in a whoosh. My heart flutters, and my whole body hums in anticipation. *Gods, will I ever get used to this?*

318

I shut the door, making sure to lock it before leaning back against the sturdy wood. My eyes drift over him, and when I manage to pull my gaze from his chest, I notice his dark eyes and the way he tilts his head as he watches me silently admire him.

"How much time do we have?" he growls, sending a pang of awareness directly between my legs.

I glance at his lips and slowly walk toward him. "Cerberus doesn't sleep here anymore."

A smirk plays at the corners of Hades' lips. "Is that right?"

I nod. "As of tomorrow, he has a room across the hall with a big fireplace, a huge bed, toys, and a full view of our bedroom door so he can keep us safe."

"And you think he'll stay there?" Hades' eyes darken with every step I take.

"Unless you want our sex life to be non-existent, maybe try to be part of the solution. Not the problem," I say with a sassy tip of my head, stopping at the side of the bed.

Hades' eyebrows shoot up, and I feel his shadows wrap around me, pulling me to him until I'm straddling his lap. "What was that, my dark spring?" His voice is low and dangerous, sending a shiver down my spine.

"Maybe I'm not in the mood anymore," I reply, trying to sound unaffected by him. "I guess you're not as desperate for me as I thought." My gaze goes to his lips, and I can hear the desire in my own voice.

New plan, P.

I try to shift off him but find myself encased in Hades's shadows again. He pulls me back, his hard body pressing against me, making me melt. The second his shadows dissipate, his lips are on me. He trails searing kisses along my neck, making it hard for me to remain anything but putty in his hands. *His big, strong hands, sinful hands.*

I moan and tilt my head to give him better access, my body arching when he bites along my neck and

319

shoulder.

"Hades," I hiss his name, completely at his mercy. I feel his claws drag down my side, and I know what's coming. I can still feel the sting of it from before, the material ripping from my skin. The sound of the stitches tearing fills the room, and the bite of pain makes me writhe against him.

"Yes, my dark spring?" Hades growls in my ear.

"Fuck," I moan as heat stokes low in my tummy, my desperation for him coiling tight.

Hades sinks his claws into the flesh of my ass, and I rock my hips, needing more of him as I feel the hard bulge of his cock against me.

Hades slams his lips to mine and kisses me hard, punishingly, bruising my lips with his, owning me. I drag my nails down his bare chest, feeling his shadows moving over me, touching me everywhere. But I can always identify which hands are truly his. The ones I crave the most.

"Deeper," Hades growls and I dig my nails into his chest harder, angry red lines trailing after them. I bite his lip hard, rocking myself against him, opening further to him. His shadows dance and lick down my spine, and I rock my hips against him, soaking his pajama pants with my arousal.

"You need me?" Hades growls against my lips.

"Always." My reply is breathless, desperate.

Hades rolls onto his back, pulling me with him, making me straddle his hips. He spanks me hard, the slap making my ass sting.

"Then take me," he moans, his hand massaging the tender flesh he just assaulted.

I pause, pulling back, tilting my head at him.

Hades raises a brow, panting. "What?"

"Take me?" I tease, my lips hovering over his.

Hades' eyes twinkle. I can tell I'm giving him itchy fingers. I can feel his need to punish me oozing off him.

"Persephone," he warns, his voice full of danger and

320

desire.

I smirk, looking down at him, playing with him, teasing him. "I'm not sure you want it enough."

His expression changes in an instant, his need to punish me at war with his desire to fuck me to within an inch of my life. In a flash, he's on top of me. "You talk too much, my queen." He reaches down, pushes his pants down enough to free himself, and meets my gaze again, waiting for the permission he will always ensure he has.

He reads the unwavering trust and desire I have for him, and with no further warning, he thrusts inside me hard, forcing a cry from me. Hades slams his lips to mine, kissing me hard, low growls rumbling in his chest as he thrusts hard and deep into my welcoming heat, the bed shaking beneath us. "Does this feel like I don't want it enough?"

I moan and drag my nails down his back. "No."

"Does this feel like I don't ache for you every fucking second?" He asks, his voice low and demanding, his thrusts punishing.

I arch beneath him. "Gods, no... Hades!"

I shiver when I feel his shadows trailing over my skin. I deepen the kiss, the sound of his cock slamming into my soaked pussy over and over filling the room. It is so fucking erotic.

Hades bites my lip hard. "You want to come, my spring?"

I dig my nails harder into his back. "Give me your wings."

Immediately, he snaps his glamor off. His wings stretch, covering us, and his tail wraps possessively around my ankle, the touch now familiar and beloved. I drag my nails down his wings and am rewarded with a shudder and a guttural growl which shoots a wave of pleasure right to my core, sending me over the edge. I scream his name, my whole world shattering around us as I come.

Hades arches above me, his cock slamming deep inside me as he thrusts hard. He sinks his fangs into my shoulder, and a second orgasm rips through me, nearly wrecking me.

Hades roars, throwing his head back, and he comes with me, filling me with his release. I shiver as he licks my neck, then presses a searing kiss there. He rubs his horns on me, and I moan, basking in his presence and closeness.

I wrap my hands around his horns. They are so hard under my fingers. I squeeze them, pulling his face to mine and kissing him deeply. Hades arches as I keep my hands on his horns. I know they're sensitive. I know he loves it when I touch him like this.

"My queen," he moans against my lips, and I smile.

"My king." Always my king. After another moment, I release his horns and relax back into the mattress. I look up at him, my heart swelling at the sight of my mate, my husband, my Hades.

Chapter Sixty
Hades

IGROWL AT HER, putting her hand back on my horn. The impact of her touch on them shoots down my spine. It's as if she scraped her nails lightly across my cock. My horns are that sensitive to her touch. She squeezes, and my eyes roll back in my head. I wrap my tail around her leg and…

Cerberus whimpers loudly at the door, pawing at it.

Persephone sighs, the sound conveying her defeat. "I give up."

I laugh, burying my face into her neck. I shouldn't be charmed by this, but it's such a domestic moment. Here I am, trying to fuck my wife, and we're being consistently interrupted by a needy dog. "You spoiled him, and now he's attached."

"Well, this is the end of our sex life." She glares at me. "So congratulations."

"What did I do?"

She shoves me off and uses her vines to open the door with a snap. Cerberus moves to his bed, and she rolls onto her side to go to sleep.

I smother my smile and spoon her back, kissing along her neck. I wrap my arm around her stomach and pull her tighter into me, loving how we fit together, even when I am just holding her in my arms. Every piece of our bodies interlock as if I was unfinished without being aware. I am only whole when I am pressed against her.

"I love you," I breathe into her ear.

Instead of relaxing in my arms, she stiffens. "Hades?"

I close my eyes, inhaling her scent. "Yes?"

"I'm leaving you to deal with Berry."

I open my eyes, looking down at her. "What?"

She doesn't open her eyes, but she cuddles into me. "If you ever want to have sex again, you'll need to deal with Berry."

How am I supposed to do that? The dog has proven to be a formidable opponent for us both.

"You started it with cuddling him," I point out.

"I was lonely and scared and stuck in a foreign realm."

Okay, that was a low blow.

I cup her cheek and turn her face to mine, her eyes opening. "No longer."

Her eyes soften. "Deal with the dog."

"Our boy."

She rolls her eyes at me. "Fine. Now I feel guilty. We'll hold a funeral tomorrow for the end of our sex life. I bet Charon is bringing it over on the ferry."

I laugh, nuzzling her face. "You're so adorable."

She rolls away from me, tensing, and I wrap my arm around her again. I bite her ear. "I'll take care of him."

She growls at me again.

"I'll send him to his mother for a bit." Cerberus is the child of Typhoon and Echidna, the mother of monsters. Typhon is locked away in a pit of never-ending torment within the Underworld, per my brother's order, but Echidna is at least cordial to me.

Persephone tenses, and I clarify. "His biological mother."

She tenses even more. "We are not sending him away."

I sigh. She wanted a solution. "Then what do you

324

suggest?" She glares at me mutinously, and I sigh again. "I'll have a talk with him. He's just very protective of you. He looks at you and thinks *Mommy*, very loud."

She reaches out of the bed and scratches his closest head. "I love you, Berry."

Cerberus pushes into Persephone's hand and shouts through my mind, "*Protect Mommy! Danger! Protect Mommy! PROTECT MOMMY. DANGER. PROTECT MOMMY.*"

Danger? Cerberus is exceptionally on edge with the coronation and my brothers in the palace. No doubt he's sensing the holes in the Underworld, warning me of what I already know.

Persephone relaxes against me. "Our boy."

Our boy. I tighten my arm around her. He is our boy. She drifts off, and I follow soon behind her.

The scent of clean linen suffuses me, a soft hand brushing through my hair. I feel the slide of silk against the edge of my ear, every swipe of the hand putting me more at ease. Comfort and safety like I've never known, surrounds me. The kind that only comes from one's own mother.

My eyes snap open, and I find my head resting in my mother's lap. I snap straight, snarling, "Morpheus, you go too far this time."

Morpheus appears in front of me, his fathomless eyes searing me. "This is not me, my king."

I tense, still sensing the presence behind me. Morpheus vanishes from my dream as swiftly as he appeared.

I don't look at her.

I can't look at her.

"You're dead," I say to the dream Olympus as if it will answer me.

My mother laughs, and the sound breaks me a little. I've never heard my mother's laugh before. It is deeper than I expected, filling me with a longing for the childhood I never had.

"You of all gods know, my son," Rhea murmurs, "death is not always the end for us."

My son. *I had once longed to hear those words from her.*

After the battle, Zeus told us what had happened to our mother. When Kronos discovered her betrayal, he unleashed his power on her, fracturing her and spreading her throughout time. She would never be whole again, only an echo of a barely remembered dream.

I close my eyes, shoring up my strength to turn and look at my mother. "Why are you here?"

She lifts her hand and cups my cheek. I barely stop myself from flinching, not used to being comforted by someone other than Persephone. Especially not from someone I never really met.

"You needed me." She smiles softly.

I yank my face away from her and stand, my hands fisting. "No, I needed you then!" I snarl at her. "When you sent Poseidon and me to be swallowed!"

Rhea's face doesn't change from soft understanding, and I hate it.

"Do you know what it was like, Mother?" I drag the word out like an insult. "To grow up in the fall? To have nothing? No one?"

Her eyes flicker slightly. "I did what I had to."

I grab her shoulders. "You spared Zeus! But not us! You left us there!"

Her face softens slightly again, and she touches my cheek. "I was scared."

My anger leaves me on a whoosh of air. "You were?"

She smiles sadly. "I was terrified of what he would do to me. I lived every day afraid of what it would bring."

I drop to my knees in front of her. I thought she didn't care and was biding her time. That she picked Zeus because he was her favorite. Never had I thought she was scared. I knew my father was a monster, but I foolishly assumed my mother was immune.

She cups my cheeks, her eyes sad. "I loved each of my sons so much."

My eyes cloud with tears. "You did?"

She nods, pressing her forehead to mine. "I did."

A tear slips down my cheek, and I whisper, "I'm sorry, Mom."

Mom. The first time I've ever said the word out loud.

She shakes her head, wiping the tear from my cheek. "Don't apologize, but don't let my past be your future."

Her past be my future? Why did that sound so familiar?

Rhea glances over my shoulder at something. "This time, my beautiful boy, give him everything you held back before."

I frown. Him?

I follow her gaze right as the dream shatters around me.

Chapter Sixty-One

Persephone

CITRUS AND SANDALWOOD, powerful arms, calloused hands.

"I look forward to seeing you soon."

A wave of unease washes through me, but I cling to the scent surrounding me, the brawny arms wrapped around me, and the calloused hands against my skin.

My skin thrums in both contentedness and discomfort. In sleep, my brain is locked in a haze of sensations that don't match. It's an internal war raging on whether I should be frightened. When I'm enveloped in that scent, I know I am home. Those arms have done nothing but protect me, and those hands have done nothing but pleasure me. But stuck in the ether, in the limbo between wake and slumber, that voice doesn't match.

"I look forward to seeing you soon," the voice repeats smugly, full of bitterness, malice, and pride.

The arms tighten around me, and I feel myself slipping back to consciousness, safety, and home.

"I look forward to seeing you soon." I hear it again, but it's fainter now, like a whisper.

I shiver as I feel a brush of the softest lips against my neck, and my eyes flutter open. The dream fades to nothing as the light of the morning sun floods my vision, and Hades kisses my neck again. I reach up to tangle my fingers in his thick, luscious hair.

This is my heaven.

I moan as he drags the bridge of his nose along my jaw, every touch, even the smallest, feeling like little bolts of pleasurable electricity trailing along my skin. He bites my earlobe, making me shiver.

"Good morning, my wife," he growls in my ear, digging his fingers into my hip as he grabs me and pulls me closer.

"Good morning, my husband," I half moan, half gasp.

I feel Hades smile against my skin, but then his whole body goes rigid, and a feeling of foreboding envelopes me.

Something's wrong.

Cerberus bolts up in bed, barrelling toward the balcony doors, and no sooner does he get there than the universe shakes violently.

It feels like someone has torn a hole in my soul. Like the Underworld has been injured, and I can feel its pain.

The glass of the balcony door shatters, the sound of the explosion deafening, drowning out the sounds of things breaking and shifting. Cerberus leaps through the now-broken door, snarling.

Hades climbs out of bed, his eyes almost black with fury. He can feel it, too.

Something's wrong.

"Stay here," Hades commands, pulling on pants and a shirt before walking to the balcony. Not listening, I climb out of bed, pulling on the first thing I can find, which happens to be one of Hades' shirts. My heart pounds in my chest, and my stomach churns with nausea, both in fear and from the pain of the Underworld.

I watch Hades' back, his body locked tighter than I've ever seen him. His shadows are spilling from him in fury as he looks out at our realm, and I brace myself for what I'm about to see.

I expect devastation, carnage, and chaos, but nothing could have prepared me for the sight before me. An angry gaping chasm fractures the vista, red smoke billowing from below as if the pits of hell have opened.

"They're free," Hades hisses.

I can't look away from the Void. "Who?"

"The Titans."

I pull my eyes away and look at Hades. His whole body is now completely covered in his shadows. As they dissipate, they leave in their wake the blackest of armor covering his skin, fitted and impenetrable.

He is the God of the Underworld, protector of his realm, and a force of nature.

"What do we do?" I ask.

Hades turns to look at me, placing his hands on my arms. "Send them back." He cups my cheek. "Can you do this?"

I place my hand on his chest, the metal of his armor warm under my touch.

"*We* can do this. Together."

"We need to prepare," Hades growls. His expression is severe, but he strokes my cheek with such tenderness.

I nod, pulling away. "Let's go." Hades slides his hand into mine, and we walk to the closet, which is completely transformed. One half is still full of our clothes, but the other is a full armory filled with swords, daggers, bows and arrows, and armor. Hades kisses the back of my hand before releasing me and walking to the wall of weapons.

I grab my fighting leathers and start to change. I was hoping not to have to wear these again for a while. The memories of Tartarus are still raw, and it feels like they mock me as I pull on the tight pants and top. My fighting skills aren't bad, but I'm not sure how I'll fare against Titans.

Now is not the time to doubt yourself, P. You are strong. You are brave. You are powerful.

I take a fraction of a moment to silently thank Josef, the servant who took the time to teach me some combat. I never had friends in Olympus, but he was close.

I used to think that being the Goddess of Spring meant I would never be considered a threat to people who wish to harm me, my family, or my realm. I'm very much looking forward to proving all of those fuckers wrong.

I braid my hair and join Hades, who is balancing a sword in his hand. I choose two short swords, a twin set, meant to stay together. Their energy practically bounces off one another. I wrap my fingers around the hilts, and they warm, softly vibrating under my touch. The petals of the flowers embossed along the shafts of the blades glow as my power welds with the steel, bonding us.

Hades' sword ignites as he lifts it. These are our weapons. They have pledged their fealty and will remain true to us and only us.

We slip the weapons into their sheaths, where they hum gently, ready for the fight we all know is coming.

I look at Hades, finding his gaze already locked on me. "Are you ready for this?" he asks.

I slip a dagger into the sheath strapped onto my thigh. "I'm ready."

Hades takes my hand, his thumb brushing over mine as he wraps us in his shadows. We keep our gazes locked as he takes me from the comfort and safety of our home into the center of the chaos.

The shadows dissipate, the smell of copper and rotten ichor filling my nose. The land is completely barren, scorch marks tracking up the barren trees. It is exactly how I imagined the Underworld would look before I came here and knew better.

The peaceful chirps of birds have been replaced by the groans and grunts of Titans breaking into fights as they battle for dominance. There are roars of agony and murmurs of discontent. With their every breath, they speak of their desire for revenge.

I squeeze his hand. "Should we summon your brothers?" I ask, feeling less confident now that I am in the center of the sheer number of large bodies threatening our realm.

One Titan notices Hades, and a snarl curls his lip. They advance on us. No longer distracted with killing each other, they want the blood of the god who has imprisoned them for millennia.

They'll have to get through me.

Hades drops his glamor, his wings bursting free, and I pull my swords from their sheaths before dropping my own glamor and stretching my wings.

Hades and I glance at each other and say in unison, "I love you."

Hades lunges at a Titan, plunging his sword into his chest as I throw myself at another, slicing his head free from his body.

Chapter Sixty-Two

Hades

OUR HOME IS SHATTERED, our realm overrun by the very creatures it imprisoned. The adamantium that once made up the cells and gates lies scattered over the Underworld. The land is torn, revealing the terrifying Void beneath. Any spirit or creature who was too close when they opened was consumed. It would crush them into nothing as they fell farther and farther, and those were the lucky ones. The unlucky ones would spiral into the beyond, never reaching the end. It is a fate I wouldn't wish on my worst enemy. The Void is the empty creation from which the first-born Primordials were spawned.

I can't think about that. The holes in my realm feel like bullet wounds that refuse to heal, the bullets bouncing around inside me, slowly shredding my power. It is less than ideal when facing an army of Titans, and this time, I don't have my brothers or an army of Olympians at my side. I am already working with only a part of my power, and everything I require to win is absent. But I am not the weak boy I was the last time I stood against them. I'm a king. This time will be different.

From the corner of my eye, I catch a flutter of white

wings, and a wicked smirk curves my lips. I'm a king in my realm, and my fucking fearsome queen is at my side.

She's wearing battle leathers the color of midnight purple vines emblazoned in an elaborate design along her arms and legs. They match my leathers, but mine are edged with shadows. Our armor is stamped with our unique powers, proclaiming us together as a couple, as rules, and as warriors.

Persephone's wings are out, and she's using them to throw Titans off her as she plunges her two short swords into another Titan's chest, pinning him to the ground. Every move is filled with lethal grace, barely reveling in a kill before she moves to the next.

She yanks the swords from the Titan's chest, her vines wrapping around his body, imprisoning him. She hurls both swords at the Titan storming toward her, hitting him in the shoulder.

Fuck, she's incredible. She's a natural combatant. She has the instinct I trained for centuries to perfect.

Her eyes connect with mine across the battlefield, and I take a single step toward her, but a Titan rams into me, slamming me against the rock. My breath leaves me on a shocked exhale, and my lungs freeze painfully for a fraction of a second. In the small moment it takes for me to register what happened, two more Titans are charging toward me. I shake my head, dust spilling from my hair, and spit the blood from my mouth without ever taking my eyes off them.

I can see the recognition in their eyes. They remember me hiding and cowering the last time we faced off. It's how they smirk at each other, thinking that I'm helpless without my brothers. I'm going to enjoy proving them wrong.

I allow them to come closer, playing up my injury and making my eyes unfocused. I shake my head again as if to clear it. They keep closing the distance, smirking at each other, preparing for an easy kill. The moment they are within range, I lock eyes on them both. They stutter in their approach, no doubt confused. Then I smile.

My shadows emerge from the ground, slithering up their bodies like snakes. They are inconspicuous at first, but then they turn into bonds. The two Titans frown, looking down at their feet when their limbs stop responding.

My smile turns wicked as they realize they've stepped into my trap. The shadows turn to ropes and from ropes to steel. I don't look away from their faces as the shadows cut through flesh, muscle, and sinew.

Like mortals, they are ripped apart, cut by that which they can't grasp. The only difference is the Titans will regenerate, but that will take time, precious, precious time.

I step forward, looking down at the two broken Titans. "I'm not the boy you knew."

I wave my hand, trying to send their remains to two of the still intact cells. My shadows can travel anywhere I can in the Underworld. They can ferry these two to the cells without me. I blink when they don't move. I wave my hand again, and my shadows flicker, but the Titans remain. Is this because the realm is weakened?

I inhale sharply and call on more of my power, straining until the Titans finally disappear into the cells.

Another Titan approaches me and sneers, "Not so high and mighty now, Son of Kronos."

He barely finishes his sentence before his head rolls from his shoulders.

"High, mighty, and with his queen," Persephone snarls at the head, her swords still singing from the slice.

Fuck, I love her.

I focus and send the beheaded Titan to an intact cell. I close the distance between Persephone and me, wrapping my arm around her back and yanking her into me. "That's right, my queen."

She smiles up at me, both of us covered in blood and

gore.

"You're perfection," I growl down at her, lost in her eyes.

My lack of focus costs me. A Titan grabs hold of my wing and wrenches me away from Persephone. I barely register the searing pain in the limb or the tearing of the fragile membrane. My eyes are on Persephone, who stalks toward me, every inch of her a warrior.

She is the queen who was promised. The Destroyer of Worlds.

A Titan grabs her foot and throws her. Something inside me snaps, and I don't just pull my wing free. I lunge away from the Titan holding me, adrenaline carrying me through as my wing is torn free. Sinew, muscle, and bone crack and snap as the wing rips from my back. I swing my sword and slice his face before turning to race toward Persephone, trying to close the distance.

Persephone's scream shatters my ears as she hurls a dagger at me. I barely hear the thud as it burrows deep into the Titan's shoulder pursuing me. Even as she is being tossed, she's trying to protect me.

There's a flash of black, and I hear her scream in agony as the Titan holding her drags his claws across her back. I roar as the pain shoots down my spine, an echo of what she's enduring. My stomach rolls. The Titan must have exposed her spine with that.

I am nearly flying, eating up the distance between us. I feel the ground shake, but it's not from me.

Cerberus thunders onto the battlefield and barrels into the Titan, throwing him from Persephone with a roar that makes mine sound like a whisper in the wind. He bites, tears, and claws at the Titans, and for a moment, they retreat.

I scoop Persephone into my arms and swing onto Cerberus's back, my vision flickering from the pain.

"Home, boy!" I order, struggling to stay conscious enough to hold on to the dog's fur.

As Cerberus heads toward the castle, I assess Persephone's injuries. They're healing, but not enough. I yank our bond and pull her injuries into me, feeling them appear on my body and vanish from hers. My vision goes dark around the edges, my fingers slipping on Cerberus, slick from both my blood and hers.

"Stop it," Persephone hisses weakly. "I'm already healing."

Not fast enough. She's hurt, so I summon my remaining strength, trying to pull more of her injuries. She snarls, even as her back closes up, her body recovering as I take them on. Her vibrant eyes narrow on me, and her power slams into mine, a torrent of life against a sea of death. She pulls my injuries into her, and I use the last of my strength to build my shield, stopping her.

The palace shimmers as we approach, the dark spots becoming larger and spreading over my vision. Awareness floods me again when Cerberus pads into our room and carries us to our bed. He leans his shoulder down to let us roll off him, and I let out a silent scream of agony.

I breathe heavily through my mouth, trying to get through the pain. "We're not... healing as we should."

We should have healed the second we got inside the palace. The infection in our realm must run deeper than I thought.

"We need a healer," Persephone groans.

I try to roll to grab my phone, but I scream, unable to stop the pain.

"Call... Z," I whisper.

Then blackness takes me.

Chapter Sixty-Three

Persephone

FUCK, FUCK, FUCK." I wince as I unlock his phone. Every movement, even a micro-movement, sends a bolt of agony down my spine. Hades took on some of my injuries, but there were still plenty of others. I could already feel them starting to knit together excruciatingly slowly.

The pain and blood loss blur my vision, and I try to open the contacts to find Zeus's number. My hand shakes, and I groan as I shift on the bed.

"Fuck," I whimper.

Hades's phone vibrates, emitting a loud shrill noise. I click the small green circle to accept the call and hold the phone to my ear.

"Why am I getting alerts about an explosion in the cells?" Zeus snarls down the phone, furious.

My whole body quakes as it goes into shock. I cup Hades's cheek, knowing I need to push every morsel of power into healing him.

"Titans…" My voice is barely a whisper, and I groan in agony. "H-help…"

Zeus says something else, but the whole room blurs and spins. I push the last fragment of power into my king before everything goes black.

"My little Persephone. What have you done?"

338

There is only darkness... darkness, pain, and that voice. There is no comfort, nothing to ground me, and my power is drained.

"You could have avoided this, you know?" The cold voice sends a chill right to my core, the hairs on the back of my neck standing. "Had you only followed the rules."

Rules...

"Mother?" I ask into the Void.

The voice laughs, but there's no humor to it. "My clever daughter. I'd been beginning to think you'd lost your brain to that monstrosity."

Monstrosity? What is she talking about?

I can feel her surge of delight as I become more confused.

"Forgetting something, sweetling?" she asks, her voice smug.

My frown deepens. "Forgetting?" I whisper. Something flickers in the back of my mind. A seed of a memory. Not even a memory, but a feeling, or at least the ghost of one.

Everything is black. Everything is pain.

"See you soon, Persephone," my mother promises, her smirk audible.

"Her first." A snarl brings me back to consciousness in a whoosh.

A warm, healing touch glides down my body, warm but foreign. It is not the touch I am used to, not the touch I long for. Heat curls along my skin, and I feel my darkness retreat, hiding from this foreign light. Not my own light, not the light of spring. This is like pure sunshine penetrating, searing through me, filling me with heat.

I force my eyes open, my vision blurry and strained. I shift and groan, wincing in pain.

"Don't move, not yet," a deep voice commands, drawing my attention.

I blink, trying to clear some of the fuzziness and meet the gaze of the person channeling their healing powers into me. Concentration furrows his brow as he seeks out my injuries one by one. His golden hair is pulled up into a messy bun, and his silver eyes bore into mine, shining and molten like the center of the earth.

But... I am confused. Helios doesn't have long hair, and his eyes are caramel brown, not the color of freshly polished steel. This isn't Helios. It must be... Oh, what was his name? I just read about him the other day. I'm sure he plays the flute or something... Oh! Apollo, God of the Sun, Healing, and Music.

A moment of clarity hits, and I turn my head, seeking Hades. I let out a whimper when I see him lying beside me, unconscious. His face is bruised and beaten, and he is still covered in dirt and Titan innards. I suppose I don't look much better.

"Demon?" I whisper, reaching out for his hand. He stirs slightly, and I sit up, nearly head-butting Apollo.

"Hades?" I cup his cheeks, my pain now bearable.

"Take it easy!" Apollo hisses, obviously pissed that I might undo his hard work.

I study Hades's face, my eyes filling with tears. "Help him. Please."

Apollo moves around the bed to Hades' side. He shakes his head. "He insisted I heal you first." Apollo hovers his hand over my head, frowning. "Your healing should have kicked in by now."

I bat his hand away. "Hades now."

Apollo replaces his hand, now at my shoulder, ignoring me.

I snarl, "Hades."

"He said you first," Apollo says. "I'm more scared of him."

My eyes flash, and I feel my blood surge in anger. "Your second mistake. Heal him." I barely recognize my voice, the timbre lower and threatening. I send a wave of my power over him, giving him a taste of it.

"Second mistake?" Apollo asks, looking a little more uncertain.

"Your first was listening to him in the first place and putting yourself in a position to experience my wrath. Heal. Him."

Apollo's confidence fades, and he shifts his attention to Hades, hovering his hand over him. I look down at my husband, his body broken and hurting. His one remaining wing is limp and sitting at an awkward angle, the other gone, torn off.

I place my hand on his chest over his heart and push a little of my magic into him. The bruise under his eye grows a little fainter, but nothing else seems to happen.

We should be healing. Why are we not healing?

"He's not healing," Apollo says, voicing my concern.

I glance at Apollo. "Why?" I know Apollo won't have the answers, but I just feel so fucking helpless.

"Well, he's healing a little, but my magic isn't advancing it. It's his own healing but at a snail's pace. I don't understand it." Apollo's lips tighten as he regards Hades.

I snarl, "What do you mean *a little?*"

Apollo narrows his eyes, but his stance gives away his uncertainty. "I mean a little."

I look back at Hades, cupping his cheeks. "Demon?" My voice cracks on the word, terror constricting my throat.

Hades groans softly, his eyes moving behind his eyelids.

"He's taking some of my power, but it's not going toward healing him. But he does feel stronger. I think."

He will heal. He will heal. He will heal.

I push some more of my vastly depleted stores of magic into him, closing my eyes as I press my forehead to his.

"Please, please, please, please, please," I whisper into him.

The silence that meets me is deafening, but I just keep pushing my power into him, tears flowing freely and falling onto his cheeks.

"I love you. Please, Hades."

I sob softly, almost missing his answering groan. "Persephone…"

Chapter Sixty-Four

Hades

OVERWHELMING WARMTH, the essence of life suffuses me, drawing me to the surface of consciousness. I need to wake up. There's danger near. The Titans are free, and my realm is under attack. I fight to awaken, to be useful. I am a king. And my kingdom is in danger. I am needed. My legs are bound, and it takes only a moment for me to realize they are not foes but friends.

Persephone.

I open my eyes, though it takes several blinks to clear my vision, finding my wife leaning over me. More life rushes into me, pure life, like the first bloom that pushes through the frost, the struggling vine just beginning to ripen. It's not just life. It's *her* life.

"Stop that," I growl.

Persephone is far too weak to be giving me her power. She's still injured. She should preserve all her strength to heal herself. I'll heal, eventually. Just like I always have. Though the Underworld has never been poisoned before, that is just semantics. I'll worry about that after Persephone is healed.

She growls back, pushing more of her power into me. "No."

I narrow my eyes, my shield slamming up against

her. "You need to heal."

It's the same voice I used to order employees and souls. The voice most beings tremble when they hear, and others pray never to hear. They dart their gaze from mine, hoping to leave my sight without delay.

Persephone narrows her eyes at me and slams her power against my shield. I grit my teeth to keep from buckling under the force of her will. It is like holding back a freight train with only my hands. "Hades Plutus. If you don't let me heal you, I swear to all the gods that I will move back into the spare bedroom for the rest of time."

My shield trembles against the force of Persephone's determination, and in small part because of her threat. I grit my teeth. "You heal first. Priority."

Her power hits against my shield, and it falters. I'm far too weak, and she's grown more powerful by the day.

"I'm moving my stuff out as we speak, husband," she growls.

True to her word, vines are uncoiling from my legs and moving to pack her things. I sigh, slowly lowering my shield. "Only a little."

She relaxes slightly, her vines dropping. Her power seeps into me, and my back slowly heals. It might have been worse than I thought. My spine might have been a tiny bit severed. Once she appears satisfied, I finally address the other god in the room.

Apollo comes to my side and pushes on my shoulder to look at my back. I sit up fully to give him a better view of my most serious injury. His magic must have sensed it when he tried to heal me.

"I won't be able to regrow your wing," Apollo says, his voice playing over the room like a melody. "That is on you, Uncle."

Apollo places his hands on my back, patching up some remaining wounds. His healing is rougher than natural regeneration, forcing bone and muscle back to where it belongs. "Where is your father?"

"Out doing your job."

Persephone growls warningly at Apollo, but he's not wrong. It is my job. I'm not just the God of the Dead or King of the Underworld. I'm the Great Warden, the keeper of those beasts too foul to be released.

I wave Apollo away, resting my back against the pillows. "Go help your father."

Apollo nods. "I've done what I can here, anyway."

Apollo bows his head slightly, his golden hair shining. Looking very much the God of Sun, Music, and Prophecy, son of Zeus and Leto. He glows slightly, a halo of light around his head. He is the Olympian version of Helios.

The common misconception of the differences between Titans and Olympians. The ones who overlap, at least, such as Apollo and Helios. While Apollo is the God of the Sun, Helios is the sun. Apollo might be able to force the sun into different positions or set it earlier or later than normal, but Helios could wipe it from existence.

That is the threat we face. The evil we battle. The personifications of the very things most of us hold slight dominion over. We bit the hand that fed us. Not all Titans warred against us. Some took our side in the initial skirmish and had lived with us for the last two thousand years. But the ones who didn't have a score to settle.

Persephone cups my cheek, and I press my forehead to hers. "I'll be fine."

She presses closer to me, careful to avoid my back. "Are you all right?"

My powers were a little too weak to sense her injuries.

She kisses me softly. "Yes."

I touch my chest, feeling the bandages. "I'm rusty."

I don't practice sparring regularly. I work out to clear my mind, but I don't train. It is an oversight I need

345

to remedy. Persephone must have had some formal training based on the way she fought.

She shakes her head. "We were vastly outnumbered."

I press my cheek to the top of her head. "Still. I got distracted."

Once this skirmish is taken care of, Persephone and I will need to dedicate time to hone our abilities as fighters.

"I got distracted," I whisper into her hair. It wasn't just by Persephone on the field. It took barely a second of watching her fight to know she can handle herself.

"By?"

The flash of green as time was shattered.

"My father was on the field," I murmur.

Her body goes rigid against me, knowing what I know. This was planned. It would have been chaotic and unorganized if this were a normal prison break. But for my father to be on the field meant someone went to his cell and freed him. His cell was completely separate from the other Titans and specifically designed to his powers to be inescapable.

I touch my shoulder, wincing. "The wing regrowth will be hard."

She rests a hand on my thigh. "I'll help."

"No more giving me your power," I growl.

She pulls back, glaring up at me. "Do you want a queen who is an equal?"

I narrow my eyes at her. Is that what she thinks this is about? "It has nothing to do with that. It has everything to do with you helping my brothers."

She blanks, her eyes trying to understand what I am saying. I cup her cheek, keeping her focus on me. "You are the queen. I'll only be a hindrance like this. They need you to fight."

She presses her face into my hand, nuzzling it. "But you're mine, and you're hurting."

I nod. "But our realm is threatened." I scan her eyes, laying this burden on her shoulders. "I can't protect it.

346

Will you?"

Her eyes flash with power, and her hair turns black. The first time I've ever seen it change that color.

"Go get them, my warrior queen."

Chapter Sixty-Five

Persephone

INOD AND PRESS A KISS TO HIS LIPS, basking in him for the briefest of moments before pulling back and climbing out of bed. A twang of pain wriggles down my back, and I hide my wince as I walk to the balcony doors. I glance at him over my shoulder. He still looks broken, but maybe he will heal if we defeat the Titans. Or maybe his healing is directly linked to the healing of the Underworld, which is still so fractured.

One thing at a time, P.

Hades' eyes sparkle with pride, and I wink at him before launching myself off the balcony, stretching my wings out to soar to the battlefield.

If I thought it was chaotic before, now the small patches of blood are pools, and the remaining Titans are vicious. Obviously, they are the smartest and strongest of the lot, having hung back while those lower in the ranks tired us out. Now their last line of defense is stepping forward.

Zeus has three Titans collared by lightning and is fighting another two simultaneously. I hate to admit it, but it *is* fairly impressive. Poseidon is locked in battle, but a wave of controlled sea water floods over the field, only taking out the Titans and leaving everyone else untouched. Apollo is off in the distance, the glow radiating off him almost blinding.

I swoop down, decapitating two Titans as I land in the center of the war zone.

Zeus's snarled words cross the hundred feet between us easily. It sounds as if he is right next to me. "Where is he?" His eyes flash in pure rage. He tears the Titan's arms off a second later, throwing them miles in different directions.

I slam my sword into another. Warm, foul blood splatters my face, but I don't have time to feel disgusted. I sense someone behind me and shoot my vines up from the ground, splitting him completely in half. His left and right sides slump wetly to the ground with a sickening thud. By the time I turn to face my victim, he is fading away, back to the cells.

A breeze of salty air passes me, and I turn my head, seeing Poseidon riding a wave to my side, sword in hand.

"You shouldn't be here, Persephone," he calls, sending the wave crashing into an oncoming enemy as he dismounts.

I grab my dagger, slamming it into the head of a Titan, sneaking up behind Poseidon. "This is my realm. I am exactly where I should be."

Zeus casts a bolt of lightning, striking three in a row before joining us. "What should we do?" Poseidon asks him.

Zeus bristles, glancing at me, but his gaze quickly darts to our adversaries, picking out his next victim.

"Don't get in the way," Zeus growls, shooting another bolt of lightning and charging back into battle.

I glare at him and wrap my vines around another Titan. I clench my fist, piercing him with hundreds of poisonous spikes.

I watch Zeus carefully. His fighting is getting sloppier as he loses himself to his anger and the need to spill his father's blood. His eyes dart, seeking. From

349

the wildness in them, I can see that it's going to be the death of all of us.

Fuck.

I launch myself into the sky and land beside Zeus. "Describe him," I demand.

Zeus's eyes flash as he glances at me. "Who?"

"You know who," I growl, not shrinking under his wrath. "I can find him."

Zeus slams his shoulder into a Titan, crushing its chest. "This is my fight. Keep out of it, spring."

"This is my realm. I can find him. I swear I won't touch him."

Zeus pauses, his hand crushing the windpipe of a Titan. He regards me suspiciously. "He looks like Hades. But taller." His lip curls. "And infinitely crueler."

I nod once and launch into the sky, needing to get far enough into the air to channel my tie to the Underworld. I need time to feel for him without being apprehended or attacked.

He looks like Hades, only taller and crueler.

I close my eyes, trying to tune out the noise from below and focus on the realm. My poor, wonderful realm is so broken.

I feel the moment the link snaps into place between us. I feel the pain from the tears in the ground, the sorrow for the new fractures, but I also feel its strength. It's still there, just inaccessible to me right now. I frown as I focus on every foreign being in the realm. Some are easy to identify, like Zeus, Poseidon, and Apollo, but the Titans are more difficult. I take my time identifying each one before I give up. He's long gone.

I fly back down to the ground, landing behind Zeus. "He's not in the realm."

Zeus stills, his hands clenching. He slowly turns, his eyes glowing in fury. His whole body seems to tremble, and before I can react, Poseidon tackles me, taking me to the ground hard.

I'm about to protest and knee Poseidon hard in the

350

balls when another explosion rocks the Underworld. This one is different. I can feel that the realm is no more broken than it was before because, this time, it's not the realm that was blown up. It was Zeus.

I groan in pain under Poseidon. He mostly took the brunt of the explosion, but some shrapnel got in, cutting my face. Poseidon isn't exactly light, and his full body weight is currently pressing my barely healed body into the ragged, hard ground.

Poseidon lifts his head after a moment and snarls, "Get your shit together, asshole!"

Zeus roars, and in another flash, he leaves, no doubt, on the hunt for Kronos.

Poseidon moves off me, offering his hand to help me up.

"Are you all right?" he asks, helping me to my feet.

I stand, looking around. Zeus's meltdown incinerated the last of the Titans. I watch them slowly fade away as they are returned to their cells. Cells that will need to be heavily reinforced when I can find the power to do so, but they will hold for now.

"Persephone?" Poseidon asks, his head tilted as he studies me.

"Hm?"

"Are you okay?" he repeats.

I nod, my brows knitting together. "I just don't understand."

Poseidon crosses his arms over his bare chest.

"I know your father is an asshole, but Zeus wasn't the one that he swallowed." I meet Poseidon's gaze.

He narrows his eyes. "And what do you know about that?" There's an edge to his voice, and I can tell he's irritated.

"I know what my husband told me," I reply, my lips twitching, enjoying how easy it is to get under both of my brothers-in-law's skin.

"No one hates our father more than Z. No one." He pauses and runs his hand through his hair. "You know

351

nothing about this, Persephone. I suggest you keep it that way."

I roll my eyes. "I'm going to check on Hades."

Poseidon sighs, looking around at the wasteland. "Many of the Titans escaped. I will start the hunt. They will all be eager to kill."

"I'll do what I can from here. I can't leave the realm, but I'll reinforce the cells as my power strengthens."

Poseidon nods, vanishing in a whirlpool of water.

I look around again, my heart breaking for my home. "We will restore you. We are strong," I whisper. I stretch my wings and take off into the sky.

Chapter Sixty-Six

Hades

WATCHING HER GLIDE OUT THE WINDOW and onto the field makes my heart thud. The way she easily took command, moving across our kingdom with a discerning eye. As her white wings ride the air, she brandishes the two swords like an avenging angel. No, she's not an angel but a queen. One made of iron and steel, her vines wrapped around this realm and its king.

I struggle from our bed and out to the balcony just in time to see Zeus's lightning illuminate the field, outlining all the Titans still in battle. Poseidon commands the Styx, pulling the haunted souls with it. Persephone is silhouetted against it all as she covers the distance to my brothers. Winged death. My brows furrow for a moment. Where is Thanatos? Hekate? Their parents?

I glance over my shoulder. The Hall of Night is in the other direction of Tartarus. If this were planned, they'd take the most powerful players off the board before attacking. It's what I would do. An enemy fighting without their most powerful weapons is an easy defeat. I close my eyes for a moment, reaching out to that area of the Underworld, sensing that the Primes are in battle themselves. This is a coordinated attack to divide us and draw our attention.

Persephone tucks her wings in, descending like a comet, slicing the heads off two Titans. I concentrate and send my shadows to gather their bodies, returning them to the intact cells.

Sweat slicks my face from that small bit of effort, but I grit my teeth. If Persephone can fight, I can imprison them before they regenerate.

I anchor my hands to the marble railing as my vision blurs. It takes several deep breaths before the dizziness passes. When I look up, Zeus is gone, and Poseidon is helping Persephone to her feet. Fuck, what did I miss?

At least it looks like the Titans have retreated, but I'm too weak to send them to the cells. Shit.

I turn from the balcony, limping to the restroom to wash the sweat off my face. Persephone's scent warns me of her presence before she appears at my side.

I hold my hand up to stop her. "I got it."

She moves past my hand, placing her palm against my chest. "Baby."

"I got it."

She stays at my side, her hand hovering over my back, waiting for me to falter, but I keep my feet under me, taking one step after another until I make it to the bed.

"What happened?" I ask, easing myself down.

Persephone sits next to me. "Zeus exploded."

I curse, glancing at her. "Are you hurt?"

Zeus's power differs greatly from mine or Poseidon's. Our power comes from our emotions, whereas Zeus's power can control his emotions. It makes his volatile, and Zeus is already an extremely volatile god, which makes him explosive.

"I'm okay, but I need to shower. I'm covered in Titan's guts," she says with a cautious smile, trying to lighten the mood.

I struggle back to my feet. "Shower?"

She stands, and the bed cleans itself when she does.

She nods, brushing her lips softly over mine. "You need to lie down."

I growl, limping back to the bathroom, even though each step sends streaks of fiery agony up my back. I lean against the counter, grinding my teeth to stop myself from crying out. "Rinse off. You need to tell me everything."

Persephone sighs, waving her hand, and her vines force me into a seat. She gives me an annoyed look before stripping out of her battle leathers and stepping into the shower to turn it on.

"Why did Z go off?" I ask, trying not to focus on her curves or the way the water is sliding off them. This is really not the time, but it would be easier if she weren't a walking wet dream.

She scrubs her hair. "Your father is not in this realm."

A shiver of foreboding shoots down my spine. Kronos is loose on the world. How long before he regains enough of his power to absorb time without even touching someone? If he is free for too long, he will cross timelines. We need to stop him before that happens.

Persephone glances at me over her shoulder. "Why does Zeus hate him the most?"

Ah, Poseidon must have mentioned that fun little fact. I rub a weary hand over my face. "Zeus was raised to hate him from infancy. Every day, he was trained to fight and destroy him." He was indoctrinated into a world where everything wrong could be laid at our father's feet.

Persephone turns in the shower, finished with her hair. "But you and Poseidon, he—"

"We didn't know why or who. Our hatred was never fostered or bred." There was a time I wanted Zeus's childhood, even envied him for it. He'd gotten time with our mother, time Poseidon and I would never have. But I eventually realized that with the way my powers work, if I had grown up as Zeus had, I would have lost myself to my darkness millennia ago. It thrived off those emotions, and I wouldn't be the man Persephone deserves.

She turns off the shower and wraps herself in a towel. I scan her body. "You sure you're all right?"

She nods and sits next to me. I cup her cheek, pressing my forehead to hers. "Thank you." She places her hands on my chest carefully. "You protected the realm when I couldn't."

She nuzzles her nose gently against mine. "My king was injured. The safety of this realm is just as much my responsibility as yours."

My chest swells hearing that. My queen.

"Back to bed," she orders, standing and helping me to my feet. "I'll get you something to eat."

I shift my weight, flushing slightly that Persephone has to help me back to the bed. "I'm not completely helpless."

She loops my arm over her shoulders. "This will be a lot easier if you stop being a stubborn ass and let me help you."

She settles me into bed, and I growl, "I'm fine."

She glares at me and pulls on a t-shirt and shorts before leaving me alone.

Chapter Sixty-Seven

Persephone

AFTER THE DISASTER I CREATED THE LAST TIME I tried to cook for Hades, I simply ask the Underworld for what I require, knowing it will do a far better job than I can.

In the blink of an eye, without even having to speak the words, a bowl of soup, a sandwich, jello, and ice cream appear on a tray in front of me. Even though the Underworld is fractured, our tie continues to strengthen.

I lift the tray and return to the bedroom to feed my injured mate. Something deep in my gut doesn't sit right, but I can't quite put my finger on it. Something about the way Hades isn't healing feels... wrong. Plus, there are my dreamless nights. Over the past few weeks, whenever I sleep, it's like I fall into a dark void surrounded by nothing.

I'm pulled from my worries when I step into the bedroom, seeing my husband, fearsome God of the Underworld, King of the Dead, completely tangled up in bandages, both new and old. His brow is furrowed in frustrated concentration as he tries to untangle them.

"What are you doing?" I ask, drawing his attention to me. My lips twitch at when his cheeks flush slightly, obviously embarrassed to be caught in such a predicament.

"I was… trying to change my bandages, but it's proving to be," he frowns down at the tangled ribbons of gauze, "difficult."

I walk over to him, placing the tray on the bedside table before gently brushing his hands away. "Let me."

I notice Hades tense a little before releasing the gauze with a heavy sigh. My king is still not used to having someone else around or being looked after. I'm not sure he will ever get used to it after being alone for so long, but I know that for the rest of my existence, I will care for him. I will show him what it feels like to be loved.

I kneel on the bed and dip a cloth into a bowl of water, bringing it to his back to clean his wound.

The second it touches his skin, Hades curses, his body going rigid in pain, and I tense in return. That I'm causing him pain makes my stomach roll.

His wound needs cleaned, P.

I softly kiss his shoulder, gently washing the angry-looking scars. I worry my lower lip as I look at it. It's healing a little, but not fast enough, not how it should be.

"It's getting there," I say encouragingly as I finish cleaning.

"Slowly," Hades groans and exhales, wincing as I wrap the clean bandages around his chest. "I'm too tied to the Underworld."

I kiss his shoulder again as I wrap him, protecting the wound.

"Poseidon texted while you were in the kitchen. He said many Titans escaped." Hades exhales sharply as I tug on the bandage too hard. I wince, apologizing under my breath.

"They're dealing with it," I say, focused on my task so I don't hurt him again.

"This was my job, Persephone," Hades says, relaxing back onto the bed as I finish.

I shift with him, cupping his cheeks. "Hades, for thousands of years, you have more than done your job. My mother was behind this. We both know that. And she will pay."

Hades scans my eyes, the sapphire a little duller than usual due to his injuries and weakness. "I haven't, though. Look what's happened. I should have expected this, planned for it, been more prepared."

Seeing his emotional pain is a thousand times more heartbreaking than his physical pain. I lean forward, pressing my forehead to his, trying to provide some comfort. Nothing I can say will convince him this was not his fault. He has worked tirelessly for this realm, and my mother is a cruel and calculating woman with allies in high and low places.

"We don't even know how she did this, demon. How were you to plan?" I ask, hoping to break his logic enough that he stops blaming himself. I need to erase that look of defeat from his perfect face.

"Fuck, I don't know," he concedes.

I pull back, searching his face. "Tell me what to do."

Hades sighs heavily and places his hand on my thigh. "It's fine. It will heal." I know he's not just talking about his injuries. He's talking about the Underworld, his ego, and his heart.

I place my hands on his chest, pushing more of my power into him. I'd give him everything just to make it better.

"Persephone. Enough. You need your power," Hades growls.

Stubborn, devastatingly handsome asshole.

I put on my most animated puppy dog eyes and pout my bottom lip. "Just a little? Please?"

I feel Hades soften a little under my touch, looking a little more unburdened, but he still shakes his head. "We need to reinforce the cells, my spring. I can wait."

I sigh heavily but nod. He's right. We have prisoners we need to keep locked up forever. Plus, we need to

359

prepare for the ones the other gods will send back, hopefully sooner rather than later. And when Zeus finds Kronos, we will need cells much stronger than the ones we had before. I imagine he won't be returned to us in one piece. Maybe we could put each body part in different cells. *Good luck regenerating then, dick.*

Hades holds out his hands to me, and I place mine into them. He smiles at me and then closes his eyes. I follow suit and drop all guards between us, feeling our power collide in a mess of symphonies, swirling and rushing, like lovers that had been kept apart for decades, only to finally reunite. Hades' immense power courses through me, and I push mine into him.

If this is his power while he is weakened... woah.

Apollo said that his power is still intact, but something is wrong with his healing abilities. That feeling of unease returns to my stomach, but I push it aside, focusing on Hades only. I let him lead as he pushes our power where it needs to go.

I feel his hand tremble slightly, his power waning but still so overwhelming. It's as if his power is still there, but the issue is with Hades' ability to wield it.

I push more of my power in, taking most of the strain. I feel a bead of sweat slide down my forehead as we work, panting with each brick we replace with a reinforced one. Even the Underworld seems to quiver at the amount of energy we're drawing from it.

I wince, groaning softly, but I push more in. "Take more from me."

Hades opens himself up a little, taking more of my power. "We got this. A little longer, baby," he pants, his voice strained.

I lean against him and focus harder, both of us trembling as we feel the last brick slot into place. I groan and slump to the side, careful not to hurt Hades. "Fuck."

"It's done. There is nothing more we can do for now," Hades says, wiping his brow.

I place my hand on his arm, trying to give him a little more of my strength, knowing how big a toll that took on him, but I only have the smallest of sparks left.

"Menace." Hades smirks, looking down at me.

I can feel his exhaustion and nuzzle my cheek against his arm. "Please eat something."

"You should eat, too."

I shake my head. "It's for you, demon. Eat."

Hades glances at the tray and takes half of the sandwich, biting into it. As he eats, I slowly see the color return to his cheeks. He obviously hadn't realized how hungry he was because he immediately eats the second one, then all the soup, then the dessert.

I exhale heavily, relaxing slightly now that I've seen him eat. "Rest." I slide my hand into his, squeezing once.

"You rest," Hades growls, and I just barely keep from rolling my eyes.

My controlling demon.

"We should *both* rest," I say with a smile, cuddling into his side.

Hades winces as he shifts in the bed, turning to face me. "I love you, Persephone."

I cup his cheek and kiss him tenderly. "I love you, Hades."

I shuffle closer to him, wanting to cuddle but knowing it would cause him pain, so I settle for just being pressed against him. Hades, obviously feeling similarly, wraps his uninjured arm around me, pulling me into him and burying his face into my hair.

I bury my face against his neck and inhale, my eyes drifting closed.

"We only have a week before I can't leave the Underworld anymore," Hades says.

"You wouldn't be leaving without me anyway," I growl.

Hades kisses my head, and I can hear the smile in his voice. "True, but it means we can't hunt down our escaped prisoners."

I shrug. "Let you brothers do the work for a change."

Hades laughs and though it's weaker than usual, it still gives me a surge of serotonin. "You want Zeus and Poseidon messing this up?"

"They won't mess it up." I kiss his neck softly. "Their realms are in even more danger than ours."

"What do you mean?" Hades says, and I can feel his frown.

"Well, where are the Titans trying to get to?"

Chapter Sixty-Eight

Hades

WHERE WERE THE TITANS TRYING TO GET TO? Where? If they wanted revenge, why not stay and focus on my brothers and me? We were the ones who usurped them. Why would my father run from the field? I bury my hand in Persephone's hair, watching as the brown becomes red in the right lighting. Red to brown. Brown to red. Red. Brown. Brown. Red.

How did he get out? If this was planned… I considered it, but how could that have escaped my notice? I might have been slightly distracted by Persephone, but I would have felt the beginning of the explosion in Tartarus. I would have felt more. It could be tied to whatever was poisoning the Underworld. My brain jumps from one possibility to another, from one plan to another. All of it brings me back to what Persephone asked. *Where were they trying to get to?*

If I were imprisoned and found myself free, where would I go?

Where would I go?

I bolt up, the sudden movement tearing my wound open, but I ignore it. "Where's my phone?" I look around, even as blood drips down my back.

"You have to be more careful, Hades," Persephone

growls. She puts her hands on my back, pushing her power into me, even as I grasp my phone and frantically call Z. I have to be wrong. Please, let me be wrong. There is one betrayal that I know cut my father deeper than any other. But he can't—

"What?" Zeus answers, his voice a gathering storm.

"He's going after Gaia."

His mother. The being who turned the tide in the war. He'll see her as the greatest betrayer, and then he'll come for us. She's the biggest threat to him returning to power.

Zeus pauses, and Persephone freezes, listening to me, her eyes widening with alarm.

"He already has her."

I hiss out a breath. "How do you know?"

"I'm looking at her corpse."

The icy hand shoots down my spine, and I whisper shakily, "No."

Gods could be killed, despite our healing abilities. A beheading won't do it, nor will fire, but we could die. It is what comes after death that can be lethal to anyone near. To bring about true death, you need to absorb their power. Most of us can't handle that. Our bodies are designed to only hold a certain amount of strength. It is just as likely you will die as your target. Only gods who are insane even think to attempt it.

Persephone shifts, moving closer to hear Zeus.

I rub my hand down my face. "If he's killed her, he won't be able to contain her power."

He's too powerful on his own to contain his mother's power.

"Not if someone else took her place, a weaker god," Zeus adds, his tone serious.

I pause, putting the pieces together, and snarl, "Demeter."

It wasn't my father, after all. All of us had wondered how Demeter could interfere with the Underworld. She killed Gaia and took her power. Demeter was strong,

364

but she wasn't at the level of Kronos. This is how she was able to trap me in the Heart of Tartarus. The pieces of the puzzle finally click into place.

I glance at Persephone. "Your mother killed a Primordial and stole her power."

Persephone pales, shaking her head. "How?"

"Any sign of how she killed her?" I ask Zeus.

I move the phone away from my ear so Persephone can hear more clearly.

"No idea," Zeus says. "But for some reason, I get the feeling she's been planning this for a while."

She must have. This isn't the behavior of a mother trying to regain her daughter. This is cold, calculated, and methodical. Fuck, it sounds like one of my plans.

Persephone gets out of bed to pace back and forth. Cerberus lifts his heads from the floor, watching her as she goes back and forth.

"I only have a week left," I say to Zeus, keeping an eye on Persephone.

A week until I won't be able to leave the Underworld at all.

"I'll come by tonight," Zeus adds.

I open my mouth to respond, but Zeus hangs up.

I look at the phone. "Bye, I guess." I focus on Persephone. "Zeus is going to come by tonight."

She doesn't look at me, mumbling under her breath, pacing back and forth in sharp turns.

"My spring?" I ask.

She looks at me. "I can make this all go away." I tilt my head, trying to read her face, but it's hard and cold. Two things Persephone has never been. "I bet this plan has been in place since my mother learned of the prophecy."

I nod. "That's what I believe as well."

It's the only explanation. Demeter would have realized Persephone's fate. She'd spent the last two hundred years preparing herself for when the prophecy came true, and Persephone met me.

365

"But I know my mother. This isn't her end goal."

I tense. Persephone's and my trains of thought are becoming scarily similar. "I won't let her take you," I growl.

She softens, looking at me. "Hades—"

"No. She won't. I'll die first."

She returns to the bed and crawls into my arms, pressing her lips to mine.

I inhale her scent and revel in her taste. "We'll figure it out together." Together, as king and queen. I'm not alone anymore, and neither is she.

She nods, and I yawn, unable to fight the exhaustion weighing me down.

Persephone pulls back, and I shift to lie down, finding the perfect position that doesn't make my vision blur with pain before pulling her across my chest.

"Sleep, demon."

I yawn again and let sleep take me.

Chapter Sixty-Nine

Persephone

I STARE AT THE NEWLY REPAIRED BALCONY DOORS, the moonlight streaming in, casting a cool white glow through the room. Hades sleeps beneath me. His body relaxed, and his mind at ease.

I can't envy his deep slumber. He's exhausted, both emotionally and physically. I am too, but it's good that at least one of us will be well-rested.

My restless mind aches with all the thoughts rolling around it. The events of the past month are completely overwhelming me. I have no idea why it's all happening at this moment, but nothing I do seems to quell the unease that's settling heavily on me. Not even the feeling of Hades' chest rising and falling below me, not the feeling of his heat seeping into me, not the way his scent surrounds me. None of it soothes the feelings of trepidation.

I close my eyes, willing myself to sleep, my brain a storm of thoughts and theories, until the blackness consumes me.

"My Persephone, my flower. What a predicament you are in, sweetling."

Nothing but black. Nothing but that voice. All of my senses are completely paralyzed apart from being able to hear her voice taunting me.

"You have made this so much more difficult than it had to be. And for that, you will be punished, sweetling."

Punished? For what?

"M-mother? I can't... I can't see."

My mother's laugh fills the void, and then her voice sounds as if it's coming from directly behind me. "Then open your eyes."

I gasp and lift my lashes, flinching at the bright Olympus sunshine cascading into the room, reflecting off the bright whites and pastels of my bedroom.

I sit up and frown when I notice my mother isn't in the room with me.

But she told me to...

I shove my feet into the slippers that are directly beside my bed, as always. I stretch, lifting my arms above my head. A slight breeze blows through the window, making me shiver and my skin pebble from the cold, my thin white nightgown doing nothing to warm me.

The usual scents of daffodils and freshly cut grass don't surround me. Instead, I smell musk with hints of oranges.

I'm forgetting something. What am I forgetting? What is that scent? It smells like... home.

I hear a snarl, and then I'm plunged back into darkness and the now silent abyss.

"Fuck."

Sleep moves to the periphery of my brain as I ascend to consciousness, but my longing to stay asleep leaves me in limbo between the two. The bed shifts following the loud curse, and instinctively I move closer to the warmth beside me. I push my power into it, wanting to repair what I can feel is obviously damaged.

I nuzzle into the warmth, frowning when my power is refused, and it snaps back into me. The bed shifts again, and then the warmth is gone. I roll toward the scent of citrus and sandalwood, burying my face into what feels like the best-smelling cloud I have ever encountered.

The latch of the door clicks as it closes, and I'm dragged back into consciousness as reality washes over me.

Hades...

I hear him curse again, and my lips twitch as I finally open my eyes. Our dark rumpled sheets are the first thing I see. I nuzzle his pillow and inhale deeply before climbing out of bed and following him into the bathroom.

He's already in the shower, his chin tilted up, eyes closed as the steaming water cascades down on him. I take a minute to appreciate him. Not only is he a god in his power, but also in the way he has been molded. He is pure sinful perfection. My eyes are drawn to the wound on his back. While it looks more healed today, it also looks worse. The gash is smaller, but the wound looks black.

I step into the shower behind him and softly kiss his shoulder.

"I didn't mean to wake you," he says, the deep timbre of his voice lower in his post-sleep haze.

I loop my arms through his and around his waist, kissing his shoulder again. "Let me help you."

Hades turns in my arms, cupping my cheeks. His eyes bore into mine, searching them. "You look tired, my spring."

I reach past him and grab the loofah. I step back and drop my eyes as I pour soap on it and rub it over his chest.

"Persephone," Hades grabs my hands as I wash the hard plains of his chest, "you need rest."

I lean in, kissing his collarbone. "I need to take care of my husband."

Hades pulls me closer, lifting my chin so I look up at

369

him again. "You need to be well rested for that."

"Not for this bit. Please, demon. Let me help you."

Hades concedes, cupping my cheek again and leaning down to brush the softest of kisses against my lips.

I take that as permission for me to continue and grab the shampoo. I step back and gesture for him to turn, both to clean his hair and also to get a proper look at his back. Hades turns, and I move in closer, brushing my fingers under the wound, worry filling me.

While the wound has reduced marginally in size, it's all mostly black now. It looks dead, and small black veins are streaking from it.

"How's it looking?" Hades asks, and I pull my fingers from his skin immediately.

"I'm not sure," I reply honestly. "We should probably see a healer."

I tunnel my fingers into his hair, lathering the shampoo into his scalp. Hades winces as he leans down so I can reach his head, but his muscles relax under the massage.

"It'll be fine. As the Underworld heals, so will I."

I eye the wound skeptically, unsure how much to push the issue. Surely, Hades has more experience with this than I do. So, he must be right.

I kiss his shoulder when I finish, and he straightens. After running his head under the water, he takes the shampoo from me and shifts our positions. He rubs the soap into my hair.

I look up at him, his fingers expertly rubbing my scalp. "Hi."

Hades smiles and presses a kiss to my temple.

I close my eyes. "I love you."

Hades angles my head back as he rinses out my hair, kissing my neck. "I love you too."

I place my hand on his chest, craving the feel of his skin under my fingers, needing to feel his heartbeat beneath my palm.

Hades conditions my hair and washes my body as best as he can without moving too much. All too soon, I pull away from him, knowing we can't get distracted. He's too injured.

"You need to eat."

Hades' eyes darken, and he licks his lips. "I do. I want to devour you," he growls.

I can feel my cheeks heat, but I push the thought away, reaching up to cup his jaw. "You are far too injured for anything like that, demon. I'll make you breakfast."

"Fine," Hades half groans, half growls.

My lips twitch, and I tamp down the flame of desire stoking low in my tummy. I step out of the shower and wrap a towel around myself before grabbing one for him.

Hades loosely wraps the towel around his waist, the tempting V of his obliques making my eyes want to drift south, where I *know* he's hard beneath that towel. I can see it in my damned peripheral vision. I turn from him, moving to the mirror and wiping it clear of condensation.

Hades rolls his shoulder, wincing. "Will you wrap it for me?"

I glance at him over his shoulder. "Of course, demon."

I pull the stool out from the vanity, and Hades sits down in front of me. I wrap his shoulder, concentrating hard to ensure it's supportive but not so tight that it's uncomfortable.

Concentration isn't easy, considering Hades watches me with desire-filled, near-black eyes in the mirror.

I furrow my brows as I bind his chest, tilting my head slightly.

"You get the cutest line between your eyebrows when you concentrate," Hades says, a note of amusement in his otherwise sinful voice.

My eyes flick to meet his in the mirror, my brow

smoothing. My lips curl at the corners, and my gaze lingers on his for a long moment before I focus on the job at hand.

"Plus," Hades' voice turns wicked, "your hands on me."

I fix the bandage and move to slide my hands over his strong shoulders. "What about them?"

"I love it," he replies, sending a shiver down my spine.

I bend, kissing up his neck to just below his ear.

"If you don't want me to devour you, my spring, you need to stop," he growls.

I bite his earlobe before pulling back. "I'll stop."

He growls again, and it's such a possessive, raw, guttural sound that I don't know how I hold myself back from pouncing on him.

I dig my nails slightly into his shoulders before pulling back. "Breakfast."

Hades meets my gaze in the mirror, the sapphire almost completely swallowed up by his pupils. "Breakfast."

I swallow and take another step back, my heart slamming in my chest and my core throbbing with need. I bite my lip and look him over once more before leaving the bathroom to dress and make him breakfast.

Chapter Seventy

Hades

PERSEPHONE'S VINES SNAP MY LAPTOP SHUT, and I barely pull my fingers back in time. I narrow my eyes at her, growling in annoyance. I had business to catch up on. The mortals in my employ did not know about the breakout. They could never know. I needed to act normal like everything was perfect.

She glides across the floor, placing the tray in my lap, the very picture of an irate Florence Nightingale.

I give her a dark look. "I can work, too."

I might be injured, but with a bit of rest, my brain is already ready to get to work. I was in contact with Hephaestus about creating a device that could track the escaped Titans. It will help to at least narrow the enormous haystack of millions of realms down a little. I also had a myriad of other tasks stacking up at Plutus Industries.

She shakes her head, sitting on the edge of the bed next to me. "Nope. Eat."

She lifts the spoon to my lips, and I take an angry bite, swallowing. "Laptop."

She glances at me, her eyes sparking. "You can have your laptop." I glance immediately at the electronic pushed to the side. But the sound of a zipper lowering has my eyes snapping back to my wife. "Or you can have breakfast with a show. Just because you can't touch doesn't mean you can't look."

Oh, my spring, I think sometimes you forget exactly who your husband is. My shadows snap to attention, the sleep having helped my power regenerate. I send them to trail along her skin, shadowy fingers tunneling into her hair.

Her hands drop from the zipper, leaving it partially open, letting me take control. What a good girl. So obedient.

My shadows move along her skin, gliding over it, and my fingers twitch with the ghostly sensation. They slip under her top and guide the zipper down, my eyes locking with hers. Her breath trembles as the shadows quickly divest her of her clothes until she stands naked before me.

I keep my eyes on her as I lift the fork to my mouth, taking a bite. Her nipples tighten beneath my gaze, the tight buds making my mouth water. She traces her hands down her body, following the shadows as they slide over her skin. The shadows multiply, touching every inch of her, making her achingly aware. Her head rolls back, and she moans as her hand slides up her neck.

"Eyes on me," I snap.

Her head comes forward, her eyes locking on me. I take another slow bite, the picture of unaffected calm, even as my cock is about to break through the tray over my lap.

My shadows explore her body, making her sway to a silent melody. Persephone moans, the palace supplying music without either of us speaking. I shift slightly, my cock aching. The shadows trail up her neck, piling her hair on top of her head. My lips tingle as the shadows suck on her neck.

"Hades," she whimpers.

Fuck, I love when she whimpers and begs. I growl,

and the shadows press her back on the bed, spreading her legs and exposing her to me.

She gasps. "Wait." She shakes her head slightly. "We should wait until... you're better."

The shadows don't stop, my lips turning to a wicked smirk. "I'm feeling just fine, and you promised a show."

She lets out a soft moan as the shadows lift her knees, opening her further to me. They mimic my cock, pressing into her pussy, but they keep themself as light as possible, allowing me to watch each thrust inside her. I lick my lips, seeing how wet she is.

"Your cunt is dripping," I groan, and she cries out, rocking and arching.

"Hades, please!" She pants.

Her body stiffens slightly as my shadows explore more of her, probing her ass for me. I'm going to fuck her there soon, but I have to get her ready first. For now, my shadows will prepare her. I slip them into her ass, savoring the tightness, imagining it gripping my cock.

I growl, shifting closer, my cock pulsing in time with my shadows thrusting inside her. I lift the coffee cup to my lips. "Please, what?"

She squirms, her breath coming in small sobs as my shadows press inside both holes. "We need... to stop."

"But I'm having so much fun."

She moans, wiggling against the shadows. "More than if you were inside me?"

I lick my lips, watching the shadows. I growl, "Never."

She rocks her hips, her head falling back, but she remembers and snaps up a moment later, keeping her eyes on me.

Good girl.

She squeezes the shadows, trying to close her legs against the feeling, but they keep her spread.

"Come for me, my spring. I want to watch."

She screams as the orgasm tears through her, her

body arching and writhing as if she only needed my permission to send her over the edge.

She pants as she slowly comes down from the orgasm, the shadows slowly lowering her legs back to the bed.

Her eyes are feral, and her breathing ragged. She turns over and crawls toward me like a tigress, sighting prey. She waves her hand, her vines whisking the tray from my lap.

Chapter Seventy-One

Persephone

MY SKIN STILL TINGLES FROM THE FEEL of his shadows, my pussy throbbing from my orgasm, but I need more. I need to give him pleasure. It is a desire so undeniable that not even the flicker of guilt that I might hurt him deters me.

I'm hurting by leaving him wanting.

"What are you doing?" Hades asks, raising an eyebrow, his eyes black.

I tug down the sheet and kneel between his legs. "I'm caring for my husband."

"Is that right?" Hades growls, his voice filled with need.

Slowly, I let my eyes drift down his body, taking in every hard plain, every muscle, every magnificent inch of him until my gaze lands on his crotch. His hard cock thrust proudly beneath his pajama pants.

My mouth goes dry, and I pull my bottom lip between my teeth.

Perfection.

I lift my gaze to meet his and stare into his feral eyes as I curl my fingers into the waistband of his pants. Hades shifts to help me pull them off, wincing slightly. Any reluctance his flinch gives me fades away as his cock springs free.

Fuck. Will I ever get used to this?

Hades pants as he watches me slowly bend to lick the swollen crown of his cock. His responding groan sends a jolt of pleasure between my legs, and I moan as I take him into my mouth, sucking shallowly, teasingly, at the head.

"You suck my cock so good, baby," Hades groans and tangles his fingers in my hair, moving it away from my face so he can watch his cock disappear between my lips.

I take another inch, teasing him with the promise of what is coming.

"Suck it like a good girl. Like *my* good girl," Hades growls, arching lightly.

His words turn me feral, and I drop my head, taking his cock deeper until I'm choking on his length.

Hades hisses, his fingers tightening in my hair. "Fuck! You looked so perfect, full of my shadows, taking me."

I work his cock deeper into my mouth, my throat constricting around the head as I gag on him, desperate for more of him, for everything. I feel my arousal slide down my thighs as I suck his cock hard, hollowing my cheeks as I take him deep again.

"Fuck… wait…" Hades growls, yanking my head off his cock.

I frown and pull back, worried I hurt him. I wipe my mouth with the back of my hand and sit up.

"Demon? What's wrong?" I ask, studying his face.

"I was about to cum." Hades pants, his eyes black.

My brows furrow. "Okay, so why did you stop me?"

"I have a theory."

"Oh?" I blink.

"I think you could heal me with that perfect cunt of yours," he growls.

I blush, my core throbbing almost painfully.

"Ride me, Persephone. We can be gentle." Hades'

commanding tone only makes the ache intensify.

"Hades… I might hurt you."

"Fuck me. Now, my queen."

I moan and carefully straddle his hips, my dripping pussy hovering just over his cock, barely touching. I pant, looking at him.

"You will tell me if it hurts?"

Hades nods, and I slowly lower myself down on him, reminded once again that the shadows are the weakest of placeholders for the real thing.

His hard, thick shaft fills me, stretching my cunt almost to the point of pain, the burn sending exquisite pleasure dancing through me. The sweetest agony is knowing that I will never be able to get enough of this man, this god, this king.

I continue to lower my hips until I'm fully seated, digging my nails into his arms as I try to keep myself from moving. I study his face, looking for even the smallest hint of pain, but there is only ecstasy.

I want to move, but I wait another moment, needing to be sure.

"Move, Persephone," Hades growls.

I groan in relief as I lift my hips and drop them again, still trying to be careful, but fuck, this feels incredible.

"Shit. You're so perfect," Hades says, moving his hands to my hips, digging his fingers in hard. The bite of pain sends a wave of pleasure through me, making my toes curl.

I move faster, losing myself to the pleasure, losing myself to him. Nothing else matters at this moment, only him, me, and our connection.

"Hades… fuck…" I moan. He guides me, slamming me down harder on his cock.

"So tight on me," Hades growls.

I throw my head back, the pleasure taking complete control over me as I bounce on his cock. The sounds of our skin slapping, his cock sliding into my soaked pussy, and our grunts and moans of pleasure fill the room.

I feel my orgasm, just out of reach, but the look of pure rapture on his face brings it closer. I slam my lips to his, kissing him desperately.

Hades growls into my mouth, his hands moving to my ass, digging his fingers in, controlling my hips as he slams me down on his cock over and over.

I pull back, moaning, my body telling me exactly what it needs. "Bite me."

Hades doesn't waste a second. He sinks his fangs into my shoulder, biting down hard.

My whole body tenses and I throw my head back, screaming as I find my release. My orgasm shatters within me, completely obliterating me. Hades slams into me and roars. His body tenses and I feel his release filling me. I press my forehead to his, panting as I slowly come down from my orgasm.

"Menace." Hades chuckles, spanking my ass lightly.

I laugh, kissing him tenderly before moving off him. "How am I the menace?"

"By being so fucking irresistible," Hades growls.

I climb out of bed on shaky legs and pull on my silk robe before covering him with the sheet and putting the tray back in his lap.

Hades blinks at me. "How am I supposed to eat after that?"

"You need your strength."

Hades shifts. "Come here and feed me?"

My lips twitch, and my heart squeezes.

My needy god.

I move the tray and grab the bowl of oatmeal before climbing into his lap. I nuzzle into his neck, kissing him softly. "Is this okay?"

Hades kisses my head. "It's perfect."

I snag his lips with mine, kissing him deeply. Hades smiles against my lips, and I pull back, offering him a spoonful. Hades takes the bite, and I nuzzle his jaw as

380

he eats.

He grabs a strawberry from the tray and offers it to me. "Eat."

I bite the fruit and then go back to nuzzling him, running my fingers through his hair, needing to be close to him.

"Eat more," Hades growls, picking up the plate of pancakes and offering me a bite. I hold a spoonful of oatmeal to his lips. He needs this to strengthen himself.

He closes his lips, glaring at me. *Stubborn god.*

"Hades," I growl.

"You need to eat more."

"Will you just let me nuzzle you? Gods." I roll my eyes but eat the bite of the pancake, and as a reward, he also takes one.

"Persephone?" All playfulness has gone from his voice.

I tense. "Yes?"

"How bad is it?"

I know he's referring to the wound that seems to get blacker by the minute. I had already planned to call a healer today.

"It's... worth watching," I reply. In the limbo between being honest and trying not to alarm him.

Hades turns his head, trying to look at it before exhaling heavily. I climb off his lap and move around to look at it. The black veins stretching from him have gotten darker and grown. I need to accept that it's not healing. It is, in fact, getting worse, and I have a sinking feeling there is nothing any healer will be able to do.

A memory flashes through my mind. Something about Olympus...

"Mother?" I look up from the ruined petals of my favorite flower in the garden. The once vibrant purple petals are now dull and rimmed with brown, black veins tracking through them.

"Yes, sweetling?" my mother replies from her vegetable garden, cutting some leaves from her pumpkin patch.

I look down at my dying flower, cupping it gently, trying to make it better, but nothing is happening.

"My flower... it's..." My vision blurs as my eyes fill with tears.

My mother tilts her head at me. "It is dying."

I look at my mother. She doesn't seem affected at all.

"But I took such good care of it. I'm trying to fix it, but—"

"This is what consequences look like, sweetling," my mother interrupts. I try to blink back my tears, but they fall down my cheeks uselessly. "Next time, you know better than to defy me."

I swallow. "But, Mother, I didn't mean—"

"Luckily, I corrected your mistake with Hera. But next time, I will ruin your entire bed of flowers, and you will be confined to your room for a month. Understand?"

I look down at my dying flower, knowing it is hurting, feeling pain for my mistake.

"Do you understand, Persephone?" My mother's stern tone cuts through me like a knife.

I swallow, trying to hide my distress. "I understand, Mother."

I continue to stare at the flower, helpless, knowing there's nothing I can do against my mother's poison. I know she could reverse it so easily, but she never will.

But she never will.

I stare at the wound on his back. My mother would need allies to achieve this. If I am right, she has poisoned not only Hades, the King of the Underworld but the Underworld itself.

There are lots of unanswered questions, but there is one that I know the answer to. There is only one way to stop this.

Hades will not heal. The Underworld will not heal.

My mother has won.

Chapter Seventy-Two

Persephone

SHE'S WON, and no matter what scenarios I think up, I can't find a way out of this.

Hades runs his fingers through my hair, nuzzling the top of my head.

Fuck. Why is everything so difficult? Why did we waste so much time fighting and actively trying to be angry with one another?

"Hades?" I ask, drawing shapes on his chest, basking in him.

"Yes, my spring?"

The pet name shatters me. I struggle to hold back my raging screams of sorrow and defeat, but it's an effort to make my voice even. "You know that you are everything to me. Right?"

I feel him nod against my head. "As you are to me."

I kiss his chest, my heart breaking. "I would do anything to keep you safe."

Hades goes very still. "Is everything all right, Persephone?"

I nuzzle into his chest, trying to find comfort in his scent and warmth. "It's just… things haven't been easy between us, and I need you to know how deeply," I swallow, holding back my tears, "how deeply I love you."

Hades gently pinches my chin, tilting my head up. I barely have enough time to school my face, to hide my agony. "I do. And you know how much I love you?"

I look into his eyes, nodding.

He scans my eyes. "Even when we fight, there is no bottom to the depths of my love for you. You could look through this world, and the next and the next, and still never find the end of it."

I cup his cheek. "I don't regret a single second of us. You," my voice shakes, "are my beginning, my end, and everything in between."

Hades' eyes shine with unshed tears, and he leans his face into my hand. "Even when I infuriate you?"

"It only makes my love for you burn more ferociously." I smile, but I'm not convinced it does anything to hide my inner turmoil. "You should sleep for a while."

"You too. You've not been sleeping enough."

I kiss him softly, and we both shift, getting comfortable. My head resting back on his chest, his steady heartbeat sounds stronger than it did previously, but I know the poison will persist.

Hades' body relaxes, his breath evening out as he falls into a deep sleep, but I don't move. Silent tears fall down my cheeks. I know what I have to do, and I know I have to do it now. I lift my head, taking him in. This might be the last time I see him where he doesn't look at me with hatred. This may be the last time I look at him, knowing he loves me with every fiber of his being. I don't want to leave him. I don't want him to be alone again, but I need him to be alive.

I will return to him.

I make it a vow to him, myself, and the universe. Even if I have to kill my mother and burn Olympus to the ground, I will return to him.

I place my hand over his heart, taking in the planes of his face, his soft but firm full lips, and how his eyelashes brush against his cheek as he dreams. His jaw, his cheeks, committing every beloved feature to memory, not knowing when I will see him next.

He is mine. I am his.

I climb out of bed carefully, wiping the tears from my cheeks before I grab my phone. The second I have it in my hand, the heartbreak snaps into pure, unadulterated fury. I walk to the bathroom, glancing back at him before I enter. In sleep, he has grabbed my pillow and buried his face into it. My heart twinges at the sight, but the anger licks beneath my skin. I need to do this for him.

I step into the bathroom, lock the door, and turn the shower on, not wanting any of my conversation to travel. The spikes beneath my skin are ready to break through, but I force them back. I am in control. I scroll through my phone, finding the number I've not used for years. My stomach knots when I see the contact roll onto the screen. I press the call button and hold the phone to my ear, the shrill ring setting me more on edge.

"Hello, Daughter," my mother's cruel voice answers on the third ring, and my blood both surges and turns to ice at the sound.

"Mother."

"To what do I owe the honor of this phone call after such a long time? Perhaps calling to inform me of your nuptials?" I can hear the smugness in her voice, and my grip tightens on the phone.

"What are you doing, Mother? You have never wanted Gaia's power," I hiss, keeping my voice relatively hushed.

My mother laughs evilly. "A mortal woman can lift a car from her infant child if she needs to. You think I would not do the same?"

I scoff. "You compare my marriage to an infant being trapped under a car?"

I hear my mother tap her nails against something. "I compare your *kidnapping* to being trapped under the

385

car."

Kidnapping?

I grind my teeth. "What have you done to him?"

"Whoever do you mean, sweetling?" I can hear the smirk in her voice.

"Hades. What have you done to Hades?" I ask, trying to quell my frustration and anger.

"Oh, dear, is something wrong with your captor?" She pauses. "How very tragic."

"What did you do?" I snarl.

"You disobeyed me. These are the consequences. You should know all about that, Daughter."

My whole body goes tense. It's not a surprise, but I'd had a sprig of hope that maybe she would be reasonable. I thought I could talk her down and get her to agree to a situation where I spent some time with her and then some time here. It's clear now, though, she would not have gone to such lengths for just a part of me.

I cling to the phone. "Reverse it."

"No." Her voice is almost bored at the request like she's disappointed in me, but I don't care. It's something I'm all too familiar with.

"Why are you doing this?" My voice breaks, and I curse myself for it. "Just to get me back in Olympus?"

"What mother wouldn't sacrifice the world for their child?"

"I love him, Mother." I don't know why I say it. It will not help my case.

"You don't know what love is, sweetling," she replies, her voice almost soothing.

Gods, here she is—the master manipulator.

I shake my head, even though I know she can't see me. "I do love him. He is the only person I have ever loved. He is the only person who has ever seen me, truly *seen* me, and he loves every inch, every flaw and quirk." I take a breath, the tears now falling freely. "If you have ever loved me, Mother, if you have ever felt

386

anything but a need to possess me, I'm begging you to stop this."

She laughs coldly. "I'm disappointed in you, Persephone. Are you begging for a man? Where is your independence? Your confidence? Look at what *he* has turned you into," she practically spits down the phone at me, her words filled with revulsion and disappointment. But I don't care anymore, and I haven't for a long time.

"Look what you turned me into," I hiss. "A woman who couldn't wait to escape her overbearing, cruel disgrace of a mother. A mother who cares more for her daughter's appearance and power than for who she really is."

My mother croons, "Now, now, Persephone. Don't forget who holds your captor's life in their hands. Maybe I should speed up the process a little."

"Mother, please," I beg.

"Please, what?" my mother spits. "Do you want me to spare him? Take the infection from his realm that will only continue to spread until he is consumed and the realm destroyed?"

"Mother," I sob, "no. Please, don't do this."

"You want to save them?" my mother asks.

I sniff and wipe my tears, sinking into the numbness, knowing what she will ask of me. "Tell me what you want, and I'll… I'll do it."

"I want my daughter home. Where she belongs."

I belong here. I belong with Hades.

I want to scream. I want to explode. I want to rip my heart from my chest and present it to Hades. It is his and always will be. Instead, I close my eyes in resignation. "Would I have your word?" I ask my words barely a whisper.

"I would swear it on Styx."

"Your word that you will stop the infection, restore Hades' wings, health, and the health of the Underworld. Then release Gaia's power back where it belongs."

387

"Of course, sweetling," my mother says, her voice sickly sweet.

"One more condition," I add, and I can practically feel my mother's frustration. A small win.

"I get a week to say goodbye to Hades."

"You have twenty-four hours. And Persephone?" My stomach sinks.

I wait for her addition, my whole body shaking.

"Try to escape this bargain, and I'll show you the exact lengths I will go to in order to get my daughter home."

The line clicks as my mother hangs up the phone. I fall back against the door and slide to the floor, finally giving in to the sadness and devastation.

How am I going to tell Hades?

Chapter Seventy-Three

Hades

THIS TIME, the dreams that visit me aren't of my past or my mother. I dream of the absence of light and sound, of touch and life, and floating into the endless ether.

There's only one place like this—the Void. I look around, not sure what I expect to see, but it is something other than nothing, I suppose.

"You've kept us waiting, Son of Kronos," a voice croons. I spin to find the source, but there is only the Void.

"Waiting?" I ask, trying to figure out who this is.

"Yes. You must prepare for what is coming," another voice echoes. This one is accented and harsh, sounding vaguely Germanic?

"It already came. Thanks for the warning. A bit late, though," I snap, still trying to find a source.

"Foolish god, you think we speak of your father?" a new voice calls, heavily accented, maybe West African?

"Kronos is a little boy pouting over a lost toy. He worries us none," comes another voice. Finally, this is one I recognize.

"Then why summon me here, Atropos?" I growl.

There's a pause in the Void, and a veil of ignorance drops from my vision, revealing what I could only hear before.

Atropos stands in front of me, her red hair coiled high on her head, golden snakes threading through the tight *curls. Her clothes are of old, the chiton an almost blinding white. Instead of her sisters at her side, a dark-skinned man wearing the clothes of the Yoruba stands there. I scan his features, and it takes me a moment to place him.*

Orunmila, the Orisha of Destiny.

My eyes widen as I take in the other beings surrounding me, and I hold back a gasp of shock. The Gods of Destiny. All of them. Even those humanity has long forgotten.

"We speak of the coming," that Germanic voice comes again, and this time I can match it with the face of the Norn of the Future, Skuld.

"I don't understand," I murmur. Outside of the gods of the separate Underworlds, I hadn't thought any of the pantheons communicated with each other.

"He is a boy. He is not ready. We have chosen our emissary. Why do we need him?" Hemsut, the Egyptian Goddess of Fate, snaps. Her headdress with its shining shield flickering.

Emissary?

"I am no boy," I snarl.

Hemsut steps closer, looking me over from head to toe. "I guess we'll see. We'll be in touch, son of Kronos."

I open my mouth to ask more, but she flicks me in the middle of my forehead.

I blink and lurch from the fog of sleep, reaching for Persephone.

"My spring?" I call, trying to clear tendrils of unease from the strange dream. It was just a dream.

The spot next to me is only slightly warm. She's been out of bed for a while. I sit up slowly, rubbing my face as Persephone steps out of the bathroom, her face pale and withdrawn.

"What's wrong?"

She walks over to me and kneels on the bed. "We need to talk."

The dream and the wound on my back that constantly aches are forgotten. Everything is forgotten. There's only her.

390

I chuckle, but even I can hear the tension in it. "How ominous."

She tries to smile reassuringly at me, but it doesn't reach her eyes. She cups my cheek, but instead of calming me as it normally does, it only escalates my alarm. "You know I would burn the world for you."

I knew that, but why does she feel the need to tell me so?

I cover her hand on my cheek. "What is it?"

A tear slides down her cheek, and foreboding shoots through me like a bullet. "You're not healing."

I wipe away her tear. "I will." It will just take longer than normal, much longer, closer to a human's. I'm not looking forward to that.

She shakes her head, her eyes showing her absolute devastation. Tears still well in her eyes, but she doesn't let them fall. "You won't. Neither will the realm. She's poisoning you."

"She'll pay dearly for this," I growl. By the end, she'll wish I put her in the Heart of Tartarus to live out her most painful memories. A small sob escapes Persephone's control, and my fantasies about revenge fade.

"I... I love you," she says, barely getting the words out before her voice breaks.

Foreboding is less a bullet and more like a knife, taking an inch of my skin at a time. "Persephone... What did you do?"

She doesn't look at me. "I ensured the safety of you, the Underworld, and the other realms."

I straighten more on the bed. "And how did you do that?"

Tears fall down her face, but she doesn't look at me. "What have you done?"

"I've given her what she wants... me." She whispers the words so softly that they are almost lost.

Me. Me. Me. The word bounces around my skull. She wouldn't. She couldn't.

391

With a feral snarl, I grab her jaw and force her to look at me. "What. Did. You. Do."

Her eyes are empty pools of agony. "We have twenty-four hours."

No. No. No. This can't be.

"Undo it," I hiss, my fingers digging into her face.

"I can't."

I release her and stand, but I have to put a hand on the bed to stop myself from falling. "Then I will."

She rushes to support me. "You'll just keep getting sicker and sicker until—"

I pull away from her. "You made a choice without me. Just like you raged at me for doing."

We just settled things between us, and now… I have twenty-four hours? *No.*

She stiffens, her eyes becoming resolute. "I chose to protect you. To protect our realm."

I move away from her. "I'll deal with this."

She grabs my arm. "Hades…"

I don't look at her. "If I had done this. Would you forgive me?"

She flinches, releasing me. "You're dying."

"I would have figured something out!"

I put my hand on the bed as my vision spins.

She whimpers. "I need you to be alive. Somewhere. Even if you hate me. Even if you leave me, I need you to be alive."

"Alive and without you."

She sobs, the sound of a soul breaking. "Please, Hades."

"I can't… She has the power of Gaia. She'll snap the bond."

She crumples, falling to her knees. "Don't you see? She would have done it, anyway. I needed to ensure your safety."

I fall with her and wrap my arms around her, cupping the back of her head as she sobs against my chest.

I can't lose her.

Chapter Seventy-Four

Persephone

I PRESS MY FACE INTO HIS NECK, sobbing.
"If I had done this. Would you forgive me?"
"Alive and without you."
"She'll snap the bond."

His words are daggers driven into my heart, but I know he's right. I made this decision alone, but it is a decision he would not have let me make. He would have died trying to come up with a solution, and I couldn't bear the thought of him being gone forever.

He's holding me. I thought he would hate me, but he's holding me. It only encourages the river of tears as they slide down my cheeks, my heart fracturing with every breath.

Hades pulls me into his lap, cupping the back of my head. I can practically hear his own heart crumbling at the thought of me leaving. I hope that one day, he will realize that I had to do this, that I had no choice.

I tangle my fingers in his hair, whispering apology after apology like a prayer.

Will this be easier for him if he's angry with me? If he grows to hate me for the decisions I've made?

"I love you. I'm sorry," I continue to whisper over and over.

"I will get you back. I will come for you,

Persephone," he growls.

I pull back in surprise to see pure determination on his face. I cup his cheek.

"I will find my way back to you," I promise, looking into his eyes. They are hardened with determination, but there is no hiding the pure devastation he is feeling, not from me.

"You should have talked to me first," he says, brushing the tears still falling down my cheeks.

I place my hand over his, leaning into his touch. "Would you ever have accepted it?"

"Never." His reply is immediate, and it almost makes me smile.

"I will return to you," I repeat, needing him to really hear my words, to hear the truth in them.

"Only if I don't get to you first," he growls.

I stroke my thumb over the back of his hand as he strokes my cheek. "Game on, demon."

Hades leans in to brush his lips over mine but tenses and gasps, his eyes flaring with pain. A heartbeat later, I scream, agony flaring through my body, my heart stuttering. I fall from his arms as he releases me, grunting in pain and clutching his chest. I writhe on the floor, the pain relentless.

"Hades!" I pant. "What is happening?"

The pain stops suddenly, but the echo of it lingers, along with the most terrible gaping feeling in my chest, like something has punched a hole in it.

"She broke it." Hades rubs his chest.

It feels like my heart has been taken and has been replaced by a phantom one.

"No! We had twenty-four hours," I whimper.

Hades locks eyes with me, both of us reaching the same conclusion. This is it.

"I have a feeling she doesn't care," Hades says, rolling his shoulder.

I roll onto all fours and crawl around him. I pull the bandages down a little and gasp. His back is almost completely healed, and his wing is regrowing. I brush my fingers over the now unmarred skin. Hades hisses in pain, and I fall back as his wing breaks free of the gauze, slicing it clean off.

Hades turns, and I move closer to him. He reaches out to touch my hand. My body anticipates the feeling, but it never comes. I frown down at where it looks as though our skin should meet, yet all I feel is a slight disturbance in the air above my hand. Panicking, I lift my hand to his chest, but it never meets his skin.

"Hades?" I whisper.

"I will come for you. Nothing will stop me," Hades snarls.

I gasp, and every muscle in my body locks up as that blinding pain sears through me once again. My body knows this is wrong, that this is where I belong, and it cries out to the realm. The Underworld fights to hold on to me. Every inch of my skin feels like it has rug burn, and my bones feel as though they are breaking as I am ripped from my home.

The last thing I see is Hades reaching for me before a bright white light fills my vision, blinding me. I close my eyes against it, trying to shield myself, but the pain continues until suddenly everything stops.

"Daughter."

My body shakes, and I keep my eyes sealed closed.

"Open your eyes, Persephone." My mother's command has a dangerous edge, and I follow her instruction.

The familiar sight of her study fills my vision, and my stomach knots. She looks no different from when I last saw her. Her blue eyes are cold, devoid of any feeling or emotion. Her thin lips are pulled into a dangerous smirk that makes the hair on the back of my neck stand on end. Even her hair is styled the same. The dull brown strands pulled into a tight bun.

"You said twenty-four hou—"

"You were not and still are not in the position to

make demands. The kidnapper and his realm are healed. That was what I agreed to," she replies, her voice clipped but laced with the smugness of her victory.

I lower my gaze, knowing I can't fight back until I know she no longer possesses Gaia's power. Once she's free of it, I shall plan my escape. "Have you returned the power?"

"I did not say *when* I would return it, sweetling." I lift my gaze to my mother once again, her smile cat-like. She glances behind me, nodding once. My stomach plummets as I feel a malevolent presence step up behind me. Cold, boney fingers grasp my head, digging into my temples. I try to turn my head to get a better look at who is holding me, to work out what my fate will be.

My mother walks over to me, grasping my chin. She tilts her head, her gaze roaming over my face. "Take it all. I want no remnants of her captor." My mother drops her hand and turns, walking back to her desk.

I feel the fingers at my temple press into my skull harder, and I'm blinded by a bright glow flooding my peripheries.

No, it can't be! She's going to...

I look at my mother, clenching my fists. "Mother, no! Please!" I beg, tears sliding down my cheeks.

My mother laughs cruelly. "You should be thanking me, Persephone. I'm relieving your mind of this whole mess."

The glow gets brighter, and a shockwave of pain shoots through my brain. I think I scream, but I can't tell. The pain increases, the light so bright I think my eyes might be bleeding. Suddenly, I start to see flashes of memories crossing my vision, the first time I saw Hades in his apartment, starting at Plutus Industries, Helios, Mellie. Memory after memory passes and then disintegrates. Every time they evaporate to nothing, a surge of pain shoots through me.

I mentally reach for them, clawing at them, desperate to keep them, but the pain is unlike anything I've ever felt. Every time I feel like I have one safe, more of that searing light is pushed into me. Memory after memory is ripped from me, and I feel myself losing my grip on the person I have become.

I am Persephone Prosperina Plutus. Wife of Hades. Goddess of Dark Spring. Queen of the Underworld.

I am Persephone Prosperina Plutus. Wife of Hades. Goddess of Dark Spring...

I am Persephone Prosperina Plutus. Wife of Hades...

I am Persephone Prosperina Plutus...

I am Persephone Prosperina...

The bluest sapphires...

HADES & PERSEPHONE'S STORY CONTINUES IN THE FINAL INSTALLMENT OF THEIR TRILOGY.
IN THE MEANTIME ENJOY THIS BONUS CHAPTER

The Coronation Ball
Helios

THE SUN BEAMS DOWN ON MY GOLDEN SKIN as I lounge on my sun deck. A little-known fact about us Titans, we are extremely affected by our celestial counterparts. It's why I am constantly tanning and absorbing the sun's rays.

I'm a mirror of a dying star that supports life on Earth. To feel the burn of the sun on my skin is the only thing that makes me feel alive. Well, that's not exactly true. There is one other thing that makes me feel alive.

My cellphone pings with an alert, and I lower my sunglasses slightly when I see the notification from Plutus Bank.

INSUFFICIENT FUNDS.

I sit up, frowning as I click the notice. Each of my accounts has been drained, even the off-shore accounts. The last withdrawn with a memo line: *Up yours, Sun boy.*

I let out a loud laugh. Speaking of the only thing that makes me feel alive. I pull up her contact and press to call. Unsurprisingly, the number is no longer connected. I lower my phone, but my smile widens, and my heart races in my chest. The chase is on.

I snicker as I stand from the lounger and head inside. My eyes catch on the embossed invitation sitting on my counter. Lifting it to my lips, I glide to my closet to prepare for battle.

Without Hades looming over us, I turn back to Melinoë, growling slightly when I see she's trying to make a discreet exit.

I smirk and follow her, chasing after my little hellcat.

"Do you like running from me? I must terrify you," I challenge, but she doesn't stop, continuing to walk away from me. "I must shake you to your core."

She waits until we're in the hallway outside the throne room before she whirls on me. "The only thing you do, sun boy, is repulse me."

I stop, smiling at her, knowing how much it irritates her when I do. "Is that right, kitten?"

My tiny little hell cat jumps the line of insanity like a jump rope. She drains my accounts and hacks my computer, flooding it with viruses. The little ways she flirts with me.

Mellie clenches her fists, but both of her eyes are black with lust. She wants me so badly. "And if you don't back the fuck up right now, I'm going to plunge my dagger into your balls."

Fuck, she's sexy. Especially when she's threatening me.

I close the distance, grabbing her hair in my fist and looking over her features. "You know all the ways to get me going." Threaten me with violence, do violence to me, or let me do violence to you. Melinoë ticks all those boxes.

She looks up at me, her dance with insanity clear on her face.

I moan at the look. "Fuck, I love when you're feral."

She grabs the lapels of my suit, shoving me hard against the wall. "Leave me the fuck alone." I lick my

401

lips slowly and deliberately. Mellie falls for it, slamming her lips hard to mine. I yank her hair hard, feeling strands come loose as I do. She growls into my mouth, "I will never, ever, ever be your girlfriend." Yet, she bites my lip and pulls back. She draws blood, licking her lips for more of my taste.

I don't think my cock has ever been this hard. She has to be doing this on purpose. I spin to put her against the wall, slamming my lip to hers, biting her lip this time so our blood mingles in our mouths as we kiss.

"You already are," I groan against her mouth.

A pained huff slips from my mouth as her knee collides with my crotch, and I crumple from the blinding pain. I wince, rubbing my balls. Mellie growls at me but hesitates for a second before leaving.

She hesitated. That's a win.

I groan at the pain radiating from my crotch. She definitely wasn't holding back. Fuck, I'm pretty sure I'm in love with her.

A soft giggle draws my attention, and I open my eyes enough to see Aphrodite lingering in the doorway. "What have you got yourself into, Helios?"

I pant, the pain slowly turning to a numb ache. "Spying? Not your usual MO."

Now, her son? That prick is constantly spying. On everyone.

Aphrodite glides over to me, her constant glow radiating off her. Very different from my own. "Spying? No. The pheromones you two were emitting were difficult to ignore."

I straighten. "She's certainly a challenge."

"It would be a Titan who is arrogant enough to believe they can tame the untamable," Aphrodite muses. "Or maybe it's the madness that draws you to her..."

I laugh at the idea. "Oh no, I don't want to tame her. I like her just the way she is." I want to run wild with her. Not tame her.

402

Aphrodite looks me over, her eyes analytical and far too knowing. "Melinoë is lost within herself, Helios. You clear her vision, but you also bring the madness." She smiles at me, placing a comforting hand on my arm. "Take her for waffles."

Aphrodite winks at me before vanishing in a puff of pink smoke.

Hm, waffles. I could do that.

Printed in Great Britain
by Amazon